James Thomson was born in Ayrshire, Scotland. The eldest of three brothers, James left school aged 15 to begin an apprenticeship in mechanical engineering. On his 20th birthday, James became a qualified mechanical fitter, he left his job before his 21st birthday and has since worked on many important sites across Europe. He moved to Dublin in 1994. He married in 1995 and has since divorced. James has two sons, William, 25, and Luke, 23. He still lives in Dublin.

This book is dedicated to my family and friends and all those who encouraged me, you know who you are and I thank you all.

James Thomson

TARMEA

Return of the Kraken

AUSTIN MACAULEY PUBLISHERS™
LONDON * CAMBRIDGE * NEW YORK * SHARJAH

Copyright © James Thomson 2022

The right of James Thomson to be identified as author of this work has been asserted by the author in accordance with sections 77 and 78 of the Copyright, Designs and Patents Act 1988.

All rights reserved. No part of this publication may be reproduced, stored in a retrieval system, or transmitted in any form or by any means, electronic, mechanical, photocopying, recording, or otherwise, without the prior permission of the publishers.

Any person who commits any unauthorised act in relation to this publication may be liable to criminal prosecution and civil claims for damages.

This is a work of fiction. Names, characters, businesses, places, events, locales, and incidents are either the products of the author's imagination or used in a fictitious manner. Any resemblance to actual persons, living or dead, or actual events is purely coincidental.

A CIP catalogue record for this title is available from the British Library.

ISBN 9781398440159 (Paperback)
ISBN 9781398440166 (Hardback)
ISBN 9781398440173 (ePub e-book)

www.austinmacauley.com

First Published 2022
Austin Macauley Publishers Ltd®
1 Canada Square
Canary Wharf
London
E14 5AA

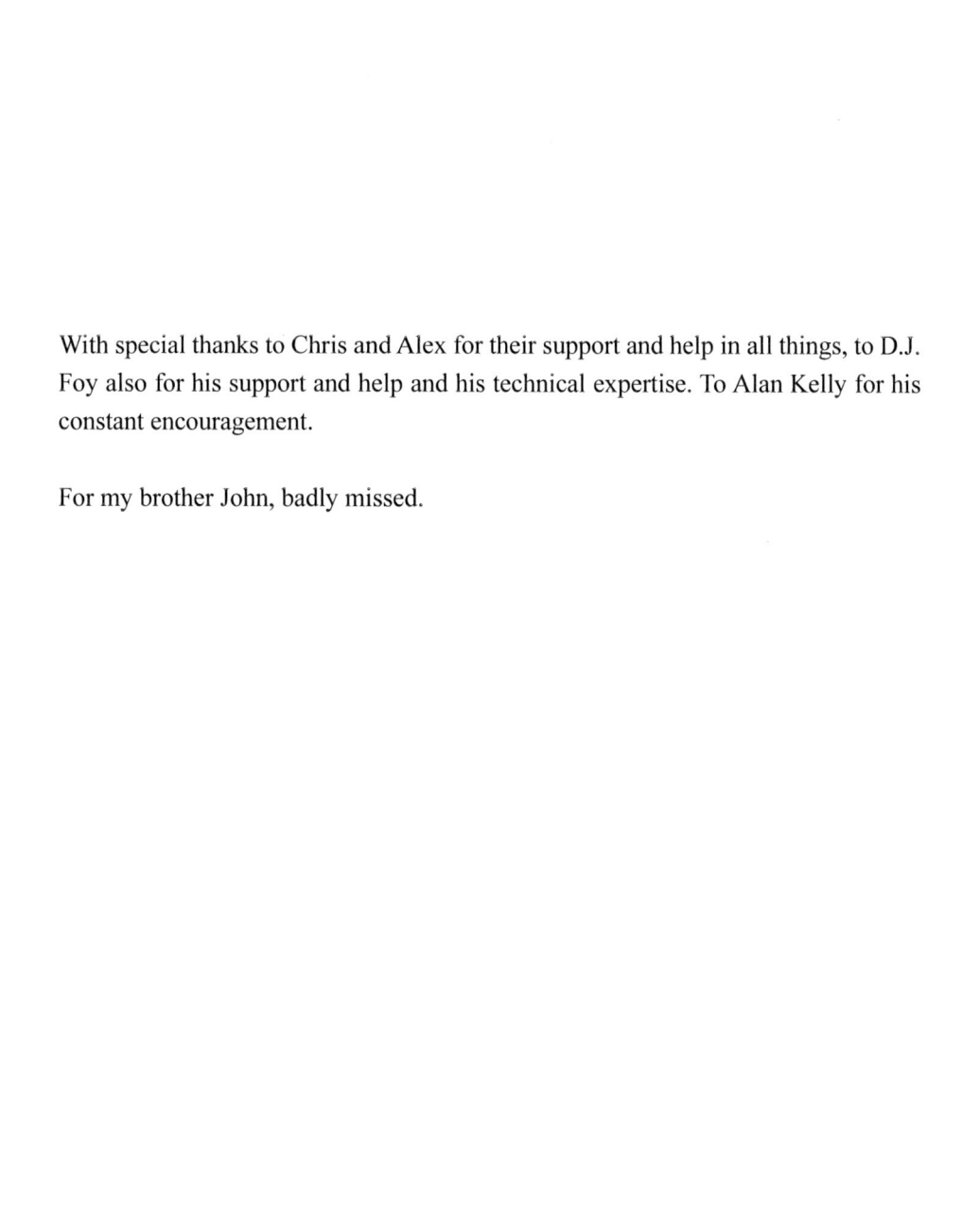

With special thanks to Chris and Alex for their support and help in all things, to D.J. Foy also for his support and help and his technical expertise. To Alan Kelly for his constant encouragement.

For my brother John, badly missed.

Chapter 1

Prince Toli woke early on the morning four days before his 18th birthday; in fact, he barely slept a wink for his father, King Toli, had granted him, and his three best friends, permission to go fishing for his feast to celebrate his passing from boyhood to manhood. This was extra special as he and his friends were to go to their special secret place and fish for rock grazing fish called peelers to the locals, who treated the fish as a delicacy as all the elements had to be right and the method used was very time consuming.

However, today everything pointed to perfect conditions for catching peelers and they would get to stay in the totally secret cave which the boys had cached all the materials necessary for not only catching fish but for a nice overnight stay in their own place.

The requirements weather-wise was a spring tidal period where the tide was low enough to allow them to take a route that was accessible only on these perfect days and later tides high enough to cover the rock face below their cave, their rock-castle.

He sprinted down the stone staircase into the kitchen where Nana, the head of the household workers—no slaves, all free folk—had three days provisions laid out for all four friends. Although he was desperate to run out the door, there was an hour to low tide proper and he knew his friends would be well awake but would be made to eat breakfast before leaving, so he sat and ate what was put in front of him although he could not tell you, if you asked, what he ate, his excitement was so overpowering.

Nana was endlessly giving him instruction to mind himself and his friends but he did not hear one single word; this was normal for Nana even if he was only going to the annual fair for he was known to be a bit on the adventurous side and often forgot, or just ignored, his orders to be back at certain times, so he just sat there chomping on fruits and oats and nodding in agreement as if he was listening, but Nana knew better than to try and press the point for she had known him since he first drew breath.

Suddenly and loudly, the door to the yard burst open and into the kitchen, falling over one another, came Ratesh, son of Tadesh, his father's best friend and general of his army. Ratesh and Toli had been brought up together and were extremely close and loyal to each other and both were known to be mischievous. "C'mon, C'mon, C'mon," he yelled, shoving Toli on the shoulder, "the tide's on the turn and we'd best be off just in case we—"

"Now young man," interrupted Nana, "in the first place, you have a good half hour left before you can leave and you'd better wait for the other two 'cos you two won't carry that lot on your own," she said, pointing to the four backpacks crammed with food and other stuff needed for their stay, at least for two nights.

The door to the yard again flew open and in ran Dovitt and Joki, who were as close to each other as the first two, and all four together were a formidable force for mischief and mayhem, they were also known to be the next heirs to their fathers' positions and would step up to be counted wherever needed.

Dovitt's father was admiral in the King's navy and Joki's father was general in the cavalry, and all four were due to begin service in full on their respective 18th birthdays; although all four were trained from birth, it was the tradition on Toli's island that all children of the royal court were schooled well, right up to their 18th birthday, not only to ensure they were able to count and spell and read and speak other languages, but to gauge their ability to handle any situation that may arise as adults. This tradition was encouraged for all peoples of the island but was only compulsory for royals and important members of court.

Although Toli's island has not been in any conflict for 30 years, the good King Toli made sure he had a well-supplied and well trained military, not a huge military machine but well paid and well fed and very very loyal.

"Right, enough of this," said Toli. "Let's get loaded up and get going, we'll need a lot of fish for the banquet." He was trying to act official and level-headed but everyone in the kitchen knew the boys were hoping to get moving and the other 3 already had their packs on and climbing staffs in their hand. Toli did the same and with shouts of farewell headed for the door and out into the yard and then to the strand Toli's Island, so-called because in all living and documented history, the only people who were allowed to be called Toli were the King and his firstborn son; should any misfortune befall the firstborn son, the name Toli would be passed on to the next of kin; if there was no son to pass the name on to, a relation would be found with royal lineage and would become Toli on the King's death. Fortunately, Prince Toli had two younger brothers, Basi aged 14 and Kali aged 12, and a little beloved sister, Shala aged 9.

Toli's Island was a massive island of solid granite only accessible from the sea to the massive harbour of the capital, King's Rock, so it was impossible to invade without entering the harbour which was heavily fortified on all sides. It was also thought that the interior was inaccessible, many tried to go up the river Dread but none came back. From the banks of the strand which was around 50 miles long of long rolling hills and meadows with crops and heavily wooded foothills with huge amounts of all kinds of game birds and animals. Above this were many mines which supplied the forges with ore and the castle with precious gems and metals.

The population was happy and loyal to the King; there were, of course, visiting emissaries and ambassadors from less well-off islands, for it was the thought that the entire world was totally made up of a collection of islands and this had never been disproved, some were jealous, none were known to be hostile, and they were, in the main, friendly.

As the tide went out and exposed more and more sand, the four pals waited for an opening in a spur of a mountain normally under water, which was known to the others but the secret was the path beyond which when found led to a ledge with a huge cave behind, invisible to anyone from below; the lads kept the path well-hidden on entry and exit.

As soon as the water was shallow enough, the boys waded knee-deep through the eye (as they called it) to the flat slab of rock thought to be impassable but the boys found a lever that when pulled caused the slab to almost soundlessly slide to the side; on passing through, they pulled another lever on the other side replacing the slab seamlessly, the friends now felt they were in their and their alone world for no-one else knew about it. The boys knew it must have been known before for they did not make it and their cave had already signs of life in it, particularly coins no longer minted and jewels known to be from different islands, rare metal chalices, platter and goblets made from metal mined on Toli's Island. So it was rightly concluded that smugglers had used this place many years before for smugglers no longer came to Toli's Island.

As they climbed the winding path, it would be too steep to climb straight up loaded with booty, they chatted about the coming festivities and they considered how much fish they would need to catch to feed the many guests at the banquet.

On reaching the cave, they rolled up a heavy waxed curtain and hung it on two jutting rocks to expose the cave entrance, revealing their very own castle-keep-treasury and they lit the wall torches with the spark flint that Nana had packed, as usual at the top of Toli's pack, lighting one on the floor and the rest from this on the wall, six in all, then lit the central fire; they had left the cave well provisioned for fire materials before leaving on their last visit.

"Right," said Toli, " let's get the net out then we can eat." They picked up a roll of light metal mesh with a bar through it and carried it out to the ledge where they hooked it on to ten metal hooks on the ledge and rolled it up and over the natural parapet the weight of the bar then allowed the 10 foot wide net to roll down the smooth weed-covered face of the rock, exposing the many hooks fixed on the net; they then went down the 30 feet on the path to a much smaller ledge running parallel to the main ledge and all four pulled the mesh off the rock face and hooked it onto the metal slabs measured exactly to pick up the end of the mesh; now secured, the boys were ready just for the tide for no bait was required as the seaweed washed over the fish hooks and the Peelers were hooked while grazing on the weed, hence the nickname Peelers.

They knew how to manage this process as there were instructions carved into the cave wall by presumably the smugglers who used this method for fresh food was extremely important on board any ship and the more clandestine the method the better, then they went back up to the cave for a nice lunch and to wait for the tide to come back on high, bringing in eager Peelers.

Chapter 2

At the same time in the castle council hall were gathered King Toli; Queen Shaleena; Tadesh; Dovitt's father, Admiral Shouk; Joki's father, General Matak; the High Sage Meer, who was the leading advisor and a very valuable advisor in times of illness and in matters of politics; and of course, Nana without whom the entire castle would fall to rack and ruin (in her own opinion), which was probably correct.

They were all in jovial humour for this situation was rare as all four sons were to be passed over to manhood on the same day for their birthdays were only days apart, Toli's being the first, as he liked to remind his friends often.

There is no need to go through every word spoken, suffice to say, each knew their duties, Meer-Ceremonial, Tadesh, Shouk and Matak in full ceremonial dress to stand and accept their sons into manhood first.

This was an especially cheerful meeting for the 3 military men for they got to pick ten men from their own ranks to go into the forest and hunt for game as deer could only be hunted by royal decree, even seasonal culling; they would obviously have an entourage of hunters and trappers and also serfs completing the party to around 50 men and horses who would make camp on the edge of the vast forest and hunt quietly on foot, although the moon was full.

Just as the boys were eager, so were the fathers to be getting on with it and were already prepared to leave as soon as this council was over; in fact, the Queen, on several occasions, had to reel in the King and remind him that he had duties right here with his wife and would not be going hunting (and drinking) with his friends for she was the only person alive who had any influence on the King at all, other than the children, who had their own way of pressurising their father.

As soon as they were dismissed, all went their own ways to their duties (some more pleasurable than others), Meer to his staff to prepare for the duties of ceremony and to prepare the grand chapel, the King and Queen off to the tailors and dressmakers to finalise small details on their robes and gowns which peeved the King greatly (he thought he was not needed for such trivial matters) but Queen Shaleena kept him in tow by making sure he knew his duties at the capital required him to be right where he was.

Tadesh, Shouk and Matak made straight for the back gate where their men were waiting and as soon as they were mounted, bolted through the gate, whooping with delight and heading through the low meadows towards the forest.

Chapter 3

Back in the castle-cave, the boys were feasting on blood sausage cooked over the fire and the huge potatoes cooked in fire embers while they talked incessantly about the celebrations; no promises were ever made by parents on Toli's Island on matters of marriage so they all speculated on the beauties who would be invited to attend, although there was never any parental pressure on any of them to marry, Toli had already met a certain Princess of the Green Isle at her 16th birthday celebrations on her home isle. Prina was the daughter of King Jai and Queen Prina and had also attended Toli's 16th birthday, both were smitten with each other and both families considered the match ideal, for both were rich and had always had a close relationship and called each other cousin although there was no blood relation.

"Well, what are we to do?" asked Ratesh.

"A fine ripe apple of her father's eye, completely head over heels for you and you for her, and the need to lengthen your royal lineage, in the eyes of the world there is no question to be asked other than the question will have to be put to King Jai, perhaps very soon, maybe in a few days?"

"Don't know, never thought about it," Toli said.

"Blinkin' liar," said Joki, "not a man here hasn't carried one of your love letters down to the captain of King Jai's merchant ships, more than a few, I reckon."

"Those were not love letters, they were letters of state from my father to King Jai," stated Toli.

"Really?" said Joki. "Then why were they all addressed to Prina?"

"Well, um…um…" stammered Toli.

By this time, Ratesh had a grin from ear to ear. "You'd better hope there was nothing untoward written in one of those," he said. "Cos you'd best be aware that King Jai read those so-called letters of state before they were passed into the pretty hands of his much loved princess."

"What-what do you mean?" Toli was now flapping like a pennant in the wind.

"What do I mean? What do I mean? Did you ever receive a return letter that hadn't been opened first? Do you really believe both Kings don't know exactly what's in your tender correspondence between both of you?"

Ratesh was now fit to burst with ill-concealed mirth.

"But, but…" Toli's face was now roaring red. "I swear by Aquos's trident I never-ever, oh by Aquos, I never thought, oh dear, oh dear!"

"Don't worry," said Dovitt. "If there had been anything at all, I'm certain your father would have let you know before now."

"Yes, yes, I'm sure you're right, yes he would…he would have, wouldn't he?"

"Yes, he would." Joki this time. "Now enough of this; we'd best check on the tide. I'm sure it'll be on the way back by now, so c'mon boys, there's royal duties to fulfil."

At this Dovitt picked up the nautical spyglass left by the smugglers. "Follow me, men, time to have a look."

They went to the parapet holding the net although from here they could not see the harbour for the ledge was not high enough to see over the natural wall; they could all gauge the flow of the tide by other natural reference points.

"It's on the way alright, and it's in a hurry, have a look," and he handed the spyglass to Toli.

"Right enough," he said, "it's rushing in okay."

The others had a look and all agreed it would not be long before the peelers would be grazing.

Ratesh, who was the last to look, said, "Have a look at this, lads, go to the horizon, look at the sky!"

They did in turn and all could see the storm approaching, huge black and purple clouds bruised the sky and they all knew that there was more than the tide coming into the capital.

To the right of where they stood, there was a stairway carved through an archway up to a platform which allowed the smugglers to spy on the city and the harbour. Ratesh went up to see what he could see and urgently called back, "Come quick, lads, have a look at this!"

As the others arrived, he handed the spyglass to Toli saying, "Look at the harbour entrance, tell me what you see." Toli took the glass and looked to the entrance of the harbour.

"What do you see, Toli?" asked Dovitt.

"I see two ships, two very fancy ships."

"Yes," said Ratesh, "look at the sails." Their mainsails were green with a blue trident at its centre.

"AQUOS TAKE ME!" declared Toli. "It's King Jai already arriving."

"Yes," said Ratesh, "and we're up here out of the way, I wondered why the good King, your father, was so easy to let us go on our little adventure, we're out of the way and lots can be said before we get back down."

"Blast and blast," cursed Toli, "oh dear, oh dear, oh dear."

"Gimme a look," Joki and Dovitt said together and they took a turn each. Dovitt, who was last to look, said, "The water's already high enough to dock, they'll be on dry land in a half hour." They could also see other ships further out to sea. Dovitt still with the glass said, "They'll all make it safe to harbour before the storm."

All the ships were full of banquet guests from other friendly islands and their parties and gifts for the Good King's son. "Bloody blast," cursed Toli, "what does it mean?"

"It means," said Ratesh, "that they were all invited to arrive today, which also means that your father will have little time to attend to any one guest, he'll have to officially welcome all of them today."

"By the blue sky, you're right; he'll be kept busy all day and every day till the job's done and we're back," Toli sighed with relief.

"Well, if I'm any judge at all, we'd best get back to our abode and batten down from the storm."

"Okay," Toli said. "You go back, I'm staying here to watch the ships come in."

"Ah yes, the ships come in and your beloved comes ashore so you can fawn all night over her." Joki laughed.

Anyway, the three lads went back and prepared to make the cave water- and wind-tight with room to let Toli back in when he was finished drooling.

King Jai's ship had already docked and the royal contents of the ship were making their way to the carriages on the dock. Toli's heart missed a beat as he focused on the Princess Prina, gown billowing in the already strong wind and her beautiful blonde hair flying, he did not see her for long, she was hustled into her awaiting carriage and up to the castle as quick as she could get there out of the incoming weather.

He closed the glass and made his way back to the cave, he could not resist a look off the parapet to check the mesh, the water was rising fast and he would be up to it in a very short time. He also looked out to sea and for a short time watched the dangerous clouds carrying with them a bedlam of a storm, he also thought way off through a break in the cloud the misty shape of a sail miles out to sea but put it down to a trick of the light for the day had gone quickly and night was fast approaching; anyway, he dismissed it and crawled through the flap left open for him; he secured the entrance properly and sat by the fire by his friends who had already had a huge pot of chicken stew with onions, potatoes, carrots and mushrooms and huge globules of yellow fat floating on top.

The friends had also managed to procure two bottles of homemade red berry wine from Nana's kitchen, thinking Nana didn't notice but Nana was sniggering to herself when they were trying to be furtive for she had left it to be found, so they threw more flotsam on the fire and settled in for a very comfortable night.

Chapter 4

In the forest, their fathers had already two large deer in the store wagon and the trappers were regularly returning with game such as turkey, grouse, rabbit, wild boar and hare. Shouk looked up at the sky and said, "Best keep a weather eye out, men; we don't want to be caught out in what's coming this way."

"You are right there," said Tadesh. "We've done enough for this day, we'd best get back to camp and get ready for it'll blow out by morning." Matak agreed wholeheartedly mainly because there was a large barrel of harbour ale in one of the wagons as well as a fine selection of wines. So in accord they packed in the hunt and returned to camp.

The campsite was a small meadow on the edge of the wood protected by a surrounding stand of oak trees; when they got back, the site had been secured by the camp workers who had made the meadow as windproof as possible by tying huge waxed blankets around the outside of the oaks left there by previous hunting parties rolled and tied at the bottom of the trees, an unwritten law was all hunters must leave the meadow as they found it, so these would have been taken down, rolled up and tied down at the foot of the trees again for any future hunters. The meadow was only left open at the forest end for easy access to the forest and back again.

In the centre of the site was the cook tent surrounded by the sleep tents; in the cook tent, they had huge pots and cauldrons full of all sorts of foraged wild food including platters of wild berries of various types and colours; in the centre of the tent, the cooks had two huge boar on spits. All these supplies, barring the food, came behind the hunters on wagons which followed the hunting party out the gate and arrived when they were all out foraging, trapping and hunting. When the wagons were emptied of the goods needed, they formed an extra perimeter around the sleep tents and the wagoners slept very well in these indeed.

Inside the giant food tent, there was room to eat for all as everyone to a man sat on a small fold-down seat with a cloth top and ate off their laps, the food was excellent, the wine better and the harbour ale better again.

As the hunting was so good, they all agreed to secure the cook tent for the night and do the clean-up in the morning so that one and all could enjoy the fare and finish their work when the hunt went out again at dawn (weather permitting).

The game was so prolific that they knew there were no more dangerous animals in this area than foxes or badgers; besides, the storm would keep even those underground. Everyone went to bed extremely happy and contented and slept with a smile on their faces.

Chapter 5

As the storm raged against the harbour's granite walls and the walls of the city, the King called for his captain of the watch and ordered him to light the stand-down fires which let the soldiers manning the port's gun stations to stand down as all invited guests were already ashore safe and it was thought that any seamen out in this weather were doomed anyway.

The soldiers were delighted and a feeling of impending celebration settled on the whole island.

Inside the castle, King Toli and Queen Shaleena were entertaining the guests they had invited and being entertained themselves as all were friendly to all others, or so it was thought.

There had, of course, been a welcome banquet prepared and after the usual formalities the guests settled in their places for an evening of jovial company and wonderful food overseen by Nana, who watched all the staff with an eagle eye and woe-betide anyone who made a mistake; none did and the event passed to the evening without incident.

As the staff were cleaning the remnants of the meal away, people could now mingle and chat and catch-up with seldom seen friends. Princess Shala, being only 9 years old, was sleepily taken back to her room in the back of the castle next to the nursery and just inside the back gate where the hunting party had left through earlier. Her personal maid and carer, Anga, worshipped the princess and had sworn an oath to herself that as long as she drew breath, no-one and nothing would hurt her ward.

Although Anga was only 18 years old herself, she had been in the room as a cleaner when the choosing of a nanny was being considered; prospective nannies had already been interviewed individually and there were 4 left, these 4 had all spent time with the child, 5 years old at the time, and this situation had been created to see which one Shala would take to the best or most. When King Toli put her on her feet on the floor, she toddled straight over to Anga and gripped the hem of her dress and no-one could remove the child from there.

It was Queen Shaleena who immediately saw what the situation was; she knew these two were going to be inseparable for life. That was 4 years ago and the Queen was never given any reason to doubt the connection between her daughter and her young nanny. Anga put Shala to bed with no complaint and the Princess was asleep even before the blankets were over her.

Back in the main hall, the chatting and dancing had begun, enjoyed with copious amounts of wine and the famous harbour ale. Princess Prina sat talking in the corner with her best friend Lattie (short for Laticia) about the things teenage girls talk about worldwide, especially Prince Toli's proposal of marriage, which was expected (by all) immediately after the passing ceremony. Normally, King Jai and Queen Prina would insist their daughter mix with others but on this occasion, thanks to the not-so-secret letters, the parents decided there would be enough pomp and ceremony to come without thrusting any more pressure onto their beloved baby (Queen Prina always referred to her so).

They chatted cheerfully and also nervously about how Toli would bring their betrothal into the conversation after all other formalities were done, they needn't have been so nervous for Toli had already worked out this process, and the entire court of both islands knew all about their plans.

As eyes began to droop and the company were all thinking "time for bed", the solid oak door which had been barred against the storm crashed open loudly and a powerful gust blew into the hall, accompanied by a black cloud and other blown debris. As the cloud cleared, the wind dropped and slowly figures began to appear in the doorway and enter the hall. As they moved steadily inwards, it became obvious that they were, to a man, armed and armoured in tough leather; no-one in the castle had been armed that evening so there was no resistance at all.

As the air cleared inside, the storm outside rapidly abated as if it had been controlled the whole time.

"Greeting one and all on this auspicious occasion," said the warrior in the lead. "I regret not having given you notice of our arrival, but many years ago my race were driven from your shores when their lord, my father, was grievously wounded. My name is Muklah, Son of Muklah, the name may ring bells in the more mature belfries."

"By Aquos, I remember your name for I was here and old enough to bear arms against your murderous father and his horde, in fact I stood by my father at the castle wall when he struck the decisive blow."

"I also was there and also old enough to bear arms and also next to my father when the blow was struck, but as you can tell, the blow wasn't exactly decisive."

"What is it you hope to gain by coming back to our homeland? Whatever it is will not be given up lightly," said the King.

And Muklah said, "Oh, I think you'll find that it is already given up, all this finery, all this royalty, all these riches and not one armed guard to be seen, the reason for my return is to avenge my father's death, for he never made it back to my mother, and to establish my reign and my lineage, and to use this magnificent island as the hub of the upcoming Muklah Empire, you and yours are finished here. I trust everyone had a good evening, please make yourselves comfortable, we're having a little ceremony of our own at first light."

King Toli knew exactly what Muklah was hinting at and he glanced sideways at his Queen who outwardly seemed very calm but inwardly she was in turmoil, not for herself but for her daughter and eldest son who were not with her.

"Go find the other children! They're not here!" screamed Muklah at his captain, Brakko.

"At once, lord." Brakko turned to his personal company and ordered them, "Go through this place like the storm that brought us here," he said, and his men and himself left the hall through the rear and began their search.

Chapter 6

Anga was awakened by the front doors flying open and had woken Shala and made her dress quickly; both then ran past every door they could, waking who they could and bid them follow. They ran into Nana in the corridor and that was enough for Anga, she gripped little Shala's hand and headed for the back gate, the rest could take care of themselves as most were milling around confused and only half awake. They ran out the gate and headed for the nearest tree cover, this whole time the Princess did not panic, did not cry, not as much as a whimper, such was her faith in Anga.

When they got to the trees, they ducked behind a large rock, which were plentiful on this island, and stopped to catch breath and check who, if anyone, was following. No-one was following. "We can't wait, we have to find the hunting party; they are our only hope, we can't find the Prince, we have no clue where to look, I only hope he realises what's going on before the boys walk right into this," Anga said and then went deeper towards the hunters' camp for they all knew where it was.

"I fear for my staff!" Nana said. "They'll need to be told what to do, they may not understand what's being said and could be slain."

"Have no fear for I heard them and they speak our tongue and they too will need people to cook and clean although I suspect they will no longer be free-folk," Anga said.

Chapter 7

In the castle, all the guests and royals were chained together by their wrists, all but one, a tall man in a hooded robe stood alone off to one side. All the staff who were caught in the hall were also chained and taken to a different room and made to sit in a huddle on the floor while being minded by a half dozen fierce looking heavily armed warriors, for these brutal invaders were an angry-looking people to begin with.

When Brakko returned to the main hall, he lowered his head before his lord and said, "My lord Muklah, the children are nowhere to be found, and we have interrogated several members of staff and I genuinely believe they do not know."

"Go now, take 6 heads and make sure the rest see, maybe that will loosen a few tongues," the invader said. Brakko gave a stiff bow, spun on his heels, signalled to his men and left without another word.

"Now," Muklah said calmly, "I was expecting the whole family to be here, shame there are just a few missing, we know about the hunting party and we'll let them bring the spoils of the hunt to us in the morning but as for your children, we know not." At this he turned his stare on the hooded man who visibly cringed beneath his robe.

This man was named Tare and he had been a spy in the employ of Muklah for the last 30 years and had been sending information by carrier pigeon for the duration of his stay; however, as the permission for the fishing trip had been granted at the last minute, he was not party to this knowledge.

Thirty years ago on the flight from Toli Island, Tare was ship's boy on Muklah's flagship, the "Black Kraken", and had been reared as an orphan by Muklah elder, who treated him as a true-born son and brother to Muklah the younger. On the realisation of his father's death, Muklah called his adopted brother to the lord's cabin and a plan was hatched beyond anything that had been done before. Passing around 1 league off the coast of the Green Isle, By dressed as a Tolian Islander, aged 15 years and already showing signs of magical ability, he was put in a skiff and instructed to tell the Green islanders that he was taken as a prisoner and as there was complete mayhem on board, he had managed to steal the skiff being towed behind the ship in the black of night; he claimed no-one even knew he was there, never mind gone, he hadn't even been shackled. On his discovery in the light of day, he lay in the skiff bedraggled, and seemingly unconscious, by soldiers alerted by a lookout in one of the tall towers built for this reason, the passing of the Black Kraken had gone unnoticed because of the pitch black of the night.

On his "recovery", he immediately fell into his role as an escapee saying that his fisher-folk parents had been slaughtered at the outset of the invasion and he had been taken as a slave on the pinnace by the returning sailors designated to go back to the flagship to defend the ship in case a speedy exit was needed. He was thrown in the hold un-tethered and as the sailors were intent on the battle ashore, the hold was never locked. As the invader in black was mortally wounded pretty early in the battle, the same crew were signalled to return to the point of demarcation with the dying lord to make their escape.

Seeing their stricken lord, many soldiers made their own shore parties to make it back to the fleet in order to gather around the flagship and hopefully protect their ruler on the way home to the Black Isles. They managed to return and crew around 6 ships of the battle fleet who immediately filled their sails to follow the already fleeing "Black Kraken".

On the shore, the rout was complete and the small flotilla made it out of the harbour under fire. There were no prisoners taken and the remainder of the fleet was smashed to smithereens; the only people to make it our alive were the people aboard the ships who left with the "Black Kraken".

This account of the battle was accurate except for Tare's story of capture and escape, and the fact that even at 15 years old, he was responsible for the pitch black of the invasion and the pitch black of the escape. He was in fact responsible, 30 years later, for the storm that brought the Black Isler's back.

His story was completely accepted on the Green Isle as many Tolians who made a living on the shore front and down at the harbour were indeed slaughtered and fisher-folk had no surname's, one of the Lord's company on entering one of the fishing cottages found a family of three cowering in the centre of the floor.

The woman cried, "What's happening, Trak!"

Trak said, "I think we've been invaded, Ella, my love." Their son was 15 years old and black-haired and it immediately struck the soldier how much he and his lord's adopted son were alike.

"Come to me, Tare," shrieked Ella and hugged her son to her bosom. Bizzo the warrior in black held his scythe-like sword under each of their chins.

"Name?" he said to the man. "Remind me."

The man said Trak, the woman said Ella and the boy said Tare. Bizzo immediately took all 3 heads and dumped the bodies in the already bloodied sea which was now filling with sharks coming in from deeper water, sensing blood and turmoil.

On leaving the hovel and wishing himself back in the battle and having thrown his victims into the sea, he made his way towards the centre of the melee and his liege lord for he was one of Muklah's personal guards and only left his side because his commander thought he saw movement from the fisherman's tiny abode.

The battle raged for another three hours and Bizzo fought alongside his lord with gusto for he was famed for his pleasure in spilling blood. Suddenly, his lord fell, blood gushing down from his neck; he had been hit by an arrow which opened his jugular.

His bodyguards instantly surrounded him and four of them picked up Muklah and carried him to the harbour pier and Bizzo took up the Black Flag that had been left in case any harm came to Muklah.

This was how Muklah came to be back on his black warship again and he ordered Tare to prepare the blackness for departure.

Tare's name at this time in his life was Sisk and after this day, he would never be called this again until now. When Bizzo and the bodyguard, to a man, realised their fallen lord had taken a fatal wound, Bizzo went to a corner of the cabin and called for young Muklah and explained what happened in the hovel ashore and within a very short time they had concocted the beginning of the plan which would come to fruition 30 years later.

Tare was so convincing in his stories he was totally accepted and when he asked if he could stay on the Green Isle as he was so traumatised by what went before to his "parents" he could not face to return.

Eventually, he was so clever in his words and deeds that King Jai sent a message to King Toli asking if it would be suitable to keep him and educate him and he could return as an ambassador who would be a valuable asset to both parties and totally loyal as he saw what happened before his eyes to the people he loved.

King Toli agreed on the condition that Tare accompany any diplomatic missions to Toli's Island as he did not want the boy to forget his roots and he wanted to meet the hero who escaped the murderous Black Lord. These two Kings were the Grandfathers of present day Prince Toli and Princess Prina and had now passed on in peace.

His final message from Muklah to the Green Isle was to tell him to make his way back to Toli Island on a permanent basis, which was easy because of his unequalled powers of observation and deception; that was ten years ago and he had been feeding Muklah information direct from Toli's Island ever since.

Chapter 8

When Brakko returned to the main hall, he had to admit, "Still nothing, my lord, I have taken heads. I don't think anyone knows."
Then a voice came out of the shadows as the spy-traitor Tare stepped forward into the light of the lamps. "No need to take anymore heads, the King and Queen know where the children are."

"AH! YOU!" yelled King Toli. "I wondered how this animal had so much knowledge of our business, you bloody traitor."

"I would have to have been a loyal servant of yours to become a traitor and I never have been. Two of you! Grab his arms." Two soldiers pinned the king's arms to his side while Tare put his hand on the king's head after knocking his crown off. A mere few seconds later, he turned to Muklah and said, "His son and sons of his general and admiral have gone fishing, he does not know where, they will return tomorrow morning, he has no idea where his daughter is, she should be asleep in bed, but as we know she is not."

"Very good, my brother, take these out and finish the job we came here to do, we won't have any trouble dealing with the rest, a few children and a hunting party won't give us any trouble when they return, we will be upon their heads before they even guess what is happening."

The royals and guests, 46 in all, were led out to the harbourside where 46 gibbets had already been erected and the entire company was hung without ceremony not even last words; they had already been stripped of jewels and finery and were left there in their underclothes.

Muklah turned to Sisk inside and said, "When we finally cleanse this place of this royal plague, we will voyage out to the other allied Isles and deal with those; we have their leaders hanging outside by their pretty necks and their subjects do not even know."

"Yes Lord Brother, all the Isles who warred against us and took our father from us must be made to pay an unforgettable price."

"And they will, Sisk, and you will have the Green Isle for you to govern on behalf of the new Empire as you wish!" said Muklah. "Now I feel the need for wine and sleep, we have another long day tomorrow I take it, those who are still living only to serve are secured for the night?" The question was directed at Brakko.

"Yes Lord there will be no trouble from those sheep for they know this night is a new beginning and we're bringing in the military from their outposts, lookout sites and their cannon emplacements as directed by Lord Sisk."

"Good, then we three can sleep easy, but we must be awake to welcome our missing friends tomorrow; now, Brother, where are my chambers?" Muklah said, turning to Sisk who extended his hand and said, "Please follow me."

But Sisk could not sleep easy, he had a feeling that something was amiss.

Chapter 9

The moon was as full as before the storm and Anga, Shala and Nana had an easy time picking their way through the trees towards the hunter's camp and were not too far off now and were quietly whispering about what the reaction of the King's friends would be on hearing the news of the invasion, of course they did not yet know of the fate of the King, Queen and their guests.

In time they could see the embers of the campfire and the two men of the duty watch were just throwing more timber on it, they were not properly on duty for any warning of attack but to mind the fire as they were surrounded with flammable waxed cloth.

The three had to make their way to the open end of the meadow enclave as they stepped into the light of the fire, the two fire-guards gave a squeak of surprise and picked up their bows to defend themselves, but almost instantly recognised all three as they were all well-known to the entire population of the Island.

"Wake the General and Admiral now!" Anga called out.

"Wait just a minute, maid!" said a guard.

"Do it now!" screamed Shala.

The other guard ran to General Tadesh's wagon and tore open the flaps; Tadesh being a seasoned soldier who had all the instincts of the warrior woke instantly and reached for his hunting bow and quiver and leapt from his wagon, bow already nocked to loose, thinking an unexpected wild animal had infiltrated the camp.

"What is it, Gogon?" he said looking through eyes puffed with sleep and wine and ale.

"The Princess is in camp, my Lord," Gogon replied.

"The what is where?" Tadesh said, still addled from sleep.

"The Princess is here in camp, my Lord," he said.

As his sight cleared in the fire and moonlight, he recognised the three by the fire and came over to them in mystified silence.

Meanwhile, Luron the other fire guard and brother of Gogon had awakened Admiral Shouk and General Matak who were both now blearily coming to the fire.

"What has happened, my Princess?" Tadesh said worriedly.

"Anga will tell you, for she knows more than us and is our saviour." Shala stepped two steps back and directed Anga to explain.

"We were invaded, my Lord," she said and proceeded to tell all what had happened, for the entire company was wide-awake and wide-eyed as they listened to Anga's account of what she had seen and the consequent journey here.

By this time, the first light of dawn was rising and Tadesh told them to strike camp and collect the weapons. "Leave the horses and wagons; we go on foot, less conspicuous," he said. "We can carry enough food for now and leave the rest to the animals of the forest."

Just then, the surrounding curtains dropped to the ground as one and they found themselves surrounded by armed warriors dressed in what appeared to be a sort of light chainmail vests and leggings. As the hunting party prepared themselves for battle by standing back to back, even the non-military had armed themselves with any blunt instrument that came to hand and set their jaws determinedly after hearing Anga's tale of disaster.

One of the unknown warriors stepped forward and called loud enough for all to hear, "My name is Soq and I belong to the lake-valley folk, we are your allies although you never knew it, you may keep your weapons but you must come with us now or we will leave you to your fate."

Tadesh was about to yell a challenge when Anga grabbed his arm and said, "These are not the invaders, my Lord, these are fair of face and I sense they are friendly."

"We go with these people!" said the Princess Shala. "And we go now!"

The rest of the company dropped to one knee and called as one, "Yes, my Princess."

Anga looked at the 9-year-old and thought, *By the sky above, a true leader so young*.

"Please follow me," Soq said and strode off into the forest never looking back and thinking, *If they do not follow, I cannot do a thing but I sense there is courage in this company and the young Princess is wise beyond her years.*

Chapter 10

As the light strengthened, the fishing party stirred in their cave and Toli lit a fire for breakfast; the tarp was suddenly torn from the cave entrance and the light blinded the companions.

"Please step outside," a voice called into the cave. "You are in no danger from us."

"And who is us?" called Toli at the cave mouth.

"My name is Broq and I am of the Lake-Valley people and we are nothing but friendly to you and your people, I assure you, you are absolutely safe."

And so the four boys slowly left the cave with hands over their eyes till the light no longer troubled them. The first thing Toli noticed was that the fish mesh had been raised and lay rolled up neatly on the ledge. "Please come with me," Broq said to the four of them; he took them up the stairs under the arch to the smugglers lookout platform. Dovitt already had the spyglass on hand and when they got to the platform, Broq said, "Please give Toli the glass," and Dovitt passed it to Toli. "Down there on the harbour wall," and Broq pointed down to the hanging figures on the gibbets.

Toli saw his father, his mother, King Jai, Queen Prina and he froze as his sight came upon Princess Prina; his eyes misted over in disbelief and grief, he moved on and came to his brothers, Bosi and Kali; he dropped to his knees in tears.

"What is it?" asked Dovitt and he snatched up the spyglass from the ground where Toli had dropped it, as he scanned the harbour, Dovitt fell silent, passed the glass to Joki who was beside him and then to Ratesh, the reaction was the same stunned silence followed by complete overpowering grief as the boys had seen their mothers dangling in the light sea breeze.

Broq laid his hand on the still weeping Toli and said, "Come, my King, there will be time for grieving when we get you to the Lake-Valley and safety."

The boys slowly got to their feet and followed Broq back to the ledge at the cave-mouth.

"I know this is hard to take but there is more, better news," Broq began. "Toli, your sister Shala is safe in our hands as is Anga her maid and Nana. Ratesh, Dovitt and Joki, your fathers are also all safe in our care, as is the entire hunting party."

The boys stared at him, still dumbstruck and unable to digest all this in such a short time.

"I'm sorry, boys, but we'll have to move now please, the sooner you are back in the remainder of your family's arms, the better; and the sooner we can all get on with the job of preparing for your vengeance."

Chapter 11

As the hunting party approached the foot of the mountains, the military men started to ask questions of Soq incessantly, did he know of any further information about wives, children, friends and especially their King and Queen but mostly their own sons. Soq, eventually feeling the truth, known so far would have to be passed on before his charges had driven themselves into a frenzied state of dismay.

"We will stop around this next bend and take some food before we enter the mountain," he told them. As they came around the bend at the foot of the mountain, there was a waterfall coming out the rock face and falling into a huge pool with no visible exit river or even a stream. They all sat down on rock or grass and then broke out the portions of food they had salvaged from the hunt and fed well enough. The Lake-Valley folk had food pouches over their shoulders and had their own fare even though they had been offered to share the game.

It was Admiral Shouk who spoke first, "Okay Soq, can you tell us what happened to our people?"

"Yes," he replied, "first let me tell you that your son and General's sons are in my brother's care, most of the castle staff are alive and most of the workers on land will be alive but have a future as slaves for we consider these people as heathens and they are known to keep slaves on the Black Isles."

"The Black Isles," Tadesh cried out. "I thought we had stamped out that black-hearted bastard."

"You did at the time but his son survived and has bred his hatred over the last 30 years, plus he has had a spy on the Green Isle for the first 20 of those and the same spy on your Island for the last 10, you know him as Tare but his real name is Sisk and he also possesses certain dark powers. We can talk further as we go but I must tell you that every person who was invited to the passing ceremony is now dead which means your wives and friends and all children except the ones

I have mentioned. Princess, this means your mother, your father, your brothers Bosi and Kali all dead."

He let the silence settle on the company for a short time for they were all stunned, still the Princess did not cry or show any emotion whatever, even though some of the grown men wept openly.

"We must move on now," he said and got up.

"Princess, please climb up on Anga's back and everyone else please follow me."

He stood on the edge of the pool and said something which no-else outside the Lake-Valley folk understood.

"TARMEA WISTWA DALAKA," and then he stepped into the pool.

Although the bottom of the pool could not be seen, the water only came up to his calf and he walked dead ahead straight through the cataract followed by the hunting party then his own kinsmen as they went through the fall of water there was no sensation of anything falling on them and they emerged on the other side safe and oddly dry in a large cavern stone chamber, Soq turned to the waterfall and said, "TARMEA WISTWA ROUTLA."

Now no-one could follow; he turned to the back wall of the chamber and uttered the same incantation as he did in the first instance and the back wall opened by sliding off to the right side of the chamber revealing a well-lit corridor. He then turned around when everyone was inside the chamber and repeated the second incantation and the wall closed again. Now they began to walk slightly uphill in the spacious corridor with Soq in the lead followed by the hunting party then the other Lake-Valley men.

"Where are you taking us?" asked Tadesh.

"To the valley beyond," replied Soq, "but I'm not taking you, you may go back if you wish, but it's time you knew this, we call ourselves Lake-Valley folk but we are all Tolians lifelong, I am older than anyone here, and although you never knew of our existence, we have been watching over you for years, we are with you now because we also have special powers and senses and because the storm that brought the invader was brought by dark powers and we sensed it coming long before you knew anything about it. It was also one of our arrows that sliced Muklah's vein, and you'd best believe that only we can bring this situation for only we can penetrate the traitor's defences."

As they walked, after an hour, the corridor floor began to level out and the going became easier. They walked for another hour in silence until Shala asked, "I see no torches, how is this place lit?"

"There are natural crystal veins through the entire mountains but they only give off light when our people are around, we discovered this many years ago when our ancestors mined these corridors, our powers were evident even then," replied Soq.

Again, Anga realised this was an extremely mature question for a 9-year-old and in her mind's eye, she could see something very special still to come.

Chapter 12

Broq, although sympathetic to the misery just heaped on Toli's shoulders, said, "We must leave for the valley now, my King, people are expecting us."

"Wait a minute," cried Toli. "You just called me your King. How can this be?"

"Your father is dead and you are his heir and we are all Tolians and have always been loyal to your royal family but you didn't even know about us, until now."

At this, Broq turned to the back wall of the cave and incanted, "TARMEA WISTWA DALAKA" and, of course, the wall again slid open and Broq led the party through then as they passed further into the, again, well-lit tunnel, the last of Broq's kinsmen spoke quietly, "Tarmea wistwa Routla" and the wall again closed.

"There are many questions to be asked and answered," said Broq, "but it is best that these are left till you are reunited with your kin and friends when we can enlighten you all together."

Then the company fell to silence and to their own thoughts, each of them felt deep regret for lost family and friends and each one of them felt encouraged by the fact that they were going to be reunited with their remaining relations and each one of them had a sense of foreboding about the uncertain future.

As they walked silently ahead, they had been walking for hours but they did not notice for each of them was deeply lost in their own thoughts. The light in the tunnel became more natural until, quite suddenly they emerged onto a shelf overlooking a huge Lake Valley. After his eyes became accustomed to the bright sunlight, Toli stood with his mouth agape and after a few seconds uttered, "By the sky" and that's all that would come out. He looked aside at his friends and they stood staring open-mouthed and silently into the valley.

Chapter 13

Muklah awoke feeling refreshed and as happy as he could ever remember being. After a fine breakfast meant for the visiting dignitaries, he sat at his huge council table and revelled in his surroundings, made all the more enjoyable because of who he had taken it from and the ridiculously easy manner in which it was taken. *Okay*, he thought to himself, *down to the business of the day*, and he sighed happily at the thought of ending this royal lineage once and for all.

He called to his manservant Crall, "You, here, now."

Crall immediately ran over to the table and stood by his side eyes lowered to the floor for it meant death for a Tolian to look a Black Isler in the eye.

"Go tell my commander I shall receive him now."

Crall ran off to Brakko's private quarters at speed and knocked on Brakko's door which was guarded by two of his hand-picked guards, one of whom was Bizzo who was now a senior and honoured member of the Black Isle military machine. Crall took two steps back, eyes always downcast for he was determined not to die on the whim of one of these black-hearted heathens, for he had resolved to wreak his own revenge upon the invader who had taken the life of his King and the freedom and happiness of his people.

The door soon opened and Brakko stepped out of the chamber dressed in black leather armour, more ornate than the previous armour he arrived in. Crall spun on his heels and stepped aside to allow the trio to pass then followed a few paces behind, eyes still lowered to the floor. They entered the council chamber in this manner of procession.

"Ah my trusted commander," enthused Muklah, "Have all the preparations been made for the return of our expected, short-term, guests?"

"Aye Lord," Brakko replied. "We have men out undercover of darkness we know the route the hunting party took, and know the general direction of the four insects who went fishing, none can return to the city unnoticed, we expect them soon, and none will escape your wrath."

"Excellent, good work, Brakko, and what of the little missing Princess? I am keen for them to all meet their fate together, we can move on then, to greater things."

"Unfortunately, my Lord, she has not been found, it is suspected that she fled with her maid and has met with her fate in the night, Sisk is applying his special ways right now trying to find her life signs," Brakko said, disappointment obvious in his voice.

"You there!" Muklah pointed at Crall. "Go find Lord Sisk and bring him here now."

Crall left the chamber at a trot, eyes down, and closed the huge door behind.

"Now, my trusted friend," Muklah turned back to Brakko. "Did you do as instructed to our other 46 friends outside?"

"Aye sire, all traces of them removed from sight, bodies thrown to the sharks and gibbets taken down and hidden, just waiting for their return, there is nothing to make them suspect anything is amiss, we even have our own men out dressed as various kinds of peasants, we will surround them before they even know about it."

"Excellent." Muklah was rubbing his hands and had an evil glint in his eyes. "I feel we should hang them all today, all but Toli, I feel we should give him a special send-off on his birthday. I will ponder this while we wait."

Just then the doors to the chamber opened and Sisk entered with Crall, eyes down, behind.

"You go now!" he waved Crall out of the room, "but always be ready when I call." Crall backed out of the chamber, closing the doors behind him.

Muklah turned to Sisk, "Now brother, what news of the Princess and the others, do you feel them?"

"There are no signs of them as of yet, my Lord, and I cannot detect any life force traces anywhere for any of them, I fear they may have all perished in the storm and robbed you of the joy of seeing them die before your eyes."

"No matter," said Muklah. "If they do not return by noon, we will send men further afield to bring them back, dead or alive, I care not as long as I see them dead personally."

"Aye Lord, but as long as I have been here I have been unable to feel any trace of life either inside or beyond these mountains, they are impenetrable but if they rest in a cave inside I will be unable to detect them until they emerge again, but you may rest assured, I will be upon them all as soon as they poke their snouts out from wherever they are."

"Excellent Sisk, I look forward to this joyous time, as to the girl, I have no worries as to her situation for she will not give us any trouble alive or dead, she is only a stupid little spoiled brat who was destined to grow into an adult spoiled brat, she means nothing important to anyone," Muklah said with arrogant confidence.

"Of course, Lord," said Sisk. "You may be secure in knowing that the future of your expanding Empire is guaranteed." He did not mention his growing unease for he had always been absolutely certain that he had been right and something was unnerving him, though he did not know what.

Chapter 14

As Soq and his companions stepped out onto the same shelf as Broq and his, each one of them had exactly the same reaction barring the Lake-Valley folk, they stood aghast at the sights before them, except, that is, Shala who looked calmly off to her left and could see off some distance away another group and she knew absolutely that her brother and his friends were among them; without a word, she began to walk at normal pace towards the other group, still holding Anga's hand, Soq knowingly followed, saying to the rest of them, "Come, we will go down now, into the valley."

By now everyone knew, because they could clearly see, that they were about to be reunited with their kin, still no-one ran, no-one called, no-one cried, for as they stepped onto the shelf and into the valley, a feeling of total calm took over them all as if they knew nothing could harm them and any grief became a memory.

When they joined in unison on the shelf, there were smiles and handshakes and hugs but no tears. Toli picked up his sister and kissed her on the cheek. "You okay?" he asked.

"Yes of course," she replied. "I have Anga," and for the first time, Toli noticed his sister's maid, the first time ever, he said to her, "Thank you for your care of my sister."

"Your sister needs no care, sire," she said and felt like she need say no more.

As they looked out into the valley, they could see they were on a shelf that went around as far as the eye could see, disappearing only under the occasional waterfall until it was far out of sight, they could not see the north end of the valley for it was too far off, but as they stood now on the south-east of the valley they could see to the east side and west side, many shelved with many stairs, carved into, the side of mountains joining the shelves on many levels all the way to the valley floor.

They could also see many openings onto the shelves for there was no need for secrecy here, they truly were safe and this place truly was wonderful and impenetrable to aggression. Along the lakeshore, they could see many small figures busying themselves for who knows what as they were still too far off, there was a sandy ring all the way around, as far as they were able to tell, then as on the habitable places on the outer side, rolling green meadows, up to forested foothills, then, the imposing mountainsides which seemed to have habitation of their own, for there was movement everywhere. They could also tell that they were on the south of the island because the so-called Dread River flowed out below them through a sheer-sided ravine which again rendered the river passage impassable.

As they descended their particular stairway, things became ever clearer, they could see men on the lake casting nets or throwing lines, men on the shoreline repairing nets or boats or baiting long lines of hooks, they saw cattle grazing happily on lush green meadows, as they came even closer they could make out that they were not all men on or beside the lake but women worked happily beside them, sisters beside brothers, wives beside husbands or just friend beside friend, they could now make out dogs and cats and children running around enjoying themselves for they had been given a full week to celebrate Toli's birthday and schools were closed for the duration of seven days starting today.

They could also make out the heavy udders of the cows and the huge heads and the shoulders of the contented bulls, they could also see movement along the treeline and at one point a huge antlered stag came out for a look at something then turned and strolled untroubled back into his domain.

Now they reached the valley-floor and with Broq and Soq leading, they made their way up the east side of the river towards a large lakeside city, the cattle stopped grazing and stood heads low as they passed all the dogs and cats were silent, and the children stopped playing and stood hands folded in front and heads bowed, any adults also did the same even the people on boats on the shoreline.

As they entered the city, the entire population took up this attitude and the party was led into a huge timber building with a huge central chimney with a faint wisp of smoke rising lazily into the almost still air. The sun was directly above the centre of the valley, it was noon.

Chapter 15

Muklah and Brakko had been plotting and planning all morning and had also been enjoying the harbour wine for nothing on the Black Isles compared with this amber delight or the deep red port wine which was supposed to have medicinal properties and was definitely making those two chuckle at their own dark humour.

"And when we're done with the royal cleansing," said Muklah, "we'll get the smiths and forgemen and cannoneers together and make plans for the manufacture of portable black powder guns and then we'll go and blow the remainder of the Green Isle army to pieces!"

"Ah ha, My Lord, and then we can leave Sisk there to rule as our ally with the best of weaponry and the second best army in existence, the best being right here with you." At this, the two men congratulated each other on this very sketchy plan.

Just then Crall came in after knocking, staring at the floor, he said, "My Lord Muklah, it's now 12 noon, you instructed me to let you know."

"Ah yes, of course, now go and get my brother Sisk and tell him to get here now!"

"Already here, Lord Brother, I figured you would require me at this time." Sisk came through the twin doors unnoticed but he had been listening to these two in the same secret cubby-hole as he had been using to spy on King Toli for the last 10 years, he was gratified to hear he was still a part of Muklah's greater plan, so far, for he had no news of any of the missing Tolians.

"Well, what news, my Brother?" a bleary-eyed Muklah asked. "Do we have a reason to plan the next hanging party or not?"

"No Lord, I cannot find a trace feeling of them anywhere, they are either all dead or are not on this Island, I suspect they met with a deadly disaster during our storm."

"Well, we will send a search party out anyway and look for signs of life or death, I care not which for I have pressing business this afternoon with Commander Brakko, you will go and pick twenty men and go out with them, come to me at sunset with your report."

"Aye Lord Brother, at once." At that Sisk left as silently as he came in.

"You are dismissed, peasant, you will not be required again this day or night," he said to Crall, he hadn't even bothered to learn his name, no need, he didn't expect servants to last too long anyway. Again Crall backed out facing the floor and closed the doors behind him.

Brakko said while pouring two more goblets of the ruby port, "What pressing business, my Lord?"

"Ah Brakko, I value your opinions greatly and so we must go from here to the ale store and make sure that standards remain high, follow me!" and the two left roaring and laughing, headed for the ale cellar for more alcohol abuse. Crall went back to his meagre quarters and wept for he was now sure that he had seen the last of the missing people and was certain all were dead.

Chapter 16

Broq and Soq led the group of escapees into the large meeting house which had already had many important valley-folk waiting for them, with them were Toli, Shala, Anga for Shala would not hear of her leaving, Tadesh and Ratesh, Shouk and Dovitt, Matak and Joki, the rest including Nana went off with the other warriors to be fed and rested while the Elders met with the King's party. A tall slim man in flowing white robes stood up when all else were seated around a table on the far side of the fire and clapped his hands twice, at once staff, no slaves came in with platters of food and jugs of wine, ale and water, they set the table and left.

The tall man whose name was Quor remained standing. "We must all take food and refreshment now, for we are in for a long day of discussion before we make a definite retaliation plan, so please help yourselves we have to keep our minds and bodies strong for what is undoubtedly to come." And sitting down again, he picked up a leg of wild turkey and took a large bite; this prompted the others to hungrily begin. As they ate, in silence, once again, the castle folk as the valley folk called them, began to realise that they had never felt so safe and secure as they did now, even in a lifetime of peace for the younger of the party and thirty years of peace for the older.

When the meal, at last, came to an end, the table was cleared and large bone mugs of a sweet flavoured, hot, malty, milky brew was set upon the table and they all supped slowly, each person savouring the excellent brew, which was made from honey and milk cream, from the happy cows they saw coming to this house.

Quor again stood. "My King, you may ask us any question you wish and if we can, we will answer."

But it was Shala who spoke first. "How did you know of our plight, master, for we did not even see it coming, and we live by the sea."

"First let me say I am no master, my name is Quor and I am your subject, Princess, as I am the King's; next, we also were preparing for the passing ceremony when we sensed disturbance in the air, all of us, man, woman and child, even our dogs were restless, so we sent lookouts to strategic lookout posts on the harbour and city side of the Island, to watch over the storm and your people and we know the storm was not a natural storm but the work of a gifted sorcerer, the man you called Tare, who we now know is Sisk by his real name, who is the bastard son of Muklah and a Sorceress on the Black Isle, a distant island from the main island of Sess with Muklah claiming that the child was an orphan of war, no one dared challenge him.

"My Princess, my King, our people have been keeping eyes on your kingdom for hundreds of years through peace and war and you never knew until the black hearted son of the black hearted father returned to wreak revenge on you, we could not stop them for we have no power of any significance over the sea or sky, so we could do nothing until they landed, and we intend to put things right before he takes a grip on your Island."

"You would have to bring life to the dead and all our dead are shark meat, so only bloody revenge will make things better for they will never be right again," Toli said this with a calmness he had never felt before, for he could find no anger inside, only a determination to reclaim his kingdom and return his deserving subjects to the peace he had known his whole life. Without realising, they all had finished their beautiful honey draught and without being told, the horn mugs were taken away and replaced with full ones, the conversation carried on into the night and many questions were asked and answered and by the end of the third honey draught, simply called honey draught, eyes were dropping and Quor stood again and spoke.

"My King, my Princess, honoured guests and all here, I feel it would be practical if we all try to sleep now for tomorrow would be a better day for making plans when our thoughts will have more clarity, are we agreed?" They all said aye together. "Then please follow the person who puts a hand on your shoulder and go to the quarters you are led to and sleep well as I know you will." With that, Quor left the meeting house and headed to his own bed.

One man touched Toli, Ratesh, Dovitt and Joki on their shoulders and they each rose to follow, the same for the three military men, and for Shala and Anga. All were shown to their respective rooms, one for the four boys, one for the Fathers and one for Shala and Anga. The rest of the meeting then left the house and retired to their own families and homes, Broq and Soq went to their own cottage for the brothers were not yet married. All were asleep in seconds, a deep dreamless, undisturbed, peaceful sleep.

Chapter 17

Muklah and Brakko were well on the way now, to a drunken stupor. They had a table brought into the ale cellar along with a pair of chairs, a barrel of wine, and enough meat to last the day, However, this was a state they were well used to, especially during sea voyages and sieges, but Muklah was prone to making wild promises when he was drunk and today was no exception.

He said across the table to Brakko, who was becoming a blur, "You know, my friend, I'm probably going to send you back to the Black Isles to govern in my absence for here is going to be the centre of the new Empire."

"I am truly honoured, my Lord, and I thank the Kraken for your good favour and will always be loyal to you alone, as I always have been." Brakko was used to these drunken promises and compliments and knew exactly what to say, drunk or sober.

"And then we will have an invincible triangle with you on the Black Isle, Sisk on the Green Isle and myself here producing weapons the likes of which has never been seen nor heard of for the weapon makers here are second to none, and their shipwrights, so as soon as I can find a way to carry those black powder cannons on board our warships, and a way to arm each man with his own personal weapon, we will be indestructible, my friend."

"We are already indestructible, my Lord." Brakko rose unsteadily and poured two horns of ale from the huge cask they had tapped, he put them down on the table then picked up a large pewter jug, emptied it into the two goblets on the table-top then went to the wine barrel and filled the jug back up to the top.

"We know this Island is impossible to invade from any other direction then the east for the mountain elsewhere cannot be breached, no more than they can be occupied, this is the perfect Capital of your new Empire, and I thank you for my part, given by you, in the forming of the greatest Empire the world has ever known or will ever know."

Exactly what Muklah wanted to hear and he knew it for like all ambitious generals, he had his own agenda which relied on him making it back to the Black Isles in one piece.

"Aye Brakko, and when we confirm that the entire royal family and those loyal to them have been eliminated we'll drag out their cannoneers and train our men to perfection, then tie them to their own guns and blow them all to oblivion."

He started laughing then, a wild, manic, drunken laugh which started Brakko off and they both laughed until their ribs hurt and they fell back into their chairs and fell asleep in a kind of stupefied coma snoring loudly. Sisk had gone out on his search for the last of the problematic royals and Tolians, he wasn't afraid of failure for he was sure if he couldn't find them then they couldn't be found and if they couldn't be found by him they must be dead, if there were no traces of death they must have been dragged into some cave somewhere and either eaten or stored to be eaten by one of the wild animals that belong to the mountains and are considered to be responsible for the disappearance of the exploratory expeditions, bears, wolves, lions, he cared not just as long as he could confirm to Muklah that they would never reappear to trouble him again, as he fully intended to do by dark this night for he was a man with his own agenda.

He took his twenty men here and there looking for signs of passing, although he knew now that he was only going through the motions for the benefit of his soldiers who would gossip when they got back and in turn one of their comrades, at least one, would be reporting directly to Muklah not even via Brakko. So he made a show of getting off his horse and checking the ground, or a broken plant, or a twig, or stone, but he had no sense of feeling that they were anywhere on the island, he knew they were gone one way or another, and that would be his report when he got back, and the light was failing so he called to his captain and said, "We must go back now but tell the men to keep their eyes open and their brains alert for there is still a little light and something may be seen coming from another direction, you never know."

The Captain strode off to tell his men who were very grateful for they had not stopped to eat or drink since leaving just after noon.

"And tell the men to light the torches, we don't want to miss the least thing."

All these actions he knew with certainty would get back to Muklah who admired thoroughness and often rewarded it. They arrived back just after darkness fell and he told the Captain to dismiss the men and himself, the tavern had been instructed to have food and ale ready to be served and not to worry about payment as he himself would deal with it. There was a hum of gratitude through the men and each of them gave a nod of respect to Sisk as they filed off to food and drink.

Sisk smiled to himself as they left, slapping each other on the back, for he knew the entire day would be recounted all night as the ale flowed and he wanted as many as possible to know of his own efforts in the name of his Lord Muklah. He then rode his horse to the stables and gave his steed up to the stablemaster and immediately made his way to the council chamber where he fully expected Muklah and Brakko to be awaiting his report on entering the chamber; all there was, was a mess of spilled drink and scraps of food on the table and floor and he immediately knew what had happened, he went to the door and let out a roar, "Crall, come here now!" and he went back into the chamber to wait.

Within a few seconds, Crall hurried in, head bowed as usual for he was expecting to be summoned again even though he had been dismissed for the rest of the day.

"What went on here?" Sisk asked, already knowing the answer, but did not know where the two revellers were now for he had not taken the time yet to mind-search for them.

"My…my Lord Sisk," Crall stammered, "Lord Muklah dismissed me shortly after y…you left for your s…search, I will go now and find their whereabouts. I…I am so sorry, m…my—"

"Never mind; have this cleaned away and scrubbed up I will have no trouble locating them myself, then you may retire for the night, you will definitely not be called upon again this night."

"Aye L…Lord." Crall cowered and left to alert the cleaning staff, now slaves, as to their duties and to supervise the clean-up himself.

Sisk then followed his own instinctual feeling straight to the ale cellar where he found the two reprobates unconscious, snoring loudly and dribbling down themselves like common soldiers after the pillage is done. He tried to physically wake them up to no avail, he then tried to wake them mentally but found, as he knew that you cannot activate something that is not there. He then turned to the cellar-master and his apprentice who stood silently against a wall shaking, eyes on the floor thinking they would be blamed for this situation and taken out to be hung.

"You two can go," he said, seeing the obvious panic in their shaking bodies, for they were frozen to the spot, "and you need not worry for your Lord cannot get into this condition without your exceptional skills."

There was an audible sigh of relief and they both grovelled their way backward from the cellar. Sisk then went to the door and screamed in false anger, "Captain of the guard, to the ale cellar immediately." The captain, having never been far away, appeared around the corner straight away accompanied by four of Muklah's personal guard all in dress armour and all wide awake.

"What goes on here?" Sisk asked, as if he already didn't know.

"My Lord Muklah dismissed us hours ago, Lord, but we did not leave him; we merely stayed out of sight, he has never been in any danger."

"Very well; station two men by the door and two by the corridors end, I don't expect that to happen before daylight so make it fresh men fed and rested."

The Captain stood poker straight and looked straight ahead as did his companions for the personal guard knew no fear. "Aye Lord, of course." He stationed his four men as requested and went off to get four replacements for these men had been on duty all day and would appreciate food, drink and sleep himself, as he made his way back to his own quarters, he smiled to himself and thought, *I can find no trace of fear in those men, they are so sure of their loyalty they would rather die impaled than betray, I must find myself some of them.*

In the tavern, his own search party were by now gorging on fine food and sculling back the finest ale any of them ever tasted, the conversation became more loud and lively, there were some very happy men.

"Well, that was some day and a bit!" said one soldier.

"Aye lad, I thought it would not come to an end," said another.

"He's indeed a hard taskmaster, my old legs are buggered for sure, poor shanks o' mine."

The Captain then stood on top of the table and shouted for quiet. "Listen, the lot of you, did any of you see himself stop to eat or drink?"

There was an uncomfortable hush in the room now. "No you bloody did not," murmurs of agreement went around the smoky tavern.

"You did not see 'cos he did not do anything we did not, in fact, credit where due, he worked harder than any two of us put together." More murmurs of agreement. "So if I was any one of you, I'd be minding what I say for we are eating and drinking on him and I'd be willing to bet my landing pay that we are all eating and drinking before him for his duties never end and you'll all, I'll bet, be sleeping this night before him, so lads a toast to our leader for the day, TO THE LORD SISK!" and he raised his horn of ale above his head, and they all stood as one, even the soldiers who had not been there that day.

"AYE, THE LORD SISK!" and they skulled their ale in unison. Then they all laughed and slapped backs and continued to tell favourable tales of the days proceeding, what a thorough man Sisk was, and how faithful to our Lord Muklah and how he rewarded those who were faithful to him, and how they hope they were picked to serve him again.

As Sisk sat in his quarters eating by himself, he chuckled for he knew he had started something very profitable for himself. He then went to his cot and slept soundly.

Chapter 18

Morning in the valley was bright and a light breeze wafted through the open windows of the rooms allocated to the castle-folk, the King and his company wakened all at the same time, and no-one could remember ever feeling so refreshed nor so delightfully hungry, a bell rang gently somewhere outside and a voice called from inside, "My King, breakfast is served in the meeting house."

They all dressed quickly and Toli realised again that by the call "my king", his father was dead along with his mother and brothers, but he felt gratitude for the lives saved more than sadness for the lives lost nor did he dwell on it, for he now had a purpose in life he never expected to feel, he had been so spoiled.

They all exited their quarters at the same time, the same guides as the night before awaited, smiling, in the common hallway Toli moved and stood before them, they all smiled, no tears, and Toli opened his arms, palms outwards, towards them they all came together in a huddle, with Shala in Anga's arms between him and Anga, Their eyes met and a palpable shiver went through both their bodies and Shala's smile became wider for she had felt the shiver too and knew there were great things to come.

Toli then straightened up and said, "Okay, we must go meet our friends and benefactors." At that, he turned to his guide and followed him with his three best friends as did the others. On entering the great house, he noticed there were more people present, and oddly that the fire was again lit though there was no need, he also noticed among them Nana and the rest of the hunting party.

Quor stepped forward and declared, "My King. The King is dead, long live the King."

Again, together they all stood and said, "The King is dead, long live the King."

"By Aquos and the sky," Toli said, "I thank you all."

A mist then came over his eyes but soon passed, he then looked around to his rescued companions, they all smiled and looked directly into his eyes, he knew then that they, everyone, felt the same determined purpose as he himself felt, and so as he met their eyes, one by one this time, he gave a nod to each one and they each of them gave a nod back eye to eye with their King and he felt great joy in the certainty that these people would be with him to the end whatever that may be.

"My King," Quor declared, "your breakfast feast is served."

And he walked behind the top table and said, "Please, my King," and indicated to Toli where he should sit, which he did, Quor then sat on his right, the other guides then brought the rest of them to their seats, Shal directly on his left, next to Anga, then Ratesh, then Dovitt and Joki, to his right Quor, Tadesh, Shouk and Matak, then Broq and Soq. On the right table going away from the top table was Gogon the fire guard and his Brother Luron with half of the hunting party interspersed with valley folk, on the left sat Nana, again with the remainder of the hunting part interspersed with valley folk.

The feast then began, the fare seemed to be inexhaustible, fruit, bread, cheese, chickens whole, potatoes piled high in huge bowls, butter, gravy, sauces, too many vegetables to name, rabbits whole and in stews, turkeys again whole, in front of each table a whole boar and a whole deer on spits kept hot by being turned over deep trays of hot coals.

"Bit much for breakfast, don't you think?" Toli asked Quor.

"Forgive us, sire, we have never hosted a King before and we also thought to the feast you will be missing today, with your family, it is the day of your passing and we wish to make it memorable."

Toli looked at Quor. "You have done that, my friend, nothing could ever be more memorable for this day is the beginning of something yet to be realised, but already destined, and together, as Tolians, we will see it to its end, today is the beginning of the end for the doomed Muklah and any other invader who dares challenge our hope and home."

"Well said, Sire, but what I had hoped for today was to familiarise you with the people and ways of us lake-valley folk."

"You'll get no argument from me this day so let's enjoy and leave serious discussion for another time."

And with that, Toli forked a huge potato and put it on his massive plate, quartered it, put a slab of butter in the centre and crumbled cheese all over, and that signalled the end of that particular conversation. As Toli ate, he raised his head to pick up his goblet and looked around the great house, every single person was chatting happily between gulping and chewing and he was gratified greatly.

Chapter 19

In the castle, it was a totally different start to the day, Muklah lolled his head in his chair which woke him with a start. "Oh, ow! By the Kraken!" he yelped, the two door guards burst into the cellar, swords in front, ready.

"My Lord, is all well?" the first guard asked, a concerned look on his face, he then bolted left and the other right, they checked the four corners of the cellar then the aisles between the massive casks, when they were satisfied there was no danger they returned to the doors, turned, bowed their heads, left and closed their doors behind themselves without another word. During this noisy action, Brakko came awake to see Muklah sitting opposite with head in hands, moaning his woes to the floor.

"Bloody seas," he said, "who put a lance through my head?" and he put his head in his hands and got on with his own misery.

Just then the doors opened and Sisk stood in the doorway, he turned to the guard on his left, "Go tell your Captain to change the guard, it's been a long night and we'll need fresh and aware men from now on," another kind act that would be spoken of. He stepped into the room and closed the doors behind him.

As he opened his mouth to speak, Muklah raised his hand for quiet, then he got up, picked up the two empty horns and walked or rather shuffled to the tapped keg and filled his own horn which he gulped down in one, he then refilled it, put it on the floor and filled Brakko's horn in front of him, he then leaned back in his chair and said, "My eyes open, your eyes open," and took another gulp as did Brakko.

"Now, what news?" he asked Sisk, turning painfully and wincing in the process.

"My Lord, we searched till the light was gone, even then we searched by torchlight on the way back, we could find no trace of any of them neither physically or mentally, but most of all there was no feeling of presence throughout the search, I am of the opinion that they all perished and cave-dwelling beasts have dragged or carried them off for food, if they were on this Island alive, they would be incarcerated under your care awaiting their fate."

"All well and good, Sisk, but I see daylight, you were ordered to report last night." Again Muklah winced as he turned towards the tiny window allowing in the daylight.

"Indeed I was, my Brother, as ordered, but you were not in the council chamber and when I found you here with Lord Brakko, you could not be awakened by any means so by my own decision, I left instructions for you to be guarded but left to rest, for fatigue is undoubtably part of the problem, you need time to rest for your voyage was long."

"Indeed, yes, rest, you're so wise, Brother, now send the master brewer and cellarman to me; they must be punished."

"Punished, Brother? Had you drank this amount of Black Isle brew or liquor, you would be under the care of the Healer or worse, the Embalmer; besides, if you kill these valuable slaves, who will keep you supplied with such pleasant products?"

"Ah wisdom again, Sisk, you truly are invaluable, hmm rest indeed hmm…very well, I'll take your advice and return to council tomorrow, tell that fellow Crall to arrange the cleaning of this place and a meal for us three in my private entertaining chamber and tell him to make sure there is plenty of wine, ale and food, I'm going to rest for a few hours, tell him to make it for four hours' time, tell my guards to wake me in three."

"Of course, Brother, but if I may I'd like to ride out alone in daylight to see if I missed anything, for my own peace of mind, I may try a different way."

"Forever faithful Sisk, of course, you have permission to do as you will, we can deal with our prisoners tomorrow if needs be, as you say we need valuable people for training purposes, the cannons pose a problem, aye Sisk do as you feel is right and we will talk again on your return, in the meantime, Brakko fill our horns and we'll sleep all the better!"

Sisk said farewell and left the cellar; he left his instructions with Crall, went to the stables and mounted his waiting horse a skin of wine over one shoulder and a satchel of food over the other, and rode out the back gate at a canter.

Back in the cellar, Muklah drained his horn of ale again and announced, "Right, I'm now going to follow my brother's advice and rest."

"And good advice it is too, my Lord, I think I will follow it myself."

With that, they both got up and went to the doors, before he opened the door he took a deep breath and straightened his spine, Brakko did the same and Muklah pulled both doors open and they stepped out into the hallway with an effort to keep up the illusion of sobriety for they both staggered and they were both covered in food scraps, drink dribble and their own dribble and vomit, all the more obvious on the black of their armour, the guards closed the doors behind them and followed stone-faced, but heaving inside for the smell was overpowering and that is saying something for sea-faring soldiers.

As they parted to go to their separate chambers, Muklah said, "Do not be late for our meeting, Brakko."

"No Lord, I will not."

When he got to his bedchamber door, he said to his guards, "I am needed in four hours' time, make sure I am wakened in three to a hot bath and a clean tunic, no need for armour this day."

The guards clicked their heels and bowed their heads.

"And make sure Lord Brakko gets the same."

He then went through the door and closed it, his armour was a trail on the floor before he reached his huge bed.

Chapter 20

The feast in the great house was coming to an end and Toli began to feel like he should say something to the assembly as a way of saying sincere thanks, most people had finished eating and drinking and were actually looking at Toli as if waiting for some kind of speech or maybe a declaration, he stood up, the house went silent, he looked around at the expectant faces.

"My friends," he began, "myself and my fellow castle-folk would like to express our thanks to our rescuers and to all Lake-valley folk for your help in this darkest of times. We are all now bonded together with a strength that can never be conquered by any invader, so with the permission of the Lake-valley folk, I would like to declare this day an annual affair, not to celebrate my passing to the valley but the coming together of all of us to form this nation, and again with your permission, I would like to call it Tolia Day and rename Toli's Island, Tolia." There was a fairly feeble reaction in the great house, a smattering of applause and no cheering along with looks of puzzlement on all of their faces.

Toli sat down and said to Quor in a low voice, "What have I said wrong?"

"Sire, you are our King, this Island, as far as all are concerned, is Toli's Island, with King Toli, always King Toli, at its head. For us to finally meet the King is almost overwhelming and to change the name we are all so proud of is beyond our understanding."

Toli immediately stood, he had to raise his voice above the muttering of the gathering, "Please friends, I apologise for my previous statement, this Island shall remain Toli's Island."

There was much cheering and clapping.

"However," the cheering quieted and there were more murmurs, "I must insist in the national day of celebration stays in place and be called not Tolia Day but Tolian Day."

Now people leapt to their feet shouting their approval; the applause and cheering lasted several minutes. Toli sat down and wished someone would say something; Quor saved the day.

"Good people, we must now consult with the King before meeting his subjects face to face so I must ask all but the top table to make their way out of the great house."

They all rose as one and left in an orderly single file from each table, one of the personal guides closed the doors behind them and called for the other guides to follow him out of the great house, what was to be at this time, the grand council, were all that were left inside. Quor said, "Please follow me," and he directed them to a previously unnoticed door of very heavy wood, jet black wood, which shone like burnished armour, it was a thing of beauty, despite only being a door.

On the other side of the wonderful door was another, this time circular chamber, carved from solid rock, well-lit despite no evidence of torches or any other man-made light source. No-one was even slightly puzzled for the rock-light had been explained during the rescue just the morning before.

There was a huge oval granite block in the centre of the floor surrounded by timber chairs, the party of thirteen took a seat each, with Toli at the top of the oval with Quor on his right.

Quor spoke first, "This chamber is a natural wonder, and is today, as it was found, as far as our documented history is concerned, you did not notice it because the great house has always been a part of this rock and has always been built around the rock, it has never been any other way, we don't even know the material of the door, for if it is wood, it is not, nor ever has been, native of this Island. Now, you will all notice there are still seven empty places at today's table, these, with your permission, Sire, will be filled with various advisors, as required, by your invitation, for you have subjects the length and breadth of this lake and land who will council you on their particular area if required, but the valley on the whole, runs itself.

"You may be here for some time, Sire, but you will never have to sit at council without good advisors around you, I also propose to you now, Sire, that the people present here now become the senior first council of Toli's Island."

"So be it! From this day on, this is the head council of this Island, this whole Island, all agreed say Aye!" Toli was on his feet now. They all said "Aye"; no-one even thought to mention the various ages of the council, for they all knew this was right, and this will win.

"Quor, you have the floor, we are in your hands, so please. Continue." And Tadesh smiled for that was exactly what his father would have said and done.

Toli sat down then and as Quor went to speak again, Toli said, "Please sit, Quor, it is to be a long day," for Toli had noticed that the chairs that had been chosen, randomly by each of the council members had left each of them at eye level with the others, and if each of their chairs fitted like his own, it was clear to Toli, these chairs are meant to be sat upon, things are meant to be done while seated on these chairs, he was certain.

Quor sat and looked around the table and thought, *By the sky, I've been in here many, many times but this has never happened before*; at that precise moment a realisation came over the entire council, they all looked at each other in a kind of awe, because at that precise moment they knew, absolutely, that a bond of trust had been formed, a chain that could never be broken, even if they were apart, and they all had a huge grin on their faces.

"RIGHT!" a palm slapped the tabletop, it was Shala. "As my brother said, Quor, we are in your hands, so please continue."

They all looked at the 9-year-old Princess, all but Anga, who sat looking at her hands grinning even more than before. Toli threw a glance from his sister to Anga, at that instant Anga lifted her eyes to meet his and there it was again, the shiver, the spark. Toli threw his eyes back to Shala, now she was, again, grinning.

"Very well," Quor broke the reverie. "I will first tell you of the lay of the valley, I will tell you of people not yet met, but will say, that you can go to any subject on this lake, or in this valley, for any reason and you will see they are all the same, all will afford the same level of welcome and assistance to King or no, for we have never had a natural enemy although, as you will soon find we have, as your father did, kept up a military force, well-armed and trained, who have kept a watch on all points of this Island.

"We have never been breached by a hostile, and forces have tried, unbeknown to yourselves, to land the wilder sides of us, they all met with death, we remain unassailable everywhere bar the harbour and the strand, there are however, certain friendly explorers who made us an oath never to leave this place, for they would never be allowed to reveal our secrets, they have lived among us ever since, now we, none of us, has a secret, there is no more need.

"We know the staff in the Castle, the trades, shepherds, fisherfolk and any others left alive, that they are necessary and if they do their work they should be left alone, we also know that Muklah, through great lack of activity, had slipped into a drunken malaise and is, for the moment, incapable of making decisions or giving orders, however, his Captains, in the meantime, were keeping duties up, so keeping, at least on duty soldiers, sober and focused.

"Thanks to them, they are unknowingly helping us, for by keeping order they are avoiding the mayhem that would come with bored, drunken, soldiers let loose, and, thankfully again, they punish off duty offenders for they did not need to be minding their own, and the possibility of being locked up, until they are needed again, which may be never, kept things well under control, which is one less thing we need worry about.

"Sire, at the north end of the lake is the centre of military matters in this valley and now, on this Island, between here and there are many villages and towns which we will describe to you as we go up to the garrison city of Bevak, it is very impressive, I feel it is best that you see it with your own eyes, the lake as we go. Now Sire, the day wears on, I kept you too long in here, would you like to meet the people who are here in Quoror? The capital? We could not take the numbers who wished to come, but we can visit as many as we can on the way up to Bevak. If you agree of course, Sire."

Toli stood up. "Of course I do, Quor, we, all of us cannot do without your council, I thank you, all of you, let's go!"

Chapter 21

Sisk left the back gate and made his way up a trail towards the strand, as he came on top of the strand suddenly he stopped the horse and inhaled deeply. *The air is different here, better*, he thought, and turned south towards the river-mouth and casually trotted along the sand enjoying being out of the city and its stink and seemingly constant heat, he could not wait to get back to the Green Isle and its open, airy, green hills, and its fruit, and its flowers, he was lost in his own thoughts when he began to notice the distant roar of white water, he was immediately alert and stopped to gather himself, he looked around, to his left the sea, waves swelling and dipping like a living, breathing entity, all on its own, to his right a scatter of various trees on basically an open meadow, which came, at this point, all the way up to the mountains, he could now feel the fresh water mist on his face and he licked his lips and left his tongue out to catch the droplets.

He rode right up to the edge of the river mouth and looked up at the gorge mostly obscured by mist from the rapid white water, there was nothing visible to suggest passage was possible, nor did he get any feeling of presence, but he looked up to the gorge and said aloud, to whomever, "I know you are there, I know, you know me, we will meet soon, it can only be a matter of time, he lingered there for a while then turned his horse and took him out of the mist for he needed a fire for food, he had been in the saddle for hours and the air had given him an appetite like he hadn't had since the Green Isle."

He started the fire first, and went into his saddle bags and took a half cooked hare and two large potatoes, he made a spit from new moist branches he cut from the local trees, cottonwoods in this case, put the hare on the spit just above the flame and the two potatoes just close enough to the centre of the fire as to be able to turn them, he then went back to the bags and took a lump of the Tolian cheese and two thick slices of nutty brown bread, he also pulled out a pewter pint flask full of good golden harbour wine, he put the cheese straight between the two slices and took a munch.

He uncorked the flask and took a gulp and said aloud, "By the sea and the sky, that is the best," and he let the horse run free and sat down on a flat-topped rock to mind his dinner and fare, paying special attention to the turning of the food. It was an hour and a half later that he had finished and with regret he packed up his little camp nothing to clean, all leftovers went to the fire, barring his flask, all else was organic, he whistled for his horse and the horse obediently walked to where he had left Sisk; with a sigh, Sisk put the flask to his lips and drained it, then put it in the saddle bag, he mounted the horse, looked over his shoulder and said, "I know you are there and I know we will meet, farewell for now."

He took his time getting back to the Castle for there was a reek about the whole city that was not there in the previous 10 years, the light was fading by the time he got back to the track leading to the back gate, only then did the feeling of wasted time come upon him. *What has been left to this land can achieve nothing by this regime*, he thought as he returned his steed to the stables.

He came back through the back door from the stables and felt the feeling as soon as he entered the building, he actually had a bad feeling since leaving in the first place but could not define the reason for this feeling which added to his confusion because normally there is no confusion, it was immediately obvious to him now that the feeling was related to what he left behind and not to what he was searching for. As he looked around on his way to report to Muklah, he noticed the lethargy in the guards, one was even slouched against the wall, he soon straightened himself up when he saw Sisk was back.

Sisk walked up to this particular guard and unnervingly stared him in the eyes and asked, "Do you have a problem with your duties, soldier?"

"No my Lord Sisk."

"Then please explain to me why you were dossing on duty?"

"I just lost concentration, my Lord, we four have been here since you last ordered a guard change, and no other orders have come from the council chamber, neither of our Lords have emerged since they went in."

"I will give you orders right now, it is your duty to go tell the change of the guard to get here now, then you four will go and get fed and rested, go now, I will be here when you get back."

Only a few minutes later, the guard accompanied by the guard-change came to attention before Sisk awaiting the order to leave, he addressed all eight guards, "From here and now onwards, there will be two twelve-hour shifts for guards from noon till midnight so you four will be here until noon tomorrow; then you will be relieved, would I be correct in thinking there are five sets of four guards?"

They all chorused together, "Yes, my Lord."

"Very well; you four go to the guard room and, whoever is the Captain here, with the leaving shift, go tell the next shift due on duty to be here at twelve noon sharp tomorrow and explain to them that from now on they will be working 5 day and night twelve-hour rotation. In other words, you lot coming on duty now will be on duty for the next five nights, you who are leaving now I will come back at midnight twenty days from now, I'm sure you can work out the details for the other guards." Then he let out a yell, "Crall, here, now!" Crall was there in seconds.

"See to it, Crall, these guards will be brought food and water at six in the morning, as the next duty will, at six in the evening and so on for the foreseeable future, I want one person per guard duty, and I want the same person to serve the same guards, in other words, the people you choose will be keeping the same hours as there assigned duty guard, you, yourself will eat the same food and drink the same water as their charges, see to it now." And Crall left at pace to fulfil his own duties.

Sisk turned back to the off-duty guards.

"You can go do as you wish now, but do not think you will be drunk for the next twenty days for as you know, the penalty for bad conduct including drunken behaviour, is severe and cannot be challenged, I suggest that off duty guards make up some kind of useful, maybe, fitness programme, for you spent many hours standing still, this, of course, does not mean that you have to be in isolation, but be aware that you are all hand-picked for this duty and are expected to set an example to the ranks, So you may enjoy your free time but always be sure that you are all above suspicion of misbehaviour, these rules are in place as of right now, do not let me down!"

At this he turned and stepped up to the door of Muklah's entertainment chamber, smiling to himself as he knew these measures would sit well with the personal guard for the hours of duty up till now had been uncertain and there had been no food allowed while on duty. The four off-duty guards headed back to the personal guard barracks to spread the great news.

"The Lord Sisk has his head screwed on alright," one guard said excitedly on the way.

"He will bring better days to us all," another said, and they all went off chattering excitedly, glad to be the bearers of good tidings.

Crall too was delighted for due to the lack of activity recently, he had been having trouble keeping people busy in the Castle, but now he could allocate new positions to staff who were struggling to justify their positions. Another positive for Sisk.

He pushed the door open and stepped into the chamber, the scene was as the scene was the night before, Muklah and Brakko both with heads down on the table, food, drink and vomit all over the table, the same on the floor. He approached the two unconscious bodies to see if he could sense any reason to wake them, there was none, both were senseless, besides he had nothing to report. He left and closed the door behind him, he turned to the Captain of the guard.

"Make sure that our Lord and Commander Brakko are not disturbed, I will return in the morning to report to them, for now they are at rest."

By now Sisk was weary and hungry himself, he had not noticed the time pass him by, he called for Crall at his chamber door and went in. Crall came through the open door with a tray of food, liver with onions and potatoes and a jug of golden harbour wine with the lovely brown nutty bread and a slab of salty butter on a separate platter.

"Make sure you have your servers ready for the feeding of the guard tomorrow at six."

"Already done, Lord, I have each need covered by a different server for each duty but the same server for the same guards. They each will be eating and drinking the same as the allocated guards."

"Very good, Crall, you may leave now, but I will be calling you early in the morning for there is another busy clean up tomorrow, wait for my call!"

"As you wish, my Lord," and he left.

Walking the short distance to his own quarters Crall thought, *He's the only bugger in the whole Castle that has a clue about what is needed.*

Sisk smiled in his chamber for he felt the compliment in the thought, then he ate and drank and then got into his bed and slept soundly.

Chapter 22

On leaving the great house, the newly formed head council were greeted by a huge crowd, all on one knee, heads bowed, awaiting the king, There were a dozen directly in front of him who seemed to be in a group of their own.

"Please rise, everyone," Toli said, and they all did.

Quor turned to Toli then and said, "The twelve people stood here in front, are the explorers your father sent to chart this valley, two of whom are Green Islanders expert in cartography lent to your father by his true friend King Jai, the other ten are Tolian and would like to speak first with your indulgence."

"Of course, that will suit, I will be greatly interested in what they have to say, although I was not yet born, I remember Nana told me and my siblings of how deadly it was to even go near the Dread River."

At this he extended his right hand and indicated where Nana stood. "The stories worked, for no child ever went within five miles of the river and to my knowledge no other expeditions were ever planned, and yet, here you are before me, please enlighten me." Toli's sense of mischief had now come to the fore and both Anga and Shala looked at him sideways, trying to contain their mirth for the two of them, at least, knew exactly what he was up to. None in the dozen had the slightest clue that the situation had already been explained in the previous council meeting. The two people stood at the front of the other ten were the Green Islands, Dauti and Doulen, who were not only explorers and map-makers but had been valuable advisors and trained officers in King Jai's army. Dauti took one step forward and began to speak without fear, no-one felt fear while in the Valley.

"King Toli," he began, "when we twelve left your father's fair city—"

Just then 9-year-old Shala poked her brother in the small of his back and said, "We don't have time for this, Brother."

Toli then held up his right hand for silence. "What is your name, friend?"

"My name is Dauti, Sire."

The hand went up again.

"So you must be Doulen," he looked directly at Doulen; another poke in the back.

"No time!"

Toli thought, *My sister has a hidden talent, a latent talent, that will surprise us all when it properly emerges, and I also think that something is happening between Anga and I, whatever it is, it is powerful, I'm sure people who live to be a hundred years old have never felt this thing.*

The little reverie took several seconds and when he looked at Doulen again, he said, "My friend, there are statues in the fountain square, you know where that is, of all twelve of you, you are all heroes, each one of you is remembered by a fair on the anniversary of the day you left, what you don't know is I already knew your situation, I was briefed by Quor, so, to clarify the whole, as far as anyone alive or dead or yet to come is concerned you will always be brave heroes, willing to do anything for their King and in the future there will be another celebration for the day you once again see home." The entire throng roared with approval and delight.

To calm them, Quor now raised his hand, he turned to Toli, "If you look across the lake, Sire, you will see a group of people, a lot of people. Sire, these are the folk who were in the outlying areas mainly cattlemen or shepherds and their wives and children, we got them through as soon as we realised what was going on, they asked to be placed on the far bank so as to get a clear view for they doubt that you are still alive."

The far bank was visible from the Capital, the lake narrowed at the south end as it came closer to the river. Toli walked to the corner of the speech platform, looked across the lake, shading his eyes with one hand, then raised both hands into the air and waved by crossing his arms and hands above his head, there were two hundred souls on the far side who erupted with joy of recognition, babes in arms and all which caused a chain reaction on this side of the lake, and Toli thought, *I hope they all feel the joy I feel here*, and now he turned to his council and saw in each of their faces the same unbridled happiness that all present felt, and, in fairness, much further afield, even the birds and animals were making a noise, and the fish were leaping from the lake so that the surface seemed to be boiling.

During this tumult, Quor said to Toli, "Sire, is it obvious that you cannot speak to all here today as individuals nor even in groups, I feel it may be best to speak to all, now, and deal with the individuals later."

"I agree, Quor, I don't want to leave retribution too long, we must plan, as quicky as possible the demise of the black-souled-rat."

"Sire, the black souled rat is a drunken mess as is his commander, the soldiers are under threat of losing their freedom if they misbehave, the Tolians, even the cannoneers, have a good reason to be kept alive for they are still valuable for a time to come, after all, there is a lot to be learned in firing those beasts, we don't have them here, nor do we need them."

"Again, I have to agree with your logic, Quor, I will talk to them all now." Toli walked back to the corner of the platform again, facing west across to the far bank and held up both hands palms out in front of him and the crowd on the bank quieted, he then returned to the centre-front of the platform and repeated the gesture, eventually there was almost total silence.

"Good people, here today, have a claim on his, the history of being a part of the new dawn coming, as do all who seek peace and prosperity in our future, unfortunately we all have an enemy to deal with first, a dirty black-hearted rock snake of an enemy, and he will never forget the reaction of this land to invasion, one way or another he will be made to regret ever setting foot here, our home, so I cannot spend too much time, on this particular day, to talk to all of you individually but I can assure you, our relationship has just begun, we are all on the cusp of the strongest, closest, bond ever known and we will never divert ourselves from the path of peace and safety for all Tolians, all we have to do is scrub the scum off the rock, never to return."

An almighty roar went up from the crowd and again there was a reaction on the far bank. Toli looked around this unbelievable scene, and for some unconscious reason, clenched his right fist and placed it over his heart, he waited for a few seconds more, just looking and smiling, then he turned and walked back into the great house.

The sun was dropping towards the west as they got back inside, there had been more to this day than is written here, their guides waited inside for them and bid them follow, they were led to yet another room, the head council dining room, and when they were seated ale and wine was served as an appetiser, and Toli thought, *Tonight's stars! I never guessed I was so hungry.*

They sat in no particular order around this table and Toli got to talk to his friends properly for the first time in days, Broq, Soq, Quor, Tadesh, Shouk and Matak got into a clique who looked like they were discussing tactics, between gulps of ale, and Anga and Shala sat demurely, talking, Anga sipping wine and Shala sipping water.

"So," Ratesh said, "any thoughts so far?"

"No, not yet, boys, but I have a notion that someone else might." He nodded towards Shala and Anga, not the Generals.

Joki gagged on his ale. "Aye, you might be right at that, Toli, or should I say, my King?"

"Only at council and in public, as you know, palomine."

The friends laughed at this for palomine meant friend of mine, it also meant that you can say as you wish as a friend but a line has to be drawn in official and public life.

The evening carried on like this for a while and before they knew about it the honey draught was being served. Shala looked up at Toli and said, "Toli, I feel we should spend more time discussing our plan of action this night than the time we have spent in idle conversation."

All present stopped speaking and looked from Shala to Toli.

"I too felt this, Shala, but I have been advised by Quor that there is a lot to do here first. Quor has eyes on every corner of the Castle and harbour from above, we also know, if not for the black-heart's Captains, we could go and walk in now today, but they are, if anything, loyal to their lord and their vocation as Commanders, we have not yet met our own army and can do nothing without them, they have been waiting for us for time unknown, we will right this wrong tomorrow.

"Quor assures me as he assured us all that Muklah is in no shape to issue coherent orders and his information is beyond question, so, I am of the opinion that the longer the invader is left to his own, in boredom, the better for us, and we will formulate a plan when we are all familiar with all our strengths, so for tonight let us enjoy moments to remember with joy, for when the dung hits the breeze, we want to make sure it hits the dung-heap."

They all laughed at this and raised their honey draughts in a toast.

"To the dung heap!"

The night ended in good spirits and as usual, they all made their own way to bed as there was no need for guides any longer.

Chapter 23

Sisk woke as dawn cracked the horizon, he washed himself dressed in a fresh robe, hooded of course, then pulled the newly installed cord which allowed Sisk to ring a bell directly to Crall, who was always ready, instead of going to the door to yell for him, Crall appeared two minutes later with a tray of food for him, two boiled eggs, a pot of the dark leaf drink, steaming from the spout and his favourite bread with salty butter.

"My Lord Muklah has retired in his bedchamber, as has Lord Brakko, allow them to sleep until you are summoned by one or the other, go and get your staff together and clean the mess in the chamber, make sure the ale barrel is removed along with any other traces of strong spirit; if any person in this Castle asks any questions, tell them you act on my orders, and if they are in need of explanation, I will be happy to enlighten them."

"Yes my Lord, thank you, my Lord," and he turned to scurry off.

"Oh and Crall…"

"Yes Lord?"

"Be sure your staff are very quiet, we wouldn't want Lord Muklah to awake prematurely now, would we?"

"No my Lord, we will be very careful, I promise."

"Never promise, Crall, things very often happen that we cannot foresee nor control, do you agree, Crall?"

"Absolutely Lord, we will be very careful."

"Very good, then, make sure you are all fed for you may have a busy day ahead."

And then again, you may not, Sisk thought to himself.

"Yes Lord," and Crall turned and left, as he walked he thought, *My staff! Make sure you're fed! Let Muklah and Brakko sleep! There is more to this mage than meets the eye.*

In his chamber, Sisk once again felt the compliment and was reassured that he was on the right path, for trust was everything, and he was building a trust in the Castle and among the soldiers. Sisk ate his breakfast with relish and thought, *I will talk to the Captains today and get a sense of what the feeling is around the Castle and the harbour, and the land around still being worked.*

He poured himself another mug of the steaming dark brew and savoured it. Crall was giving instructions to all his allocated 'staff' as was given to him by Sisk; when he was done, an elderly man called Saso, known for speaking his mind, spoke up, "In ten years I never knew that man even had a voice, now it seems he is the voice to listen to."

"Aye and you'd better listen, all of you, he's the only one making sense out of any of them, now come on, move your bum-hole, and remember you'd all better remember to move your bum-holes quietly, as requested."

Sisk, still in his chamber, once again, felt the reaction of the workers and sighed happily. He rose from his table and stretched then made for the door, he paid no more attention to the breakfast table for that would be spotless before he returned. He stepped out the Castle doors into the huge square leading into the harbour and the city proper, as he looked around, he saw, on the far side of the harbour, and on the natural walls surrounding the harbour, Tolian cannoneers being brought out to man the big guns and give instruction to the Black-Islanders.

He drew a long satisfying breath and headed for the causeway that led to the top of the harbour wall and cannon emplacements, he took his time, he was savouring the day and thanking the sun, stars and sea for the respite from listening to his drunken Lord and his drunken Commander. As he reached the top of the ramp, he looked around himself, out to sea, along the emplacements, into the Castle and around the land visible from here, he could see soldiers drilling, and could hear their officers shouting, he could see the Castle staff and harbour workers coming and going about their everyday duties he could also see people minding animals and coops in the distance, replacements for the ones lost in the storm.

He made his way to the end of the natural parapet and nodded to each of the gun crews and had a word to say to each of them as he passed, when he came to the end, where the Captain in charge was stationed, he was standing above the harbour entrance, looking north, to the other wall protruding at a right angle from the land manned by three stations going through the same training.

Good, he thought, *all are occupied that are on duty, and all are within a certain level of sobriety, that are off duty*. Everywhere looked busy and efficient, he also knew that soldiers were learning to make the black powder, about to learn to forge cannon, they had no access to the materials are ores required on the Black Isles, so had none of these skills.

He then spoke at length to the captain about the progress of his charges and gave permission to actually fire the cannon into open water today, and reassured him that on watching the sea level again he would ensure that a few captured ships would be made available as targets, with Lord Muklah's permission of course, the three teams on the short parapet could come over to here and have their target training at the same time for their cannons only covered only the harbour entrance, As he left he briefly to all ten of the gun crews, promising to keep them busy and to keep up the good work, although the Tolians looks could scald skin, the Black-Islers were gratified, to a man, for this recognition of their efforts.

He watched the bottom of the causeway and headed straight to the Castle and Muklah's chambers, inside, Crall, who had been watching and waiting stood in the hall, head bowed, with the personal guard.

"Any signs of life from our Lords Muklah and Brakko yet?" Sisk asked, already knowing the answer.

"No my Lord, I have been here since you left the Castle, in case I had to get a message to you but there hasn't been a squeak from inside, my Lord."

"Very good, Crall, well done, I like a man who can think for himself."

Crall was shocked by this praise.

"Now I must council my Lords, stand by, Crall, as I know you will, for you may yet be needed this morning."

"Aye Lord" and Crall took one step to the side to allow Sisk passage to the door. If anything, the scene was worse than before the two of them comatose bent over the table in a puddle of their own drool and vomit, with spilled food and drink all around, there were several daggers sticking out of the front of the ale keg and the lower ones seeped ale from the wound and a massive puddle was underfoot. Sisk had no intention of waking these two up for they would be completely incoherent so he went to the door and softly called for Crall. Crall came to him, head still bowed.

"Crall, you can and will raise your eyes from the floor when dealing with me, for you and I cannot do what we must do without looking at things and that includes each other, is that clear?"

Crall lifted his head and looked at Sisk and said shakily, "Aye, my Lord."

"Good; now go get whoever you may need to clear this up, clear the ale off the floor and anything else that my Lord may slip or trip on or over and do it quietly for I wish my Lords to get a chance to fully recover before taking on the day ahead." He said this with calm authority and loud enough for the soldiers to hear.

"I will stay here with all of you until we are done and my Lords are safe from harm, just in case a problem may arise, and bring two cots with fresh blankets."

"Aye Lord," and Crall left quickly to organise 'his staff'.

The cots arrived first and Sisk with the guards lifted the two, Muklah then Brakko, into their temporary bedding, there was barely a murmur on getting them horizontal; they began to snore loudly. Next there was two racks of fresh clothing carried in, everything from robe to boots, taken from each of their wardrobes, the clean-up was done, perfectly, in no time, without disturbance, and they all left together heads bowed, except for Crall, who looked dead ahead.

Chapter 24

Toli and his fellow council members from the Castle-side of the Island woke at the same time and dressed at the same time and left their quarters to a waiting guide, Toli's guide, Lor.

"Breakfast will be served in the council dining room, if it pleases my King." He stepped aside and fell in to follow them, for they all, now, knew the way. On seeing them coming a silver-mail clad warrior thumped on the door twice and the door was opened by another on the inside, Quor, Broq and Soq were already there, Quor in his official robes and Broq and Soq in chain-mail with hoods down, all had mugs of water in front of them with a pitcher of water each, as there was in every place. As soon as they were seated, the breakfast service began, bacon, eggs, black blood sausages, bread, butter, scones and pots of the same black leaf brew they were used to on the Castle-side, always at breakfast.

Again they were all chatting away merrily about things unimportant until Quor spoke when the meal had finished and cleaning up was going on around them.

"Sire, as you are, none of you, in any way armoured, we would like, first, to take measurements from each of you in order to prepare you for the coming conflict."

"Of course, whatever it takes, Quor, we are in your hands, as well as your debt."

"Sire, all you see, and all you don't see, on this Island is yours, you can be in no-one's debt for that or any other reason, the measurements are for necessary garments, but all are taken from materials all coming from your land."

"You leave me with no question nor complaint, Quor, so let's get this done and move on, we have a lot to get through today."

Several people came in with measuring tapes and note books and fussed around each of them, it all took less than an hour and then they left. They sat back at the table in turn, as they were finished, and when all were seated, Quor spoke, "Sire, we have a ship ready at dock for sail and provisioned for the voyage to Bevak."

"Well and good, Quor, but I have just one request to make before we leave on our journey proper, I would like Nana and the rest of the rescued hunting party to board with us, for I would like Nana there for her organisational skills and Gogon and Loron to oversee the new building, already begun but mostly to have words with them before I leave them once more."

"All already aboard Sire, we foresaw these wishes and acted accordingly, the expeditionary party volunteered also to help the folks integrate, as they have been here, involved, for some time, so we took the liberty of boarding them also, I hope this is agreeable to you, Sire."

"I could not have planned better, Quor, thank you, my friend."

"Okay then," Shala enthused, "shall we make our beginning now!"

Anga smiled down at her ward and thought, *Always anxious for action, little one, I hope I survive this to see your greatness come of age.*

"Yes Sister, we shall, so without further discussion we'll head to our duties and deliver to the people the peace and justice they deserve, we all deserve!"

As they exited the great house to board, they walked onto the platform and the same throng as yesterday stood before them, with right hands clenched over their hearts, Toli was moved and looked around to the council, and each one of them stood in the same manner, he turned slowly back and raised his right fist over his heart. The crowd once again erupted raising their left hands and punching the air yelling "Toli! Toli! Toli!" Toli then turned, tear in eye, and led the council off the platform towards the waiting ship. Anga felt his emotion right through her being. As did Toli feel hers.

Toli looked behind him; Anga was staring at him with misted eyes and he thought, *We must address this soon, Anga, for this is something not to be ignored, this, whatever it is, has to be cherished.*

Then he came back to the present to find himself stock still, staring at Anga and Anga staring back, she gave the slightest of nods, barely perceptible, then he realised everyone else was bobbing their heads between himself and Anga in confusion, except Shala, who had the biggest grin on her face that a 9-year-old girl could possibly get on her face. Toli looked to each of them, all confusion then he turned again to the ship and caught Quor, Broq and Soq in the eye, these three too were grinning broadly.

He boarded the ship somewhat confused himself but resigned to carry out whatever necessary acts it required to free his land, everyone he passed held the same fist to chest salute until he had gone by. He held his own salute and the crew and all others aboard held their salutes until he dropped his own. Without any more ceremony or "Bumf" as Shala called it in the Castle, the crew attacked their jobs. The Captain whose name was Storq came up to Toli and placed his fist on his chest in salute. *From here on, this is going to be the normal thing*, he thought.

"Yes Captain, is all well?"

"Oh yes, Sire," he said. "I just—"

"Wait Captain, you may lower your salute now, salute me when I come aboard your vessel and do not salute me again until I disembark, if we go on like this the entire voyage we'll get bugger all done while we're aboard, is that okay with you?" and Toli laughed and slapped Storq on the shoulder.

"Now what did you want to say, Captain, or may I call you Storq!"

"O-Of course, Sire," Storq smiled back. "I just wanted to welcome you aboard the galleon 'Queen Shaleena', launched and named on your mother and father's wedding day." Toli was stunned to think that these folk ever knew of his parents' wedding day, and then, *Hold on, you fool, they know every single thing about our history.*

"Thank you, Storq; my mother would have been hugely honoured by this amazing gesture, she is a beautiful vessel." And she was.

"Sire, we leave for the bank shortly, as there is no breeze today, as often happens in the valley in calm weather, we have to make the crossing under oar Sire, if you don't mind, of course?"

"Storq, as you know, on the other side of the mountain, we are sea-faring folk and since I was old enough to understand, I was taught there is only one man on board a ship in command, and he is not a King, you may go about your business as you wish, for it is the Captain who commands on board, no-one else, and that is you, Storq."

"Yes, thank you, Sire," and he saluted, Toli did not return it.

"And spread the word about the salute as well, once getting on and once getting off, that is a royal decree you best not disobey." Again he slapped his shoulder and laughed.

Storq grinned. "All your wishes be met, Sire" and bowed gallantly and they laughed together, another friendship formed.

They cruised the lake in no time at all and docked at the temporary jetty that had been constructed for them, all the rescued castle-side folk were by the little jetty, just about big enough to take the gangway and there were valley folk come to help with the building of new dwellings, each one of them stood in the same salutation as the near bank folk.

Toli lifted his fist to his chest and dropped it immediately, he called to Storq and said quietly in his ear, "Storq, we are only 20 minutes on the water and look, see what I mean," he indicated to the gathering all at salute and then turned to the ship where the entire crew stood at this position. "See," he said in Storq's ear.

Storq returned the whisper, "My king, you said salute on embarking and disembarking, my crew obey as are all here, and they will salute again when you leave."

"By the trident of Aquos, you're right, I suppose I have to get used to it as well as others."

At that Toli signalled the crowd to lower their salute and spoke to them, "Tolians, our land has been invaded, Kings rock is occupied by the son of an old enemy and as you now know, the lake-valley people are our saviours, but also our kinsmen, as they have been for centuries, we are now gathering our forces and advisors and the re-patriation of you all is in process."

There was loud cheering and shouting, Toli raised his hand for silence.

"I have brought with me people you all know from the Castle-side. Nana who will listen to, and give counsel to, all here who need reassurance or advice, she will be my advisor and keep us all up to date on proceedings, please listen to Nana for she has kept us in line, in the Castle, for a fair number of years." Another cheer went up.

"We also have with us Gogon and Luron, again you all know them, they will be in charge of any problems with building and developing this beautiful site into an acceptable place that suits our benefactors as much as ourselves for we must integrate, the people here owe us nothing, we owe them our lives, so therefore our future, so I must introduce you to Roqi, brought to you by us as your chosen representative of the valley folk he will reside here with you with you and will be available to carry messages and information and requests to the main administration on the near-side, and as a consequence return the same to you.

"I and the head council must leave now on the pressing business of organising our retaliation and to consult with our allies for this is also their Island. I swear to you that all is being done that can be done and you all will be kept abreast of all developments as well as every other individual on this Island, so farewell my friends, I know we will all be reunited as one and when we drive the enemy from our land we will make sure that it is permanent, we have more power now, I think, than any of us know."

Toli saluted and turned to Roqi, "Please spread the word on this salute thing we discussed on the ship, or at least Storq discussed with you and the crew, once on arrival and once on departure, and when I drop my salute, everyone does, please Roqi."

"Aye Sire, I will, without question."

Toli walked up the gangplank and stood side on to the shoreline, Nana came first, Toli shook her hand and spoke quietly and briefly to Nana, then Gogon, then Luron and all the rest one at a time. Quor, Broq and Soq had disembarked with Toli just to speak with the valley folk to find out how morale was among the castle-siders and how well they were coping.

All news was good in this regard, they had a sick baby but he was in the hands of a lake valley healer and recovery was rapid and the child was expected to be screaming for Mothers milk by the next day or even sooner, he is a fine healthy specimen, all is well, no need to worry.

"Very good, then we won't." Quor then shook the hands of the valley folk and finally Roqi's, saying, "We will return soon, my friend, and when we do, the bloody Black Kraken worshipping, tobastards, will be made to regret the day they left their filthy poisonous homeland." Then he made for the ship, followed by Broq and Soq who also shook hands and spoke to their kinsmen.

The gangplank was raised Toli gave a short, sharp salute as did the others aboard, then the oars come out into the lake and with both sides of the lake cheering and waving they turned north to begin the voyage of freedom as it is to become known, as the oars were dipped into the lake the folks on both banks began to chant "Toli, Toli, Toli", and it seemed to match the rhythm of the rowers.

As the galleon peacefully made way north, Roqi called for quiet in the camp, at this time it was really only that and related the King's wishes to all, then he went to the oiled-canvas tent given to him for the duration of his stay, at least until more structures were up, inside was a cot, a table, a small chair, on the table was ink, parchment, a quill, drying powder and a finger of wax in a box with a new seal, the King's seal, which could only be broken by the King himself, or by another head council member in the presence of the King.

At the back of the large tent, there was another table with two bowls, two plates, two mugs, knives, forks, spoons, two of each, and various condiments, underneath this table there was a large basket crafted from hickory stalks, he slid it out and put it atop the table, next to his eating utensils, and opened it, there were six pigeons inside, each with a different colour band on its right leg signifying one of the five main cities on the lake, on four of these birds he banded the King's instructions to their left legs and released them, the fifth he carried back to the loft that had been built for the royal messengers, for he was one of the birds of Quoror, the Capital.

They had received this information already, for Storq had sent the ships lad ashore to leave the message with the acting council, which he did and was back aboard before the last line was released, he wasn't even missed by the ships company he was so quietly efficient, his name was Tak, he knew his duties without being told and any other services he was designated were carried out without complaint nor comment, he was fourteen and lived to be on the water.

As they made their way north, the lake widened so they could no longer clearly make out people or even buildings on the eastern bank; but, on the western bank, they regularly passed by small villages of very few inhabitants, even small holdings, which may only have a man and his wife working their little plot, however none of these were in Quoror for the feast of the King, for there had been no more space for any more subjects to attend, so they patiently waited for a glimpse of their King, many made their way to the nearest city in the hope of a closed view, and to hear his words.

Shala soon became bored as Anga seemed to be deep in thought, she knew why, so she got up from the hatch she was sitting on and walked over to Tak, who sat near the bow, on his own, tying knots in several lengths of rope, he looked up to see Shala stood in front of him.

"Learning your knots, eh?" Shala had seen this practice before with navy cadets working to pass exams and the fishermen teaching their sons.

"No need for learning, I'm just keeping my hand in, we're underway and my duties are done, but Captain Storq doesn't like idle hands, so, unless I'm sleeping, I'd better be sure I'm keeping busy."

"Can you teach me please? Only the boys get to learn anything interesting on our side."

"I-I don't think I can", and he turned to look at Storq who stood well within earshot. Storq turned to Tak and nodded approval, she was a Princess after all, she could demand it, and anyway, two sets of idle hands occupied at the same time was always good.

"Okay then." Tak looked up smiling, Shala smiled back. "Sit yourself down and we'll get started, Princess."

"When you and I are together, you shall call me Shala, Tak."

"As you wish, Shala, let's get going by untying this little lot," and he indicated to the pile of knotted strands of rope piled high in a chest beside him.

"Wow, you've been busy."

"Aye, as I said, Captain, idle hands."

So they both began untying knots and throwing the untied strands back into another chest.

This is going to take some time, Tak is very good at this, Shala thought.

Going up the lake, the people on the banks became rarer although there was more animals he even caught a glimpse of a huge mountain lion looking from behind and beside a massive craggy rock sticking out the land, thrown there by the mountain eons ago, the lion stared at the passing ship with curious interest, then as the ship went all the way passed the rock the lion turned and jogged off towards the thick forest at the foot of the mountain on the other side of meadows and low hills. Toli turned there and saw Anga sitting on her own, seemingly miles away, then, further up the ship he saw Shala and Tak engrossed in the art of knot tying, Shala looked around and nodded towards Anga, then went back to their knots.

Toli sat down on the hatch next to Anga, Anga came around then.

"Oh-Oh my King, I'm so sorry, I didn't—"

"No need to be sorry, Anga, I know how you feel, I've been off myself, and please call me Toli, as I feel like we're going to be together, alone, a lot," and he nodded sideways at Shala seemingly deeply into her studies but who had one eye on the two of them at every chance, as did Tak.

"But this is more than Shala, Toli, and I think we both know it, I am actually in fear that this, all this, is a dream, my feelings are running amok and I don't know what I will do if I wake."

With this Toli took Anga's face in both hands and kissed her there and then, long and lingering, and the kiss was returned; on parting, Toli put his arm around Anga and whispered, "Now we both know, my love."

Anga pulled away. "Aye love, now we know" and kissed him full on the lips again.

Shala grinned at Tak and Tak grinned back. Storq turned away and raised his eyebrows, puffed up his cheeks and blew air through pursed lips, the rest just carried on as if they hadn't noticed anything, when, in reality, they had all been watching slyly, sideways, around corners, and they all were delighted. Shala said to Tak, "Well, it looks like we're going to be having more lessons then we bargained for," they both laughed and Tak wondered at the maturity in Shala's humour.

The other members of the head council sat around a timber table up on the deck, high in the stern, that was built for council, tactical discussion was little or nothing all discussion of war, it was thought, was pointless until all military leaders had their views heard, not views on the upcoming war, that was inevitable but views on how to go about it, the Castle-side people were as safe as they could be, as long as the Black-heart has no opposition there is no conflict, any progress he makes, weapon wise, will come into Tolian hands for he will not be around long enough to see his plans come to fruition.

They sat sipping the beautiful lake-valley wine, talking about the upcoming visit to the first city of Tabunti, when out of the blue, Quor shouted, "Look" and pointed west. "Can you see that small green patch at the foot of the mountain off in the distance?" And they all could, for it stood out, surrounded in pines, but in a place where the sun was on it all day.

"That, my friends, is the vineyard responsible for the wine you are drinking now, it is much larger when you're there, you can't even make out the big house from here." Closer to the shoreline trotting across a field of flowers, up to their chests, somewhere between the trees and the beach were a pack of wolves moving parallel to the ship and glancing intelligently at them, stopped and sat and began howling, heads in the air, then as the ship passed by they all stopped and the lead male stood, he was huge, and turned towards the forest and trotted off, the rest of the pack in tow.

"A greeting from the wolves, a sign of good fortune indeed, that was Gris, leader of the western wolves, there are other packs, Gris leads them all, formidable allies, Gris has just committed them all to our cause, we expect others to follow," Quor explained.

"What do you mean others, Quor?" asked Tadesh.

"We expect similar tributes from all inhabitants of this land, flying, walking or crawling, we are all in this together, all Tolians, as our voyage continues you will find this kind of thing will happen frequently, especially from the truly wild things."

Quor rose then and went down the stairs to the main deck he went up to Toli and Anga who talked quietly, still stunned from the speed of their revelation, and said, "Beg your indulgence, Sire, Lady Anga." He bowed his head to Anga. "Could you please join the council to be briefed on the city of Tabunti?" And raised his voice so Shala could hear.

"My Princess, could you join us at council, we are coming close to Tabunti."

"Yes Quor." She turned to Tak. "Okay Tak, I have to put my council head on now, speak later, yes?"

"Yes Princess, if I have my chores done."

"It's Shala, and I'll help with your chores if they let me."

"They can't stop you, Shala!" and Tak winked.

"My grief, you're right, Tak, okay then!" and she left him to attend her duties.

When they were all seated, another round of wine was served and Quor spoke, "Tabunti is a small city, the city responsible for your wines and ales, and the thick black rum the garrison prefers. They have a local apple drink, made only in quantities enough to supply Tabunti, they call it Cider, you will see rows upon rows of grapes and hops, an orchard for apples, and fields of sugar cane, we already passed some of the grapes.

"The population is dedicated to the perfection of their product and most believe this has been achieved, the city also houses a small garrison of soldiers to relieve, on rotation, the warriors on duty, every city has at least one, there are also garrisons between cities but those are right up at the foot of the mountain and can't be seen for the trees. Behind the city a little way off is the huge distilling and brewing houses working day and night to supply the whole valley and it will be in sight very soon."

And then, abruptly, the landscape changed from a row of fields full of wild flowers and bees, to row, upon, row of hop fields, with bushes, heavy with cones, which were also boiled and went into the making of the honey draught on which we all sleep so well. As they looked at the rows of plants growing through the trellis fences, in the distance the city began to come into view.

Chapter 25

After he was satisfied that Muklah and Brakko were suitably ensconced in their cots, he ordered Crall to have two baths prepared for the lords for although Muklah had his bad habits, uncleanliness was not one of them, and this applied to every single person on the Black Isles, although always in black garb including armour, which gave off a dangerous, as well as morbid, aura, the Black-Islers were personally as clean and hygienic as any other subject on any other Island, in fact even more so, in many cases.

Happy all had been catered for, for the awakening of the two drunks, Sisk gave the usual order to let him know as soon as they woke, he would be up at the forges and would return after his visit to check up, completely unnecessary, he would know exactly when the two of them came to, without the telling. He left for the stables, the forges were almost up at the mountain, close to the mine entrances, so too far to walk, but at least the mountain was closer to the harbour here and the logistics worked perfectly, rail lines mine face to forges, forges to smiths, smiths to stores, stores to supply as necessary.

Now, as there had been no conflict for three decades, the forges has been busy in the making of farm tools and hand tools, stores of weapons were plentiful for the needs of the Tolians, which allowed development of agriculture and industry, also, weapons had been advanced and plans for even more advancement for these had been hastily buried in a very safe place in the mine supplying the ore for weaponry as the plans for the hand-cannon were further advanced than anyone, outside weaponry could have guessed.

He mounted his horse and headed for the forges which were situated towards the north end of the harbour, so as to re-fit ships as they needed, with speed, as generations of families had been born into their particular vocations from fisher to smith, farmer to soldier, mason to cook, even during these dark times they took pride in everything they did, it helped to take their minds off the barbaric death of their King and Queen and Princess, it also helped to distract them from the doubt about the missing Tolians, some of when had simply disappeared during the night of the storm, including Toli, Shala and the Generals.

He decided to begin at the harbour end, at the loading bays, built to supply and deploy the ships as quicky as was possible, these were in preparation for the new cannons arrival, for they had not been manufactured for a long time, over twenty years ago in fact, and he could see carpenters fitting out the black ships to be able to accommodate the new weapons.

The black ships at anchor in the harbour, were of such a design, that, at sea during a storm, the sails could be reefed and stowed in lockers that were all around the deck then battened down, the three masts were then dropped, on a hinged bracket the foremast first, then the mainmast dropped and fastened to the foremast and the deck, then the mizzen, all secured to each other and the deck, then there was a large fan-like object coming off of a shaft going directly into the stern of the ship, inside the ship the shaft continued through the bowels of the vessel and through twelve bushes were eleven cog-wheels about five feet in diameter and two feet long, into each fitted an identical cog on its own bushed and greased mounting.

These machines were an extremely sturdy design and was the basis for all future mechanically driven ships the black-islanders called it a propeller, for it propelled them along, on each side of the second cogs were fitted drive handles, one high one low, enabling two men to push and pull at their station, twenty-two men on either side of the driver shaft, forty-four at any one time, all slaves, these ships could move at pace in foul weather, and manoeuvre with deadly ease, not needing wind or oar, the only thing on deck was a raised cabin, for steering, with double thick glass shaped to slice through foul weather, there were also two paddles each side of the glass driven off a smaller cog and shaft these left the glass as clear as possible and as all movement came from the same drive system.

It was also a pretty precise indication of the ships progress, this little cabin seated two men with spy-glasses whose voices could be heard throughout the ship through a system of pipe lines. Officers accommodation was below the main deck, towards the stern, crew accommodation, the galley and, in between these, the Captains dining cabin where he ate with officers and discussed any subject to do with the ship. Below this was what was known as the drive deck with all the machinery just described, there was room left on either side of the drive, and carpenters were down there too cutting gun-parts and fixing gun emplacements on this deck as on the top deck.

Under this deck was the hold, fed from one hatch on the main deck at the bow which went through the drive deck and man-handled from there, these hatches were water tight and invisible when closed, this was situated in the bow to allow cargo to pass the drive, which stopped just before the hatch. On the main deck were positioned air vents, open end to stern which fed fresh air to all decks and any excess By ended up in the bilges which was pumped out, again, by the operation of the propeller, these were going to be invincible at sea when fully armed and being piloted by seasoned Captains directing, with his first mate, from the deck-cabin.

As he rode up to the dock, he noticed the three captured Tolian ships to be used as target practice, being rowed out to sea, each towing two pinnaces to get the crews back to shore after the ships were anchored in position.

They'll have to wait for Muklah's direct order to fire on those. Maybe tomorrow.

He was pleased to see people going about their business efficiently, each doing what he's meant to be doing. He called down to the duty Captain, "Captain, is all on target for supplies?"

"Aye Lord, we have enough dry dock crew and craftsmen for three ships at a time, we'll be ready long before there's enough cannon to arm them."

"Very good, Captain, keep it up, it won't go unnoticed."

"Aye Lord, thank you, Lord," and the Captain bowed and raised his head, greatly flattered.

Sisk nodded and turned his horse to follow the road by the side of the rail track towards the forges where the ship's cannon would be made, it took half an hour or more to trot five miles to the forge-village, just outside the forge compound with its four separate forges with double doors, like barn doors, thrown open with flashes of fire and spark lighting the darkness inside each of them, and smoke billowing in rolls of dark clouds spewing from slotted vents just under the eaves of the building, made not of rock, but of timber. *How do these not go aflame?* a question to be asked later.

The four forges each had a separate function, the first was specialised in plate metal, forged, heated to nearly white hot, then sent through rollers powered by a giant water wheel, one of two in turn powered by the fast flowing river which came from the mountains in steps and rapids running parallel to the back of the buildings on its way out to sea.

The second was to make specifically naval products, like bands of steel for masts and yardarms for cutlasses and pike heads, arrowheads, they even had their own moulding area for cast iron cleats, all powered by the river.

The third was called the little forge specialised to make farm implements, ploughshares, scythes and the like, again, powered by the river.

The fourth, behind which was the second water wheel, connected by a common shaft which in turn powered each of the buildings by a system, almost like the ships, of shaft and wheel and belt and gear, had been semi-idle for a time for it specialised in cannon-making, which had been a redundant trade for a very long time, but fathers had taught their sons how to cast cannon, as a project each apprentice, usually sons of tradesmen had to, with only the help of drawings, materials and manual labour, if he could lift it himself he had to lift it alone, design and build the mould, cast the cannon and make the cast fit for firing. If the cannon fired without incident the son or apprentice was declared, there and then, a master cannon smith and would never be ordered around from that day forth.

He got off his horse and let him wander to the river's edge to munch on the lush, damp grass. Inside, there were two people deep in discussion.

"But you promised me this would be my cannon year, you flaming promised!" The younger raised his voice.

"Aye son, we are now under a pain of death order to design ships cannons and I can't pass you unless you can do this thing on your own and there are no completed drawings for reference."

"There are drawings of the harbour cannon and we still have the original pattern mould, I could scale down, in fact I bet I could cast two in the same time, in the same sand."

"If you could do that, I'd declare you King O' the smiths, for all to hear."

Sisk came up behind them unnoticed and said, "If this boy can do as he clearly thinks he can, then let him!"

The father and son jumped in surprise, the father was called Troi, as was his son, common on Toli's Island.

"Wha? Who? What?" Troi, the eldest, was completely flummoxed, this was unannounced, unexpected.

"If he can do as he says, let him I said."

Troi both senior and junior could now see who stood before them. The man who was now Sisk, the traitor.

Sisk turned to the youngest Troi, "Do you believe you can do this thing?"

"I do, Lord."

"Very well then, I will set you this task, if you can show me a pair of ships cannon in the same time as the forging of the harbour canon, and they are capable of firing shot, causing the required damage, now, how long does it take to forge one of your big lads?"

"At best six days, lord." Father again. "Two days to set up these two new moulding patterns, two days to cast a bathe then temper and another two to finish, the bore will have to be re-tooled to suit the new cannon, this is all after altering patterns and scales, my lord."

"Very well. I'll give you five days to rearrange your measurements and weights, after all you have the references, don't you? I shall return here in eleven days and expect two functional ships cannon; now, Troi, if your son achieves my wishes and his ambitions, would it not be within your power and profit to declare your son a master smith? For if he does this, he has done something no-one else has, including you."

"Yes Lord, if he does this, there is no doubt he will be a master and no argument, we just didn't think it was allowed."

"I turn on you now, young Troi, are you confident you will fulfil this tall order?"

"I am, Lord, I will not let you down, no more than I would let my Father down."

"Very well then, eleven days from today, be warned, the Lord Muklah and his Admiral will be in attendance."

He left the cannon shed then and took his horse by the rein and mounted, rode out to follow the rail tracks up to the mine head. As he began along the road he had a feeling of mild disquiet, not enough to be troubled by it, what he did not know is that young Troi had been putting things on paper for a while now and had become a very capable planner, and was very confident in the outcome of the undertaking.

His father looked in his eyes and asked, "Son, are you sure you want to do this thing for the invader?"

"Father, we have no choice as long as they are here we are in their power, between you and I, Father, we can test every gun here to the highest order, we can prove they are well made powerful cannon, but will they perform under battle conditions after being stowed for potentially weeks at sea?" He winked at his father.

"Son, you have the mind of a true smith, if it can be made to work, it can be made to not work, eh?" Then he almost split his apron laughing. "Right then," he said when he recovered his cool, "I'm off to see what the guild have to say, they'd best know before we begin."

"Sorry Father, already have begun," and winked again.

"By the sky, boy, I swear you'll have us all hanging off a gibbet if we don't keep a weather eye on you." They both laughed fit to bursting.

Sisk, now left to his own thoughts, said to himself, *I'm getting some confusing feelings lately, don't know why, I'd best pick a little team to act as apprentices and keep an eye on things here, I have men learning trades all over now, now they are planning the new forging method, two guns in the same mould, he knew, had never been done, I'll pick them up on my return to the Castle.*

Troi eldest brought the proposition to the other six members of the smith and forgers guild. The Grand Master, the oldest living smith, no one could ever remember him not being around, was sat on his forge-side stool drinking black leaf tea from a tin mug he made himself, as they all did on the first week of their apprenticeship, said to Troi, "'Bout time, you've held back long enough, that son o' yours has been long enough waiting, yours is the only forge here without two full forgers and there are lads waiting for a place, so you are holding more than one back, we'll hold the ceremony when he passes the cannon-casting, as we all know he will."

The other smiths had already discussed the delay in Troi younger's passage to full trade status as he had passed his time a year ago, he was twenty-two and had to learn to forge in each of the forges and had to create every single tool or weapon completely before he was allowed to move on, he had proven time and again that he was well above competence, soldiers would request one of his swords farmers would ask if Troi would make a plough-share or a scythe for them, his tools and weapons seemed to be more resilient, stayed sharper longer, broke less easily, in fact, thus far, Troi the younger hadn't a single bad comment said against him or his work.

The Grand Master, whose name was Launt, said, "Right, so we're right on this, the day those two cannons fire, your Son will be inducted into the guild, and most welcome too, I'll notify the other guild members."

There were other forge sites along the length of the harbour but situated well back from the harbour, another four, two situated in around the centre of the harbour, and two up at the closed end of the harbour, Trois forge was built to supply ships from friendly island nations who did not have the resources to form or forge iron and steel, the centre forges were to keep the trades and farms, around that area, with sharp tools they also had a wagon go around with small supplies and sharpening equipment to tend tools on site, lots of hammers, axes, nails and the like.

Eight more guild members, there were two in each of these forges, he would get word to Manni, the wagon master, who often came up for naval goods; he was a good friend and as reliable as the tide.

Chapter 26

Sisk rode up to the mine entrance and tied up the horse to a hitching rail which was outside the mine managing Captain's office, he stopped and thought, *I've never felt so uncertain of myself, it has me puzzled, I know something is afoot, but I could detect nothing in the forges but confusion.*

What he did not know yet, for nothing brought it to light, that the ores in the mountain rock blocked his senses, he had never detected any life on the mountain other than the animals who populated the foot of the mountain, lions and goats mainly, he never knew for sure the lake-valley even existed, never mind its people, likewise in and around the forges there were multiple slag piles which cause the same result, still able to function, but the dark feeling of doubt nagging at him.

He gave himself a mental shake and went up the single step into the Captains office, the Captain had seen him outside his window, deep in thought, so he was already on his feet.

"My Lord Sisk," he bowed his head, "it's an honour that you come so far to inspect."

"Please Captain, sit, I intend to, it's been a long day in the saddle I'd appreciate a seat that doesn't move."

"Please Lord, take mine; it's got a cushion!"

"Captain, you are a cure for the plague, thank you, I won't forget you, I assure you."

At this the Captain whipped up, poker straight and stammered, "Yes Lord, many thanks Lord." He was beside himself with pride.

"Please Captain, pull up a chair yourself and sit opposite and we'll have a chat." He indicated a wooden chair against the wall.

Again, "Yes Lord, thank you". and he picked up the chair and sat opposite on the opposite side of an orderly desk-table.

"Well Captain, you keep a neat office is the mine in as good order?"

"It is indeed, Lord, the men gain competence every hour of every day."

"Good, tell me how you run your man hours please?"

"Certainly, my lord, firstly there is myself and another Captain, we change shifts at six morning and six evening we have two other Captains who relieve us every seventh day, Sunday we come back to opposite shifts, I'm on days now, I'll be on nights next Sunday."

"If this is what works for you, the men and the mine, then it works for me Captain, and if it works for me, it works for our Lord Muklah, now my friend what of the mine itself, no need for figures, I mean the men in the mine, the output figures I trust are a matter of record."

"Oh yes lord, every detail."

"I knew it, Captain, I knew it, so, to the men."

The Captain was bursting at the seams by now. "We have sixteen men in training, Lord, four at a time, there are, for now, twelve Tolian miners on duty for twelve hours at a time, they share the same shifts as the mine Captains so we all know our own miners, there is room at the mine face left for four men training so we have incorporated those to daily eight men rotations seven days or nights on and seven off always changing on the Sunday, even replacements will be vetted and watched to be sure they are actually miners, however, at this stage, that has not arisen."

"My Captain, sorry, what is your name?"

"Mungo, Lord," he almost choked.

"Then Captain Mungo, I can only say that if the other Captains are doing their jobs as you obviously are, I can report to my Lord Muklah that this mine at least is in good hands, and, good Captain Mungo, that is my favourite report to give."

"Thank you again, my Lord, we are all here to serve."

"We are indeed, my friend, and with people like you at the helm, this ship will always sail a steady course and weather the storms."

Mungo nearly fell off his chair, his head spun with what can only be described as joy.

"Well Mungo, my Captain, meeting you had reassured me of absolute success, I do not feel the need to inspect the mine workings, your report was good enough for me, so, I must go to the city now, it was a good way here and it will be a good way back, and things to do before respite, but you have made my part in this some way easier." Mungo made to move.

"No need, Captain, I will see myself out, you deserve your cushion back." Mungo was almost wetting himself by the time Lord Sisk left, he was glad there were non-mining soldiers around 'cos the next shift would never believe this.

Sisk turned his horse seawards and headed downhill, as he passed between two large mounds piled high with ore, the same feeling of unease as before came upon him.

Chapter 27

As the Queen Shaleena closed on Tabunti, the multitude of workers in the hop field began to head in a single file, between rows of tall trellis, towards the city was behind, in the main, the brewing houses, again built in timber allowing direct loading and unloading from brewer to ship and vice versa, stopping briefly on the dock for the purpose of unloading and loading the stevedores making sure things got to where they were supposed to be, past the city was a ferry pier to bring passengers between cities, different city every day there and back, there were five main cities including the capital, Tabunti. Closest to the capital although on the west bank of the lake, up the east side, first city and last before the garrison city of Bevak was Beeth, on the east bank, Dalri on the west then around the north end, the mighty city of Bevak.

Approaching the pier made for the Queen Shaleena, Anga stood on the council deck next to Toli and slipped her hand into his, Toli turned his head and they looked each other in the eye.

"Well," she said, "I suppose we need to worry no longer about our feelings, the confusing ones I mean."

"Yes, I have no doubts whatever about our future but, WOW, it all happened so quickly."

Anga put both her hands around the back of Toli's neck, gently pulling his face closer to hers, when they were face to face, she said, "Really, my love, I have a feeling that this has been going on for years," and kissed him full on the lips. The rest of the council, stunned to silence by Anga and Toli's little vignette, cheered and clapped as one, closely followed by the rest of the ships company, by the time they were tying up to the capstans on the pier the cheering and clapping became infectious, though for a different reason than on board, the clamour caused by this visit had never been seen in this valley in known history.

The gangplank was dropped and Toli came to its head, in salute, behind him all on board came to salute, then slowly at first, the noise receded as the salute moved through the crowd like the ripple of a receding bow wave, Toli came to the top of the gangway with Anga beside him and they dropped their salutes simultaneously, as did the rest of the ships company immediately after, then like another receding ripple, the throng dropped theirs. Toli and Anga walked down the wide gangplank on to the large pier, the greeting party stood far enough back as to allow the whole council to disembark, right behind Anga was Shala, and behind Toli was Quor.

When they came to a halt before the greeting party, Shala stepped between Anga and Toli and took a hand of each, the crowd who were everywhere, as far as the eye could see, waiting, silently, for maybe some kind of cue, erupted in a roar, so loud, had the mountain not been there, it would have been heard on the Green Isle.

A stocky man dressed in a cotton shirt and britches with cotton stockings all of these immaculate, pristine white, on his feet, black shoes, laced tight, shining in the sun, all the other four welcoming party were exactly the same, the stocky man said, head bowed, "My King, welcome to Tabunti, I am Keli, head master brewer and mayor of Tabunti, please follow me, Sire."

He turned and led them passed the bowed heads of the welcoming committee who fell in behind the head council, they were all led then, between rows of bowed headed soldiers and workers alike, to a large timber building with a grand, semi-circular, porch in front with columns holding up an identical platform above.

"This is the guild house, Sire, this is our centre, all city pronouncements are made from here, public announcements are made from the upper circle there," and pointed at the top circular balcony, open to the sky.

"Before the tour and dining, Sire, would you perhaps give our citizens a few words from the upper circle, it would mean so much."

"I had thought of nothing else, Keli, it's the main reason we are here today, I will indeed be the honoured and I thank you."

Keli squared his shoulders and jutted out his chin with pride. "Yes Sire, if you'll follow me," and he brought them through the open doors, up the massive staircase and out onto the open balcony. For as far as Toli could see, there were waving and chanting people, and many he could not see.

"TOLI, TOLI, TOLI!"

He walked front, centre of the balcony and raised both hands for silence, the racket receded to murmurs.

"Dear friends," he began, "I regret not being able to meet you all individually today, but we are under no illusion what must be done, you have brought me here, rescued from an invader, and have taken me to your hearts as I have taken you to, you declared me your King and declared your allegiance, you have been loyal and mindful of us for centuries, and we never knew it, it took the scum of the Black Isles to bring us together as a real nation, and as my beloved subjects, I hereby swear to each on one you we will never be parted again, this is the very dawning of an invincible Island nation, together, when we deal with the invader, our last, we will build a peace everlasting, a peace broken by no-one, we here have only known peace all our lives also, other than our Generals and Admiral Shouk who were very young last time these black hearts invaded and we all now know, that the lake-valley folk were minding us even then."

"We will never let that situation rise again!"

Another eruption. Again Toli asked for quiet.

"My friends, citizens of Tabunti and the lake-valley, I thank you for your support here today; unfortunately, I have many duties to perform this day and so I must say farewell for now." He turned and led the rest into the large meeting room where food and drinks were spread over a big pine table facing to the floor to ceiling open windows, the lake breeze was wafting a little now, and was perfect for cooling the room.

They were seated in their own order. Anga now at Toli's right hand and Shala next to her, Quor on his left and Keli next to him, the rest sat as they wished and the rest of the welcoming party sat at the furthest ends of the table.

Keli stood, "Thank you Sire, for finding the time to visit your subjects, we are all overjoyed to welcome our King at long last, however Sire, we are well aware of the urgency of this, your first, voyage up the lake, so we will delay you as little as possible, with your consent Sire, we will partake of some local fare and then, if you so wish myself and the other masters will guide you around our little brewing house."

"I thank you and your fellow Tabuntians for your welcome, master Keli, but, be sure my friend, that any time deliberately spent, with any Tolian, will never be considered a delay, and we came here deliberately, so, although you are right about the urgency of our mission, every city, will be visited with equal attention given to all, in spite of our present situation, please ensure your citizens that the lake-valley will carry on unaffected by the invasion, all will carry on as normal for all but the military, I would like to speak with the senior soldier at this garrison before re-boarding, in the meantime let us enjoy, the fare you have kindly given, and then, you can, if you wish enlighten us ignorant Castle-folk how our favourite luxuries are made."

There was, on the big pine table, ales and wines which were avoided, in any volume for the day had many more hours of diplomacy before sleep. There roast pork, the pigs raised on apples and hops, and indeed, grapes considered below brewing or distilling standard, but produced the best pork any of the Castle-folk had ever tasted, with piles of potatoes, and vegetables so tasty they all had trouble stopping.

Then came dessert, apple pies and cakes and flans, strawberries with cream, massive peaches baked and topped with a heavy syrup made from the sugar cane and more treats, too many to name, all of this was washed down with the dry, or sweet cider of choice, and although they had tasted, and thoroughly enjoyed the ales and wines in moderation, none of them could resist draining their tankards of cider, and then having a second of the alternative dry to sweet or sweet to dry.

The Tabuntians were very pleased with reaction of their visitors to the hospitality provided and Keli said, "Everything you have seen on this table now has been brought to the royal ship twice over, one lot to feed the crew now, and another to stow and bring to the Capital on your return there."

"Thank you, master Keli."

Then they nibbled and supped and chatted about things related to Tabunti, Quor and Keli along with the other master brewers seemed to be friends of old and seemed to be catching up with personal news.

Broq, Soq, Tadesh, Ratesh, Shouk, Dovitt, Matak and Joki were having a relaxed conversation of their own, as they were supping the last of the second ciders Tadesh finished and got up and came around to Toli and asked, "Please excuse me, Sire, but Broq and Soq had suggested that we military men go up to the garrison for an inspection as they both are senior officers and would like to keep in touch with their Captains.

"Although the reports were always right up to date, the personal touch was always best, for the written word does not give the same clarity and they are personal friends with the Captain here, and the fact is Sire, that we have had enough peace time to have toured the brewing houses, distillers and wineries on our own side of the mountain several times, please Sire, we don't mean to offend, but to save precious time we would like to go ahead up to the garrison barracks and meet what is effectively our front line."

"Absolutely, General Tadesh, you may of course and the rest of the council will join you after the inspection, please carry on."

The Generals then left to follow the duty soldiers up to the garrison barracks relieved to be addressing military matters again. Keli, side by side, with Toli, Anga and Shala, led the remainder out the doors they came in, straight into three awaiting carriages, Toli, Anga, Shala and Keli in the first, the Quor and the lads in the next, then came the welcome committee. Quor noticed, as did Toli, the dark expressions on the three, so a look from Toli to Quor told Quor to get in the same carriage as them, and as their carriage followed the first, Quor spoke, "You know you three are the future of the military on this Island." All three gave a start for each had been under his own cloud and did not even notice that Quor was with them.

"Fear not, lads, your time is coming, your King hasn't forgotten you, it is because of his friendship for you, and his trust in you, that he wants you in his company at all times, well almost all times," and he rolled his eyes.

The three friends immediately caught his meaning and laughed out loud, the clouds of doubt lifted then, the first time since coming to the Valley, and the boys were staring at each other again, and Ratesh said, "Exactly, do you actually believe that your lifelong friend does not have important military positions for you, do you see a Toli's island without yourselves around, so you'd all better be aware that you and the rest of the council have all our own functions, confidants, he cannot, and will not, through any choice of his own, be without you, things will become much clearer when we get to Bevak."

The three carriages made their way through the cheering and waving crowd the short distance to the brewery, they could have walked through the guild house, but, at Quor's suggestion, they would go around the building in order to give citizens who could not see their King from where they were, but not walking, this would slow down progress too much, so they all stayed in their respective places, everyone smiling again. Toli and the party stopped at the entrance to the brewery to turn and wave at the people, who were ecstatic, he did not make a speech again, the whole population knew every word of it by now, the tour of the brewery, the winery and the distillery went along very quickly as the whole party barring Anga had done this before, they had all the same processes on the Castle-side.

Toli, Anga and Shala walked around the tour hand in hand with only Anga asking questions, "How is the molasses for the rum made? How does the sugar turn to alcohol? How do grapes become wine? How do apples become cider? The same for hops and ale?" Keli was more than happy to answer all of Anga's questions, delighted that somebody was asking something, he knew the urgency of their journey up the lake, he was also delighted to have the ear of the new Queen-to-be, for it was now known the length and breadth of the Island, that the new King would not be a bachelor for much longer.

The tour finished in the winery and they left by the back door where their carriages waited for them. They boarded their transport and left along the road towards the city, it would not be called a city on the other side, there was only one on the Castle-side and it was several times the size of Tabunti, the road into the city itself was again lined with brewing workers, distillers, and wine makers, there were farmers, growers, gatherers, all the folk you need for this part of the valley to be productive. The waving and cheering continued to the end of the road, at the back of the city on alighting from their carriages, Toli, Anga and Shala were introduced to the local butcher, baker, barber, shopkeepers and last but not least, Tobi the overseer of the six taverns in the city, the biggest being the 'Garrison Inn' which stood at the road end.

The off-duty soldiers used this tavern, for the ever present rail line running alongside the road continued up to the barracks with only a single horse track running parallel to the single line of track here, the centre between the tracks, had been beaten to a rock hard surface in order to allow the single file of four garrons stocky, tough horses, used to bring ore out of the mines, these four were shining in the sunlight, in livery never before seen, hurriedly made for this visit, and to their left there was a fairly large field with four more garrons in it with a stable, annexed to the inn. Tobi was responsible for the care of the horses at this end of track and there were four on the other end cared for by the soldiers, these horses were much loved and molly coddled by all.

The party boarded the man-rider, as the rail carriage was known, while Toli, Anga and Shala spoke to the businessmen briefly before boarding, there was no question of being delayed unnecessarily, no-one wanted this invading filth on their land, so pleasantries were kept to a minimum and no-one took any offence, the quicker they got to Bevak, the better for all.

Toli thanked them all and the three boarded the man-rider one carriage, on this occasion, more for the military, with rows of benches, six in all, each bench able to seat three. The soldier-driver clicked his tongue twice and gave a gentle flick of the reins and the four set up the gentle slope to the garrison at a fast walk.

Toli sat in the front with Anga and Shala, with his arm draped on the outside feeling the breeze, when he saw a man on a wheeled plough, being pulled by a huge horse with hairy hooves, called Sire, horses on this side because of their size and strength, they must surely be Kings of horses, he was sitting on a single seat swaying to the rhythm of the plough.

"Who's he?" he pointed through the gap to the man, oblivious, on the plough, they all turned to look. Keli smiled.

"Ah Sire, that is old Bri, old Bri is known to all on this side of the mountain, west and east, at this moment he's preparing that field to lie fallow, when he's done with the tilling he'll cover the field in a damp mixture of animal waste, pigs, cows, horses and sheep is mixed with straw, not used for any other purpose, waste straw really, from stables to sties, spread over the field with a similar machine to the one you see now, except it spreads instead. This is collected and mixed on the other side of the city and brought up here on carts when needed, on the other side of that far wall is another field green with potato growth, then the same again on the other side of his farm, occasionally the growers will use it to boost their plants before fruiting."

"That sounds similar to my limited knowledge of our side, we have the horses."

"Yes Sire, Bri is not especially famous for his potato prowess, it's his secret recipe spirit that does it."

Bri had passed out of sight now and Toli turned on his bench a bit more, so as to better see Keli, so did Anga and Shala.

"Tell us more, Keli."

"Your wish, my King," and Keli smiled. "Old Bri distils his own spirit, a clear spirt he calls gin, he distils it from potato skins in a still at the back of his farmhouse, accessible only through the house, it has a sweet flowery taste and smell, and its recipe is, we think, the only secret in the whole valley, he simply refuses to part with it, he has an eighth of an acre of lavender off to one side of the house, he says it helps him sleep, but there is something to it none of the masters can copy, they have a similar spirit made from sloes but it's not this, Sire, Bri was there when you alighted to the pier, after you passed he put a cask of it on your ship and now you see him back to his work, the swaying motion of Bri just then was, more than likely, Bri catching up on lost sleep and energy, he works himself very hard."

"I will keep Bri in mind, Keli," and he turned with Anga and Shala to face forward and they all fell silent then, thoughtful, enjoying the wonderful view as the man-rider rose higher they could see far off into the distance rows upon rows of green goodness followed by tree tops, first beach and oak, elm and sycamore then, as they got closer to the mountain, tall pines, majestically stood like the guardians of the mountain, Toli looked up to the sky and the silhouette of a massive eagle passed overhead flying north in the direction of Bevak.

The track levelled now and came onto a ledge, wider here than the ledges running north and south, enough to take the horse and the man-rider with room to take more, there were ten soldiers waiting to greet them, in salute, Toli saluted before leaving the carriage and stepped down and walked to the far end of the ten warriors, allowing the rest of his company to follow when everybody was off, Toli walked down the line of warriors, shaking each hand and thanking each of them personally for their service.

Last in the line was the duty officer, Captain Corq; after thanking the officer, he said, "Captain, may I trouble you to be taken out to the other side, I wish to speak to all our warriors."

"Yes Sire, of course, we are preparing your passage now," and the Captain bid Toli to look behind him. The beautiful garrons were being unhitched and led one at a time, into the corral already keeping another four horses, who were delighted to see their pals back.

Toli turned and one of the soldiers was coupling up the man-rider to a steel rope at the front and another on the back where a drum of steel rope, on a mainframe of steel, was being sat upon the rail and fixed there with specially made clamps. Through the centre of the drum was a shaft which rested on two saddles, heavily greased, with two handles, one a side, so as to allow for soldiers, two a side to bring the man-rider back. On the other end of the same system applied, except the shaft was driven by a water wheel which was filled by a waterfall coming from higher up the mountain, the wheel was braked to allow control of speed, this system turned a six hour walk into a half hour ride.

When all was ready, the part re-occupied the carriage and the Captain hit the near rail twice with a steel bar, the, only a few seconds later, the slack of the rope was taken up and they began to move off, soon the carriage was moving at a gallop's pace. Anga, who had never ridden a horse so had never gone this fast in her life, gripped Toli's hand so tightly she stopped the blood flow in his left hand, by the time, less than half an hour, they emerged at a similar landing area, this time the rope drum being operated by the braked water wheel.

The brake operator, bringing the wheel to a halt, then rushed to join his fellow warriors at salute, salutes over, Toli again thanked them all individually, then he said to the Captain, "Please Captain, explain to us city dwellers what you do here."

"Yes Sire, the watch point at this station is one of three manned from here, one to the south, one north, each manned by two of us, there are ten below at any one time, the four extra for horses, cooking, maintenance and duty Captain, we work on a seven man rotation, two here, two south, two north plus the Captain, when out shift is over the seven replacements will come up to this level, two will go south, two north and relieve the watchers there, we then get in the man-rider and go back down, it is about a twenty minute walk to the other stations so myself and the other Captain can exchange any information necessary at the time."

"Can I see from this point, Captain?"

"Please Sire, follow me." And he led Toli and the others to a small door in a rounded rock face, he opened the door, stepped inside and, holding the door open, bid them enter.

They walked into, one at a time, a large, round chamber, on the sea side of the chamber ran a horizontal slot, a foot high, running south to north curved, off the floor it ran parallel to the height of the soldiers heads, they all seemed to be the same height, there was a cavern step below the slot to allow the watcher to het his head through in order to look below, the room was softly lit by the rock-glow, the slot nor the glow could be seen from outside, the mountain sees to that. Toli stood on the step to look out in a direction he had never done before. As soon as he saw the sea, a heavy melancholy came upon him, he hadn't smelled nor seen the sea since the day he saw his family swinging on the end of ropes.

Anga stepped up immediately, feeling it, Shala turned pale, the other six Castle-siders, on smelling the sea, rushed to the slot to have a look, they all stood silent, a deep feeling of revenge came over them. Anga whispered to Toli, "My love, we mustn't dwell on what has passed, we must concentrate on what is to come, and how we will make it happen."

Toli looked her in the eyes and nodded in acknowledgement, then he looked down on Shala, her pale face turned upward to look at her brother, eyes misting over, not with grief but rage and frustration, he looked in her eyes and instantly reacted.

"Captain," he said dragging himself and the rest of the Castle-folk back to the present, "please excuse me not visiting your other points and my apology goes to the four warriors I will miss, but we have some urgency on our timetable and I fear we must return to the Queen Shaleena and continue on our way."

"No need for apologies, Sire, I sent replacements out, one south, the other north, to send them in, they will be out there now, for they ran to get them, and they ran back, we are fast runners, Sire."

The Captain left first and one of the lookouts held the door, the other had never left his duties except to shake the King's hand and accept his thanks. He stood looking out to sea, through a pair of short spy-glasses, fixed together side by side and raised to both eyes, they called them bi-spies. The four soldiers who were at their posts before, were stood at salute, in a row, at the rail side. Toli again gave each of them his personal thanks and boarded the man-rider, when all were aboard, salutes again done, the carriage moved forward slowly, pulled by the cable they pulled up behind them, and braked by the drum that pulled them up, now disengaged from the water wheel and under the control of its own brakes, it travelled at the same rate downwards as it did upwards.

Feeling the dark mood, Keli spoke up, "Sire, these are watch stations at the lowest level on the mountain, your first line of defence, at least regarding things unseen from your side, during your thirty years of peace there have been three separate attacks, attempted landings, on this side of the Island, not one invader survived, not one ever will, our warriors are ruthless in this regard, but as they take no prisoners, we have no idea exactly where they sailed from, only that it is far off to the west and by their sigils that it was the same nation, we have been attacked twice on the north end and twice over on the east, far enough from the harbour that even these eastern attacks went undetected by yourselves.

"There is not much noise to our defences, we have no black-powder weapons, so no big bangs, but the mountain looks after herself, she sends rocks, gravel, water upon anyone who dares set foot upon her, added to the accuracy of our bowmen, the invading fleet is set afire while waiting to land, the last attempt was 9 years ago and they left a ship out on the sea to observe, not to invade, and when again the invaders were dealt with this ship turned tail west and that was the last time we were invaded anywhere, seven attacks in 30 years, not counting this attack on the harbour, tells us we must always be vigilant, always be ready.

"Up at the garrison, you will meet one of the three non-Tolians on this Island, not an invader, but a shipwreck, first spotted many leagues out to sea, floating on a raft of flotsam, unconscious, close to dead. His name is Xing and he came from far off in the west to land at our north end, he had a bag on his raft with instruments and bottles of potions unknown to us, and powders and leaves and bones, you'll meet him soon, Sire."

Now, coming to the tunnel end, the Castle-folk felt the cloud lift, although Shala had a look of determination or concentration on her face which belied her age. On arriving at the open platform on the lake-side, the rope was unshackled and the rope began to retreat back into the mountain, sliding on a metal tray to avoid snagging, the front rope, going down, was left attached and rolled back onto the drum on the descent.

The four horses, facing down the incline, were harnessed into the man-rider, and after the usual ceremony of salute, began moving down at a walk, the horses pushing rather than pulling, driver sitting atop the last horse, on the way down they spotted old Bri taking the giant horse out of harness and although he was far off they could see old Bri face to face with the horse, who had to lower his head to listen.

"Now Zacko, my old pal, off you go and have your rest, same again tomorrow," the horses then wandered off towards a trough of water for a well-deserved drink.

"There's old Bri again!" Shala stood and pointed out across the perfectly ploughed field.

"Yes Princess," Keli said. "Tomorrow the townspeople will send up Bris fallow mix, enough for the whole field, he likes to call it silage, and the drive will stay with Bri and load the spreader for him it could have been brought up days ago but at this time of year, he has much to do, so the elders like to give him as much rest as they can."

Back up at the sea side station, a young warrior said to his Captain, "My grief, Captain, did you see the look on the King's face?"

"Aye lad, all of their faces, I wouldn't want to be a dirty Black-Islander when the King comes to regain his throne."

On reaching the bottom again, they all boarded their carriages and, ceremony and salutes over, made their way back, through the cheering crowd, waving and smiling, the pier was clear of citizens and workers and Toli spent a few minutes talking to Keli, thanking him, the welcome committee and all the citizens and field workers.

"And please be sure to thank old Bri for his gin and to expect a royal visit when what is necessary to be done is finally done."

"I will, Sire, you may be sure."

Toli turned and walked up the gangplank to re-join his party.

Getting underway, turning north-east to head for Beeth, Toli sat next to Anga up on the council deck and looked to the sky and said to Anga, "Look Anga." There were small flocks of many different kinds of birds, around five or six birds to a flock, all flying north, collectively they occasionally blocked the sun, now on the downward arc of his eternal journey.

"They are all heading to Bevak to give their reports to Redwind, King of all birds who reports to the garrison sage, who speaks fluent raptor can communicate with all other birds on the Island," Quor explained.

There was now a light westerly breeze blowing east across the lake, and Toli called to Storq, "Storq, how about we raise your mainsail and break out old Bri's Gin and give us all a tot."

A cheer went up from all of the crew, the only people abord who had tasted the spirit were Quor, Broq, Soq and, of course, Captain Storq, who never left Tabunti without a flagon of the stuff. This was the crews first and probably last taste of the famous spirit. The crew attacked their task with unbridled enthusiasm, singing a lake shanty, not unlike the sea-shanties he had heard on the Castle-side as he was now calling the sea-facing side of the Island.

"HO HO HO AND UP WE GO
TO CATCH THE WIND
BOTH HIGH AND LOW
ACROSS OUR BOW
LET WATER FLOW
HO HO HO AND UP WE GO."

This was the first time they had heard a lake shanty or any song since coming to the valley and it affected them greatly. Admiral Shouk actually had a tear in his eye.

"HO HO HO AND UP WE GO
UP THE LAKE
OUR SKILL WE'LL SHOW

TO SAIL THE LAKE
WE ALL MUST KNOW
HO HO HO AND UP WE GO."

At the end of this verse, there were many more, a big cheer went up, for Tak had emerged from the galley with a tray of leather cups. Stacked one inside the other and joined his Captain. Storq took the tray from Tak and laid it on the deck as he tapped the cask, underneath this tray Tak had another, on which he placed twelve cups, one for each council member, only a splash for Shala.

"A little taster for our Princess, I think," Storq said to Tak.

Tak brought the tray up to the council deck and unloaded his tray on to the table, as he turned to go, Shala called, "Wait for me, Tak, I'll help you," and she gulped her small sip down and followed Tak back up to the bow and the cask. Tak laid down his empty tray and picked up the tray with full cups.

"How about you do starboard and I do port?" she said.

"Okay, great stuff, thanks." Tak made off up the starboard of the ship and when Shala's tray was filled, she headed bow to stern up the port side, when all aboard had their half-filled cups, Captain Storq lifted his own above his head and toasted loud so all aboard could hear, "To Toli, our King, and Victory!"

The rest of the company including head council, raised cups above heads and yelled the toast, "Toli, King and Victory!"

They all swallowed their cups as one, as they lowered the cups from their mouths, they all looked around at each other, even Shala who had been in too much of a hurry to help Tak, looked around, now tasting gin, even her small sup was now making a previously unnoticed reaction.

The sweet liquor danced on their tongues, made their cheeks and lips tingle with pleasure, the eyesight, already sharp, sharper, their touch more sensitive, then a sailor jumped onto the middle of the deck and began a jig, shortly followed by the entire crew, except Captain and the Helm:

"HO HO HO AND UP WE GO
TO RAISE OUR SAIL
TO SLEEP BELOW
AND WHEN WE WAKE
WITH GIN ASTOW
HO HO HO AND UP WE GO!"

And it continued until the light faded and the crew were ordered to light the deck lights, Storq could see the city lights in the distance winking on in the distance.

Toli and Anga the whole time sat together away from the rest unnoticed, even the Generals and the lads clapped and cheered, while Broq, Soq and Quor kept them up to speed on the lyrics.

"Anga, we have a dilemma when we land in Beeth," he said as the crew danced and sang.

"Not really, I know your thoughts, and I can assure you, my King, that nothing need, nor will, change until this conflict is done with and we are properly wed in your city and under the mountain, under the sky and before the waves, as generations untold of, have done before you, and Shala will be always within reach of me, even after marriage, until she is my grown daughter."

Toli was struck dumb for a few seconds, then he kissed his love on the lips and whispered in her ear, "My thoughts exactly, I'm glad you agree." And they broke into a fit of hysterical laughter, made worse by the fact that no-one even noticed, such was the celebration aboard.

"Look, Anga, the city lights are coming on and the sun will soon set all the way, lets watch the sunset from here with the council then we'll go up and watch the approach, if you'd like, of course, only if you'd like."

"I'd like nothing more, my King," she said and laid her head on his shoulder now both looking west.

As the sun sank, Toli called out just before and called to the rest of the council, "Look men! Nothing better!" Even the crews stopped to look. As they watched the sun slowly sink, but as it sank, it eventually turned a blood red and cast the lake a scarlet hue; the ship was silent now, even Captain and Helm staring west, the Queen Shaleena sailing herself, the sun then disappeared completely behind the lowest peak of the mountain leaving a blood red glow reaching upward to the stars.

"My sky, I have never seen the like before!" Toli exclaimed.

"Nor have I, Sire." Quor stood stock still. "For the like of that has not been seen before."

Now, the pier for the Queen Shaleena was coming into view and as Toli and Anga walked to the bow, they noticed that only one person was standing alone on the pier, as they came closer they saw the man was in mail, a sword at his side. There were no committees, there was no-one at all apart from the warrior.

Chapter 28

Old Bri brought Zacko's harness and tack into his small barn, hung them up on pegs, picked up a large metal bucket and headed up the track beside the recently ploughed field, as he walked into the wood at the top of the field he walked into a clearing, in the middle of the clearing there stood a tall plant, some sort of herbal bush, with big palm shaped leaves and big yellow flowers, in the centre of each of the flowers were large gooey seed pods, already having shed their seeds old Bri picked the flowers and the pods together and they filled his bucket and another box in the clearing which he would reclaim later.

These were the secret of old Bri's gin, he also dried the leaves and added them to his pipe bakky, it gave him a nice mellow feeling at bedtime. The plant would die now, its seeds were sown, and regenerate on the same spot as it had done as long as Bri had known of it, there was not another like it anywhere, although it shed multiple seeds, it had grown only here. Old Bri was happy now, another harvest done for the year.

Chapter 29

Sisk was heading downhill, back towards the Castle and his drunken Lords, when he decided to call in again and surprise the two Trois, keeping them on their toes, never knowing when he'll show up. But they knew he would be passing en-route back to the harbour and were poring over the drawings Troi the younger had already drawn as part of his guild final exam.

"Hello again, men." The two Trois acted startled as Sisk silently appeared at their shoulders.

"My Lord, you have returned." Sisk could detect no malice or deceit in Troi senior's tone unknown to him, the reason for this was in the slag piles all around.

"These drawings look like final drafts, like they were already prepared before my visit, can you explain please?"

Young Troi was ready for awkward questions.

"My Lord, these drawings were prepared for my final presentation to the guild, should have been last year, Lord, but because of circumstances at that time these were stuck in my desk drawer, in class, ever since, but, my Lord, on myself and my father mulling over these details we can find no reason to delay the making of the mould pattern, and we are confident we will meet your deadline and even surpass it."

"I shall still give the eleven days as agreed, if I make a commitment, I'll see it through, so you know in eleven days' time I'll return to you with my Lords Muklah and Brakko plus at least four of our soldiers as apprentices to yourselves, only for the making of cannons, nothing else. Your drawings are excellent and I can see no reason why full production cannot begin now, today; however, two working guns in the time given will be enough to satisfy my Lord, I can assure you, no need to let anyone else know these were already prepared, so now I will say my farewells and very well done Troi and I'll see you both in eleven days, tomorrow being day one."

Sisk then turned and left, on leaving the forge site he stopped to speak to the soldier on guard at the entrance/exit, "How are you finding the duties up here, soldier?"

"Fine Lord, we keep ourselves busy in our duties, we can have no complaints, for this is our easiest post since I've been soldiering."

"Good man, your name, soldier?"

"I am Sito, Lord."

"Well Sito, you and your comrades are doing an exceptional job up here, be sure to tell your fellow guards I said so."

"Aye Lord, surely Lord, I will, Lord."

"Very good, Sito, I'll leave you now, but I'll be back in eleven days with Lord Muklah and Brakko, so be on your best form when we next appear." At that Sisk left, again, very pleased with himself; he complimented anyone who needed it and was laying a solid foundation for his personal plans when the time becomes right. As he and his horse walked back to the harbour, his thoughts went to the problem of the condition of the two below and how to deal with the rest of today, as he distanced himself further from the mountain he had a feeling of clarity slowly coming over him too slowly for an instant impression but a definite easing of thought, by the time he got to the back gate he was up to speed on his next manoeuvre, the light was beginning to fade now as he stabled his horse, he thanked the stable-master for the attention to his mount and thanked him again for the way he turned the horse out, all horses, in fact.

On his way to see Muklah and Brakko, he walked to the barracks looking for the off-duty Captain whose name he knew to be Kile. Kile stood outside the barrack quarters talking to a fisherman who was handing a large basket of fish to Kile. Kile gave nothing in return, it was not necessary.

"Ah Captain Kile!" Sisk called. "A word if you please."

"Of course, Lord."

"Kile, I want you to pick four young very quick learners, good workers, to go, in eleven days' time, up to the cannon forge with the visiting delegation from the Castle, no Kile make that six, five plus your good self, I also expect you to promote your choice for the new harbour Captain, do you understand, Kile?"

"I do, Lord."

"Then do it now, we may leave before the present deadline."

"Immediately, Lord Sisk." And Kile left to make his decisions, happy to be getting on from the boredom where he was. *Ah well*, he thought, *at least we are all training hard and staying sharp.*

Sisk opened the doors to the Castle-keep to find Crall waiting for him.

"Well, what news, Crall?" he asked.

"I heard movement, Lord, but I fear the movement was towards drink, I cannot properly say."

"Very well, thank you, Crall, now come, time to wake the Kraken."

Sisk stopped at the chamber door and spoke to the guards, did any of them hear anything?

"Only brief movement about two hours ago Lord, but we have not been summoned."

Sisk could tell the captain was ill at ease and sensed his relief at the presence of himself.

"Well, you may relax now, Captain, whatever has gone on in here, it is not your fault; you are blameless."

"Yes Lord, thank you, Lord," and his spine turned to jelly with relief.

Sisk pushed open the doors and stepped through into the stink and mess. Muklah was head down on the table grasping a mug on its side, head in the puddle; he didn't...he didn't seem to be breathing, Sisk rushed forward and grabbed Muklah by his shoulders and pulled him upright on his chair; he called the guards to come quickly, Sisk felt for a pulse, which was weak but steady, he then got a pewter goblet and held it to Muklah's mouth, there was breath.

"My grief!" he declared. "He's drank himself into a coma; quickly, get him stripped and washed and into his bed. Crall, get your staff to clean this swamp up, I want two at the door, closed, and one of you in here on a chair, paying attention to our Lord Muklah, is that clear?"

"Yes Lord," the guards said in unison.

"Good lads, now Captain, you come with me."

And he marched out followed by the Captain straight to Brakko's chamber, at the door he said to the Captain, "Anything to tell me, Captain?"

"There has been movement inside, Lord, but that was a while ago, it's been silent for about an hour and a half now, we dare not go in unsummoned, my Lord."

Sisk again felt the relief at his presence and again assured the guards that they were blameless. Sisk pushed the doors open, again the stink, again the mess, as he entered the room, he said to the guards to follow and the Captain with him gave a nod and a wink to his fellow Captain as if to say, *This fellow is worthy of respect.*

"Okay lads, get him up, washed and to bed, it seems our leaders didn't stop when they parted at least when they were awake."

Brakko was the same condition as Muklah, it was an act of stupidity which played right into Sisk's hands. He stationed the guards as before and told them to find him if anything should happen. At that he left to go back to Muklah's chamber, he went across to the bed where Muklah lay comatose, he checked his vital signs again and straightened up, saying, "Well, this is not going to pass tonight, men," he said to the guard in the room.

"Stay vigilant; try to be aware of any changes during the night, the same to the rest of you; be as vigilant as I know you always are and come for me if need be. Crall, make sure there is nothing to drink in here but water, that way we will be alerted when he wakes, and do the same in Lord Brakko's chamber, do not attempt to disturb me unnecessarily, I have much to do in the way of preparation. Crall, I go to wash now, see I get some food in one hour," and he left.

After he washed himself of the day's grime, Sisk sat writing his daily report which he kept to himself, unless asked for a written report which could not be given verbally; there was a gentle knock at the door.

"Come in, Crall." Crall came in with a platter of food including the ever present nutty bread and placed it on the table.

"Thank you Crall, how was your day?" Crall was taken aback by this interest in his day.

"Same as always, Lord, not going anywhere, including backwards, so can't complain, my Lord."

"Yes, not going backwards is always a bonus, eh, Crall?"

"Yes Lord, always."

"Well, goodnight Crall."

"Yes goodnight, Lord."

Crall left thinking, *Well I never, a Black-Isler you can talk to, beat that!*

Sisk in turn was very pleased with the day's proceedings, something or somebody seemed to be looking out for him, not literally but things certainly were coming together more smoothly than expected, suddenly there was a loud cry at the castle door as it flew open,

"Come, come quick!" a voice yelled and staff were already going out the door. Sisk noticed a strange reddish light in his chamber and on hearing the cry, got up and went outside people stood around, silently staring at the horizon, even the air seemed to be stained red and as they all watched, the sun dropped, blood red below the horizon but just before it disappeared the sea, the harbour, the castle, mountain and the whole city turned scarlet and it struck them all dumb and when the sun finally dropped beyond sight, they all stood staring at the blushing sky until it faded completely. After eventually uprooting themselves from their spots, the people and the soldiers slowly went on their separate ways, mostly silent.

Sisk turned back to his chamber mulling over what he had just seen, trying to make sense of it; every seaman and shepherd knows the saying, "Red sky at night, shepherd's delight; red sky in the morning, sailor, take warning," but this was something different, something he had no experience of, finding no clue in his extensive memory as to what just occurred, he finished his report and by the time he finished, the night was black and he sank into hid bed gratefully, still puzzled, but happy with the way things had gone on this day.

Chapter 30

The warrior stood alone on the dock at salute, brief salutes over, he explained to Toli directly.

"Sire, we apologise for this interruption in your plans but we have received a message that, although not immediately pressing, my Lord Briq would bid you dwell here with the welcome committee tonight, and speak with them, but leave for Bevak at first light, the good people of Beeth have agreed to stay quiet tonight and allow you space till morning when they will see you on your way with as little ceremony as is possible. Dalri is so close to Bevak, citizens have agreed to make their way to greet you there, please Sire, the elders of Beeth await you inside." He indicated to the guild house and to follow him, when he led the party inside, he turned to Toli and said, "Sire, I will leave you now. I must report back that the message is delivered, not even the pigeons will fly tonight after that sunset."

"Your name please, warrior?" Toli asked.

"Forgive me Sire, in my haste—"

"No need for forgiveness, friend warrior, I merely want to know the name of the warrior who rode to his King on the night the birds refused to fly."

"My name is Luq, Sire."

"Then Luq, your King thanks you sincerely for your service, please tell the garrison Commander that I will follow his advice to the letter and the Queen Shaleena will depart Beeth at first light with all aboard and thank him for his prompt action, farewell, Luq, till tomorrow."

"Aye Sire, till tomorrow," and Luq mounted his massive Destrier, a beautiful animal with an intelligent face, and galloped off into the black of night.

Inside the guild hall, the four city elders stood waiting alongside the city garrison Captain.

"My name is Sori, Sire, I am head elder and Mayor of Beeth, these three gentlemen are my council," and he turned to introduce them in turn.

"I am lucky, Sire, to have three right hands, this is Mauri, Mossi and Toi, and this, Sire, is Miq, the garrison off-duty Captain." All four bowed their heads briefly.

"If you wish Sire, the table is ready for supper," and Sori led them through into the dining hall. The meal was a little less extravagant than meals before, but it was appreciated, for it had been a busy day, all were tired, and they appreciated the lack of ceremony, they sat down, in what was now the established manner for the head council, Anga and Shala at his right and Quor to his left, next to Quor, the senior city elder, the rest as they chose. The table in this room was shaped in a semi-circle so as to make cross-table conversation less troublesome.

"My King," Sori began, "the entire population of Beeth regrets not being there at your arrival; however, partly due to the sunset but mainly as a request from the garrison, we will leave our celebrations until it suits your own purposes, there will be a small gathering outside at dawn, but most people who are able are making their way up to Bevak as are Dalri folk so that at least they may be able to catch a glimpse, so I propose that I give you a tour of Beeth from the dining table."

"Your proposal is accepted with thanks, Sori. I thank you for myself and every one of us in the head council, we could all do with a rest for the short voyage here was not as restful as I had hoped."

Sori took this to mean the inexplicable sunset, he did not know of the gin nor the singing and jigging.

"Yes Sire, we understand, so if you wish it, Sire, I'll give you an explanation of our workings here, we won't delay your bedtime any longer than we must."

"I thank you for this, Sori, as I'm sure the rest of the council do." There were thankful sounds around the table then, although somewhat muted.

"Sire, we here in Beeth are mainly responsible for the upkeep and health of the Islands forests, we also prepare timber for building material, we have some in the lake now to go south for the new settlement, we have to cut and shape the timber to measurements sent to us by Roqi, your Nanas advisor, previous to going in the water for the lake water and the river water of our mountain have an effect on the wood so as to prevent any other work or tooling, carving and the like, Sire.

"After soaking in our water for a very short time, the beams in the holding pond now were cut and tooled yesterday and today, they will be taken, tomorrow after our departure, down this lake to our new township, these timbers will never break, never be punctured by any weapon we know of, and will never burn, the water is the reason your forges never burn down and your carpenters have been using this method unknowingly as your workers tool the timber on the river's edge, it matters not which river for by the time the finished timber is across, it is as indestructible as the toughest stone, maybe even more so, and your tradesmen know now all holes, grooves, joints, pegs, etcetera, must be worked before the crossing, although they think it is to do with the cutting of the trees and the trees themselves giving time to your men before becoming too hard to tool.

"They have no idea that it is the brief river crossing, and the method you use to cross, still pulling them over in single file, roped together, because your ship timbers are cut from trees close to the sea and do not cross a river, this does not apply to them, although I sense this might change Sire. Every tree cut down is replaced by a seedling the same day, less these days, for we have built all we need and our buildings last a very long time, the workshop were very happy when Roqi's drawings arrived, there is a purpose in Beeth again, a sense of rebirth."

Quor then spoke, "Aye, rebirth, Sori, good choice of words, I think everyone here would agree with that sentiment, I feel for the people on the outside as they believe the situation now is permanent and they believe the entire royal family is gone forever along with the Generals in Command along with Admiral Shouk, they also believe that as soon as they are no longer needed they will be destroyed and their memory erased forever, we are going to make certain that never happens." Quor's face was bright red now and he seemed to be somehow bigger.

"By the time this episode in history is over, the rest of the world will know that this land will never be conquered." He slammed his fist down on the table, he looked around the table then and saw the surprise on the faces of the assembled company, he muttered, "Forgive me, Sire, please."

"Quor, your passion for our land is an inspiration to us all and should not be dismissed easily, never ask forgiveness of me for your passion or you will be asking forgiveness for asking forgiveness."

"Yes Sire, of course, forgi—" And a burst of laughter went around the table, relieving Quor, he was not accustomed to bouts of temper, but, as they got closer to Bevak, he felt his warrior instinct come out, for although he had not mentioned it Quor was a warrior of some repute before becoming the Mayor of the Capital, the other lake valley folk had said very little on this trip, they knew all was to be revealed up in Bevak.

In fact there had been a noticeable change in Anga as the garrison became closer, now she sat silent seemingly far away, her brow furled in what appeared to be a confused expression. Toli took a mental note to speak to her alone before bed, Shala too had become distant since the sunset.

"With your permission Sire, we of the Beeth elders would like to travel on the royal ship with you, purely to save us from travel by road after your leaving, I myself will be attending the large council meeting and would delay my attendance by road travel, and as the council will progress without me, and would leave me missing information which I would have to catch up on after council is suspended."

"I would not have it any other way, Sori, we can catch up on things as we make way, now let us enjoy the fare of Beeth and leave tomorrow to tomorrow for we can do nothing today."

And the company went back to chatting among themselves, the Generals were almost touching foreheads and talking rapidly as if one was preventing the other from voicing an opinion, the Generals and Quor, Broq and Soq seemed deep in something that made them oblivious to all around, Ratesh, Joki and Dovitt were the same as were the Beeth elders, and so it was that Toli, Anga and Shala were left to their own, everyone else had an agenda of their own for now.

Anga still had a confused look on her face, and Toli said, "Anga, what is on your mind that is enough to cause this concern?"

"I know not, Toli, but I have a feeling in my very being, tomorrow is going to enlighten me as to this unrest inside me, it is becoming stronger by the hour and I can't say what my state of mind will be when I wake tomorrow."

Then Shala said, "Me too, I have this too." Although the whole company felt the change, even in the atmosphere, none had the same turmoil inside as Anga, unexplained, worrying.

"Tomorrow, as I said, is tomorrow, my love, for the rest of today let's try to enjoy our company and the fare. I think that everyone here has sensed the difference as we close on the garrison, big things to come, I'm absolutely certain."

"Yes, me too, there's no denying it."

The rest of the evening passed cordially with various conversations around the table, Toli quizzed the Beeth elders about the method of wood treatment, "Sori, would it be feasible to treat our ships in this way."

"Definitely Sire, no doubt, as I said your smiths have been doing it for years, but for shipbuilding you have options, you can have your timber cut and tooled here then brought through to the City side by way of one of the many streams or rivers passing out of the mountain, then assemble the vessels as the material arrives, or Sire, and you may find this more pleasing, the river passing behind your forges has been treating your wood for many years and it runs down to almost beside your fitting docks.

"If you built a soaking dam, doesn't have to be huge, then you could soak a complete ships timbers together, after tooling of course, then, after drying you could have your builders, building, and ship fitters fitting, at any pace you feel like, you could float the material for one ship at a time down river without the need for a dam, the bigger the dam, the more ships completed in less time."

"Sori, one of these methods will happen, I thank you for your knowledge and the sharing of it."

"It is my duty, Sire, and my great pleasure."

The night was coming to an earlier than usual end, and when Toli was served his third honey draught, he said, "I think Sori, I will take to bed after this one as I feel we all should be prepared for the day's proceedings tomorrow with clear heads."

The entire company muttered agreement and nodded heads, they seemed to be falling headlong into the comfortable softness of sleep approaching. Toli drank his draught quickly and then stood up abruptly.

"I will bid you all goodnight now," he said loudly. "Would you all please allow myself and Anga to exchange a few short words before retiring yourselves?"

Now Toli and Anga stood and walked from the hall, Shala got up to follow and Quor gently but firmly put his hand on Shala's, looked her in the eye and shook his head very slightly. Shala understood instantly and nodded back, then sat back down.

Toli and Anga walked out onto the porch of the hall and sat on the top step together, the night was now pitch black, the moon was, for now, behind a bank of clouds and very few stars were visible, only for the porch lamp they may have been invisible to each other.

"Anga, I feel your concern inside of me and I know Shala feels it too, something huge is coming tomorrow, and I get the feeling things are being kept from us, I could go back in now and order Sori or Quor, or anyone to tell me all they know and they would have to obey, but I also get the feeling that they have not been told anything that we already know so as not to let slip, but then I may be imagining everything, after Bris Gin then the sunset, then the messenger at the dock.

"At this moment, I just need sleep and to tell you that my love for you is boundless and no matter what, me and Shala can never be parted, except of our own choices, I feel tomorrows dawn cannot come quick enough for this day to be over." Then he stood up, taking Anga's hand and helping her to her feet, they stood face to face, they shared lingering eye contact, then a lingering kiss and swore their undying love for one another and went back inside.

"Okay friends, without wishing to be rude, I feel we should bring this day to its end and I, at least, am going to bed, so I bid you all a goodnight." And he gave Anga a kiss on the cheek and simply left. Immediately, the lads Ratesh, Dovitt and Joki got up and followed, then Anga and Shala followed hand in hand, the rest of the company dispersed within a few minutes, thanking the elders and the elders thanking them.

Leaving the chamber, Toli realised he had no idea where to go; fortunately, as he walked into an atrium with several doors heading off it, a guide stepped forwards and directed Toli and the lads to their door. As the group were undressing and re-dressing for bed, Ratesh, sitting on the end of his chosen bed, said, "Strangest of days, eh lads." There was kind of a mystified murmur in answer as if no one knew anything else to say.

"Aye men, and I've a feeling tomorrow will be even stranger, well g'night." Then Toli rolled under his bed cover and was asleep in seconds.

In Anga and Shala's room, they lay in their beds staring at the ceiling then Shala turned to look at Anga.

"Anga, you know something big is coming tomorrow in regard to yourself I mean, are you able to talk about it?"

"Yes I know, but I don't know, I'm very confused."

"Anga, you will never leave me, will you, for I could never imagine life without you."

"Shala, your anxiety is misplaced, you and I and Toli are forever, only death can split our bond and I have no plans to take my leave just yet, my unusual emotions, as far as I can tell are not fatal, we can only let tomorrow tell us what we must do, goodnight Shala."

"Night Anga," and both went off into a deep dreamless sleep.

Chapter 31

When they were sure Sisk was definitely gone, younger Troi said, "Father, we can have two cannons poured today, soaked in oil bath tomorrow, tooled the day after, and tested the day after that, if we do each process on a daily basis one after the other and one team casting, another tempering, another tooling and you and I testing, after four days we can produce two working cannons every day after the fourth day, we'll have sixteen working cannon in eleven days' time, that's almost enough for an entire gundeck!"

"Aye lad but Sisk doesn't know that so let's pour two now, leave them till tomorrow and we'll decide what must be done tomorrow when the Grandmaster and the others here."

"Aye Father, that makes sense." With that the two Trois went to work, the work they were born to, they would cast the two tonight, let them cool overnight, break them out in the morning, clean any slag off, place them back on the forge to reheat the weapons to the correct temperature for soaking in oil to temper the alloy mix of the guns meanwhile reset the pattern and pour again, when the two cannons came out of the oil bath they will be mounted and clamped to a level table one for each gun, they must be worked when still warm, then a central boring tool would lightly and precisely bore the cast shot-hole, on the same table the outside would be finished including the powder pan and firing hole, and now it can be test fired.

After casting the test pieces on the way to their small stone cottage on the same site as the forge, Troi senior stopped to speak to Sito at the gate, still on duty, "Guard, can you please tell your Captain the forge masters will be here early tomorrow to assist in the making of your Lord's guns, we need them here because it is our tradition that all drawings and patterns and processes are passed by the guild masters, it will not interfere in any way with us making Lord Sisk's deadline."

"Very good, master Troi, I'll make sure he knows."

"Thank you, guard."

"Sito."

"Sorry, what?"

"My name is Sito, you can call me Sito as long as an officer doesn't hear."

"Okay then, thank you Sito."

"You are very welcome, master Troi."

"You can call me Troi, Sito, I'm not your Master."

"Then you are welcome, Troi."

"Goodnight Sito."

"Goodnight Troi."

Walking back to the cottage, elder said to younger, "You know, son, some of these invaders are not all bad through and through, that chap was positively friendly."

"He certainly was, Father, we must keep that in mind, it may come in useful, later."

Chapter 32

Sisk went through his usual morning routine so washed, fed and groomed, he left his chambers to go speak to the guards on night duty, Crall, who had cleaned away the breakfast tray while Sisk was washing, waited at the door to follow Sisk in case he was needed, it was not unpleasant working for Sisk, and he dreaded Muklah's awakening. As they walked the red sunset briefly came into Sisk's thoughts but were dismissed as unsolvable, there were more important things to deal with, things he could control. He went first to Muklah's guard, "Anything to report, Captain?"

"No Lord, disturbingly quiet, again I am relieved to see you, we are all confused, we cannot enter without a summoning or danger to our Lord is suspected."

"Have no fear, Captain, as I have already said, you are under no threat nor accusation about your ethics and I am in the front line as far as decisions are concerned, I personally guarantee you that neither you nor any of your men are in any danger of being chastised for anything; are we clear, Captain?"

"Yes Lord, I won't mention it again, Lord."

"Right then, so let's see how our Lord Muklah is today."

Sisk pushed the doors open and, followed by Crall, walked into the chamber he could see Muklah prostrate on top of his bed, as he approached he could hear an even breathing, peaceful, serene, he looked down on the errant Lord.

"Crall, we must leave our leader to properly awaken, we will go and check Lord Brakko, who, I'm sure, won't be too far from this state, then I can see what's to be done."

Brakko was in exactly the same condition as Muklah.

"Once again," said Sisk, looking down on Brakko, "I'll have to start the day without directions."

He and Crall left the chamber and closed the doors behind and making sure the guards were within earshot, said to Crall, "Crall, I have many things to attend to ensure my Lord's plans are executed properly, so, to that end, I must go and check the other forges, but I will return in four hours to wake up the good Lords, in my absence if anything happens, once again send someone to find me I'm going around the other forges and mines today, as much as I can anyway," he said this with feigned weariness as if something was weighing heavily upon his shoulders.

"But I'll be back in four hours when I must wake our Lords, so have black leaf brew ready for both, if they request more wine or ale you must, of course, give it to them but come find me quickly, I do not think there will be any need as I believe I will have to wake them on my return, and Crall, have some hot food ready just in case, but I fully expect the pleasure of the waking ceremony."

He didn't wait for the reply, he just sighed audibly and left to carry out any duties he could.

As he watched Sisk's back heading for the door, the guard Captain said loud enough to hear, "What a man, he's doing enough for ten men easily."

And all the guards along with Crall said, "Aye." Crall noticed a softening in the invaders' manner recently and thought, *I doubt this will be the case when the Black Kraken rises.*

Sisk thought to himself leaving the castle, *If I go up to the forges again today, I'll never be back to make my report from yesterday and I said I would not go back up for eleven days anyway, so I'll stay around here for a few hours and pick up some loose ends, like it or not I will have to bring Muklah back to reality in order to progress with my own agenda.*

He walked down to the harbour and asked a soldier the whereabouts of Captain Kile, now on duty.

"He's just gone up to the causeway to the cannon emplacements Lord, he said he had something important to do, he didn't give me any time till his return, Lord."

"Never mind, soldier, should he return before me, please tell him to make himself available for a talk with me, but I'll probably bump into him anyway."

As he walked the length of the harbour up to the causeway, he thought, *I'll go up to see Kile and have a bit of target practice at the same time, the noise may help wake Muklah and I can easily convince him that he gave me permission.*

As he came to the top of the causeway, he turned to face the mountain, sun glistening off the time polished rock, he felt some kind of pang in his chest and he muttered to himself, "I do not know who you are but I know I will, I just know."

Just then he heard a call from the closest cannon emplacement, "Lord Sisk, are you okay?"

He turned to see Kile standing atop the emplacement rampart with a genuine look of concern on his face. "Aye Kile, come down, we'll have a chat."

"Yes lord, right away." He was beside Sisk in seconds.

"Did you pick your men, Kile?"

"Yes Lord, the sixth man just now."

"Excellent Kile excellent, I need not vet your choices, Kile, you have my complete trust."

"Thank you Lord, we will not let you down."

Kile was far from a stupid man and he thought, *Where is this coming from?*

"You're frowning, Kile, I know a person I can trust the second I first speak to them, I know you will not let me down, come." He began to walk to the first cannon.

"I'm glad you're up here, Kile; for the first time ever you're going to see a Black-Islander destroy a Tolian ship with their own cannon." He walked up to the gun crew, three Black-islanders and three Tolians training them.

"We have permission, men, to fire on those three ships today, one shot from all ten positions so load up and prepare to fire!" The Tolian expressions were fit to kill, they offered nor gave any help; they would die before firing on one of their own ships.

"Don't worry, men, you may step away if you wish." Sisk anticipated this reaction the first day up here so he spoke lightly as if he were a concerned uncle. "You may rest assured nothing will come of it." Then he had another notion. "Kile, will you please go tell the other crews to ready their guns, send a message across to the other three over the way, to stand down and man the flags, tell each of them to fire at five-second intervals, the first shot from here and so on up to the tenth."

"Aye Lord." And Kile was off.

"Oh and Kile?"

"Yes Lord."

"The first shot will be at your arrival back here, so they know how much time they have."

"Yes Lord." The three Black-islanders stood staring at Sisk in dumb surprise.

"Well lads, is it going to load itself?"

"Loaded Lord, today is loading practice, Lord, we just finished as you arrived."

"So unload and do it again, loading practice, remember?"

"Yes Lord, at once."

They unloaded the weapon in no time; there was no spark present today so there was no real danger. The first man picked up a long staff with a double pronged and twisted end they called it the worm, he rammed it up the bore of the massive gun and simultaneously pushed and twisted, then began pulling and twisting a large block of cloth called wadding came out, another man then turned a large screw moving the back end of the gun up and down for aiming, very advanced for its age.

He pointed as low as possible and the worm was rammed up again this time to loosen the ball, eventually the ball rolled into a basket placed to catch it, the man with the worm moved it aside as the barrel was raised again for reloading, the third man made the action of clearing the powder pan and extinguishing an imaginary taper in case of accidental ignition.

The first man was now ramming another staff with a brush on the end to brush the powder back out, there was no powder allowed on these days so they were only going through the motions.

"Okay men, now load it for real, show me the real thing."

The man who was in charge of powder and taper ran to a metal box and took out a small keg of powder, a taper, and a flint, ran back, handed the keg to the loader, he lit his taper by first lighting a bowl carved in the rock, full of loose wadding soaked in gun oil, the keg of powder fitted loosely into the barrel and he rammed it home until the keg burst its sides and the powder leaked into the barrel.

He rammed the ramrod home twice more till he was happy the powder was where it should be, the barrel was now aiming slightly upward and the loader rolled the ball into the bore of the gun and rammed it home on top of the broken wood and all, now he shoved a different ball of wadding in the gun and rammed that home.

He stood back and raised his hand and called, "Ready!" The taper man dropped an amount of black powder in the firing pan, stepped back, held his taper up and called, "Ready!" The aimer, on the screw, sighted his gun for height then punched a bit to his left with the ramrod and looked up his barrel again then stood back raised his hand and called, "Ready!"

"I'm very impressed, men, you've been training hard, now all we have to do is wait for Captain Kile and we can begin." Kile came back quicker than anyone expected.

"All ready, Captain?"

"Yes Lord."

"And the three opposite?"

"Yes Lord, I flagged them myself."

"Very well done, everyone, the Tolians will be shaking in their boots. Okay READY?"

"Yes Lord, READY!"

"FIRE!"

The taper lit the powder in the pan and with a slight delay, the cannon went off in an enormous cloud of smoke and let off a roar like an angry bear but much, much louder. The five of them on the rampart coughed and rubbed their eyes, the rest of the cannon went off exactly as ordered; unfortunately, the first position was downwind of the other nine and they remained in acrid smoke longest of all; when the smoke eventually did clear, they looked out on three perfectly intact ships at anchor broadside to the guns a cable length between the first bow and the third stern as they all watched sullenly as the bowsprit of the middle ship slowly dropped forward, swung once, then dropped into the sea.

"Well," Sisk stood with tears leaving tracks down his face mucky with gun smoke, "one hit in ten shots, I must be honest I expect better, please bring the Tolians here, I wish to speak to them." The three Tolian trainers stood heads bowed in front of Sisk.

"My Tolian friends, I could be excused for thinking my men have been deliberately misled, that they were deceived, anything to say?"

A big man, less cowed then the other two, raised his eyes to Sisk. "My Lord, when you shoot a stationary cannon at a moving ship, the first shot is the range finder, if you look up to the positions out of the smoke, you can see a single red flag, red means long and the single flag means we were all long; had we mixed results, there would be mixed flags; it is the best system we have, ten flags for ten positions, it is good that there is only one flag showing."

"Yes, makes perfect sense explained, I completely understand now, well I can't shoot anymore today much as I would love to, I'll have to consult with my

Lord Muklah and arrange more target time, okay, I must return to the castle now. Kile, go and tell the gun crews to stay at their posts for relief, but they may rest for the rest of today, then bring your last choice down and wait for me in the canteen, I will delay no more than I have to."

He left the gun position and walked down the causeway and along the harbour and back into the castle. Again, Crall was waiting inside the door.

"Ah Crall, what news?"

"My Lord Muklah and Brakko are now awake, my Lord, they are both drinking black leaf tea and eating like bears just out of hibernation, my Lord Muklah requests your presence and your report to date as soon as you can."

"Very well, Crall, thank you, please tell my Lord I have returned to the castle and I shall submit my report as soon as I wash myself and change my clothing."

"Straight away, Lord Sisk."

"Please make sure my lord knows I would come immediately but I am in no fit state to see him right now."

"Of course, Lord."

When the first cannon went off, Brakko leapt out of bed and grabbed his war sword from its scabbard and staggered out the door in his bed shirt, head still reeling, Crall was in a position to attend quickly to the first of the Lords to appear, he heard Brakko's roar and moved himself and the prepared hot tray of food and drink outside Brakko's door, but enough distance away to avoid being skewered or beheaded. Brakko burst out of his chamber doors, looked around and pointed his sword at Crall.

"You there, what just happened, are we under attack?"

"No Lord, Lord Sisk is up at the cannon emplacements to examine their progress, he will be directly joining my Lord Muklah to submit his reports, shall I bring your food inside?"

"No, I'll do it myself," and he took the tray inside and slammed the door shut behind him.

Muklah, just as the tenth cannon belched fire and steel, sat up abruptly in bed and looked around, finding his bearings he crossed the room to his wash basin and filled it to the brim, then grabbing the basin rim with both hands, ducked his head under and held it there for as long as he could, he shook his long black hair, like a dog whose been in the river, then dried himself on a fresh towel; he felt better already, and he had no idea that it was cannon fire that woke him as there was no more.

"Crall!" he yelled.

"Yes Lord." Crall came into his chamber pushing the hot tray in front of him. "Some food and drink, Lord."

"What just woke me, and where are Lords Sisk and Brakko?"

"Lord Sisk is just returning from cannon practice and has gone to wash and change and pick up his report for you, and Lord Brakko is in his chamber having breakfast, or early lunch, my Lord."

"Go get Brakko now, he can eat here and we will take food together and take Lord Sisk's report together, wait a second, did you just say cannon practice?"

"Yes Lord."

"And was it cannon fire woke me?"

"Yes Lord."

Crall knocked on Brakko's door.

"Enter."

"My Lord Muklah requests your presence in his chamber, to take food and to take Lord Sisk's report."

"Yes Crall, tell Lord Muklah I'm on my way." He was washed and dressed in that short time, and was supping on a small cup of black brew. He had just went in to join Muklah when Sisk came through the door.

Crall went to the door of Muklah's room and then knocked. "Yes."

Crall pushed the doors open stepped in and said, "My Lord Sisk has returned, he has gone to his chambers to get his report and make himself presentable, the cannon smoke made quite a mess of him, he sends his apologies but feels the sight of him may offend my Lords, he will be here soon."

"Thank you Crall, please bring a tray in for Lord Sisk, oh and bring a dozen oysters."

"Yes Lord." And Crall thought, *My grief, what's happened, I must feed them more of the black tea. I got a please and a thank you from Lord Muklah all in the same sentence.* And he went off to prepare a tray for Lord Sisk.

Sisk knocked on the door and went in without waiting, as he turned to close the doors, Crall arrived pushing his tray and pulling another with a dozen oysters on a platter and a large pot of hot black leaf brew. "For you, lord," and he nodded at his tray in front of him. Sisk looked over Crall's shoulder and asked, "And that?"

"Ah, that is Lord Muklah's oysters and I thought I'd bring a fresh pot of black leaf tea," and he looked up at Sisk's face, "Very good for hydration, Lord."

"Of course it is, Crall, please, I'll take this, you bring the other." And they wheeled both trays in together.

"You can leave now, Crall, thank you."

As Crall closed the doors behind him, he thought, *By the sky, they're even pushing trays for me now.*

Sisk looked at the two Lords. *What a difference, now we know, a near death coma and black leaf tea changes lives.*

"Now Brother, please join us and we can take a little food together while we mull over your report, please have an oyster, the black tea is excellent."

Brakko was also in fine fettle and spoke through a mouthful of oyster, "If you don't mind, Sisk, can we begin with the cannon fire today?"

"Certainly Brakko, yesterday morning I climbed the causeway to inspect on your behalf, Brother," he indicated Muklah, "I felt there was nothing to gain by constant drilling and no idea how to destroy a target so I ordered three captured Tolian ships as targets anchored out to sea within range of your cannoneers. I then returned to the castle to ask permission for live target practice, which you happily gave, Brother. Brakko, you also seemed delighted at the thoughts of destruction so that was the noise that woke you today."

"Yes I remember now, Brother, so tell me how did the men fare?" Muklah had no idea he was being led.

"Brilliantly. I had three short-wall crews spotting the rest as their cannon were covering more of our ships than Tolians, the spotter flagged all cannon fired long, what he did not see from his position is that we blew the bowsprit on the centre ship clean off, had that been a few feet left it would have wreaked havoc on deck, Brother, I'm told it is almost impossible to hit a moving ship from dry land ever, never mind on your first try."

"In that case, I don't mind at all that I was rudely awakened and almost cut the head off Crall, by the Kraken, who would have brought my morning black leaf tea?" All three had a brief laugh at Brakko's comment.

"So Sisk, anything more to report?"

"Aye Brother, all written for your perusal whenever you wish."

"No need today, Sisk, I'll just take a verbal report for now and we'll have your written report put on record."

"As you wish, Muklah." And Sisk proceeded to list his actions from early till close of day, the only thing he left out was the fact that no permission had been given for live target practice, when he eventually had covered everything to date they sat around in a relaxed way, chatting for hours about the bright future they were about to enter into and how Muklah was going to establish an Empire which would carry on through history forever. As the light was fading, Crall came in and lit the wall lamps, a prearranged action between Sisk and Crall.

"Ah that reminds me, my Lord, I must away to meet Kile and his six future forge smiths, I had almost forgotten, would my Lords like to join me?."

"Not at all, Sisk, you have absolutely everything in hand, you are now, and will be in future, invaluable to the Empire, so please carry on, and Crall?"

"Yes Lord."

"I feel so good today, I think Lord Brakko and I will have some supper and a nightcap, bring us a small keg of harbour ale and a flagon of the golden wine, early to bed tonight, eh Brakko?"

"Yes Lord." Always using Muklah's title in front of any Tolians. "Lots of work to do tomorrow."

"With your leave, my Lord."

"Of course Sisk, please carry on." And he waved his hand in dismissal.

Sisk and Crall left together, when outside the chamber, Sisk said, "Make sure our Lords get an uninterrupted sleep tonight, understand?"

"I do, Lord."

"Good. I'll speak to you again on my return," and he left to see Kile and his men.

Crall went off to fulfil his order and again the Captain of Muklah's guard looked around his men and said, "I wish we had more of them," meaning Sisk. And his men nodded their agreement.

Sisk found Kile, as ordered, in the canteen with his six recruits. "Kile, reliable as ever, please introduce us."

"Yes Lord, these five reprobates are called, Pri, Dri, Cort, Lant and Burt these men and I grew up together, came through military school together, and we have been minding each other's backs for as long as we can remember, we are a formidable force, Lord, and this, Lord, is my Brother Miles, the best swordsman and archer alive, he was your aimer on cannon this morning."

"Very good to meet you all, I'll get down to business, men, as Kile has already told you; you did, didn't you, Kile?"

"I did, Lord."

"Good, in ten days' time we will all be heading up to the forges to learn the art of cannon making, at least, you men will be doing the learning, we will be accompanied by Lords Muklah and Brakko on the trip up, on day one, when myself and the other Lords leave the two Trois, Father and Son, will take you through the process, beginning to end, of making cannon, men you will be the only Black-islanders ever to be able to make cannon, in turn when you are all proficient you will begin to train the others, as soon as we have trained in a sufficient number of forge workers and the fleet is armed, you will all be given command of your own ship." There was an intake of breath in the canteen then and grins all around.

"Kile, you will be promoted to a Commander of the fleet." Kile straightened up and pushed his chest out, shoulders back.

"You will be in command of these five Captains to begin with and, of course, their ships, your flotilla will expand in time, with the Empire, and you seven may expect to move up the rigging, I ask you to keep this quiet I do not want to spread unrest among the other men, 'why not me?' and other such complaints, so as far as anyone else is concerned, you go to learn to make cannon and that is all you know, clear?"

"Aye Lord," was the chorus reply.

"Good men, remember you are my first choice and Kile's first choice, no-one else's for now, this is a new beginning for us all, we will be written into Black-Isle Folklore."

They all leapt to their feet now, blowing up with pride, "Hail Lord Sisk! may the Kraken bless and keep him!"

"Thank you for that, but I have just asked for a certain amount of secrecy, and here you are on your feet yelling for anyone to hear, this is not a good start, is it?"

Kile, who hadn't jumped and yelled, said with a severe scowl, "No lord, it is not, maybe I made an error of choices, would you like me to make other choices."

The other six were no longer grinning, in fact they were panic stricken, all gone in one stupid gesture.

"No need, unless you believe they were heard in which case, yes, make more choices."

"No lord, fortunately, the nearest soldier to the canteen right now is on duty, the canteen staff won't be here for another hour to cater for the soldiers coming off duty later, those off duty are mainly in the tavern, I can assure you, Sire, no-one heard." His scowl had not gone.

"Very well, if anything like this happens again, the outcome will be very different, if anyone should be approached just say you're happy to be chosen cannon makers, now I must leave you it has been a busy day, do not forget what I say!" And he left.

Kile turned on his and said clearly but in a hushed tone, "By the eels Mother and Father, this kind of chance comes once in a lifetime, and ten seconds after agreeing to the secrecy of our mission, you all jump up shouting! I can't contemplate what would have happened had we been heard."

His men suitably cowed, each one was ashen. "Sorry Brother, can't apologise enough." Miles was staring at the floor.

"If it happens again, you and I, Brother, and all of us will be written into history for a different reason."

As Sisk made his leisurely way back to the Castle, he thought, *It was good to give them a shock that early, I won't have any more trouble in that quarter.*

He walked to the Castle and went in, as usual, Crall waited just inside, "Crall, how are our lords now, all good, yes?"

"Yes Lord, they are having a little snooze, an after wine snooze," and he smiled at Sisk.

"Will you bring a bottle to my quarters, Crall? I'd like a glass while I wait and think."

"Yes, of course, lord, you've had a big day."

"Fine Crall, I think I'll take a walk for the sake of the walk, would you also bring some supper for me?"

"It will be done, Lord Sisk," and off he went.

As he strolled along the harbour in the moonlight, he said to himself, *That Crall man is becoming a very fine servant, he seems to know exactly what I mean without me having to say it.* As he walked, he thought, *No red sunset tonight, anyway, no point in dwelling on things I have no control over*, and dismissed the thought, then on his way back, his mind fell on things he could control and was controlling.

Before retiring for the night, he stopped to talk with both Brakko's and Muklah's guards.

"They are both sleeping peacefully, Lord, my Lord Brakko is back in his own chambers," Brakko's Captain said, the same answer from Muklah's Captain.

When he got to his quarters, Crall had already left his supper on the table with a bottle of golden wine and a glass, he had also laid out Sisk's writing material; he ate a little bread and cheese and supped on black leaf tea. Then he sat back and sighed contentedly, after a few minutes he leaned forward and poured a glass of wine, and then looked at his quill, ink and paper and said out loud, "Not tonight, my friend." He drained his glass and washed again before getting into bed and falling into a deep sleep.

Chapter 33

When Toli woke up, the boys were already washing and dressing.

"Happy birthday, Toli!" They all said and Toli stood and said, "I forgot again, just like Quoror." He looked and felt confused, the three pals gave him a birthday hug, each in turn.

"Well, get ready, my friend, it's up to Bevak for us, and the sooner the better."

Ratesh was already dressed, keen to be off to the garrison city, the others just about there as well. It did not take long for Toli to catch up to his pals.

"Okay, it's time to move, I can't place nor fathom my nerves today, this far anyway, so we'll get on with it," and they left their chamber.

As usual, the rest of the council waited in the atrium plus the four elders all on one knee except Anga and Shala. Shala ran and jumped into Toli's arms and whispered in his ear, "Happy birthday, brother, I love you." Toli stepped forward to take Anga into his arms along with Shala.

"Happy birthday, my love." She was cold and Toli could feel her trembling like a leaf on a sapling.

He whispered, "Anga, are you unwell?"

"No, I don't know, but something is definitely going on, time will tell."

As they parted, Toli, still with Shala in his arms, looked to the others. "Happy birthday, my King!" they said together, none of these birthday greetings were any louder than spoken, no celebratory actions whatsoever.

"Thank you, friends," he said quietly and he put Shala down on her feet, took hers and Anga's hand and led them all into the dining room. The table had already been set and food had been served and the hall had since been cleared of staff, outside it was not yet even daylight, somehow they all had wakened early for first light departure. During the meal, Toli continually glanced at Anga, she wasn't eating she just supped on her tea, her face a mask of confusion, not pain, confusion, she sensed Toli's concern and quietly said to him, "Toli, please don't worry, the answers to all our questions are up in Bevak, I do not know what they may be, but I know the answers lie there, so, no point in getting worked up now, it will not be long before all is clear, I know it."

"Okay Anga," was all he said, for he had no more to say about the subject that might help.

Meal over, each person there felt a sense of urgency come over them. "Well, are we all ready for Bevak?" Toli was already on his feet, joined by Anga and Shala, he turned to the doors where a guide waited to open it.

"Sire," it was Sori who spoke.

"Yes Sori?"

"Sire, as we leave the hall you may expect a huge gathering and a speech before leaving Beeth."

"Yes Sori."

"Sire, everybody in Beeth has been making their own way up to Bevak, some for days, but we only have the people here who must stay because of duties or age, I'm sorry Sire, I should have mentioned this last night, but you may expect a very small crowd, who expect no speeches, they are all just glad to lay eyes upon you and to wish you well."

"Thank you, Sori, but I will not board without thanking the good citizens of Beeth, here, now, briefly, I won't delay our departure too much."

"Of course, Sire." Sori smiled to himself, delighted.

On leaving the hall, they walked into a mist floating about knee height on the small crowd lining a path to the Queen Shaleena, as he came to the handrail of the hall porch, he stopped, as expected by all but the crowd.

"Good people and friends, I regret not being able to spend more time with you all, but promise you all now that I will return when the invader is dealt with and we can then enjoy each other's company properly, I thank you."

An immediate cry of "Happy birthday, King Toli" went up and everyone dropped to one knee and became silent.

The company walked, also silently, to the gangplank and boarded. "Captain Storq, cast off and make way."

"Aye, my King" and immediately Storq began issuing his orders.

The ship was moving off the dock when the people ashore stood up and began chanting, "Toli, Toli, Toli!"; although it was a small crowd cheering their departure, it was quite a while before they were out of earshot.

The mist on the lake was thicker, somehow heavier, making way only for the ships passage, making first light a hazy affair, but the ship, under oar, clipped along at the usual pace, it was impossible for a person born here to get lost, the ship was silent, the only sounds were the ships oars splashing in a hypnotic rhythm, adding to the strange atmosphere. Headway was deliberately slow.

As they made way up the lake the light slowly began to change getting brighter with every stroke, eventually they came into broad daylight, the rising sun quickly burning off the mist left behind them. Anga seemed to perk up as the sun warmed the ship, she had been deep in thought, with her brow furrowed, now she looked as though she had come to a positive decision, she looked up at Toli beside her upon the council deck.

"Toli, I know absolutely that there is something big for me in Bevak, but I don't think I am in any danger, don't ask me how I know because I couldn't answer, so I've decided to enjoy our time together on your birthday for I feel this is as much privacy as were ever going to get until the invader is vanquished."

"I was just going to say that!"

"I'm sure you were" and she shoved him playfully with her shoulder.

Toli leaned back, folded his hands on top of his head, and looked around, the rest of the council, excepting Shala, were in an open discussion about how to deal with the invader, Shala was happily playing knuckles with Tak up near the bow, the crew were chatting among themselves, even the oarsmen, the going was so easy. Toli leaned back again then after a few seconds said, "Look, Anga." His eyes were up to the clear blue sky.

"What's wrong, Toli!" Anga was alarmed by Toli's urgent manner.

"Sorry Anga, I shouldn't have done that, but look at the sky."

"Yes, what about it?"

"No birds, not a one."

"You're right, another first, for me anyway."

Quor who had been listening since Toli let out his yell, said, "Only the leaders of birds and their advisors are allowed any further north today, and they are already there, Sire, any more must stay south of Beeth."

"Thank you, Quor," and he reclined again, " do you fancy a short walk to a place guaranteed to come with great company and a stunning view, my Queen?"

"Why yes, I would, my King, please, lead the way."

Toli stood and offered his arm to Anga, which she took, and they both made their way, with exaggerated mock regality, down the deck to the bow where they burst into laughter; the rest of the ship's company finally cottoned on.

"They're making fools of themselves," Storq said through his mirth, and the ship's company shouted, "Happy birthday King Toli!"

When the laughter died down, Toli and Anga went up to the bow to find two comfortably carved wooden chairs with a tall bench-like back higher than both their heads, so as to allow complete privacy when seated. The couple hadn't noticed it until now, and Storq said from behind them, "The carpenters of Beeth carved this for you and the crew fitted it for you overnight, we hope you both like it, it is our gift to you on your birthday," and he opened a small door to allow them into their bow space, when the two of them saw the chairs for the first time and Anga out her fingers up to her mouth and let out a small gasp.

Toli turned to Storq and walked past him. "Come," he said, Storq followed and Toli addressed the crew:

"This thing that you have all done for us is more valuable than any amount of any other riches, we will never forget it or you or the people of Beeth. Storq?"

"Aye Sire?"

"A tot of rum for all, sorry lads, no gin o' old Bri today, we have urgent business in Bevak."

The tots were quickly dispensed to everyone but Shala, she didn't even want a taste of it, the smell was enough, so she had a tot of water for the coming toast, when all were ready, Toli lifted his tot and toasted, "To us all, long may we prosper."

And the ship's company repeated the toast plus, "Long live the King."

Toli and Anga locked the skinny door behind as they took to their new chairs, they had never sat on anything like them before, fitted to perfection they had no central armrest and their two individual chairs seemed to blend into one, they sat back side by side and Toli said, "How do you feel, my love?"

"I have to put my worries aside for now, no point to it, I have no real reason, I just have this, I don't know, sensation, anyway we will know all soon enough, so let us enjoy the best birthday present ever made, totally alone."

"Do you know something, Anga, my love?"

"Were you about to tell me you were about to say that?"

"Yes, how did you know?"

"Just a lucky guess, I suppose."

"I'm doomed; you can even read my mind." He kissed her and sat back down and they both fell into a companionable silence, the rhythm of the oars and the breeze on their faces almost lulled them to sleep, they were so relaxed. The rest of the journey went like this saving a break for food up on the council deck as they rowed up the lake, the land was at its furthest for the lake widened all the way to Bevak, and they were going up the middle, they could not see the hordes of people trying to get to Bevak for the Queen Shaleena's arrival. Then a shout shattered the peace, "Bevak Ho!"

Toli and Anga jumped up and looked ahead, Toli squinted and said, "I can't see anything."

"I can, it's a long way off but I can see it, how can I?"

"Don't know, my love, but the answer lies there," and he nodded to the north.

They had been coming up the lake and it was drawing towards evening, Storq knocked on the door.

"Come in, it's unlocked now," Toli called.

Storq stepped in and said, "Beg your pardon, Sire, we had a bird, the garrison begs your indulgence, they feel it may benefit us all if we move straight to council and eat later, he wishes to apologise for the lack of Birthday celebrations for now, but feels this must be done first, the reason for this, no-one on this ship knows." Anga squeezed Toli's hand.

"So to this end, Sire, we have served a meal on the council deck, if you wish to join us."

"Yes Storq, we'll be there shortly, thank you." Storq left them then and Toli asked Anga, "Are you alright, Anga?"

"Yes love, bit peckish actually, c'mon then." And she led Toli out of the cubicle and let Toli lead her up to the deck.

The conversation was plentiful but pointless no one knew anything but something was urgent. The food was excellent as usual, and they sat supping on a tankard of ale, which Shouk downed in one and immediately called for another.

"Another, Shouk, really?" asked Toli.

Shouk did his best to disappear into his big bushy beard and grumbled, "They wouldn't give me anymore rum." The laughter was long lasting and easing when they began to hear very loud, distant cheering.

"We have hove into view, Sire, we must prepare for landing," Storq yelled from the deck.

"You have the ship, Captain." And Storq and his crew went to work.

By the time they reached the dock, the clamour was incredible, there were people as far as the eye could see, and farther again.

"Long live the king! Long live the king!" was the shout.

They tied up at the dock of solid rock, Toli had thought the approaching dock had a menacing look about it. *Like one of those dungeons we heard about in history lessons*, he thought now, before alighting he felt he would be walking into the dragon's maw indeed! There were warriors all over the city on different levels standing to attention, watching on the dock was Briq, the garrison and city Commander, with a guard of honour, he dropped to one knee in front of Toli, Anga and Shala.

"Forgive me, Sire, your highness, would you please come with me?"

"Lead the way Commander, please."

Before following Briq, Toli stopped to wave both hands in all directions, the crowd erupted and birds watching from perches outside the buildings and on the mountain, advisors, plumed up as one into the sky like a cloud blowing up from below.

He followed Briq, one hand in Anga's, the other in Shala's, into the large tunnel with warriors, they climbed a staircase which had curved treads at the top, two guards opened the massive double doors into a cavernous chamber, brightly lit, by nothing, apparently, with another big single door by the other end, the room was arched and had rows of pronounced arches supporting the ceiling. There was a large circular table in the centre and there were warriors lining half of the chamber nearest to the entrance, and a single warrior out in front, without ceremony, standing next to Anga he called to the warrior, "Bri, come here please."

Bri walked directly up to Anga, he did not appear to be as stooped as before.

"Anga, I am your father, would you please come with me?"

Anga cried out, "At last, at last," and threw her arms around Bri's neck, then, "I knew it, I always knew I was different!" Then she took his hand and said, "Right, where will we go."

"To the Dragon's tail, if that's ok?" and he pointed to the door at the other end and they walked through the door arm in arm and closed it behind them.

Toli, stunned, asked Briq, "What has just happened?"

"Bri is Anga's father, Sire, I intend to explain to you as Bri explains to Anga, it should take around the same time although father and daughter may be given grace if they should take a shade longer, I'm glad Queen Anga took it that way, she must be incredibly strong, it could have gone very differently."

"Right then, Commander! Down to explanations now I think!"

"Immediately Sire, please be seated in the Kings Valley Throne."

And he led Toli to a throne which had never been sat upon, he wasn't aware of where anyone else had sat except for Shala who was at his right holding his hand and grinning like a cat.

"What are you grinning at?"

"No idea, but I know this is going to be good."

The circular table was not solid, rather it was a ring and Briq now stood in the middle facing the council members and began.

Inside the room Anga and Bri hugged each other in silence until Anga broke it,

"Let's get down to it, Father, I can bear it no longer."

"Thank you, Anga, but how can you be so calm?"]

"Because all of my life, I was treated differently, first by the people who acted as my parents, always kind, always distant, but no-one ever harmed me, up at the Castle my only friend was Shala, because I've waited for this day never knowing it would actually come."

"Very well, Anga, if the truth upsets you please try to forgive me, your mother died giving life to you, it destroyed me, so much so that I could no longer bear my own child about me, one night after the nursemaid brought you back to me you would not stop crying, you loved your nursemaid more than me, I was so sick of living without your mother that I thought of bringing us both to the woods, to end it and leave our bodies to the wolves, but I thought of a visiting friend, seeing my distress he told me of a couple on the other side who had lost their child at birth.

"They lived out at the extreme edge where the land stops and the mountain reaches the sea, it was close to his watch and he witnessed the burial and heard the cries and wailing, so I took you out that night and left you on the doorstep and knocked on the door and watched until you were picked up by the overjoyed couple, then I came back to tell what I had done, could I have given you to a family here? Yes, well maybe, if a couple take on someone else's child here they risk never having their own, but we'll explain that later.

"I was so demented with grief I could never know what was going on around me, so I wouldn't have, couldn't have, known or even cared what happened anyway, so I came back to my punishment, we cannot leave the valley without orders or by being on duty upon the mountain upon pain of exile from our order, they had no other choice, however, seeing how distraught I was they gave me a small holding to grow potatoes and as Briq had been my Captain and had just been made Commander of the garrison, they told me you are hereby exiled from this garrison and this city to grow potatoes, but knowing your worth in the past, and seeing your anguish first hand, should the day come that your offspring returns to us, on that day you may set foot back on garrison rock not a day before.

"We all felt your presence while you were crossing from Tabunti to Beeth. I camped in the woods last night until I was sure, and I was sure since I saw you sitting with the King in the bow of that blessed ship, so now you know it all, barring the fact you could never be detected by anyone with powers on the other side because you had none yourself until you left Tabunti after seeing me, so Anga can you ever forgive my insanity, if you can't, I'll go, without another word."

Anga got up and put an arm around Bri's shoulder and sat on his lap and whispered in his ear, "I've missed you, father."

Bri held her at arm's length, still on his lap and looked at Anga with tears in his eyes.

"What? You don't like me calling you Father?"

Bri hugged her so hard she thought her ribs might crack, until she said, "Come Father, my future husband, the King, awaits us."

When they came through the door arm in arm, there was complete silence. *He may just be escorting her back to her seat before returning to potato exile*, was one of the thoughts going around at least one of the castle-siders' minds, Anga walked up to Toli and said, "Toli, I want you to meet your future father-in-law, Bri." Toli stood up immediately and grasped Bri by the shoulder at arm's length.

"So happy to meet you, Bri." And he embraced him in a hug. The chamber was full of clapping and cheering people, with warriors banging spears on shields and the giant eagle, who had been introduced earlier as Redwind, raised his wings high above his head and cried loudly in the language of the eagles.

When Anga calmed them down enough to hear her, she said, "My Father and I thank you for your kindness but there is work to be done so we must get to it, Commander, would it trouble you if my Father joins his comrades at arms."

"Not at all," Bri said smiling.

"We are prepared for this eventuality, please Bri." And he stepped aside to let a warrior set up and hand Bri a spear and shield and a new helm, he already wore his mail. He would have had to remove it again had Anga rejected him, he bowed from the waist and spun, military style to a place made for him by two smiling soldiers, old comrades, he was reborn.

Anga sat next to Toli, now seated again, Shala had shown everyone to the right, along a place to make room for her next to Anga.

"You may begin, my King," she said out of the side of her mouth.

"You may begin, Briq." Briq still stood in the centre of the table.

"Yes Sire, Queen Anga, if I may call you Queen?" Anga looked at Toli, Toli nodded.

Anga said, "Your King gives you permission, Commander Briq."

"Thank you, now please let me introduce you to the people you missed while you were in conference, the King has agreed to convey the details to you later if that's okay with you?"

Anga nodded.

"This is Joi," and he introduced a tall female warrior who bowed at the waist. "Joi is leader of our female royal guards, the Bevalla, brought up from very young to serve the King, even if he never comes. This is Luq, your messenger at Beeth, and Commander in charge of the royal guard as a whole." Luq bowed and stepped back.

"This is Xing, our master at arms as well as many other things." Xing bowed.

"This is Worq, our sage and sagest of all." Worq bowed.

"These warriors here are Kings guard and belong to the Royal guard." Each warrior banged their shields once with spears.

"And this, my Queen, is Redwind, King of Eagles, King of all Birds." Redwind lowered his head and screeched.

"Now, I believe, my Queen, we are all up to scratch, I will continue from here." And he spoke directly to Toli. "My King, let me begin by saying the reason for the recent urgency, was the situation between Bri and Anga, so I must tell you that your subjects on the other side are perfectly safe for now, and the situation won't change anytime soon, the reason you had not been fully informed of today's situation was that Anga and Bri, this council felt, must resolve the problem, with no encouragement from any quarters, face to face, the people aboard the Queen Shaleena had no idea; only the people here now, excluding yourselves, of course, knew about it, Bri was, and is again, Kings Guard, we had to let them meet before anything.

"The only relevant military information is that one of Redwind's eagles intercepted a pigeon on one of his rest stations with a message for a man called

'Lord Vakkra', the Commander of the Black Isles' second fleet, ordering him to prepare his fleet of twenty ships for sea and await further orders, the pigeon is now our bird, as is every other, as they will find out when they try to leave this Island, and we have access to every message sent from here on, we can send this same message at your leisure, we know how long it takes to get there, and we now know, it takes twelve weeks to reach us, we can control things all the way to their dark, beating heart, so, my King, with all under control, and time on our hands, I personally feel there is no more to do this day, but to address your people, then we can all get on with Birthday celebrations tonight, and forget the rest till tomorrow, what say you, Sire?"

"I say aye, Briq, may I drop the Commander just for tonight."

"You are my King, you may do as you wish."

"Very well, by my decree, after I meet my people, there will be no mention of rank in conversation for the rest of the evening."

"Except for royalty, Sire."

"If you insist, Briq."

"Indeed I do, Sire."

"Shall we, my Queen?" And he put his right hand up to allow Anga to place her left hand on top, the kings guard were all clapping each other on the back and smiling, being kings guard and royal guard, rank, was always respected on duty, but they were all good friends anyway and to be able to relax so, at the banquet for the first coming of the king, would be kings guard legend, they would make sure of it.

As Toli and the growing council were led through a door to a climbing staircase, the kings guard gathered around Bri with welcomes and congratulations. Joi threw her arms around his neck and said, "We are all very happy, Bri."

"Me too, Joi, me too." Then a roar went up outside and they ran through the doors and down to the harbour to watch.

As Toli, Anga and Shala came out onto the large balcony, large each enough for everyone and more, an almighty roar went up, and again the birds exploded into a plume this time close enough to hear the whoosh, audible above the crowd, now cheering, "Toli, Toli, Toli!" or "Long Live the King", or "Happy Birthday to the King." Toli stepped up to the low wall, up to Shala's waist, and raised both hands, the crowd eventually ceased, Toli had complete silence.

"My friends, unfortunately the circumstances of our happy meeting, here today, are the results of an unhappy event, an invasion, an invader who would come here to poison our Island with hatred, we will not allow this!"

The crowd once again erupted, "Toli, Toli, Toli!"

"As your King, I promise each and every one of you now, the invader has no chance of the victory he thinks he already has, the valley, as we know, will always be safe, but there are things out there that we know nothing about, maybe things we don't even understand, we on the other side were caught unawares by a traitor mage, we had no chance, fortunately, you lake valley folk came to our rescue," and he indicated to the other Castle-siders.

"You call me King, and I am honoured beyond belief, and we are now united as one, we are unshakable, undefeatable and can never be conquered." Again the clamour, again he had to raise his hands.

"And now I believe some of you have some sort of celebration planned for tonight, so please do not let your King keep you from it!" Toli waved his goodbyes in different directions then turned and led the way back down the stairs, getting to the bottom he said to Briq.

"What have you planned for us now, Briq?"

"Now Sire, I suggest you all go and refresh yourselves and your clothing, then we can have the celebration you should be having with your parents."

"Yes Briq, I should, but the thought of cold revenge makes me sing inside, and of course you are right, washed, changed and end the day on a high, yes?"

"Yes Sire, absolutely." Toli turned to Anga and Shala.

"My queen, my princess, with your permission I will retire with my friends in order to prepare ourselves for the upcoming celebration, do I have it?"

"I think the Princess and I may allow it on this occasion, what do you say, Princess Shala?"

"Very well, on this occasion, as long as these occasions don't arise too often, we shall allow it!"

"Thank you both, do my friends and I have quarters, Briq?"

"Yes Sire, follow me please." And he led them through yet another door, into a circular, like a bubble, atrium, with three doors off of it, after being directed to their own chambers, again, rounded, the only thing flat in these rooms were the floors. Toli was ready, first of the lads when a soft knock came on the door. Toli opened it, Anga stood in the atrium alone, in a silver dress, which fitted perfectly, on her head she had a tiara of silver ferns, she radiated beauty.

"Anga, you look beautiful." He stepped forward to take her hands. "Is something wrong?"

"No my love, I am bursting with joy, joy for my love of you and your love of me, and joy at the meeting of my Father, my life had been fulfilled in a few short days."

"No Anga, not yet, we have some fulfilling to achieve ourselves."

"Ah yes, I'd forgotten about that…Not, ha-ha!"

Just then Shala came out like a queen, not a Princess, all in silver with the same tiara as Anga's, gracefully atop her head.

"Well, give 'em a shout then," she said.

"Shala, you look wonderful."

"Oh I'm wonderful and Anga's beautiful, is it."

"How do you know what I said to Anga?"

"Never mind that, call the lads and I'll get the Generals." There was no need for they all appeared at the same time dressed in long purple tabards made of the finest materials they had ever touched, underneath were cotton shorts and leggings with soft leather slippers on their feet, they walked into a huge chamber and everyone was dressed in a similar fashion, except for the six duty guards, they were still in mail but no weapons, Bri also wore mail but covered in a deepest blue tabard, he could not bear to remove his mail so soon. They all snapped up to salute and Toli bid them to be at ease.

"Now let the festivities begin," but before he sat on the throne, he walked up to Storq and said, "Where is Tak, Storq?"

"I know not, Sire, I'd guess he's on the wander, taking in the festivities, eating a lot I expect."

"Please send someone to find him, my sister seems to have taken a shine to him."

"Right away, Sire." And went out the door, as he passed through a voice said, shouted really.

"Looking for me, Captain?" Storq turned to find Tak stood dressed as a smaller version of himself, he was speechless.

"It was the Princess' idea, Captain, honest!"

"Eh? What? Yes fine, now get inside, your presence is required."

While this was going on outside, Toli asked Briq, "Is this the entire royal guard, Briq?"

"No Sire, the entire kings guard is here, but not the entire royal guard."

"How many are they?"

"Twenty more again, Sire."

"I think the place looks a bit empty, what do you think, Briq?" And he winked.

"I think you may be right, Sire."

"Right then." He called up the hall prepare another twenty places, and then, "Please mingle, relax, we will all sit down as soon as all our guests arrive, ah! Here's one now, oh and prepare a place next to the Princess for Tak please."

As Storq and Tak approached, Shala ran up and grabbed Tak's hand. "C'mon you." And led him away.

"That reminds me, I'd better go and spend some time with my bride-to-be and her Father."

The staff were running around setting extra places, they had to find two curved tables, able to seat ten each, and find a suitable place for them, which they did, facing each other so as not to look at someone else's back. Toli joined Anga and Bri, deep in conversation.

"I was just saying to Father, Toli, about how much we enjoyed his gin aboard the Queen Shaleena and how it would be a shame if his recipe went with him 'to his grave'."

"You needn't worry, Anga. I will give it into your trust the day before I die, so you'd best make sure you're around for a while."

Anga looked into his eyes and said, "I will, Father, I will."

Then twenty men and women walked into the hall breathing heavily, as though they had sprinted here from Beeth.

"Ah ha! The last of the guests." He put up his hand for Anga to cover and went to welcome them. "Come with us if you like, Bri."

"If you don't mind Sire, I'd like a few words with my old friend Quor."

"As you wish, Bri."

Toli and Anga crossed to the twenty royal guards, Toli thanked them for their service and bid them welcome, it was now time to sit down, Toli could feel the lads eyes boring into the back of his head, as he seated Anga, he said, "Hungry, lads?"

"Aye and thirsty too, my King." Ratesh was grinning, he knew the game. Toli made to sit then seemed to change his mind at the last second and stood again. "Toli!" a warning from Anga, he sat down instantly, and the rest followed suit.

There were six empty places at the opposite end of the table. Toli still seated called out to Joi seated around to his left, "Joi."

"Yes Sire?"

"Tell me Joi, have we enough guards outside this chamber should we come under attack?"

Joi feigned puzzlement. "Yes of course, my King."

"Then would you mind if your King filled the last of these empty seats with the standing warriors in here, they are making things very untidy." The standing guards were throwing glances at each other and shrugging shoulders, bewildered, the door opened from the kitchen.

So many doors, Toli thought, and six serving staff come out carrying one deep blue tabard each, palms up out in front of them. They all stood agape not knowing what to do, when Toli called up to them, "Well, hurry up then, your King's food is getting cold." The first guard came to first and snatched the tabard and began making a meal of getting it over his head, the other five grabbed theirs and had put theirs on before the first was finished, eventually they took their places, then Toli stood and said with his goblet raised and toasted, "To friends." and everyone stood and toasted, "To friends," and sat back down all but one; it was Tadesh.

"My friend, the King, is dead, long live the King." And the return toast was an emphatic, "Long Live the King."

Then Anga stood and said, "We have forgotten the most important toast friends, so please allow me, HAPPY BIRTHDAY, KING TOLI!" And again the reply toast raised the roof.

The fare was extraordinary, too many of everything to describe and a keg of Bris very own spirit, enough for the night. Toli sat on his throne centre top of table facing the exit, to his right Anga, Shala and Tak, who was dumbstruck at first, to be in his position, at this banquet, with a Princess, now chatted happily with Shala, so naturally, you'd think they had known each other forever, to his left Quor, then Bri, who chatted so happily because they had.

"Has Redwind gone, Quor?"

"Yes Sire, he has gone to his convocation to keep the eagles and in turn all the birds, up to date, they are our sentinels in the sky, Sire, our ears in the wind, he shall return at first light Sire."

"Of course, a King has his own responsibilities to his own subjects."

The night was superb, music, dancers, dancing jugglers, jesters, magicians, Toli noticed a few people around the table reluctant to relax, particularly Xing and Worq so he sent a round of Bri's gin around the room and called for another toast.

"Death to the Invader!"

"Aye! Death to the Invader!" And the gins went down in one. Five minutes later it was all in, even Xing was laughing at a joke told to him by Worq.

"Look at those two," Toli said to Anga.

"I know, it must have been the one about the shipwreck and the sage." Toli looked at Anga.

"You know a joke about a shipwr…oh no! Walked right into it! Ha ha." By now it appeared the entire guestlist had heard a good joke.

The celebration went on late into the night and Toli called for honey draught all round, which went around twice, then he called it a night bidding the guests "take no notice of us Castle-folk" and please to "carry on", before Toli reached the door to the chambers the room had already fallen quiet, guests were leaving, staff already beginning the clear up, Shouk was last to his bed, he decided to help with the clear up for a bit, he didn't like a good ale going to waste, it had gone silent outside, the King was trying to sleep.

Out in the atrium, Toli and Anga were alone.

"Anga, I missed my own father, my mother and my brothers very much today, they would have been so proud to meet you and to see my coming of age, I have tried to do today, what my father may have done today, make everyone happy."

"I am happy, and very much in love with you, Toli, but the fact is, if your mother and father were still alive none of this would be happening, we probably would have never spoken and by this time you would be promised to Princess Prina, also I would never have met my Father, so good comes from every bad, and it is left to us to make sure the good, stays for good this time, and end this threat forever."

Shouk came out of the hall then and burped loudly, said "S'cuse me!" and went to his bed.

"I must go to Shala now, Toli, goodnight, my King."

"Goodnight my queen." And they kissed and parted. As Anga dressed for bed, she noticed Shala had one eye open hoping for gossip.

"Tak's very nice, isn't he, Shala?"

"Suppose so, don't really talk to him much."
"Goodnight Shala."
"Goodnight Anga."

Chapter 34

The two Trois were in their forge at first light, they broke the two casts out of there moulds, to see two perfectly cast, to a smiths eye, cannon, lumps of slag to be broken off, lots of cleaning still to do, but perfect. Troi the elder began chipping and scraping at the casts while Troi the younger set his moulds for the next two, normally this would have been the other way around, but these were young Troi's drawings, young Troi's patterns, young Troi's passage into Tolian Naval History. Young Troi's moulds were ready in a couple of hours and he and his Father poured the next two cannons together, the alloy mix already melted to pour temperature, which all smiths knew by eyesight, by consistency, then mixed the ores required to make cannon metal and put the pot back on the forge.

Young Troi joined his Father back at the cleaning horses, made for these guns' four legs formed into two Vs, one for the barrel, one for the rear end, these were braced by two more with these Vs taking the lugs to keep the weapon stable for cleaning, when the top is finished the guns are turned over and the cleaning on the outside is finished, they are then clamped back onto a level table one for each of them and two drill bits on two water driven trucks grasping the drills dead centre to the bore of the guns. The tables were then hand-screwed up the length of the drill bit and back again, the cannon were then taken to another forge to reheat to soak, the oil baths would be at a certain heat when the guns were lowered in, they were left to cool to the temperature then removed and a bigger drill bit, just by a scrape, would make the final cut on the bore, back onto the forge after tooling the firing mechanism, then into the bath to cool overnight, when it came out of the oil, it was ready to fire.

Thirty years ago, the remainder of the Black Isles fleet was smashed by catapult and rock and Toli's Grandfather Toli, set the smiths a task to make a weapon, so fearsome, as to ensure the Island could never be invaded again. Troi's grandfather obliged, he also invented the drill bit, super long as to accommodate the long narrow bore of the big cannons they called Culverins which were not poured with a bore hole, but solid. With the heavy lifting equipment made for the giant Culverins they could easily cope with two ships cannon at one time, and to a smith, it was all so easy.

All this took most of the day and the plan was, to set and cast the next two, but that already done they removed the two cast in the morning, put them one at a time in a specially dug pit, dry inside and hidden on the outside, big enough for a hundred ships cannon, this was used for the storing of extra Culverin awaiting tooling to be shipped to their allies in the Green Isle, in much more need of defence than here. Young Troi set his moulds again, they both poured again, and all was done till tomorrow, two cannon up on the Invader and the same every day, if they don't get caught and it'll all stop when Sisk sends his fools up to learn how to pour bad cannon.

It was still early for a smiths day, so old Troi thought of a diversion. "Come, Troi, got an idea, tomorrow we'll have brand new guns ready to shoot, we must stay on the right side of our Lord Sisk." They left the forge and walked to the guards station.

"Is Captain Sito here?" he asked the guard stationed at the gates.

"He is, what do you want of him?"

"I have been instructed to give my progress to Captain Sito only, it may benefit you to get him now!"

"Very well, wait here."

Sito came out in a few minutes, wiping his mouth with a cloth. "Yes Troi, what is it?"

"Please come with me, Captain." And he turned and headed back to the forge.

"What you up to, Father?" young Troi asked through the side of his mouth.

"Wait and see, son."

Entering the forge, elder Troi led Sito straight up to the soaking cannon in the oil baths, he pointed at them. "See those in there?"

"I do, what of them?"

"They will be ready to fire in the morning, and I had a thought."

"Really Troi, and what might that thought be?"

"That thought would be, instead of asking Lord Sisk to send up carpenters from the ship fitting, maybe it would behoove you to take the initiative, and put your men to work building a firing range to test the guns when our Lords come up in ten days' time now, you could tell our Lords that you put your men to work in order to stifle boredom, to keep them alert, to keep them fit, or you could tell him you've been up here doing nothing but sleeping and eating, cos you couldn't be bothered to think yourself."

"Yes Troi, of course, that was my plan anyway, I'll expect your drawing in the morning."

"You will have it, Sito, and thank you for the excellent idea."

"You're welcome, Troi, good evening."

Sito left the forge to tell his men about his revelation, and they were delighted to a man, something to do at last, no sitting around for your tour on duty.

"That'll keep them out of your hair for a bit."

"It will Father, clever boy."

The Trois spent the rest of the night mulling over the drawings already drawn from big gun days, if it could take shot from them, it could take anything, whole trees not from the far side of the river, these were never in the river water, and they would splinter and burst when hit by a big ball, but would stay upright, these smaller cannon, would barely scratch the old range, so it must be built weak enough to create a big impression. They pored over the drawings for a while more, deciding how to weaken it just enough for their own ends, and went to bed early.

Chapter 35

Sisk rang Crall's bell after washing and dressing himself, Crall appeared as if by magic, in a matter of seconds. "Good morning Crall, how are our fearless leaders today?"

"Already awake, fed, washed and gone, Lord."

"Gone? What do you mean gone?"

"They rose, they ate, they washed and then left for the gun emplacements, my Lord."

"Ah, good, involved at last, I shall join them shortly, I will not start a single day without one of your breakfasts."

Sisk was in no hurry to join the other two, his plans required Muklah's presence, or rather Muklah's participation, he felt he had already laid the foundation for the support of the people he needed, and word was spreading that he was a reasonable man, for a traitor, and reasonable is not a word that could be used to speak of Muklah nor his Commander. He finished eating at his leisure and happily strolled along the harbour to the causeway up to the emplacements, reports up to date, left on his table for Lord Muklah's perusal.

Big, grey winged gulls were mewing and screeching, as if laughing, milling around, high and low over the harbour. *Strange*, Sisk thought. *Maybe a storm out to sea, I don't remember this number of birds before*. He hadn't noticed, leaving the Castle, that there were more thrushes, finches, sparrows, blackbirds and other smaller birds, more discreet than the gulls, attracting less attention than the raucous gulls, all of them obeying the orders of Redwind, all of them gleaning information right up to the mines.

Arriving at the first gun emplacement, Sisk could hear Muklah's voice, "Seven shots! Seven bloody shots on three full-sized bloody ships and all we got was a bowsprit," he was ranting at the Black-Islers, the first crew minus Miles, Kile's brother.

"Good day, my Lords." Sisk stepped out onto the gun emplacement. "Is everything ok?"

"No, by the Kraken, it is not, Sisk, if we cannot hit a stationary target from land, what hope against moving ships at sea?"

"There are no stationary targets upon the sea, Lord, the sea constantly moves as it wishes and our guns do not, I am assured, Lord, that at sea there will be no misses, we will be so close to the enemy without return fire."

"Nevertheless, Sisk, I will be demanding a better outcome today, I have ordered all seven crews to concentrate on the middle ship, The Green Swift, the deceased King Jai's flagship, I wish to see it blown asunder before my eyes, the crews will fire in order from one to seven immediately after the cannon before has fired, spread the order!"

Sisk did as he was told, personally going to each crew, on his arrival back to number one gun, he said, "At your command, my Lord."

Wasting no time, Muklah screamed "FIRE!" And the seven big Culverins boomed and blazed in perfect time. When the smoke eventually cleared, the Green Swift was gone, except for smoking flotsam it may have never existed. Muklah was beside himself.

"Wonderful, wonderful, now reload and let's dispose of the other two, first three guns on the nearest ship to us and the other four on the farthest, let's get it done!" Sisk did, and when he got back to number one gun, Muklah did not wait.

"FIRE!" And the guns roared again.

This time the near ship was only splinters on the sea but the far ship looked to be intact.

"Go and get those crews here, now," Muklah commanded a Tolian gunner. "All of them." The gunner ran off like a scared cur. As they stood looking out to sea, the last ship keeled over and began to sink, the bow was slipping eerily, silently, below the waves, as the stern kicked up to allow the ship to nosedive, two cannonball holes could clearly be seen below what was the waterline, then there was a sound of rushing water as sea water and smoke began rushing out of any hole they could find and quickly the ship disappeared forever.

Muklah and Brakko stood speechless for a few seconds only, until the water's surface calmed to its natural swell.

"Well, my Lord Commander, what do you have to say about the noise now?" Muklah teased Lord Brakko, who was still agape, looking at the sea where three ships had once sat quietly at anchor.

"I will learn to ignore the noise," he said as if enchanted. "We are invincible, even our biggest ships with our biggest assault bows could not cause that to happen if we hit our target a hundred times."

"Indeed, my old friend, and you will be on the Black Kraken alongside me, causing mayhem among our enemies and establishing the empire that will rule the world forever."

The gun crews arrived then, with Muklah in a considerably better mood. "Okay men," he said briefly. "I am suitably impressed, I shall see to it that more targets are made available for destruction, do not let the standard fall!" He walked towards the causeway then, and his Lords followed him unbidden.

Halfway down the causeway, Muklah said loudly without turning back, "You reports are very precise, Sisk, I thank you for that, I believe you have picked six men for cannon-forge training, I'd like to meet them now."

"Of course Brother, they have been waiting eagerly since their choosing and an updated report lies on my table for you now, I have sent the six up to the dock to learn about ships gun ports and positions, it's all new to everyone and cannon should start arriving as soon as we have tested them, the quicker we can fit and arm them the quicker they can go out for sea tests."

"Yes Sisk, agreed, so first on our agenda is to get on out into open water and see if it fulfils its promise, what do you say, Brakko?"

"The quicker I'm out on open water smashing things to smithereens, the quicker I'll be happy!"

"I think you will both be surprised at the progress already made, the Tolians are anxious to prove they are worthy of life and our men are anxious to get to grips with the new ships and weapons, everything is going along fairly swiftly."

"Good, good Sisk, you may send the six forge recruits to their new duties as you see fit, you do not need me to check your decisions as long as it is always reported."

"Thank you Brother."

They strolled along the harbourside at a leisurely pace in silence enjoying the day. *The gulls are much quieter now*, Sisk thought. He did not know Redwind had sent an eagle to tell the gulls to "make less bloody noise." They had been attracting attention from people who knew about the sea and the habits of its birds, so some went back out to sea and the rest stayed quiet, for gulls that is. As they came up to the dock where the Black Kraken was tied up, it looked as though the deck was covered with two-legged ants it seemed to be moving, the noise getting louder as they approached, a cacophony of hammer, saw and plane. Kile, who was duty Captain, left the ship to meet them at the dock.

"My Lords, we are honoured by your presence." He stood at attention before the three Lords.

"Lord Muklah," Sisk said, "this is my chosen Captain of the six future cannon forgers who are all aboard now, I thought it would be beneficial to know the process from forging to firing."

"Yes, indeed Sisk, once again your planning is ahead of us all, these soldiers will be at the forefront of training our navy at arms, they will be the most important seven soldiers in our immediate future."

"Yes Lord, they will be the catalyst for our invincibility."

Kile was so surprised and shocked by the magnitude of these words, his breathing became short and his legs shook. *The catalyst for invincibility*, he thought. *Lord Sisk is a genius!*

"Now Captain," Brakko asked, not willing to be left too far behind, "would you be kind enough to show us the progress so far?"

"Yes Lord, immediately." Kile's six men stood on deck, in a line at the top of the gangway, "With your permission, my Lords, I'll lead the way in order to introduce your six cannon forgers, soon to be cannon experts." Muklah nodded his consent and Kile led them aboard.

"Please allow me to introduce my Lord to the six who are to accompany me to the forges," he introduced the soldiers in turn, Muklah simply nodded to each of them. Brakko was already on the deck watching the workers but not willing to ask questions until Muklah was beside him.

As the four, Muklah, Brakko, Sisk and Kile, walked around, Sisk said, "Captain, if you could, will you educate us as to the workings of the gun deck, and where are we now as regards progress?"

Kile began his practiced report. "We have maximised the top deck according to dimensions given to us from the forge, ten guns a side on four wheeled carriages, roped by the front of the carriage to the strengthened bulkhead pulled tight to the bulkhead for firing and rolled back to stop on the chocks you can see on the deck for loading, we know now from our days up on the harbour, how to safely load and fire the weapons, the ship however cannot accommodate another gundeck because of the propeller crew below, but up here the deck is totally committed to cannon warfare as we only require the gun crews on deck under battle conditions.

"We now have to train gunners from scratch as this is all new, we will be able to take guns as soon as we can get them, we have six stations ready now, three to port, three to starboard, we expect to begin fitting out the next ship in three days' time."

Muklah and Brakko were absolutely delighted at this unexpected progress. Brakko stood quietly with a stupid childish sort of an expression; Muklah said, "You are very efficient, Captain, you have done well, you will go far in the new Empire, you and your men, now, we have taken enough of your day so we'll leave you to your work, expect to hear from Lord Sisk very soon." And then he walked to the gangway and left the ship, again Brakko and Sisk in tow, again unbidden, as they walked towards the castle, Muklah turned to Sisk and Brakko and said, "Straight back to the castle, men, we have much to discuss, things are going so well I can barely take it in." Re-entering the Castle, Muklah and Brakko's guards were obviously relieved they had returned, they had been told to stay behind and did not like it one bit.

"Crall!" Muklah yelled. "Bring food and wine to my chambers, enough for three!" He went to sit at his table saying, "Well Sisk, you've been busy and I thank you for it, Brother, your organisational skills are exceptional, thanks to you we are far ahead of schedule, and can move on rapidly. Tomorrow you will take your new recruits up to the forge to begin training, if we can increase the number of cannon coming out of the forges we will have an armada ready to conquer in no time."

The doors opened then and Crall came in pushing a trolley laden with food and wine, enough of each to keep men going all day and night; after he had left, Brakko said, "Maybe now would be a good time to send a bird to Vakkra and tell him to set sail, by the look of things our ships will be ready by the time he gets here, he should be ready to leave we sent a message to prepare his fleet already, did we not, Sisk?"

"We did, Brakko, it's a long flight and there are stops on the way but I'd say Vakkra began his preparations the second the first fleet left and will be ready for sea the second the latest bird arrives on Sess, in any case its looking like we can bring guns down daily, tested already at the forge, I will take the men up in a wagon in the morning and load any cannon ready and bring them down for fitting and testing aboard ship, we don't need them all for sea testing and Brakko gets to smash a few Tolian ships to pieces for fun, now my Lord if you will excuse

Brakko and I for a short time, we will go and send the bird now for Sess, another job done."

"Please do, men, but return quickly there is much to discuss and the day is wearing on."

The two men left to go to the bird loft and left Muklah alone for a bit, a crow who had been on a high sill with an open window, who understood man-talk, flew off to the mountain then to report what he had heard to one of Redwind's eagles, in this case Blacktail, Redwind's mate, as soon as the crows left the window, another silently landed on the sill again to begin his own vigil, Blacktail listened to the crow and thanked him in the language all birds understood, and flew off to pass the information on to her King and partner and in turn the War Council in Bevak.

Message sent, the two men returned to Muklah's chambers and sat with him at the table, and they ate, drank and talked with for the rest of the day until the light was gone and all three were tired enough to sleep, before retiring Sisk sent Crall off to the stable to make sure a wagon with four horses was ready for him and his men at dawn, then go and tell the men to be at the stables at dawn with all they need for a stay up at the forges, and of course, to make sure he himself had been fed before meeting with anyone.

Brakko and Muklah stayed awake a while longer chattering like novices the night before their first battle and they drank a considerable amount of wine before finally parting company for the night. Sisk, as always, did any writing he had to do, and had his supper before getting into bed and falling asleep.

Chapter 36

When Toli and the lads woke the next morning after his celebration, there had been suits of chainmail at the foot of each bed on a standing hanger, there were also four new tabards, deep purple with a golden crown over a golden ship, each member of the head council had the same clothing left sometime overnight, they each washed and dressed and, as was becoming normal left their chambers at almost the same time allowing Toli and Anga a few minutes alone before emerging to begin the day, as they all gathered in their own atrium, they looked at each other, in admiration, aware of how fine their clothing looked, down to the soft sandals with tough soles covering their mailed feet, Toli, the lads and the Generals had all been in mail before but nothing like this, so beautiful, so comfortable.

"I feel like I'm naked," Joki said. "I can't even feel this upon my skin; it's incredible." Then there was a chorus of agreement, as if everyone was waiting for someone else to say it.

"Right, we have a serious day's decision making ahead of us, so let's have at it!"

As the nine Castle-siders entered the grand chamber, with Anga on Toli's right arm and Shala holding Angas right hand and the rest following in no particular order, they saw that the food for breakfast had already been served and every member of the war council were already seated, plus three more faces, absent the night before, they all seated themselves in the same places as the previous night, before they began their meal, Briq stood up and said,

"My King, please allow me to introduce you to Qwill, Brother of Luq, Shqin and Shivi, Brother and Sister, the three Commanders on the three north end tiers." The three warriors stood at attention on facing Toli, Toli then stood to speak, he said directly to the standing warriors.

"My friends, I have not the words to thank you for your diligence and loyalty. I am very pleased that you have joined us here at council, and I look forward to speaking to you all in person in time, Briq, I feel the meal should begin soon, then we can begin the serious business of how to rid us all of the plague that has infested our land."

"Your wish Sire, what say all here?"

"All here say Aye!" was the loud reply, and everyone sat again and began breakfast. Dovitt noticed his Father Shouk seemed to be agitated, concerned, he went to Shouk and whispered, "Father, what is wrong? You look as if you are about to drop!"

"No wine, son, no ale, just tea and water, what under the sky is going on?"

"Father, by your King's order, there will be no wine nor ale until this war council has finished with its deliberation this day, fear not Father you will have your chance at pleasure after business is concluded."

"Aye Son, you're right, I may have got too used to peace, you may relax now, and thank you Son."

Dovitt took his seat again and the meal continued with talk of the previous night, while Qwill, Shqin an Shivi were brought up to date by their fellow warriors.

As the meal ended and they all sat sipping tea. Quor said quietly to Toli, "Whenever you say, Sire, Briq would like to begin."

Toli stood immediately, silence fell instantly.

"Good people, Commander Briq would now like to begin the day's proceedings so I ask you, Commander, to take your place at our centre, with our thanks."

Toli sat down and Briq strode to the centre of the table, he faced Toli and saluted and the whole room stood and followed suit, Toli then stood and quickly returned the salute and sat back down, as the others did, except Briq who moved to the gap on the outer ring of the table so as to address the whole council.

"My King, Queen and Princess and the other comrades at arms, first let me give you what I can about our history for it is, in fact yours too, you now sit in the carcass of the Dragon who once ruled this Island, the door at the back is called the Dragon's Tail because it is, or was, the Dragon's Tail, two doors to the front, his forelegs, two at the back his rear, the four doors between are magma chambers, caused by the destruction of the beast, you may have noticed the likeness of a Dragon's head on the dock when you landed, it is the Dragon's head, trying to get him to the water before TARMEA took him.

"Tarmea is the mountain, for it is one mountain, not many as some believe, Tarmea means Mountain Mother, you have heard it spoken, 'Tarmea Wistwa Dalkaka' means 'Mountain Mother please open'; and 'Tarmea Wistwa Routla' means 'Mountain Mother please close'. From now on, you will notice we are all calling our home Tarmea for we are the mountain because without her, there would be only desolation, we worship no gods but live in complete harmony with the mountain, the lake, the sky, the land, not forgetting the beasts and birds and we know you have the same harmony on the castle side, we believe that the Dragon, long before our time, had been terrorising the seas and islands around us until Tarmea became sick of the death-reek off the beast and for the good of all, melted and melded the Dragon forever and no Dragon has ever come here since our forebears arrived on the harbour side together.

"There is no historical record written that can be found, our valley ancestors, at least one anyway, must have found the words to open and close for it is the only way we could have got here, it could only have been Tarmea's wishes, we are all here because of her, inside and out, since then we have developed more spells over the centuries, beneficial spells, beneficial for us, not for anyone else unless Tarmea wishes it, certainly not for our most recent visitors, these spells will become evident as we go, your chain mail, given to you today, will fit you for the rest of your lives, it is now part of you, it comes from the mine behind Dalri.

"As to mining, the Black-Islanders will never mine the mountain alone, without Tolians, already they are learning that they cannot mine a single rock unless one of ours is there to finally free it from its place, we also know that the cannon forges are up and running and are producing four cannon in a day, although one of our birds reported to Redwind that they are only declaring two a day and hiding two, so as to have an extended fitting time, slowing down sea tests, but our treacherous friend Sisk has plans to bring men up to train in order to speed up said sea tests, even at two a day they'll fit a ship in ten days at four a day, his entire fleet of thirty ships in a month, that's without the coming help!"

"So you're saying the sooner we act, the better, eh Briq?" It was Matak, General of Toli's cavalry, who, up until now had been very quiet, he had been silently struggling with coming to terms at the loss of his wife, but having seen the garrison and its warriors and horses he saw hope of revenge where before there was none.

"Aye General, that is my thought on the subject," said Briq. "But the final decision must lie with our king."

Toli stood then, "I accept mine will be the final decision, but I will decide nothing without listening to everyone in this chamber who has an opinion, so forgive me if I fall silent during council, I assure you I am aware of every word you are saying, every opinion you are stating and will give my decision when I make it, in the meantime I will listen and pass an opinion if I feel I must."

"Then I will voice my opinion now," said Matak calmly. "My opinion is call the army to arms right now, then march out and destroy them all today, as soon as we are able to march, ride or sail we should be on the move!"

At that Shouk leapt to his feet. "Aye Matak, the sooner the better, they don't even know we exist, they'll never know what hit them!" Shouk had been hiding his sorrow behind drunk eyes and now his purpose in life had come back.

"We still have Tolians out there," said Tadesh. "Our main priority, as I see it, is to devise a plan which ensures the absolute safety of our own before the demise of others." A murmur of agreement went around the council then.

"We have other considerations we must address," Quor this time. "The Green Islers are expecting their own royal family back the day after tomorrow, if they do not return as planned, and no notification of delay reaches them, they will send ships to find their beloved rulers, and their navy will be murderous in their hearts when they discover their most revered Admiral, Admiral Tors, was hung from a gibbet along with the rest of the royal delegation, the navy will be implacable as will the land army over General Miro's execution."

"Aye Quor, you're right," agreed Briq, "we will know better what to do when that day comes, for today, I will bring you all up to date on what we know now, Redwind and his birds have been gleaning information from Sisk for some time now, the fool thinks he is sending his birds off protected from detection by his spells, he has no powers on this land other than that which Tarmea allows, all his messages have been intercepted and examined and most have been allowed to be delivered to prevent suspicion.

"Sisk has been messaging his Mother, Tuvaa, who was supposed to have been murdered on the day Sisk was born, she is very much alive, and is on an Island with many magii waiting for word to set sail and bring their powers to Toli's Island to begin their own dynasty, that Island is completely masked from discovery by the combined powers of the sorcerers and sorceresses on that evil place, however we found of its existence, but not location by simply following one of his birds with an unimportant message, composed by Worq, whom you have met and we are now more privy to every word of every page between them.

"Sisk and his Mother have been plotting against Muklah since the day he received a strange bird with a strange message telling him of his beginnings and the attempted murder of his mother by present day Lord Muklah's father, their plan to establish the centre of an empire here on this land as is Muklah's, with his Mother and her evil band of cohorts here and Sisk on the Green Isle, ruling between them all the surrounding known Islands then onto previously uncharted seas to spread their Black arts throughout the world, much the same as Muklah's plan, domination by whatever means.

"Sisk has been endearing himself to everyone on the Island and is gathering support as a fair and steady man, a good leader, a good listener, all a ruse of course, once established he intends to revert back to totalitarianism directing operations from his own beautiful palace on the Green Isle, he is misled, his loving Mother, if it is indeed his Mother, is making similar plans with the numbskull Brakko, who is under the impression that he will have his own territory and will, on his return to the Black-Isles, raid north and west to claim even more land for their new Empire, Brakko who was thought to be Muklah's most loyal friend and Commander would be relieved of his duty as soon as he served his purpose and, of course, executed if he can turn so easily on his so-called friend, he must not be allowed to exist." The chamber was silent, concentrating on every word Briq said,

"So they are destroying themselves from within already, but we cannot wait for their self-destruction we must be the cause of their demise so as to discourage any future potential aggressors from thoughts of invasion ever again, it also appears that his army is made up mainly of men who were pressed into service and the majority of those are unhappy at having been stowed on a ship for months and packed off to war, and nothing for their families to live on, most of them were the only provider, but hollow promises of lands in the new Empire had kept them at bay this far, but there are rumblings of unrest and Sisk is taking full advantage of the situation, endearing himself with Tolian and soldier alike, pointless of course as he would not be staying long enough to establish anything, we here just have to agree on the method of his and his murderous leader's end."

While Briq had been speaking, Shala had whispered something into Anga's ear. Anga stood up.

"Commander, could you please enlighten us Castle-siders as to the powers made available to us, for the coming conflict." And she sat back down.

"Yes my Queen, our powers include managing wind, rain, river and rock, or rather Tarmea's powers, we can create fog or disperse clouds, create our own storms as well, the land-born version of the storm that brought the invader from the sea, while you are in your mail no weapon of an enemy can harm you, we also believe, but this is untried, untested, that if we leave this land, as long as we are in our mail we carry Tarmea with us, we can wear it and float, on the lake at least, you, yourself, have every power we do and we fully expect every Castle-sider here to be given the gift as well, this will take practice of course, but we feel Tarmea has already given her blessings, otherwise we could not have brought you here, specifically here, this chamber.

"It means Tarmea has accepted you as our King, not her King Sire, for she needs no ruling, but our King, and with her grace we will reclaim her from the invader, for she was duped by the off Island storm as we were, but we are wiser for it and will take these steps to safeguard against a recurrence."

Discussion came and went with the Castle-side military condoning immediate mobility, march out and slaughter every Black-Isles lowlife and chuck them all in the harbour for the sharks, call it a returned favour.

"Except for the three morons supposedly in charge."

"We will have a special ceremony for those buggers, I fancy we give Sisk to the Green-Islers and let them have their sport with him, at their leisure naturally, and it won't take us long to debate the final day of the other two." Tadesh was so infuriated his face was turning bright red as his blood boiled.

"Aye Tadesh, but destroying them all makes us as them, the information that not all his soldiers are loyal to his cause may become valuable, maybe even vital, to us, I urge careful consideration before mass extermination, we cannot split our own population in order to go off governing lands we know nothing about, we don't have enough people, and the Black-Isles will have to be brought to heel, we know there is a malevolent force there and as long as that heart beats it will forever be plotting against us, so let our heads rule our hearts while planning, what we do now becomes history tomorrow.

"I for one will always advocate mercy over execution where deserved, this of course does not apply to the bastards who slaughtered our innocents, they will be weeded out by their armour, they have a silver Kraken placed on their black breastplate over their black hearts, they are supposed to be the elite of the elite, we shall see how the elite die!"

Loud agreement rang around the council, slapping the table and shouting, "Death to the elite, Death to the Kraken!"

The council members then fell to discussion with their nearest neighbours at the table when the kitchen staff brought out food and drink, water or tea were the choices of liquid refreshment, Shouk did not bat an eyelid, his focus had shifted. When he had finished his food, Toli stood with a mug of water in hand and said, "I don't know about anyone else but I'd like to stretch my legs for a while, I feel there is more sitting and listening to come, so please, join me, we will reconvene in half an hour." He put out his arm for Anga, which she took and with Shala in hand they moved to mingle around the chamber.

Anga said to Toli, "Would you mind, Toli, if I spent some time with my father, I'd love him to get to know Shala better."

"Yes, of course Anga, I want to have a word with Xing and Worq over there by Redwind." And he gave her a kiss on the cheek and made for the three by the door, open to the mountain to allow Redwind to come and go and to allow his many messengers to contact him from another perch outside the door, he had just made it to the three when an agitated Thrush landed on the perch and began chattering loudly flapping his wings nervously and hopping up and down on the rock perch, Redwind turned to Toli and shrieked loudly, he bowed low so the tip of his beak tipped his talons, he shrieked again, spread his massive wings and flew out the door, as Toli watched him go and he sighed, "If only man could fly."

"Man can fly!" stated Xing.

"What are you talking about, Xing?"

"Man can fly, I can fly, you can fly."

Toli looked at Worq who stood with his ever present serene smile, his eyes twinkled playfully and he gave a nod and said, "I myself have flown, Sire, most people in this council have, we thought it was best explained as it was being demonstrated."

"Then demonstrate it now please!."

"Yes Sire, we are ready when you are."

"NOW, PLEASE!."

Xing saluted and left the room through the door down the Dragons throat and onto the pier the aboard the Queen Shaleena. Toli stood by Worq feeling totally bewildered when Briq's voice rang across the chamber,

"It appears our King's demonstration is imminent so members of the council please make your way aboard the Queen Shaleena and await the King's boarding, the King's entourage will join you presently."

"This is all very mysterious, Briq, tell us what is going on."

"You must see to believe, my King, suffice to say you may remember something similar as a child."

Shala was beaming. "Are we ready then, can we go?"

"Yes, we can go now, Princess, all is ready."

The head council headed down to the ship, the Tolians completely baffled and valley-folk smiling knowingly, when they arrived on the pier the people aboard and on the pier stood at salute Toli quickly returned the salute and boarded the Queen Shaleena, on boarding the ship he noticed, towards the stern, a ten foot high timber wall across the centre of the deck, unnoticed before because of the throng on the pier going about their business once again, Briq bade them follow and the castle-siders did that fascinated, they valley-folk stayed where they were.

Behind the wall in the stern of the ship there was, bolted to the deck a large drum of cable, very fine cable, with brakes and notches and two even larger wheels with a man standing at each of them all this made from the same ore, given up by the same mine, and fabricated by the same magical craftsmen who made their mail.

Following the fine cable, Toli's eyes came upon a strange frame holding what looked like, giant bat wings, with Xing in the centre with another, this time triangular, frame, a breeze got up, coming up the lake from the south, Xing felt the breeze and raised a hand, he then dropped his hand and pulled a lever between his legs, the triangle was now free, the wings began to fill in the breeze and Xing's feet lifted and fell to the deck, two men then pulled levers opening the wall in a fashion so as to push the wind downward onto the deck and creating lift under the wings forced there by more angled upward facing boards.

Xing's feet cleared the deck and he hooked up his feet behind him, the two men on the drum wheels fed out the cable at a steady pace, keeping the cable taut the wall slats were raised at a matching pace until it was closed again, this time in an upright position, that's when the breeze caught Xing and he soared upward and outward until the cable men stopped, the pull on the ship had her straining on her anchor, Xing controlled the wings from his triangle and he dipped and soared from side to side, the drum on the deck was on a swivel and followed the direction of Xing exactly avoiding snags.

"It's a kite," said Toli. "A kite that can carry a man!"

Briq was now beside Toli. "Yes Sire, we have a few of these on high stations on the north side with the help of Tarmea, we can fly out over the sea and look down on our enemies before they come to our shores, we know from the birds they are coming, but to look into their ships unseen is another thing."

Suddenly, Redwind came out of nowhere and screeched at Xing who immediately signalled to be brought in, Redwind dived to the deck then and flapping and screeching at Worq, he turned and went in his door to the chamber and waited.

Toli asked Briq, "What's going on, Briq?"

"Not sure, Sire. Worq!"

"Yes Commander, here."

"What's going on, Worq, what's gotten into Redwind?"

"He has not one, but two, new messages meant for the Black Isles, it seems to be important, Sire."

Xing was brought to the deck in exactly the reverse fashion he had been fed out, and Storq took the Queen Shaleena the short distance back to the pier. They tried to be as dignified as possible in their rush back to council, but everyone had seen Redwind for everyone within eyesight had been watching Xing fly. Worq went straight over to Redwind and took the two scrolls Redwind had been carefully carrying, Worq took them directly to Toli who sat in his Throne before unrolling them, they were in cipher, Toli dismayed, Worq saw his concern.

"Never fear, Sire, I speak this cipher fluently and have done for ten years since the fool Sisk began sending them believing them to be protected, please Sire, allow me." Worq examined the first scroll and said, "This is a message to fleet Admiral Vakkra, ordering him to sail here immediately for refitting and this is a message from Sisk to his Mother telling her to stand by, for the next message will be to make her move, fool does not even realise her 'move' involves his death, no maternal instincts there."

"Right!" Tadesh leapt to his feet. "This means we must bring a solution to the council all the more urgently."

A shout of support filled the chamber, Shala stood on her chair and whispered in Anga's ear, who in turn whispered in Toli's. Toli stood up and raised his hands for silence.

"My sister wishes to say something to the council." And he sat back down.

Shala began, "With due respect to my elder council members, which means all of you, I would like my opinion heard before it gets lost in argument." All eyes were rivetted on Shala except, as always, Anga, who simply stared ahead as if expecting a revelation. "There is no need to advance any plans in a hurry, in the first place this Admiral has not yet received his bird telling him to prepare his ships, never mind to set sail, second place, our folks are safe if busy, and Tarmea will see to it they all remain vital, not giving anything to anyone but Tolians, is that correct, Commander Briq?"

"It is, Princess," was all Briq could say.

"How long would it take for this fleet to reach us Commander?."

"About six months, it is only a reckoning."

"And how long before a bird can reach them from here?"

"About three, we reckon again, we think a bird may be twice the speed of an average ship at sea, but these ships look much faster, having said that both ship and bird must take stops, at least for fresh water."

"So let's assume for now it is nine months between message being sent and fleet arriving here, yes?"

"Yes Princess."

"So quicker again, do you see, my King? All our folk are safe, busy, why not let them, the Black-Islers, fit out and test our new fleet, and we take it off them when were properly ready and wait for his second fleet, when they appear on our horizon we'll go out and greet them as friends and blow them to the depths of the Tolian Sea!" Total silence fell on the room.

"Commander, what say you, it will work."

"What say I, Princess? I say we have us a new Commander of Operations, and yes it will work, we are in charge of everything, yes Princess, watch, prepare, let the scum play themselves into our trap, your trap, my Princess."

"Well then," she said and sat down, she whispered to Anga from the side of her mouth, "What do you think?"

"Wait for it," she whispered back. It was the new warrior Qwill who stood first and rhythmically began thumping on the table, a warrior's sign of approval. Soon they were all thumping a war-like beat on the tabletop.

"Told you," Anga whispered, Toli stood again and asked for silence.

"Please talk among yourselves, I wish to speak with my sister." He sat down again and asked Anga, "Would you mind, my love, if Shala sits between us?"

"Not at all, my love, not at all." And she swapped seats with Shala.

"Now Shala—" Toli began.

"Before you start, my King," Anga interrupted. "I have something to tell you of your little sister, if it suits of course, Sire."

Toli drilled his eyes into hers, "Anga, now is not the time for mockery."

"Actually, thanks to Shala, we have lots of time for mockery, instead I'll tell you an interesting story; when I first came into service with Shala I noticed she had lots of dolls and she loved to play with them, she was a perfect little Princess, then I began to notice she was making the dolls fight and die, she even made them march, the toys were being broken regularly and the Queen wondered what was happening, so I covertly went to the royal toy maker and asked him to make enough toy soldiers for two armies of twenty and when they were finished, I brought them to Shala and she would stage little battles and give names to the soldiers she had overheard when you and the lads were playing.

"Soon, she had me going to the library to find books on real battles and read them to her, her collection grew and soon she was staging mocks of real battles, she would have me read positions and movements of the victor and the loser and every single time she turned the loser into a convincing winner, all with the benefit of hindsight of course, but I began to stage battles without telling her the outcome I'd give her an army and I'd play the exact strategy of the victor and Shala would defeat me with her own, she has sent many a famous general home with a sore face, your baby sister is the best strategist in your army."

Toli blinked and looked at Shala, and Shala said, "Oh and there is something else, we must get a message to the forges and tell the Trois to declare all cannon and warn them of their surprise visit, I would suggest we send a bird to the settlement and have a Tolian taken out to get a message to them."

"Ah how are we do that, Sister? There are guards night and day at the forges and the mines."

"Well Brother, we could have Manni the waggoneer told at his cottage when he comes home for the night, no guards there, we could send him up to the Trois, with new tools of some sort and he can warn them before Sisk and the rest get there."

"Well and good, but how will he explain his knowledge of this?"

"Tell him the Generals are in hiding and planning a coup, send Gogon or Luron, they are known to have been with the Generals that night."

"Brilliant." He stood to call Briq. Briq came over. "Please listen to my sister again."

Shala repeated her plan in its entirety once more to Briq who immediately turned to the chamber and yelled, "Somebody bring a bird for the settlement!"

Briq turned to Shala again, unable to keep his delight hidden, "My Princess, in the last few minutes, you have solved the problem of many endless, anguished hours of argument and hurried decisions, you were born to this, I have never been more positive of anything in my life and my life is not much troubled by indecision."

"Good, Commander Briq, I have one more decision to ask of you this day."

"Anything, my Princess, just ask."

"There is an hour before dark and I would like you to decide, right now, that I should be taken from here and given a go on Xing's kite, have you come to a decision yet, Commander?"

"My decision lands in your favour, Princess, and with the King's consent, I will accompany you to ensure that the wishes of my final decision are met with." He bowed.

When he straightened up again and looked at Toli with a look of inevitability about him, Toli said, "Okay, I give in," and Anga kicked him under the table across Shala. "In fact we'll all go."

Shala said to Briq, "Would you be kind enough to ensure my personal guard is there please?"

Briq looked puzzled and he looked at Toli for help, but it was Anga who spoke. "Tak," she said.

"Ah Tak," Toli said. "Of course, what was I thinking."

The royal party went down to the Queen Shaleena and it was beautiful basking in the late sunlight. Shala was 9 again and she chattered incessantly to Tak, barely drawing breath; for Tak's part, he was an avid listener to anything she uttered.

Soon the youngest person ever to fly was buckled in and up in the air, she screeched with delight and after a short time Redwind joined her with Blacktail gliding at each wing tip, soon the sky was filled with birds, raptors to ravens, screeching and cawing, smaller birds whistling, all around her like a protective cloud, the whole time Shala in the eye of the storm of birds squealing and laughing along with them.

Eventually, Shala had to be reeled in as darkness was falling and they wanted to await news from the settlement. The warriors had been deep in discussion during Shala's flight of fancy and no-one could find a flaw in her plan, as she and the others entered the chamber they all rose and began their war rhythm beat until Shala sat down then they all sat, after the King and Queen were settled of course.

Again the conversation was General in nature and soon more food was brought in, this time with wine and ale, no one could believe the day had almost gone. Admiral Shouk, his son noticed, sent his usual measures of ale and wine back to the cellars and asked for a large pitcher of water, as Ratesh was talking with Tadesh, and Joki with Matak, Dovitt moved to the place next to his father made vacant by someone else moving around.

"Well Father, what do you think about our little Shala?"

"I think I will pay attention to her every word from here on in, any relevant word anyway, it seems like she anticipated the progress of the situation and had it solved, I mean it was as if she knew, girl's a genius!"

"Yes, it's like the mountain brings out the best in us, Father, for sure, there is a clarity of thought here, I feel stronger and wiser than I ever did."

"Me too, Son, me too."

Just then a squawking bird landed on the outer perch, and passed a very loud message to Redwind, Redwind passed it onto Worq, and Worq came over to Toli, who said, "Please Worq, speak to everyone."

Worq went to the gap in the table and addressed the council, "Roqi has returned with Gogon from Manni's cottage, Manni is going up to the forges at first light, any time before would be suspicious, he will be carrying big saws on the premise of the saws being requested for the building of the new firing range by Troi through a message left at another forge he was visiting today, Gogon said he knew nothing of the king when asked and said only that he knew the whereabouts of the Generals, the Trois will know long before the traitor and his friends appear the word will be kept out of the capital, but the forges and mines are a different matter, a different community they will keep it up the hill, as they say, apparently."

"To keep it up the hill," Toli said, "means that it does not come lower than the forges; it's 'up the hill business'."

"Well, it seems we are in the hands of your Castle-side 'up the hillers', and all that's left to us is to plan the final days of Muklah and his reavers, and, of course, time for our warriors to learn the art of firing a cannon."

"Something to think about, Briq, which brings me to the matter of Dalri, you master armourers and elders of Dalri are not here, why is that. I hope I did not offend them by coming here straight from Beeth."

"My King, it is impossible for you to offend under any circumstances, the elders and our master armourers are one and the same, they have been rushing to make mail for our Castle-side visitors, they were under the impression war was imminent, as we all did, and would not leave the forges and workshops until all was done, the mail will be on its way up the lake to the settlement on a supply barge at first light, the elder armourers are on the way here now, hoping to meet you before you retire tonight, they have, Sire, just finished the last suit of mail no more than an hour ago, ah! here they are now, Sire."

Three tall men, even for valley-folk, in mail covered with a white tabard with a golden anvil on the front crossed by a black hammer, were escorted into the chamber by the two other door guards. As the guards announced them, Briq, Toli, Anga and Shala walked across to the door to greet them.

"My King, please allow me to introduce you to Slaq, Craq and Tilq, elders and master armourers of Dalri, loyal subjects and, when required, valuable warriors."

"Once again I find myself in debt to the Valley-folk, I thank you, friends, for remaining at your posts in time of need, your efforts will not be in vain."

The three men dropped to one knee then, and, looking at the floor, Slaq, the senior of the three spoke.

"My King, there is never a need to thank us, our purpose is to serve our King, we always knew you would come Sire."

"Please Slaq, all of you, stand up, no need to speak to the floor my friends." Once standing, Toli put both his hands on Slaq's shoulders. "I have a request of you, Slaq."

"As you probably already know, thanks to my sister's foresight, we have time on our hands, and I know my Generals," he was now including the lads in this category, "would love to see your method of making all things military from one metal and to that end, would it be possible to visit your facilities tomorrow?"

"Why yes, Sire, we would be honoured anything you wish Sire."

"Then can we say after breakfast on the morrow?"

"Yes my King."

"Then I shall see you on the morrow, and look forward to it, but for the rest of the night please partake of the food and ale or food and wine if you prefer, and catch up with your friends, no need for the urgency we once believed was necessary but your industry will never be forgotten I can assure you." Toli's party returned to their places and the night continued in a lighter mood then the day had begun, the Generals were excited to hear they were going to see the source of the marvellous versatile metal, as were the lads, more serious now, less interested in playful pursuits.

"Didn't see Tak on the ship when I was flying, nor was he there when Xing was flying," Shala said quietly to Anga.

"I noticed," she said. "So I asked Storq before we left the ship last time, he is helping to load the barge for the settlement tonight, he be back on the Queen Shaleena tonight later, he sleeps aboard, it is his home."

"Yes I know. Anga?"

"Yes Shala."

"I'd like him to come with us tomorrow, can that be arranged?"

"Already is, he'll be waiting by the pier in the morning to join us, that is you, me and Toli, in our carriage."

"Thank you Anga, I must thank Toli too."

"Toli doesn't know."

"What!"

"Our King has enough to worry about, without having to think of the comings and goings of a simple cabin boy." And she winked at Shala.

A tear came to Shala's eyes then. "We are forever, Anga, I know this for certain."

"Me too, Shala, forever and certain. I'm going over to speak to my Father before bed, come with me, he already loves you."

"And I him, let's go!"

Toli was too engrossed in a conversation with Quor to bother, so the royal ladies captured Bri for the duration of the night, eventually Anga realised that no-one would be sleeping this night until the King had retired, and Shala's eyelids were dropping, she gave her apologies to Bri and took Shala across the floor to Toli.

"My King, I fear it is time for our chief tactician to get to bed."

"Forgive me Quor, but Anga is right, we'd best all keep ourselves in good fettle, so I must bid you goodnight."

Toli stood and Anga took his arm and they led a sleepy Princess from the chamber. That signalled the end of council for the day and the council members drifted off to their own beds, there was a serene atmosphere all over the valley, even the night creatures were quiet.

Chapter 37

The Trois were already in the forge before first light in order to remove the two overnight casts and put them into the secret cache, as they came back into the forge after stowing the rough cast cannon, Father began the cleaning and finishing the other two while Son set the Moulds again ready for the pour. In the quiet of the morning they heard a guard call a halt to a visitor at the gate, the two men went outside, curious to see what was what.

Manni was saying loud enough for the Trois to hear, "I was intructed by master Launt, Grandmaster Launt actually, to deliver two log-saws here today, by the request of master Troi, in order to begin the building of the new firing range." The guard had heard about the new construction and drowsily waved Manni in without further question.

Manni, on foot now, led his horse and wagon over to the forge doors where the Trois stood, baffled, how did Manni know about the range? Launt did not know to tell him, what is going on? The Trois greeted Manni in a loud and friendly fashion, with Father Troi calling.

"Manni, you're early! You must have fallen from your cot, leave the saws here we'll bring them up to the range in the wagon after a brew up."

The guard went back to his bench then and the two Trois went into the forge with Manni. The Trois actually had a brew of tea ready to drink, and the three of them sat on stools around the forge with metal mugs, steaming in their hands.

"So what are you up to, Manni?" Young Troi asked.

Manni learned forward and spoke secretively, "Brace yourselves, men, the Generals are still alive and are planning a coup!"

"Bugger off, Manni, it's too early for your japes!" Father said.

"Do I look like I'm japin', Troi? Eh? You'd best listen to what I have to tell and soak it up, I had a visit at my home last night, a visit from Gogon!" The Trois gasped, Gogon was well known up the hill.

"He told me he was with the Generals and they were in hiding with the rest of the hunting party, he knows nothing of the King and Princess or any other missing people, believe me, I asked, he says the Generals are planning a coup and it is imperative that you send every gun made, down to the harbour as quick as you can, even the ones hidden outside."

"How do you know about those?"

"I don't know. I told you they are in hiding, now listen, sometime this morning Sisk, Muklah and Brakko will be coming up the hill with seven extra men, a Captain and six soldiers, to learn and to help, you must declare your cannon thanking him for the help to speed things up, now, as we know, what's up here, stays up here, yes?"

"Yes," they answered, joyous at the news. A curious soldier on his rounds heard their voices and came into the forge, Troi junior caught the movement from the corner of an eye, so he jumped up and shouted. "Right, let's get these big boys over to the range, shall we!"

"We shall." said Manni. "I've to head along to Launt now he's broke his big hammer again, lucky I had one in the shed eh?" The soldier wasn't to know Launt was more than capable of making his own hammer, big or small.

Troi senior, acting as if he had just noticed the soldier, said to him, "Guard, would you mind giving Captain Sito a message from me?"

"Of course not, Troi." The soldier was a decent fellow. "What is it?"

"Will you tell him we have all we need to begin work on the firing range and we're heading up there now, oh, and tell him we have cannon ready for testing."

"I will Troi, no bother."

"Thank you guard, what's your name, soldier?"

"My name is Sol, I'll go deliver your message now."

"Thank you Sol."

Going up to the range, only a few hundred yards away, Troi senior said, "What a pleasant person that soldier is, if only he knew we have always had all we need up here."

"Nice to have some new saws all the same." And they arrived at the range roaring with laughter.

They unloaded the saws and said their farewells, and Manni clip-clopped out the gate waving to the guard on the bench who did not move. The Trois were busy checking where everything had been stowed and the condition of the materials to be used, the attitude had changed and they were forging for their own again.

After a short time, Sito rode up with two of his off duty guards and they dismounted at the Trois who seemed to be making a list. "Are these the supplies we need, Troi?"

"No Captain," he gave his military title in front of his men, "this is a list of what we have, it seems we need nothing, we can test cannon today, as soon as the range is ready."

"What do we have to do?"

"Come, I'll explain," and Troi senior brought him to the entrance of the long range, a corridor of very thick trees on each side, stacked horizontally between heavy steel beams braced back to ground on more steel beams buried deep in the ground, from where they stood at the open end of the range they could see the same set-up at the far end, about halfway up the range there were four more steel beams braced back to the far end again piled into the ground, Troi walked up the packed earth floor with Sito to the upright steel. "We have a stack of cut trees that fit between these two beams." He was talking about the two beams that took the girth of the trees.

"All you have to do is cut the trees to length, there is a measuring stick up at the stack, we'll bring the new saws up with us and I'll show you what's to be done up there, Troi, would you mind having a look at our pile of cannon-rocks and grade me a few for our test firing?"

"Aye Father, I'll bring over a barrow load." Young Troi had already made a gauge to find rocks that suited their new-gauge guns so he headed to the forge for his gauge and a barrow and headed for the rock-pile. Up at the log stack, Old Troi was explaining the process to Sito and his men, he stood between the stack and a very long six-wheeled trolley with a V-shaped top; the six wheels were chocked with wedges to disallow movement.

"Now what we have to do is pick up a log and get it into the Vs on the trolley, leave the leading end hanging over for cutting." Then the four men, two on each end picked up one of them and placed it in the V trolley leaving the end nearest the range hanging over more than the other. Troi picked up a long stick from the underside of the trolley frame with a right angled plate on one end, he placed it on top of the log, plate against the end, then he told the two helper soldiers to pick up one of the two handed log saws, he told them to place it up to the end of the measuring stick, a man on each side of the trolley, he then lifted the measure off and pulled a bar with a spike on it on a hinge and bit the spike into the log to stop it turning under the big teeth of the saw.

"Okay," he said, "cut the end off now and make sure it is cut square!" The two burly soldiers made short work of the cut, and stood grinning, saw still in their hands.

"Well done, lads, now lay the saw handles at your feet," he said to the far soldier. "And mind your fingers! Make sure the wheels won't go over the saw when we move. Right, now a man on each corner please." The soldiers each grabbed a corner of the trolley and Troi removed the chocks then took a corner. "Okay men, let's move." The road to the range was packed solid from use, the weather did not seem to affect it, it was also on a slight downhill gradient and the walk was effortless.

Troi made them set the trolley parallel to the outer-near wall of the range, there was a lifting rig which reminded the soldiers of a gibbet, and for a second they were nervous, Troi picked up a ring of strong rope, wrapped it around the log and fed it through itself, he then swung the lifting arm around and lowered the block, he hooked the rope and took the weight of the log, dead centre, as it cleared the trolley, he stopped and said, "Right lads, take the trolley to the path and chock the back wheels." The soldiers obeyed and came back to stand by Sito. There were two timber frame staircases up to the top of the side walls, one a side.

"Captain Sito, would you be kind enough to take this from me?" And Troi handed him the rope that lifts and drops the log.

"Right," he said, "you up this side and you up the other, Captain, would you raise the log please?"

Sito pulled on the rope and the log climbed up close to the wall, when Troi determined the log was high enough to clear the wall he said, "Now, pay attention."

He picked up a loose end of long rope attached to the end of the swinging arm and he walked around the front of the range, he walked to the foot of the stairs and said to the soldier, "Take this and pull slowly." And the soldier pulled and the log swung into place, perfectly balanced, dead centre.

"Right Captain, lower, nice and easy, you two, guide your ends between the steel." As the log entered between the beams, he called, "Okay, hands off, Captain, lower all the way." When the log was on the ground, he said, "Okay stop there." Then he picked up a long steel bar and went inside.

"You two," he called to the men on the stairs, "come in here now please." The men came into him and he placed the bar below the log next to the rope, he held the bar at waist height and called to Sito. "Okay, all the way down now."

Sito did, and Troi took the weight of the log, without straining. "Okay, one of your remove the rope." One of the soldiers unhooked and untied the rope, Troi shoved the bar upright and the log dropped into place, the bar, the rope, and the swinging arm were returned to their starting places and Troi said, "Easy, well done men, now wheel the trolley up and do it all again, the three of you should do, four is better, but I must work in the forge now, and for the foreseeable future."

"No problem, Troi, I'll walk down with you and pick another man to help me, in the meantime, you two get the trolley up to the logs and prepare the, next one." As they walked, Troi junior passed with a barrow full of round rocks, muscles bulging under the weight.

"Can't stop, sorry." And he struggled on up to the range.

Waiting back, Troi said, "It'll take ten trips to fill that wall, keep at it and we'll be able to test fire today."

"Keep at it? Try to stop us, Troi, being a constant guard does not suit any of us, some, in fact most, of my men are not soldiers and never will be, they all want a crack at the range."

"Well, when this is up we'll try to find something to keep your men busy, how many do you have off duty at any one time?"

"Four on, four off, four spare, twelve men, all bored beyond insanity, even when on duty!"

"May I make a suggestion, Sito?"

"Of course Troi."

"Go get all your off-duty men, all eight, let two work with the existing two, set the other four to building a permanent saw horse up at the log stack, a team sawing, a team building, rotate them to suit your needs when this one is built you could bring sawn logs to the range and stack them ready for fitting, you, of course, will supervise."

"Absolutely brilliant! That's the way to go, Troi, thank you."

"Please finish this one first, Sito, we would want something to report to Lord Sisk fairly soon I feel."

"Understood Troi, we'll finish this today and I'll make plans for tomorrow."

"Perfect Sito, tomorrow is another day, am I right?"

"Yes you are Troi, and its looking better than today, I'll give a shout when were done."

"Yes, do, please Sito."

Troi went back into the forge then and Sito carried on to the barracks at the gate, he bumped into Sol about to start his rounds for the second time.

"Go get out of that armour, Sol, and get into your work overalls, you have five minutes, I'll be here counting the seconds."

"Aye Captain, straight away." He was back in three, but Sito wasn't actually counting. Troi junior came back to the forge seconds after his Father, sweat pumping from every pore on his body, he flopped his saturated body on a stool at the forge side.

"My stars, Son, how did you find so many suitable rocks in such a short time?."

"Strangest thing, Father, when I went up to our usual place, to our usual rock pile, there was a separate pile right next to it and all of them were perfectly round and of exactly the correct gauge, and heavy too I can tell you!"

"Aye Son, strange times, but at least we are not lost yet, our Generals are alive and have a plan, we must trust in our Generals to save us from the fate I feel Muklah has planned for us; for now, Son, let's make ourselves invaluable to the invader in order to be invaluable to our Generals."

"We are already invaluable to both it seems, Father." Young Troi now had steam rising from his clothes. The noise of a wagon at the gate caught their attention, after a few sharp words the wagon moved and pulled up to the forge doors.

The Trois busied themselves by discussing the method they would use to manufacture cast shot for the new guns, they were occupied, engrossed even, in this discussion that, apparently, they had not noticed the entrance of the three Lords—Muklah, Sisk and Brakko. Troi senior turned around as if suddenly surprised.

"My Lords, I'm very sorry, I didn't notice you were there, it's only been three days."

Sisk stepped forward. "Yes I know, Troi, unexpected visits are usually the most productive, please allow me to introduce my Lords Muklah and Brakko, whose names you most probably know."

The two smiths lowered their heads respectfully together, "My Lords."

"This surprise visit revealed to us that you are developing a new type of cannon shot, is that correct?"

"No Lord, not a new type, merely a new size, we have moulds and method for the making of a large shot for the big Culverins on the harbour, it's simply a matter of working out how to make them smaller, no-one here was involved in the original making of mould or shot, the plans have been secreted by my own Father and they have not been seen since."

A pack of lies, his Father had showed him everything he needed to become the best smith on the Island, even if the plans were lost altogether it was a simple job to scale down sizing from an original mould. Sisk could not trace the lie, he could trace nothing up here.

"Very well, so what progress, Troi?" He was addressing junior now, believing him to be vital to the new regime, his regime. Muklah was becoming agitated by his lack of involvement in the conversation and butted in.

"So tell us what we have please, not what we don't have." He was also agitated from the effect on his soft pampered body, even the long sea voyage did not have the same painful result. Brakko too looked like he'd been beaten, his lack of activity had taken its toll. Young Troi walked over to the two finished cannon.

"Simply put, Lord, these two can be tested now, the two at the cleaning station will be ready later today, the process, as it stands, is producing four cannon per day, two a day are ready to shoot, please follow me, my Lords," and he took him out to the pit-cache, "we have four in here, again waiting for finishing and testing."

The unpleasant expressions of the Lords Muklah and Brakko changed to one of divine revelation, all pain was gone or at least forgotten, Sisk was nonplussed, he had expected this much.

Muklah, who looked like a man who had just been told he was going to live forever, asked, "So when you figure out the shot and build the range, you can begin testing?"

"No Lord, we intend to test today." Even Sisk was taken aback.

"Please tell me how?"

"Your own Captain up here, Sito, has given his off duty soldiers the job of building the range, so after some simple instruction, he and his men are building at this very moment."

"But what of the shot?" Brakko asked of senior.

"We have always tested with rocks up here, we don't waste valuable shot, and we have enough up at the range to begin now, or as soon as Sito and his men are finished. We only have to knock up a cannon saddle to fit our new guns, with help Lord, we could be sending four cannon a day, ready to fire, down to the harbour."

Muklah went weak at the knees. "Do you hear, Brakko, four a day." And he put his hand on Brakko's shoulder, as if for support. "We'll be sea testing the Black Kraken this week." Brakko just stood in his spot, grin spread from ear to ear.

"Good, Troi," Sisk said to senior. "Your help is waiting outside, and as well as that we have brought up two saddles from the harbour, at this moment excess to requirements, the flagship is ready for cannon right now, please follow me."

Outside, Sisk introduced his seven new apprentices saying, "Any trouble from this lot, just tell Kile, he is in command of this little crew, although each one of them comes to you willingly."

"Then let's get the cannon up to the range and see how Captain Sito's building is coming along," Troi senior said with genuine enthusiasm. "Please follow me."

Troi brought the soldiers back into the forge and instructed them to sling the first cannon with four ropes, the seven new soldiers took the end of a rope-sling each with Troi junior on the eighth, with instruction from senior they took the weight then in unison took one step to the side, senior then positioned a wheeled trolley below the gun and they dropped the cannon on the trolley, "Follow me out now." And senior went ahead to open the doors, when the trolley reached the open doors, junior bid them stop, senior dropped the tailgate of the wagon, and took eight sacks of straw, one at a time, and made a soft bed to transport the guns up to the range.

Up the side of one door and across the top there was exactly the same lifting gear as was at the range, only different dimensions, they picked up the first cannon and dropped it on one side of the straw bed, while senior adjusted the gun for safe transport, junior re-entered the forge with the seven soldiers and the trolley, soon they emerged with the second gun which was quickly loaded and made safe. The soldiers, who had come up on the flatbed of the wagon and were in considerable pain themselves elected to walk up to the range behind the wagon.

Getting up to the range Sito and his men were dropping the fifth log of ten into place, Sol inside, now on a ladder removing the rope sling and bedding them in with the bar, there were two logs by the side already cut and ready for fitting, senior was amazed, after the Lords alighted the wagon, he said, "Sito, how did you manage this so quickly?"

"I took your advice Troi, would you like to see?."

"My advice?, yes I'd very much like to see, perhaps our Lords might like to see your process too." Troi was careful to shift some credit on to Sito, he liked Sito, he didn't dislike any of the soldiers up here.

"I'd very much like to see, Troi."

Muklah was so keen it was almost as though it was a different man. As they approached the cutting crew two of them were lifting a cut log off the ground at right angles to the stack, they put them across the path in line with the ground logs and chocked it, then they went back to the stack and all four of them lifted another log and placed it atop the two runner logs and left it there for measuring and cutting, then the two on the cut log de-choked it and began kick-rolling it down the slow incline, too slow to let the log get away from them.

The group followed the rolling log to the range where the two soldiers up ended the log and tipped it over its length to place it with the other prepared logs then went back up for the next one, the tenth and finishing log, the fitting crew had number six already slung awaiting Sito's return for fitting.

"We'll have this wall finished within the hour, my Lord, and extra logs cut for the next one." Even the Trois were amazed.

Muklah and Brakko could barely contain themselves, and all the Black-Islers were pleased they were happy, it could have gone so differently, but Troi's organisational skills and his hints had won the day.

"An hour!" Senior declared. "We best get these cannon off the back and into the saddles; aboard ship and with wheels they'd be known as gun carriages."

"Troi, go get the paint, will you?" And junior went to the shed between the range and the log stack and come back with a bucket of white wash paint and an old brush.

"Land that saddle there, Kile, right in the centre of the range if you please."

Kile and Miles hopped up on the wagon and easily picked up the saddle between them and handed it over the side to two of their comrades who placed it as close to the centre as they could guess by eye, the other five slung the cannon, and, with Troi junior helping slid the first gun off the back, carried it to the saddle and left it resting in its cradle, junior then fixed the caps on to stop the gun jumping out of the saddle. Senior, picked up the paint and slopped it on the bottom log, then the fifth log up. The wagon driver backed the wagon to the entrance of the range, they slung the second gun and dropped it into the other saddle, just off to one side.

Senior began sighting the gun onto the reference line on the fifth log, the range was fifty feet long, he was set at twenty-five, junior then loaded the gun, the round stone was ideal, he could not have forged any better himself, when senior was happy with his sighting wedges he drove two round, heavy, steel bars deep into the ground a foot behind the saddle to allow a certain amount of recoil but to stop gun and saddle flying up the range.

"Ready?" He asked junior.

"Aye, ready!"

At the wall Sol shouted, "Done."

Sito had his men unsling the gun and now the last log was in.

"Well, what do you think?" Father said to son.

"I think we are as ready as it gets, no more man-handling Father, buggers are heavier than I though, we almost had six broken backs, so lifting tackle, wagon and trolley from now on."

"Fair enough, now who has the honour?"

"Father, you know I could never claim to be a master forger and smith; if I let someone else fire my weapon, I'm primed and ready to fire, please father, could you clear the range?" Junior picked up a long stick with an unlit taper on one end, he lit it from a small brazier several feet away behind a small wall, he re-entered the range and stood off to one side. "Ready."

Senior made sure everyone was in a safe position and called, "Ready!"

Junior touched the taper to the flash pan, the was a big flash and a very big blast, the range was filled with smoke, obscuring junior.

"Troi, is all well?"

"Aye Father, all is well." And he walked from the range, and the smoke, the only features visible, his eyes and his teeth, which were very visible for he had a huge grin on his face, he looked at the Black-Islers who, although they had seen the big harbour guns in action, they all stood agape, eyes and mouths wide open, it took several minutes for the smoke to clear; there was a scene of devastation when it did, as far as they could tell the gun hit the fifth log in the middle, there was a large hole with ragged edges, all ten logs were damaged, the edges of the blast area were simply shredded, the look of astonishment on Muklah and Brakko's faces changed to one of joy.

Senior bid them follow him up to the wall, "We'll inspect the damage and see the effect on the stone shot."

The wall was ruined, had this happened at sea one shot on target would sink any ship, there were chunks of black rock shards embedded all over the wall, but the splintered ends were the worst, nothing like this had been seen before, Junior said, "When that shot struck, the stone must have burst into these shards, these logs are ten times thicker than a ship's planking, that single blast would not only sink the ship but slaughter anything on the other side within twenty feet!"

"It'll win wars, son, that is certain, my lord, we'll repair the wall immediately and test the second gun."

"Bugger that!" said Muklah.

"Aye. Bugger that is right," Brakko interrupted.

Muklah turned to Sito, "Get these guns on the wagon, all future testing will be done at sea, Troi, a wagon will be here every day expecting to pick up four finished guns at least, any less is unacceptable, do you understand?"

"Yes Lord, I do."

"Good now, it's getting dark and these men need food and sleep, they'll eat and sleep in the barracks tonight, but there is a limit as to how much that can accommodate or so I'm told, so instead of rebuilding that wall, Sito and his men can begin work on a stout cabin build with your range logs, the forge crew will be too busy, and get those shot stones up on the wagon as well, I will be expecting more ammunition of this type, spend more time on that than forging iron, I'll expect two per gun for sea trials."

"Could I speak, Lord?" Junior was so proud of his guns he couldn't bear the thought of anything going wrong in his absence.

"Make it quick, lad."

"My Lord, please make sure you strengthen your ships in all the right places, that bad boy kicked up on his backside, when he hit the back-stop rods he bent them, tell the carpenter—"

"No need Lad, go and get your gear, enough for a couple of days and grab some food for the trip, you're coming too."

"Thank you Lord, thank you!" And he ran off to the cottage to collect what he needed, and tell his mother he was going to the capital. By the time he came back the wagon was up at the forge waiting and Sito's men were bringing down a log on the single log trolley, they dumped it on a quarter acre of level ground, lying vacant by the side of the existing barracks, he hopped ain the back with his guns and sat himself down on the straw stacks. The wagon driver clicked his tongue and flicked the reins and the wagon moved off slowly, sluggish with the weight and the driver thought, *Stars above, I'll be on the brake the whole way down.*

The guard saluted them through the gate and Troi waved to his Father and Mother who was by his side now, his mother was crying and his Father thought, *First time in the capital, Son, and no way to enjoy it.*

But Troi junior was thinking, *I'm going to be in forge-lore forever, right next to Grandfather.* He was right and he couldn't care less about the capital. *This is history*. Troi said, "Carry on men, I'm just gonna walk mother back home."

Mother was still looking longingly at the leaving wagon when it stopped, but it was only the driver lighting his front lanterns before going downhill, it would be pitch black before the bottom.

"Come Mother, he'll be okay, he's a very valuable man, you should be proud, I know I am. Please Captain Kile."

"Yes Troi."

"Will you join me in the forge when I return?"

"I will, Troi."

"Good, we have two cannon waiting to be poured before it's too dark." Troi dropped his wife at the cottage door and returned to the forge.

"Thank you, Captain, this ladle has been ready for hours." He pointed to the ladle on top of a furnace filled with molten metal, bubbling exactly as it should be. He walked over to the open top furnace and picked up a pair of heavy leather gloves, "Put these on, Captain." And he handed them to Kile.

"Kile's my name, Troi."

"Right then, Kile it is." And he put on the pair of leather gauntlets.

"When I say okay, pull this chain downward till I say stop." And he demonstrated but let his hands slip over the chain, "And when I say down, you pull this other side of the chain, it's the chain so down for up and down for down yes?."

"Yes." Troi then grabbed the forked end of the bar attached to the ladle perfectly weighted on the other side.

"Okay; up." And Kile did as he was told.

"Stop." The lifting block ran on wheeled overhead trolleys one going across and one running length wise. Troi took the few steps to come to level, ladle spout to mould hole he placed the spout, centre of pot ladle on the bottom of the pot he aimed it precisely by eye and slid a lever at the bottom of the pot, to allow the liquid metal to precisely fill the mould, he cut the pour off when he was satisfied, and moved across to the next mould and repeated the process, happy he returned the ladle to the furnace.

"Absolutely flawless, Kile, did you see what I did there?"

"I did, Troi, very interesting."

"Good 'cos you're pouring in the morning."

"Very good Troi, as you say." Kile had a huge grin, and Troi thought, *A lot of grinning Black-Islers around here today, grinning because they're not being soldiers, I do hope we don't have to kill them all.* He showed Kile the routine for closing down the forge safely for the night and they left together, no need for locks when they stepped outside across at the barracks the others were having a heated debate about the style of the new accommodation, it seemed the forge boys fancied a seven bedroom log cabin with the others insisting it had to be military, as they walked up, Sito said, "It's a military billet and that's it."

"Agreed, Captain Sito, that is it, is that clear?"

"Yes Captain." Unanimous.

"Everybody starts at first light, yes?"

"Yes Captain."

"Right, get yourselves fed and watered and get some sleep, goodnight," Sito said abruptly.

"Goodnight Captain." This left Troi, Sito and Kile.

"Well men, if we can get through that amount of work every day we're on the right road, we have two finished cannon in there, Kile, we need four, you and I need to get in there finishing two of the rough casts early, I don't know when the wagon will arrive, after we send that load down we are cruising."

"Then we will be cruising."

"Sito, when you finish the new billet, I'll make sure I find something else for you and your men to build."

"Thank you Troi."

"Right, food and sleep for me, my Captains, I'll see you at dawn's first blush, Goodnight."

"Goodnight Troi."

Arriving at the harbour in pitch blackness, Muklah had the wagon driver take the wagon straight to the stable yard, when they came to a halt, Muklah hopped off the wagon like a teenager.

"Right Brakko, Sisk, Troi, come with me, you." He said to the driver, "Leave this here for the night and await my call in the morning, right boys, it's down to the castle for us, I feel like a drink!" He led the way out of the yard and through the back gate.

He burst through the back doors like a bull, a very happy bull.

"Crall," he yelled, "where are you!"

"Right here, Lord," Crall said walking around the corner, closely followed by both sets of relieved guards.

"Crall, bring copious amounts of ale and wine to my quarters, and see our young genius here gets all he desires." And he put his hand on Troi's shoulder and told him, "Troi, go with Crall here, he will look after you, right Crall?"

"Right Lord, please follow me, Troi." And they left for the kitchen.

Muklah headed to his chambers then with the rest trailing behind, again he burst into his chamber and began pacing back and forth, he was muttering to himself too. Crall came in with his pre-prepared tray and left, but not before Muklah and Brakko filled and drained their big horn mugs and were starting on their second.

He had left Troi one of everything that was on the tray, from his pantry, and a mug of ale; Troi had a mouthful of fish pie when Crall got back, he'd never tasted the like of it before and, his ale-horn was empty. Crall filled a pitcher of ale for Troi and filled his horn as well.

"Well Troi, what have you done to please our Lord into such generosity?"

"I made his new cannons."

"You did what?"

"I made his new cannons."

"Why?"

"Because as my Father says, we are providing jobs at the mines, the forges and the harbour, as long as they need us, we're safe just like you, I'll bet you created a few jobs yourself, no?"

"Yes, of course I did, I just never thought of it like that, guns being involved and all sorry, I misunderstood, but what happens when he has all the guns he needs, or is making them himself?"

"Nothing works for them without Tolians around; whenever they try to mine their own, they can't get a stone chip out, so they are beaten from the start."

"Sounds good to me, well, that's your cart in the corner you can eat or drink anything on the table, I do not expect an early start from our lords Muklah and Brakko but Lord Sisk is regular as the dawn in summer, thankfully he's no work at all really, he can even be kind, goodnight Troi."

"Yes Crall, goodnight."

Sisk had already made his excuses and left, thinking on his way to the nice supper that he knew waited for him in his quarters. *Let them make a mess again, let them sleep the morning away, I'm even barred from moving the cannon to the harbourside and that's the only wagon capable of carrying four cannon, ah well, I've got some writing to do anyway.*

Chapter 38

Toli, Anga and Shala strolled into the council chamber wearing normal day clothes except over their cotton shifts and leggings they wore their royal tabards, for their visit to Dalri, the atmosphere today was much more relaxed and only the Kings guard and members of the head council were present this morning, everything else in the valley seemed tranquil, not so behind the scenes everything was being geared for war, the elders of Beeth and Tabunti had gone to their own people to bring them up to date, and they were greatly relieved, they all thought war was going to be immediate and were glad to hear they had more preparation time.

Shala hopped into her usual seat and, as Toli went to sit, Anga grabbed his arm and said to Briq, "Commander, the King and I would like to have our morning meal outside on the veranda today please." The head of the serving staff saw a light nod from Briq and bolted from the chamber to organise a setting on the veranda.

"As you wish, my Queen, things are in hand as we speak."

"Wait a minute, what about Shala?"

Anga smiled at Toli and called at the door, "Tak!" And in came Tak in day clothes with his light blue tabard, emblazoned, now, with the purple ship of the King's navy; he was the happiest person in the land, it did not occur to him yet that he was about to become a member of the King's entourage, he sat down next to Shala and the two began gabbling straight off. Anga took Toli's arm and encouraged him to the stairs up to the veranda, it wouldn't do for the King to be seen being led by his intended Queen. They walked onto the veranda in the light of a perfect morning, right up to the wall, Toli blinked as he looked at the beauty before him.

Funny, he thought, *I swear I can see past Beeth, must be the clear air.*

Anga sighed as she looked up the lake then she turned to face Toli and said, "My darling King, there is no happier being in the world this day." And they hugged and kissed and were looking over the lake, arm in arm, when a commotion behind them caught their attention, they turned around to see six people hurriedly setting a table, close enough to the edge of the veranda, but not so close as to be disturbed from below, it only took a few seconds for this to be completed and they left.

Toli and Anga sat down across the table from each other, sideways to the lake, so they both had a view. Toli ate in silence enjoying the serenity of the morning, when they were finished eating, Toli reached across the table and took Anga's hand in his, he leaned forward and said looking directly onto her eyes.

"So let's fill the King in on the story of the cabin boy and the Princess, if you please, my queen!" And he sat back and folded his arms across his chest, Anga threw her head back and laughed.

"My King need not be concerned about the relationship between the cabin boy and the princess, I know it, my love, those two are on the same path and on it together, they will be faithful friends forever, what develops from that friendship in the future, is in the future, and you and I cannot, must not, interfere with fate, but if you believe I love you and Shala, believe me now when I say that Shala will come to no harm when that boy is around, oh and he's not a cabin boy any longer; he's now a full member of the King's navy, and is now the Princess's companion and will be with her a lot, not during council, of course, but you and I are going to be seeing a lot of that young man, so we'd best get used to it, don't you think…my King?"

"Whatever you say, Anga." And he took her hands again. "My Queen."

Briq came out onto the veranda then and said, "I apologise for the interruption, Sire, but your carriages have arrived from Dalri."

"We'll be right out, thank you Briq, please tell the others on board."

"Yes Sire, if you will permit Sire?"

"Yes my friend, what is it?"

"The Valley-folk of the council request you will allow them to remain here, just in case an urgent message arrives in your absence."

"As you wish, Briq, and thank you."

"No, thank you, Sire." And he left.

Toli leaned over the table, then kissed the back of Anga's hand. "Duty calls, Queen Anga." And they walked arm in arm down to the pier where two carriages waited, the Generals and the lads in the back, all still in mail, with tabards, they loved their mail! Shala and Tak were in the back of the front carriage already, they did not even notice Toli and Anga climbing into the thing they were engrossed in their own chatter, the driver flicked his reins and the two jet black, long-maned Garrons, moved to a walk, another flick and they moved to a trot.

They followed the well maintained road, the beautiful horses rapping a pleasant rhythm on the hard packed chips. Going along was so pleasant even the constant chattering behind them faded to nothing, about halfway through the short two mile journey the horses slowed to a walk then stopped in the middle of the road. "Is there a problem, driver?"

"No Sire, some of your subjects wish to pay homage." And he pointed to the tree line with his crop, which had never been used as a crop, more like a prop.

Toli saw them coming out of the forest then, close to the road at this point, and they formed a line and each of them bowed their heads once. Toli stood up in the carriage, he did not have a clue what to say, so he raised his right hand and called out, "Thank you, my friends, very much indeed."

There were wolves, deer, mountain goats and lions, wild boar, all the animals of the valley forest, one male, one female, save one exception, a massive black bear stood off to one side on his own, the driver gave the horses a flick, and the horses moved off slowly enough so as not to cause Toli to stumble, Toli raised his hand again and the beasts of the forest bowed once and disappeared, like mist, back into the trees. Toli sat down and the horses moved up to a trot again.

"Well, what do you say about that?"

"You are a very popular person, my love, a very popular King."

The episode with the animals had silenced the two in the back but approaching the city they were back to their gabble-chatter, before they reached the city Toli turned around to them.

"Right you two, pay attention." They shut up instantly. "From here on in, and for the rest of the day, you will speak only when it is relevant, when you are asked a question, or if you wish to ask a question, and I do not mean questions of each other, questions of relevance to our visit today, do you understand?"

They lowered their eyes and mumbled in unison, "Yes."

"Good because if you want to be part of the royal party, you'd best act like it, or they'll be no more kite flying or any other favours, is that clear?"

"Yes."

Toli smiled, "Good, all is well then."

Very soon the road forked, left, for the pier, and right, up to the door of Dalri guild house. The three elders were waiting, hardly able to contain themselves, they had met the King and the royal party before, but they were so proud that royalty saw fit to grace their very important city. Courtesies aside, the elder Slaq bid them follow the elders into the hall, no need for time consuming introductions, and, since the entire population were otherwise occupied, there was no throng and no speeches.

Entering the buildings atrium, they were met by ten mannequins facing them, each wearing an ornate belt with an ornate scabbard containing a sword with an ornate pommel. The Generals nearly leapt at them.

"Please!" The elder Tilq said and directed each of them to their own mannequin, royals first of course, and bid them fit their own swords, there was one there for Tak too. Each sword when in its scabbard, stopped at the same spot on every individual's calf, just below the knee. Tilq said, "Adults needn't bother, but like your armour, Tak and Shala, your sword will always fit you thus, always stay the same length in respect to your own growth."

The lads, the Generals, Toli and Tak all drew their swords and looked at them in wonder, beautiful, weightless.

"They will never be blunt or chip, if you misplace them, you will find them, or rather they will find you, and no other person can touch it if the owner forbids it." Anga and Shala drew their swords then and immediately became entranced in their own sword's beauty.

After a minute, the third elder, Craq said, "Please sheath your blades and follow me." They reluctantly did so and followed the elders to another room, gleaming clean, where two men stood, each at a wheel, winding wire onto a drum, the wire came from a hole in the wall opposite, about ten feet away, the men on the wheels simply kept the wire taut and guided it onto the roll. *Torture*, thought Matak, but the men were engrossed in their task, working the metal they call Tarmin.

"This is the same wire drum as you saw on Xing's kite, this one is our special gift to you, Princess, it is almost finished."

Shala was 9 again and let out a squeak, trying to be royal, "Thank you." The words barely audible, she thought she might scream.

"Please, this is a good time." And Craq showed then into another, bigger room. "In a minute, you'll see how it is done, we cannot fabricate another one until yours is replaced by an empty drum, but I'll explain the process to you."

A second later there was a click and an arm which had been pushing something began to return, in a smooth action, when it came to the end of its backstroke the operator pulled out a lever and the whole thing stopped. Craq brought them to the end.

"If the stroke is allowed to operate this lever here," and he indicated to a small lever a hairsbreadth from a trip-bar on the piston, "It opens this furnace door which allows our metal to pour into this channel, the channel is a kind of mould, then when the time is right he pulls his lever and the trip closes the furnace again, the metal is allowed to cool to yellow-hot, he pulls his lever again and the bar is forced through here, it's a tapered die through a heat chamber which keeps the correct temperature for pressing and it comes out in the next room as you seen it, your kite will be ready tomorrow, Princess."

Shala nearly choked, again in a squeak, she said, "Thank you."

"Now to the mail room, the mail you are about to see being made now is for your people at the settlement." Stepping out the back between the two buildings, there was a water wheel, only the upper half showing, almost the full width of the gap between buildings, but no stream, the wheel was free spinning in the underground stream invisible above except the water dripping from the paddles.

Slaq pointed to the ratchet on top of the push rod outside the building, when engaged this one operates the press out here and this one he indicated the other side, is geared to press in here, and he brought them into the press room with Slaq saying, "Same process, different gauge, it's through here that it changes, the wire comes out the hole when it exits, once again this little trip operates and the soft metal is chopped the next one forces it out and the trip back, and it goes on until the whole bar is links of chainmail, the links are put into a warm tray then next to a mail-tailor who built his or her suit on a mannequin with the dimensions of the wearer, guess whose is Nana's?" Shala giggled.

"Then they build the suit with warm malleable links for a perfect fit, closing the warm links as they go, as the suit settles and cools, instead of the links opening in contraction our links close, permanently, and its wearers forever, these are going down on the barge tomorrow."

"What a place!" declared Tadesh. "What an army you must have!"

"Yes General, the King's army is unbeatable, as we will prove very soon, now if you are hungry, food and wine are waiting in the guild house." And he led them back the way they came.

The fare again was tasty and plentiful, and Anga and Toli had a chance to talk, for Shala and Tak were back to chattering, albeit muted, and the three elders were being bombarded with questions from the Generals and the lads. The day wore into evening, with everybody talking on the subject they enjoyed.

Anga said, "We'd best be getting back now, we got lost in the day and there may be messages, although if there was anything urgent, Briq would've sent a rider, but still no time now for the mine."

Toli stood up. "I apologise to our host, but I have to ask my company to make ready for Bevak, we will not make it to the mine this day, I am so sorry, please pass my sincere regrets to your miners, I'd like to be there if anything changes and the sun is dropping west."

"No need to apologise, Sire," Tilq said. "The ore is special Sire, the mine is just a mine, and our miners will thank you for even thinking of an apology, Sire, your carriages are ready as soon as you are."

They all climbed into their places while Toli and Anga thanked the elders. "Thank you for a perfect day, I've never seen my friends and Generals so interested in anything."

And Anga said, "And thank you for your wonderful gifts, you have made your Princess extremely happy, goodbye for now, friends."

"Goodbye for now," the elders said together.

Anga and Toli climbed into their carriage and they moved off at a trot waving and calling their thanks, as the carriage swayed along the road rocking the contents gently, Shala yawned and said, "What a wonderful day." And put her head against Tak's shoulder and went straight to sleep.

"Yes, it really was." And Anga fell asleep on Toli's shoulder, Toli rested his head atop Anga's and he too fell asleep.

Not even dark yet, Tak thought, unable to move.

When they got back to the garrison, the lads and dads were still having an animated discussion about the amazing things that could be done with that amazing metal. The front driver jolted to a stop to wake his passengers without having to shake them, they all opened their eyes, brought themselves awake rubbing eyes and shaking heads except Tak who spent the whole trip terrified that the King or Queen would turn around and see Shala snoozing on his shoulder, all three got off too dozy to notice, and gratefully Tak followed them out of the vehicle. Toli, pulling himself together now, said to Tak, "Tak, there may be council business to be aired up in the council chamber tonight, if so, you may join us for supper if the business is done by then, I shall send you a message either way."

"Yes Sire, thank you," and as he turned to go, Shala called after him, "Goodnight Tak."

"Goodnight Shala," he called back, and went for his own snooze in his new cabin aboard the Queen Shaleena.

An escort of royal guards brought them up to the chamber; when they were all seated again, Toli said, "Any developments?" Briq, Quor, Bri and the Kings guard were the only people left in the chamber, the rest had gone off to fulfil duties or visit friends and family.

"No point in us all being here for one bird, maybe even none Sire, I hope you don't mind, Sire."

Briq explained, "I gave the permission myself."

"Not at all, Briq, we are all weary, our brains need as rest as well as our bodies, nothing important then?"

"The only thing of significance, Sire, is that there will be four new cannons a day going for fitting, it looks like they will be tested at sea, more men have gone up to the forge to speed up the casting, and young Troi went down to help with fitting and testing, both Trois are a party to our 'Generals in hiding' plan and can be trusted, so, no, nothing important, nothing immediately urgent, all of this is to our benefit, Sire."

"Yes for now, Briq, tomorrow we must face the problems of the Green Isle and the Friendly Isles, both meant to sail on first tide tomorrow."

Shala yawned and said, "At first tide tomorrow, send a bird to the Friendly Isles and the Green Isle telling them that they are having such a good time they have decided to visit with their seldom seen friends a little longer, have you sent out the bird to the Black Isles yet?"

"No Princess, we were waiting for your return."

"Send them all together tomorrow, that way we can more easily keep track of the day's problems in a matter of minutes."

"It will be done as you say princess." said Briq.

"Well, we did a great deal of talking in Dalri, and not so much eating," said Toli. "I fancy some supper and an early night."

"Yes to both." Anga had seen how tired Shala became. "Shala, maybe we should let Tak rest too."

"Tak is expecting to supper with me tonight, and he will, we're all retiring early any way."

"Briq, could you send a guard for Tak please?" Anga knew argument was pointless.

Dark outside now, supper was being served when Tak arrived and placed himself beside Shala, supper was a fairly quiet affair, the last few days had taken a heavy toll, and the sudden relief of pressure to act had deflated them all, pitch black again outside. Worq came striding through the door immediately on the left of the Dragon's Tail, he strode up directly to Toli and Anga, "Please forgive me, my King, I know about the red sunset, I know for sure!" Toli and Anga were alert now, Worq seemed very agitated.

"Please explain, Worq." Anga felt concerned, she could not explain why.

"I have been looking at the stars tonight," by now he had everyone's attention, "as soon as they showed their light, as I studied them last night after your late council, I could not find any clue as to the reason of the red phenomenon, I was so frustrated, I decided to call a halt for tonight as my eyes were closing with fatigue, I sat at my table and poured myself a small glass of wine, white wine Sire, and while I was still studying my star chart, I inadvertently knocked it over, it slowly turned red, Sire, then my chamber began to throb, or so I thought, and the walls, my chamber is a magma bubble, Sire, part of the mountain, as the throb continued, the walls began to blush red.

"I ran to my window thinking it was happening again, all was normal, so baffled I sat on my cot and the blush deepened to blood red, it cast a hue on everything, then bang! like a punch in the head, it hit me, Tarmea was telling me, the sunset was the choice of the mountain, Tarmea's aura caused the sun to redden, the message was Tarmea welcoming back a lost child, lost blood, the same night as we felt your presence." And he bowed his head. "My Queen!"

Anga felt an overwhelming sense of joy at the news, she instantly knew it to be true. "Thank you Worq, I can say no more than that." Anga was lost for words.

Worq begged his leave saying he was tired before, he was drained now, and went back to his cot.

Anga turned to Toli. "It seems, my love, that we have more than our love to thank the Invader for." There were tears on her cheeks.

"It would seem so, my love…still going to kill him."

Anga sniffed and said, "Ah yes, that's a given."

Tak asked Shala politely for permission to take his leave, sleepily granted, he left for a good long sleep, he'll be up when Shala is up, that's for sure. The rest of the council members said their own goodnights, somehow less formal tonight, and wearily made their way to bed.

Chapter 39

Khoul, the wagon driver from the day before, woke up in the stable hay loft, he was too exhausted to go any further, his arms and chest were aching from the effort of yanking on his break all the way downhill from the mine, could his horses talk, they would tell the same tale, horses do not do well downhill at the best of times, and the idiot Muklah could not have cared at all if they had both dropped dead, as long as it was after the cannon were down the hill.

Crall had left a tray of food for him while he slept, he mentally thanked Crall, for he knew he had three buggers inside that required attention at the drop of a hat. *Worse than new-born babes*, he thought. *I'd rather deal with my horses any day.*

He had finished his food and was grooming his horses, after their food and water, when Sisk came up to him from the castle, the sun was already up, so Sisk was up.

"Good morning Khoul, how are your arms? Don't think I did not notice your pain yesterday, we will have a special bogey made for the forges after today and the guns will come down by the rail, there were none available yesterday, and Lord Muklah was in no mood for delay, but I'm sending you up when Manni arrives, all we can do is wait, my Lord Muklah forbade me move the guns one inch without his presence, so for now we are in the hands of fate, I'm going back to the castle now to see if I can hurry your day along, I'll do my best but don't count on it."

Well, maybe the traitor has a conscience after all! Khoul thought. *At least he had the grace to let me know.*

Just as Sisk got back to the Castle, Manni drove his team into the yard.

"Hey Khoul, nice to see you again, are you okay? you look a little green about the gills."

"Aye, fine as I could be after yesterday," and he proceeded to tell him all about the day before, and the reason Manni was here.

"Okay, we'll bring up a second brake with us and get it fitted up at the forge, that way we'll brake two wheels instead of one, it'll stop us skewing all the way down and your big wagon is set up for a second brake already."

"Brake's already on the back, I never thought I'd actually have it done, I've been putting it off for ages, I'd do it myself now while we wait, but I don't have the nuts or bolts down here, never asked for them, stupid really." The first guards Sisk came upon were Muklah's.

"Well men, any movement inside yet?"

"Yes Lord Sisk, Crall has since gone in with our Lord's food and has gone to get Lord Brakko's now, he's roaring for his, blaming Crall for not having the sense to wake him on such an important day, his life may be in danger, Lord, Lord Brakko is screaming mad."

"Is he now?" Sisk had no intention of taking any waffle from the man he called the Oaf, and regarded him as exactly that, an Oaf.

Crall came from the kitchen with Brakko's breakfast trolley, huffing and puffing, sweating profusely, and muttering in panic.

"Ah Crall," Sisk said pleasantly, "allow me to escort you to Lord Brakko's chamber."

"Thank you Lord, I appreciate it."

In the time it took to get to this stage of the day, mid-morning, Crall had fed both sets of guards, Sisk himself, first naturally, Muklah and Troi junior, still in the kitchen, well fed and ready to go, again not going anywhere until Muklah calls him. Brakko's guards were nervous, normally when their Lord is in this humour, someone gets hurt or worse, killed, luckily today it looked like Crall.

"Is our Lord in a bad mood today, men?" he asked, not caring at all.

The duty Captain answered, "Yes my Lord, better to be on this side of the door today I think."

"Where is that lazy dullard Crall, if he is not here in one minute, his life is forfeit."

The doors swung open, no knocking, and Sisk led Crall into the chamber.

"What is the problem, my Lord Brakko? Did Crall offend you?"

"Offend me? Yes he bloody offended me, I've been waiting hours for this minion to feed me so I can get to the harbour to blow something away."

"Is that so?" What Sisk really wanted to say was, *Is that so, you feeble-minded moron.*

Brakko looked puzzled. "Yes it is, what do you have to say about it?"

"Not much really, except to say, my Lord, that last night, if I recall accurately, our Lord Muklah expressly forbade us all to do anything until he ordered us to, is that correct?"

"Well yes, but—"

"I believe his instructions were, to all of us involved, do not do anything until I call you."

"Yes but—"

"Did he call you?"

"No." Brakko looked at his toes.

"Then I suggest we, that is we, who were instructed to wait, lest we spoil my brother's good humour, wait, agreed!" Sisk had used the term "my brother" deliberately, to stunt the flamin' oaf's ardour, Brakko on his part had seen the performance of the cannon and stupidly had thought his chance was, at long last, on the horizon. *Take it easy, Brakko*, he said to himself, *Reef in your mainsail.*

"Yes, agreed, wait."

"Very well then, I myself am going to wait Lord Muklah's call with the smith, in Crall's kitchen, I shall see you at my Lord's convenience, let's go Crall." He shooed Crall out and closed the door behind them.

They had only been back in the kitchen two minutes when there came a knock at the door, one of Muklah's guards was at the door, "My Lord Muklah wishes you and the smith to join him now to go to the stables, someone has gone for Lord Brakko, Lord Muklah awaits you in his chambers." He turned and went back to his watch.

Before Sisk and Troi reached Muklah's chamber, Brakko and his guards came up behind them at marching pace, Brakko could barely stop himself running. Muklah stepped out into the corner as Sisk arrived.

"Aha," he said. "All ready, let's go, guards you stay here." He pushed his way through the throng and went out the back door and they hurried themselves along to the stables. Crall had gotten a message to Khoul, Lord Muklah had wakened and was eating, now might be good time to have things prepared.

The Lords and Troi came into the yard like a rushing wind, the horses stood in harness ready to go, Lord Muklah did not seem to care he hadn't given the order, in fact Khoul had a feeling it would have been much worse had he and Manni not been ready, *Good old Crall*, thought Khoul. When all were boarded, Khoul clicked and flicked, and the horses whinnied in protest, they too were sore.

"Who's this?" Muklah asked Khoul of Manni.

"It was my idea, Lord," Sisk admitted. "Coming down yesterday, our driver, Khoul, took all the weight on one brake coming down from the forge, luckily he had the strength and the ability to control it, had the single brake snapped or had Khoul allowed us to slew, we might never have seen the light of this day, so today, since four cannon are coming down, I thought to ensure a smooth trouble-free descent, we could fit a double set of brakes on and ensure our cannon smash our enemy ships instead of our own supply-chain, and two brake men will manage slewing as well as stopping."

"Yes Sisk. Very good." Muklah hadn't heard a word, just the noise of speech, he was eyeing up the Black Kraken, majestic, awaiting her guns. Khoul pulled up under the lifting tackle on the dock, before he was at a stop he shouted at a stevedore, "You, get more men and get these beauties aboard, right, Troi, with us, you two up the hill as soon as they're off." Then he leapt off the wagon and sped up the gangway into the ship, with Brakko breathing down his neck. He called to the harbourmaster, "Hi, you, go and tell your men to take out another three captured ships for sea trials."

"Yes Lord." The harbourmaster already had three ships manned to take out for the harbour guns to destroy, all he had to do was tell one crew to stand down and send the other two out. No sooner than the guns were off the back of the wagon than Khoul had his garrons backing off the dock, he reversed the horses into a forward facing position and he jumped back on next to Manni, and got out of there before the lunatic changed his mind.

The stevedores dropped the two guns on the deck. "Right, what now?" Muklah asked.

If Muklah or Brakko could fire these guns on their own, right now, they would just because they could, but they couldn't, not yet.

"Well Lord, first let me say, your craftsmen have the same idea as me about this setup. They have gun carriages, not saddles, so you can run them out for firing, tight up to the bulwarks." Troi had been up later than the rest, studying the names of things on the ship, a ship's top deck anyway.

"And run them back for loading, I presume we have ramrods and powder aboard, and a pail of water."

"A pail of water, what for!" Brakko was impatient to destroy something, anything, with 'his' new weapon.

"We don't want to ignite the next charge with the sparks left in the barrel, from the last shot, the early smiths learned that one pretty smartly, after two of them were obliterated on the same day."

"Okay then, a bucket of water it is."

The carpenters were, by now shackling rope pulleys from the bulwark to the front of the gun carriage to run out and in and aid with aiming, also to stop the gun running across the deck, they had the basics all figured out. The two guns were ready in no time, at least it felt like it, watching and talking had been so fascinating.

"Don't worry about ramrods either," Troi said, "I've two with me, one to load, one to douse and two leather buckets for powder, they hold the same weight as the shot weighs, I think we should halve the charge for testing."

"Absolutely not!" Brakko declared.

"Move on now, Troi, that's not happening." Muklah was having none of it either.

"Right then, I'll load these two now, then refill my charge buckets, so no need to carry extra powder today, but we'll need it aboard as the guns come down the hill." He loaded both guns then, refilled his buckets from the giant powder keg on the dock.

"Okay bring it out to sea."

"Bring *her* out to sea, all ships are females," Brakko said without thinking, he was mesmerised by the entire process. The two target ships were at anchor out to sea, bobbing gently, in line, only twenty feet from the tip of the bowsprit to the transom at the stern, the harbour walls were lined with off and on duty soldiers, waiting for the never before seen spectacle.

Troi landed the starboard gun first, then ran across the deck to the port side gun, the helmsman steered, to keep the harbour wall safe from bombardment, between the wall and the targets, the targets forty feet to port. Troi unwrapped a coil of taper card from around his waist and cut it in half, he lit on of the halves and shook out the flame over the small brazier, he handed it to Muklah who blew on the end of the glowing taper making it flare, they stood by the port gun.

"My Lord, when I shout fire! Touch the burning cord to the flash pan here," and Troi indicated the flash pan, "everybody to the side now, please."

Troi walked ten feet up the deck and crouched down till his eyes were level with the rail. "Ready Lord!"

"Ready."

Troi, who knew how to hit a target, called, "Wait for it"; from the rail he could only see sky, but the ship was rolling to port now and he liked a target he could see, the top rail of the target hove into view.

"FIRE!" he roared. Muklah touched the taper to the pan, there was a huge flash, a delay, then a roar and boom, and plumes, clouds even, of dark smoke, they could see nothing, nor could they hear, nor see, the soldiers on the wall jumping up and down in delight and celebration, their ears rang, so loudly, they had to shout at each other, the ship had come to a halt, the propeller crew were below, holding their ears in pain, the smoke cleared, as the pain in their ears lessened, they laid hands on again and slowly made way again.

The target had been hit midship and there was a ragged hole in the ship, down to the waterline and fifteen feet across, the hole went straight through the ship and the horizon could be seen through the massive gap. Muklah and Brakko were enraptured by the sight, as their ship moved off the target began to sink, she heeled to starboard and slowly disappeared to the depths. Troi, all business again, took the taper from Muklah, saying, "Excuse me please, my Lord." Muklah was none the wiser, he put the taper in Brakko's hand, Brakko had a demonic look on his face.

"Please tell the man who steers to turn around and come back this way," Troi asked him.

"The man who steers!"

"Yes, the man who steers, you do want to fire the other gun."

"Bloody fool, helm! come about!" The ship came about and took the opposite heading.

"Are you ready, Lord?"

"Aye, ready."

Down on the prop deck, as it is known, the lead man called as loud as he could, "When you hear 'Fire', let go and cover your ears."

"Wait for it."

Troi lined the second ship up in the very same way as the first. "FIRE!" The effect of the gun going off could end life, again the ship came to a halt as the prop crew covered their ears until they were certain the racket was over. The ship had been hit midships again, but the shot had hit just above the waterline, causing massive damage, the shot again carried on through, as the sea rushed in she sank so rapidly she broke her back, while she sank. Troi went to reload.

"We can't fire again today," he said running in the port cannon.

"We can and we will." Brakko looked fit to kill.

"Lord, we cannot, the bulwarks are split, and besides, two targets, two shots, two sunken wrecks, we don't want to pull the flagship apart, bring her in, strengthen the bulwarks today and fire six tomorrow."

"Aye, six tomorrow, better," smiling again.

"Aye tomorrow." Muklah was coming out of his trance. "You're not pulling my ship apart just to hear a bang, Brakko, I think Troi is right, do it now, before any more damage is inflicted on my baby, helm, bring us in! We'll discuss it over a horn of ale."

"Aye, a horn of ale."

When they docked again, Muklah said to Troi, "Troi, do what you think is best and report to me when you're done, before bed preferably."

"Yes Lord, I'll come before supper to report the men here know exactly what they're doing, the setup is perfect, Lord, your baby needs a refurbish, as far as the bulwarks go, we'll put a plate of hardest wood outside and in, bolts all the way through, including the shackle bolts for the trolleys."

"Yes, yes, come before supper, thanks Troi." Muklah was still entranced, he hadn't heard a word after supper.

The Lords left the ship and made their way back to the castle, each lost in his own thoughts which were surprisingly similar, murder, mayhem and domination, but Brakko thought, *Just not with you, you fool.*

Troi left the carpenters cladding the Black Kraken, in the fashion he had instructed, all the materials required were in the harbour storehouse and were soon found, he instructed the men to clad the ship bow to stern and two men to go ahead clamping the timber together, two more hand drilling the holes, and two more placing and tightening the bolts, they were working at a decent pace, these ships will be ready easily for the new cannon before morning, the guns won't be down before dark, they'll be fitted in daylight, I'll not make a mistake to suit greedy Lords, anyway, they will not be keeping them.

"Bloody sun," he said aloud, he and senior had made this curse up, and used it when something couldn't be explained. "First time on a ship, now I'm building the buggers."

Someone ran up from the Castle then and called him up to the dock, "Crall says he is serving supper soon, he invites you to wash before your report, Muklah notices cleanliness."

Troi called to the men on the deck, "Tolians and Black-Islers alike, you boys okay to carry on?"

"Aye Troi, we'll be ready for your guns, don't worry." Already the men had taken to the hardworking Troi, able to think on his feet.

He went straight to the kitchen, ate and washed, and changed his clothes, trying to put the General's secret behind him in the meantime.

"Come on then," Crall said, "follow me." And he pushed the supper trolley out the door, he knocked and entered, left the trolley and left Troi with the three Lords. Sisk had explained on the wagon that he 'had to go back to the Castle to do paperwork, it was building up'; he could have said anything, no one heard him, except the Tolians, the other two hadn't even noticed his absence, truth be told, he hated the noise, smell and smoke of the things, and there was no chance of putting to sea with them! But he had seen their performance, from afar, there was no paperwork of any kind, but one watching the ship destroying their targets from a hidden spot, he was genuinely amazed, as the ship was coming in after just two shots, he made his way, covertly, back to the castle and sent a bird to his Mother. He was back in the Castle with his Lords again, his 'paperwork' done.

"My Lords tell me you are quite the marksman, Troi."

"Thank you Lord, I found it easy; the ship is aiming for me I could not hit a moving target with a stationary cannon on land, I suspect though, that ships further off and not at anchor will not be so compliant."

"What is your report to date, Troi?" Muklah bluntly interrupted, ships further off and not at anchor could wait.

"My Lord, your ship will be fitted with six working cannon, by noon tomorrow, I guarantee it, if I have the cannon of course."

"We'll send six captives out first thing," said Muklah.

"Only got six left," grumbled Brakko. "I counted them on the way back."

"Any ideas, Troi?" Sisk asked, trying to be involved.

"Actually, my Lord, I did think that thirty ships with twenty cannon each would require a lot of targets, so we should test at random every tenth gun, otherwise we'll expend enough powder and shot to win a war, we must never forget these things are expendable, for target practice, we could have a team of carpenters building rafts, with various size targets atop, just a timber wall, Lord, we could string a few, or many, out beyond the harbour and blast away at your convenience, but I recommend we keep an eye on supplies."

"But we're doing all six tomorrow, right?"

"Yes, we'll test every gun on the flagship, we must know the bulwarks will hold up under battle conditions."

Brakko lifted his ale, gulped it down in one and said, "YES!"

"Okay thank you, Troi, you may go."

Thank you, Sisk thought. *That lad's blessed.*

Troi went back up to see how the men were getting on, and did they need any help.

"You hit the hay, Troi, we're well on the way, we'll be home to see the children tonight, off you go and goodnight."

"Aye goodnight, I'll see you at dawn no doubt." He walked back to the kitchen, and spent a very pleasant evening listening to Crall waxing lyrical about how Sisk minded his staff and what it was like being a city dweller.

Sisk made another excuse and went to his own quarters, where, as always his own supper awaited, the other two had taken no notice of his excuse, as they were too busy plotting the fall of the world, another lie-in for the drivers in the morning.

Chapter 40

Troi senior had shown his new help around the furnace workshop, after he and Kile broke out the cast cannon up and set four of them to cleaning and finishing, they were already wheeling them out when the wagon with Khoul and Manni on it, trundled into the yard, unchallenged, they were all at the building of the new billets, on duty and all. They pulled up at the forge doors and hopped off.

"Kile, get these up on the wagon, more straw sacks over there," Troi said. "Come in, you two reprobates, we'll have a brew up while the lads load up."

"Rein in there, Troi," Khoul held his hand up, "I am not bringing these down with one brake, I'll have to fix this, before dark, I'm not the quickest." He was holding up the second brake.

"Go and have your tea, friend, we'll be loaded and have your brake fitted in no time."

"I won't say no, friend, but I will say yes, and thank you."

Troi, Khoul and Manni went in then for a brew and a late lunch, packed in the wagon by Crall, plenty for all. The talk was general gossip, nothing special Khoul could not know, he was from the harbour, even with the best intentions, he could be overheard. lKile yelled in the door, a while after they were led to believe it would be ready.

"Okay, your wagon is ready, would you like to see?."

"Yes, thank you, Kile." The three men stood and stretched their backs, and then went outside. Not only had they fit the new lever and block they had reversed the brake action and a bar set above the kick-board allowed a solo driver to operate both brakes, from the centre of his bench without even taking his hands off the reigns.

"You're very bright, boys." Khoul turned to Troi and said, "My friend, we should've thought of that, I say we, but you should have thought of that!"

"You never asked, Khoul." Troi was a bit miffed at the outburst. "And anyway, you're only up here every blue moon when you must, how's anyone to know if you don't talk to us!"

"I apologise, Troi, I never would offend you knowingly. I've been in so much pain, for so long, I lost my place, please forgive me."

"Forgotten, and forgiven, and for my part I'm sorry too."

"Right then, we'll be off to our downhill torture, made less torturous with the help of our new friends here." He lit his lamps, they both climbed aboard and left at a slow walk.

"My horses don't like it up here," he said to Manni.

"Its gonna kill them, I'll have to have a word with that Sisk fella, he seems reasonable."

"Aye Khoul, reasonable for a traitor." It took a long time to go down, but a lot better than the previous night, being both wagon masters, they looked after the horses before themselves. Crall had left food and ale for both of them, they ate and drank with relish, and keeled over and slept.

Chapter 41

Toli and Anga sat out at their new breakfast table with Shala. Tak had duties this morning but would join Shala later, they had finished their food already and Briq came up to the veranda as the three royals were silently soaking up the ambiance, the lapping of water below, the soothing breeze, warm sunshine, and the cheerful singing of the ever present finches.

"The three birds have gone off to their respective destinations, my King, and word has just arrived that they are fitting their first two guns on Muklah's flagship, and the wagon has left the capital and is headed up to the forges for the next consignment of four, he has set a target of four fitted cannon a day, he has sent help, as we know, up to the forge, which will only speed up the armament of his fleet, what are your wishes Sire?"

"Call the war council to the chamber, please Briq."

"They are all on the way now Sire, I took the liberty of summoning them already."

"Thank you Briq, we'll join you directly."

"Very good Sire," and Briq left.

Toli who had no more reservations about listening to his sister's advice, said to Shala, "So what do you think, Shala?"

"I think we'd better begin mobilisation or at least begin planning for it."

"Agreed, let's go!"

The chamber was already full, every member of the war council already there, when the three took their places, silence fell on the gathering. Toli stood up and said, "Bring the council up to date please, Briq."

Briq only spent a few seconds in explanation, a buzz of anticipation filled the air, restless military minds feeling the approach of action. There were many opinions flying around, various tactical decisions had apparently already been made by different veterans, they all clashed in some way, there was no absolute agreement being reached, it was all speculation and argument.

Anga spoke out the side of her mouth, "Shala, long enough, please speak up, this 'meeting' has taken up enough time." It had gone on thus for the last two hours, and Shala had spoken of her thoughts to Anga before sleep last night. Then Anga shifted her mouth to Toli.

"Toli! Shala wants to speak." Toli instantly got to his feet, the disorganised clamour was hurting his brain.

"Members of the council!" He had to raise his voice to attract the attention of the council.

"Princess Shala wishes to speak." And he sat down abruptly, confused in himself, feeling revenge approaching and feeling frustration that it was not now, right now! Shala climbed up on her seat, total and immediate silence fell.

"My personal feeling is this, all our troubles are on the east side of our Island for now at least, If we send a decent-sized company through the mountain at Beeth, we can go into the castle by the rear and surprise the temporary tenants, I suggest we hold their upper echelon, until the east side is under our control, I personally would like Briq and Soq, our rescuers, to pick twenty men each to take care of this task, their leaders must be dealt with in an altogether different fashion from the rest, your only trouble will be the fanatical guard of both Lords, these misguided fools are known to fight to the death for their Lords, but we will surprise them in the dead of night, when their Lords are comatose, they will be relaxed, unsuspecting, but as our Generals will tell you, they were young, but they remember how ferocious these maniacs were, gathered around their leader, their only purpose in life, to look after Muklah and ensure safety, even at the expense of their own.

"I'd like Joi and the Bevalla to take the ramp up to the harbour gun emplacements and take them back, again holding the soldiers as prisoners, if they decide to fight, show no mercy, if they decide to jump and feed the sharks, let them, but reports are saying most of the army is unhappy, they are fishermen, farmers and craftsmen and were forced into serving the Black-slug, as Muklah is known among his detractors, quietly.

"Some of these soldiers built the machinery that derives these ships and could be very useful, we don't have thirty helmsmen to take immediate charge of the converted ship, there is information to be gleaned from these people, and word is, from the forge at least, is that the Black-Islers, in the majority, would rather slaughter than save their leaders, their information will be invaluable, Tarmea will detect any deceit, am I right, Briq?"

"Yes, Princess."

"The rest of us will come directly through the forest, quietly until we can be seen coming through the meadows when we will announce our arrival with gusto, then we will see who is willing to fight for the slug and who is not!"

The room was stunned to silence, Shala looked around the staring faces.

"It's not perfect, so sorry." And Shala sat down again, feeling 9 years old again, she lowered her eyes and took Anga's hand. It was Shqin who started it, he stood up and began the rhythmical thumping, closely followed by Qwill in a few seconds the whole chamber was vibrating, Shala raised her eyes again, tears were streaming from Joi's eyes, all the Bevalla were weeping openly, thumping harder than the rest, they had always wished, even dreamed of, being in the vanguard of an army going into battle, all the action up until now, were mere skirmishes, Tarmea herself, made it clear to all who was and was not welcome, folk had very little to do with it.

"See, I told you before," Anga said. "Wait for it!"

Toli picked up his sister up and stood her on her seat, he threw his arms around her then kissed her on the cheek and went back to his place, the council cheered loudly, Toli looked around, even the lads and the Generals were crying, each one of them thinking, *Our little Shala, well I never!*, or something along those lines. He held up a hand for quiet, they all sat down.

"Well, all that is left for us mere kings, queens and warriors, to do, is work out how to get down from here to there, and when!"

"Road, lake, walk, ride, any means we can, take the rest of today and to choose who's coming and who's not, prepare for departure tomorrow and head south at first light the following morning, well if you no longer need me, I, have to go and test my kite, my Xing wings." She stepped out the door with all eyes following, in awe and wonder.

Tak's absence at breakfast, Shala knew, was that he and Storq with the crew had to fix a new kite on to the deck, he had said it half asleep last night, he was meant to say something else entirely, Storq had a full crew aboard for a trip like this, a bit excessive, but, as it was known, Storq's mantra about idle hands had passed on to any crew member he had ever had, and they would never have to be ordered, only told, what to do.

They set sail out onto the lake and Tak strapped Shala in, she said, "You next, Tak."

"Oh! Thank you Shala." Tak had not flown yet.

Back in the chamber, watching Shala leave, Toli said to Anga, "I'd like to have a go on that as well, you know."

"I know dear, I know, me too." Then Redwind screeched on his perch, Worq listened to Redwind and came over to Toli, he said, "They have tested the first two guns, the targets were destroyed with a single shot each, Sire, the Black Slugs' flagship,"—it seemed the name had stuck—"was damaged during the testing, it's under repair now, the wagon is almost up at the forge for loading, that's all for now, Sire."

Shala was up above the lake, screeching like an eagle and laughing heartily, she had been joined by Blacktail and a few others from Redwind's convocation, screeching, dipping, soaring, Blacktail suddenly tucked in her wings and dove like an arrow towards the surface of the lake, a split second before she struck the water, she pulled up, still swooping and struck the water with her Talons and swept them backwards lifting a fat, brown, lake trout from the surface, where upon she dropped it on the deck and went back to Shala. Shala signalled to come back in now, she was hurting from laughter and exertion, as soon as she hit the deck, she said, "Right, get up there, Tak, you'll love it," and he did, he had to be reeled in as light was fading.

The eagles continued to drop fish, flopping on the deck the crew dispatched them quickly, and soon the deck was awash with dead fish, slime and scales, as were the crew. Getting dark now leaving the ship, the crew were buzzing around the deck, scrubbing and splashing, laughing and joking the whole time, Shala, Tak and Storq were the only ones to escape the slimy onslaught, they had two sailors carry up half of the fish to the council kitchen, early enough so as not to disturb them in cooking supper, they had lunch already aboard ship with the crew, first, swab the deck then up to the wash-pool to scrub-up, fresh clothes and cook the fish over braziers on the dockside, up at the wash-pool one of the crew said.

"What a day, shipmates, flyin' a kite all day, eagles droppin' trout on our heads, and we're having them for our supper!"

"Aye, had I not been there and seen it with my own eyes, I'd be callin' you a liar right now, shipmate!" Another shouted, he got splashed in the face for that.

Shala walked in alone, most of the council had gone, again, to carry the councils instructions to their own folk.

"All done?" Shala asked. "Can Tak come in?"

"Yes Shala, all is as you said, Tak can come in, everyone in the Valley is party to the plan by now anyway." And he filled her in on the cannon testing situation.

"Okay, Tak, come in." Tak came in with Storq who had to pick up his own instructions.

"Please have supper with us, Storq, and we'll fill you in."

"Yes do, Storq, I believe we're having fish," Shala said and the three of them laughed their lungs out, under the astounded stares of the others.

When they calmed down a bit, Toli asked, "How do you know we're having fish, Shala?" This set the three of them off again, bursting their sides, when they caught their breath enough to explain, Shala was about to speak when a tableman came in and set a plate in front of Toli and Anga.

"Fresh lake trout, Sire," he said with pride, and the three went off again.

Shala jumped up and said, through the laughter, "Please excuse me, I must use the privy" and she ran through the door to her bed chamber, squealing in an attempt to stop laughing, for fear of having an unprincessly episode.

It took a while for Shala to contain herself; when she came back in, Storq was saying, "…and by the time we got back, the ship was awash with fish." Now they were all splitting their sides, and it took a while for them to contain themselves.

Chapter 42

Sisk and Troi came into the yard at a leisurely pace. "Please get the guns up to the ship, and get them unloaded for Troi, no need to wait for our Lords, permission is granted, I promise, I will be coming up the hill with you, but on my horse, as soon as you're done head up the hill, I'll be along, if I'm not already gone." *Which I will*, he thought. "Troi, you're in charge of operations, better to get a head start on the ship fitting before gun-play."

"Thank you Lord." Troi picked up on the sarcasm of gun-play.

Sisk went back to the Castle, to seek the promised permission, not yet granted, but would be. He explained himself away to Muklah as he ate. *Good*, Sisk thought, *another distraction*. He finished his tale with, "If we build and man another forge, we'll be able to send even more down, we might as well be ready for the second fleet as well."

"Right, off you go, Brother." Muklah had no interest in anything but making guns go off and making ships disappear.

Sisk went back to his quarters and picked up his knapsack, with food and a skin of wine in it, his horse was ready and waiting, he mounted and walked the horse out of the gate, he intended to take his time, and let the wagon catch up, he didn't care when. He was hungry a bit later and decided to eat and wait for the wagon, it would be a while, four cannon this time. *Poor bloody horses! What must it have been like for the harbour guns.*

The harbour Culverins had gone down the hill by rail, Sisk never knew, all the guns were installed by his arrival, ten years before his arrival in fact, the question of weapon transport crossed his mind, Troi would enlighten him today; now, the Tolians were in a hurry.

He finished his repast and lay flat on his back, hands behind his head, he let his mind wander to his own near future, Lord, no King of the Green Isle, Mother here, close to him, he had never met her, somehow a bird had reached him from the Black-Isles telling him she was alive and well, and that he had been lied to for the first fifteen years of his life, he was seventeen when the bird found him, and the message also described the murder of his wet nurse, mistaken for his mother, by unfamiliar soldiers; only Muklah's Father knew what she looked like, the affair was kept secret, he did not want his army to know he had been consorting with a sorceress; however, a child with magic powers will be invaluable to his plans, Sisk had harboured a well-hidden, burning hatred ever since, and had been plotting with her to mete out their revenge on Muklah since first contact was made.

The slow clip clop of the uphill side of the horses journey brought him out of his daydream he sighed, tidied his lunch site, and remounted before they reached him. The wagon appeared around a slow corner and Sisk hailed them. "Hello men, nice day for a rumble, eh?"

Khoul and Manni were startled by this sudden appearance, and Manni thought, *My stars, lucky Khoul knows nothing of the Generals, I could've been saying anything then!*

They finished the trip with conversation about the general logistics of transporting heavy guns down a hill, by wagon, if numbers increase, would it benefit the forges to use the rail line? They could use it in coordination with the mine, all it would take would be to a spur line, then another forge up and running, everybody wanted more cannon, but, now, more so the Tolians.

Coming through into the yard, Sisk took a mental note, *No guard, must look into this!*

Then he saw soldiers swarming over the new billet and thought, *Well, at least they're busy, no danger anyway.*

They pulled up outside the forge, the four cannon and shot were ready to load, and Kile and Miles, on hearing the wagon came out to load, they had loading down to two men already.

"Where is Troi?" Sisk asked Kile.

"Up beyond the firing range, Lord, he said he had something he wanted to take a look at, didn't say what."

"Very well, get these loaded, boys, no brew up today, we're heading straight down."

He rode up to where Troi was counting rail tracks, overgrown and neglected, since they stopped sending down the harbour cannon.

"My stars Troi, you must have read my thoughts, what's all this then, will these be of any use to us?" He was actually excited and making a poor job of hiding it.

"Yes, provided they haven't rusted to the point of rotting, my Lord."

"These look alright, Troi, are they?" And Sisk pointed to two rails Troi had already exposed from their weed-bed.

"These are perfect, Lord, if the rest are like these, we're on the way to laying soon, I suggest immediately after the billet is finished, keep them all busy, Lord."

While Sisk had been in conversation with Troi, he hadn't noticed the time go by, the wagon was ready, and Khoul and Manni had a brew and a bite to eat, and both were snoozing up on the wagon, fortunately, Kile who was paying attention to the movement of Sisk, shook them awake when Sisk began his return trip.

They spent more time talking about laying the spur line to Sito and his guard-builders, they were pretty pleased about the news of the track, and even more pleased when he mentioned plans for a new forge. Light fading once again, it had been a later start for the wagon, up the hill, so again Khoul lit his lanterns before clicking and flicking his beloved beasts into movement.

Sisk said to them, "Same as before, men, stable tonight, harbour in the morning, I'll see you then, I'm heading to the Castle in a hurry to give my report, I'm sure the news of the rail line will please Lord Muklah greatly."

And Troi had a thought of his own, *Aye fool, and so will our Generals.*

Arriving back in the Castle, he found Crall, pushing a supper tray for two into Muklah's chamber, he followed him in.

"Ah Sisk." Muklah was slurring his speech again, Sisk had no patience for this habit. *Just as well I am keeping a finger on the pulse of progress*, he thought.

"We have fired six cannon today, and we have destroyed six targets, comprehensively, I might add, what do you have to say to that, Brother?"

"I have this to say, Brother." And he went on to explain the proceedings of his day, the spur line and the new forge, and how the men were performing, leaving out the absence of a guard, no need to give a reason for anger to a drunken Muklah, and after he had done that, once again he excused himself saying he hadn't eaten yet and wanted to put his report in writing, he also expressed his wishes to go up to the forge again tomorrow to 'discuss plans for the new forge'.

Muklah was so pleased with everything going so well, he would have granted anything Sisk asked of him, so Sisk left and went to supper, wash, report and bed.

Chapter 43

Bevak was a hive of activity on this first day of mobilisation, Broq and Soq had already chosen their forty warriors and were loading wagons with necessities, mainly personal, for their stay in the capital, before their attack via Beeth, on the Castle. They were ready to leave now, they would be the first to leave the garrison, the warriors mounted their beautiful Destriers and set off in a column, two horses abreast, twenty ranks long, followed by five wagons one to be dropped at Beeth containing sundries, nothing to do with the coming conflict, there was a large keg of Bevak rum, among other, less important things.

Toli, Anga and Shala stood on the breakfast veranda watching Storq and his crew load the Queen Shaleena; Shala's kite had been stowed in one of the leaving wagons, there would be no room on deck for it today much to her annoyance.

Soon after the last of Broq and Soq's column cleared the garrison city limits, Shqin and Qwill led out another two-abreast column then Joi and Shivi leading the Bevalla, forty strong and the mobilisation would continue thus until the road south on the east bank was a glinting ribbon of Tarmin-clad warriors and supply wagons.

Briq and Quor were already aboard the Queen Shaleena when Tak came onto the veranda.

"My King, my Queen, my Princess, the ship is ready for departure and awaits your presence aboard." Tak too was resplendent in tabard and mail with his Tarmin sword at his side.

"Okay Tak, lead the way." And he held his arm out for Anga to take.

"I cannot Sire, it must be you."

"Very well then, follow me." And he made for the stairs. Tak fell in behind and Anga noticed Shala did too, and had taken Tak's arm instead of her hand.

They boarded without ceremony other than the usual salutes, only when the royal party were seated on the council-deck did Storq shout, "Up gangway, full sail for the capital, let's be havin', you lads." And they were underway in no time, it would take the whole day to get to Quoror even in these favourable conditions. It was just over sixty miles to Quoror and they were clipping along at six knots, slightly overhauling the soldiers on horseback who must pace their mounts.

The journey was uneventful, with Shala groaning at Tak, "We could have had my Xing Wings up, no reason not to, this is boring!"

Redwind and Blacktail were perched on the starboard rail, in case any bird had to get a message to the ship, the only message of the day was six cannon fired, six ships destroyed, the general consensus was, 'All going as planned then!' The journey was interspersed with food and drink, they all enjoyed a mug of rum at the start of the cruise and a mug of Bri's gin later in the day. Bri and the other military men were going on about the best way to go about surprising the main force, and after the gin, it became a bit silly, so Anga and Toli went up to their seat in the bow.

"We're getting one of these when we get back," Anga said with her head on Toli's shoulder.

"Absolutely, no doubt about it," replied the King.

They continued the cruise in companiable silence up until Beeth, when Anga said, "We're going to have to talk about Shala's expectations regarding the battle, Toli."

"I suppose she expects total victory, like the rest of us."

"That is without doubt, she also expects to be with us in the vanguard going through."

"Have no fear, Anga, she's definitely not coming through with us either."

"Oh I'm sorry, I didn't mean to confuse you, when I say us, I do of course mean the Bevalla, I'm going with them, in the first wave, up to the big guns."

"You are not, I will not risk my Queen and my sister's lives in battle, any battle, and I will not allow—"

"You misunderstand, my King, I ask no permission, I am going."

Toli groaned, "Then I have no say in this."

"No, my love."

"Will this always be the way?"

"Yes my love."

"Then I'd best concentrate on the considerable problem of breaking the news to Shala, I'm guessing she has her heart set on it?"

"Maybe Toli, it may be an advantage to have Tak a part of our strategy, he may be able to soften her up a bit."

"Yes, good thinking, Tak spends more time, than even you, in her company, as soon as I get a chance I'll break the news to Shala, the earlier the better!"

"And I'll have a word with Storq about Tak, I've an idea."

"Storq? Pray tell?"

"If Storq commands Tak to stay aboard the Queen Shaleena, it would be mutiny to do otherwise, then I'll go to him and bring him into our plot, if Shala knows he's not going, she may not be so adamant."

"I like that idea, but we have to wait for Quoror, we won't get them apart aboard ship."

"Agreed, but I'll have a whisper in Storq's ear before we dock."

As they continued up the east side of the Lake, just after Beeth, Toli pointed south-west, "Look Anga, I can see Tabunti now!"

"Yes, your eyesight is gaining strength, Tarmea is empowering you, you will soon be as me."

"Bring 'em in, lads, oars out, helm, make for Tabunti!"

The crew swarmed up the rigging and the sails were reefed in, a short time later, they made way under oar, for Tabunti.

"What's going on, Storq?" Toli had come back with Anga.

"Forgive me Sire, I forgot to mention, Bri asked to pick up his horse Zacko, he wishes Zacko to be with him, come the time."

Anga was delighted. "Nothing to forgive, Storq, I too am looking forward to meeting my Father's favourite friend."

As they approached the pier, the young silage-cart driver could be seen standing, waiting, with the big, patient, animal.

And Bri said to Shala, "Sorry Princess, he's the reason for the absence of your kite on deck, I could not leave him behind."

Shala's eyes were wide open and the size and looks of this stunning horse. "Please don't bother, Bri, he's amazing." Both Anga and Shala were wide-eyed as Zacko was led up the ship, to the place behind the council deck where the kite would have been.

Bri barely had a chance to reacquaint himself, as soon as he had spoken to Zacko, Anga and Shala began fussing over him, apples were called for, water, brushes, even Tak was forgotten, by the time they reached Quoror all three were firm friends. They finished the cruise under oar, Storq yelling, "Don't worry, lads, you'll get a go before we tie up at Quoror, idle hands, lads, idle hands!"

By the time they reached the Capital, the sun was heading towards the western peaks, it would be completely dark before the first of the mounted warriors got there.

Toli had planned for the Castle-folk to visit the settlement after everyone else had disembarked and the ship unloaded, but the unloading would take too long, so he had to send a bird, they message being they would 'be there for Nana's breakfast in the morning.' Toli knew Nana's kitchen would be the first priority, the highest priority, as soon as she got the message, the preparations began.

When the horse was being boarded at Tabunti and everyone was distracted, Toli saw a chance to have a word with Storq, Storq had no intention of letting Tak go to war unless the King himself signed the decree, he was glad to hear their plans accorded and guaranteed his cooperation, in a quiet moment though.

"I'm not going to embarrass the lad before his peers."

"Agreed Storq, no more than I wish to embarrass my sister."

When they were alighted, they—Anga and Toli—began the explanation planning, when Toli told her Storq was already on board, and his feeling about Tak going to war, she was greatly relieved saying, "That may just be the help we need, good man Storq."

When the council members aboard alighted, the Valley-folk went to their different duties in preparation for the arriving army which would stretch from Beeth to Quoror on the day of battle, or rather the night.

There was only the head council inside until Bri came from putting Zacko in his field to wait for company, the company of horses, the stables were full, so for now he was alone, as usual, so no problem for the unflappable Zacko.

Eventually, Storq came in with Tak, Storq sat next to Broq and Soq and Tak stomped over to sit by Shala, a shadow over his face, bottom lip out, cheeks flushed in anger.

Anga and Toli were paying close attention to the proceedings, Storq had said his piece and Tak was cornered.

"Storq won't let me go out, unless I get a royal decree, Shala, I cannot join you in the battle!" He looked at Shala hopefully.

"Join me!" Shala was now surprised. "You can't join me, Tak, I'm not going out, I'm 9, that would be one hundred guarantees disallowed, Tak, why did you think that?"

"You always say 'we' and 'us' in your plans, I assumed you included yourself in this." Tak was distraught at his mistake.

"'We' and 'Us' refers to our race in general, I myself in battle? No Tak, I'd only be a child needing looking after, you and I will be witnessing it from there!" And she pointed up and east towards the mountain.

"Maybe I have no powers," Anga quietly said to Toli, "I definitely did not see that coming!"

"Couldn't have said it any way better myself, pretty mature for a child who needs looking after, eh?"

They all agreed to recommence council business in the morning; as they retired, they could hear the first of the mounted columns coming in.

Chapter 44

The Lords Muklah and Brakko had fallen once again, into the habit of laying on in the mornings, and allowing Sisk to oversee the smooth running of everything, he watched the four new cannon being loaded, Troi had fitted them all with a stout rope slung from the bulwarks around the cannon to bring the recoil to a stop for loading, he called it the breech rope, he had also adopted a long hollow stick, with the taper fed into it, the cord could be lengthened or shortened by a long notch cut from one side which allowed the gunner to thumb the cord to suit, he simply called it the taper, it kept the gunner at a safer distance from the deadly weapon.

Sisk and the wagoners left the harbour at the same time, but Sisk was soon ahead of the slow wagon and did not slow down to wait.

By now Muklah and Brakko were having the late, early meal, with ale of course.

"Won't be long now, Brakko my friend, till we rule the world." Muklah had a half-eaten blood sausage in one hand and a horn of ale in the other.

"Aye Muklah, and when we do, it will last forever." Brakko had heard the same thing every day since the first cannon was fired, and several times before that.

"And when Vakkra gets here with the second fleet for arming, you can take a couple of the first fleet ships and go raiding for a while in whichever direction you choose, just for fun my friend, I know you're bored beyond suffering."

"Aye, I am, and I appreciate your thinking of me, Muklah, now I have something to look forward to before we set sail with the invasion fleet." But he was thinking, *When the second fleet gets here, 'my friend', you'll have bugger all to do with where I go raiding anyway.*

When Sisk reached the forge, again there was no guard on the gate, he no longer cared, there was no danger, if there had been he would have sensed it or so he believed.

Troi was out in the yard in conversation with Sito. "And then we can clear the track the whole way down!"

"What's this about clearing a track? I am intrigued, Troi, please enlighten me."

"Above the spur tracks you saw yesterday, in good condition, as are all the tracks, Lord, an old buggy that used to bring the big Culverins down the hill, it's the lead bogey Lord, and is fitted with a very sharp, arrow head, slicing bar, designed to keep the tracks clear by slicing or pushing obstacles off the rails, if we get it in position at the top of the slope, and we weight it heavily, we'll attach it back on the old drum and wheels and run it downhill, I'm sure it will, at least, make track clearance easier."

"Keep talking Troi, I'm liking this."

"I was just saying to Captain Sito, if he could lend me two men, your men are very capable in the forge, and the billet is almost finished, we could clear it out of the bush its stuck in, and when the wagon gets here, we'll pull it out to the road with his horses, our horses are strong Lord, and get it to the top of the track, the fact that we found the drum here is full, should mean the wire rope pulling drum at the bottom is empty, so the wire rope should be all the way up here, this will take four cannon a day easy, we could have more men up for the new forge build."

"Okay, Sito, pick two men, send them up to us." Sisk dismounted and walked with Troi up to the bogey, overgrown, barely visible at all.

"I'll have to make a slicer for the back, if it's coming up on its own, other than that its ready to go, I've had my head in there." And he pointed to the camouflaged bogey.

"Until that is ready, a man can accompany the load down and back with the relevant tools to keep it working, we can work out 'stop and start' signals."

Sisk was keen. "I'm going down to take Kile's report now, I'll send the horses up." He then led his own horse back on foot saying, "They're not having you, my friend, no chance!" to his horse.

On his way back, Sisk had another soldier come past him carrying machetes, one each and one for Troi. Sisk had just reached the forge door and was letting his horse off, to go to the verdant riverside, he knew he was safe, when the wagon came into the yard.

"Leave the wagon here for loading and bring your horses up to Troi, he has a job for them." He went into the forge then to take Kile's report. "How are you progressing, Kile?"

Kile jumped in shock, he had been concentrating on cleaning a cannon bore, slowly feeding the bit inside, he stopped and brought the bit all the way out.

"The four cannon outside for loading were poured and finished by us, inspected by Troi, of course, before passed for transportation to the harbour, in just a few days Lord, each of us is confident in the tasks we are given, and Troi is confident enough in our ability, to go off and create even more innovations, I believe he is working on something now, Lord."

"Yes Kile, indeed he is, we have a very valuable man in Troi, and his son below, him, his son below, he never asked me about his son, that's odd!"

"No, Lord," Kile corrected him, "the wagoners are quizzed every day, he knows they are definitely here every day, that's now his habit, Lord."

"Ah yes, makes total sense," Sisk mused. "Well, I'll be here again tomorrow, I find it fascinating up here, better than that noise and smoke, anyway I'm going to get back to the innovator and see how he's getting on."

By the time Sisk got back up to Troi, they had dragged it to the roadside and were tipping it on its side onto four legs in order to roll it right up to the rail side on logs, by taking the rear of the four logs to the front as soon as it cleared the bogey at the back, they went all the way to the rail-head in this way, and sure Troi was taking the latest news of his son with a big grin on his face.

"So the gunner is a safe distance when the gun goes off, and it stops his taper cord flappin' around when the ship's rollin'," Manni enthused.

"Clever boy!" Troi declared.

"Oh he asked me to ask you to have a look at this." Manni handed him a letter to be read with his Mother, but inside there was a drawing and a note at the bottom.

"Father," it began, "I have written a personal note to you and Mother, but I ask you to look at this drawing and consider its feasibility." It showed a section of a cannon with the flash pan atop it and by the pan it showed a lug with a hole, above this there was drawn a, supposedly steel, cap, and an arrow with instructions for fitting, the cap had a hook for opening and closing. The note went on,

"I'm having a brutal time keeping my primer powder dry, when our guns hit water we often get soaked, it's not going to work at sea in any way, unless we protect our primer we won't get a single shot off in battle, or even bad weather, Love Troi."

Easy, thought Troi, *so easy, good boy.*

The horses were hitched again to the loaded wagon, and Khoul lit his lanterns, the forge had eaten up the hours.

"I'd like to get that bogey on the rails in the morning Lord, can I use four of your men to help?"

"Do as you wish, Troi, as long as Lord Muklah sees, at the very least, four cannon a day coming down the hill."

"Your own men are on top of that, Lord. I have total faith in them."

"Good Troi, glad to hear it," and Sisk urged his horse out the gate at a nice canter, calling back, "I'll see you all tomorrow."

Troi re-entered the forge and asked Kile, "Kile, I'll ask you to finish up here, if you can do without me I'd like to go up to mother and read our letter together, it's from our son, would you mind?"

"No Troi, I would not, not one of us here isn't missing family, ours are only safe as long as we serve, I'll shut down safely, you need not concern yourself, go, read."

"Thank you Kile, I'm sorry for your family, I did not know." And he left.

Troi and Mother sat at the kitchen table with a pot of brew, and Troi read the letter to his soulmate, Mother wept to hear her son was happy, well fed and, best of all, well treated; she was so proud of his ideas.

"Just a shame it has to be for the use of scum," she said through gritted teeth.

Troi almost let slip about the Generals, but stopped himself, not for lack of trust, but for her own safety, they sat chatting for a while, Troi spent some time, after dinner, doodling a plan for a pan cover for his son, but they soon called it a day and went to bed.

When Sisk got back, he met Crall, who was waiting for him inside the back door. "My Lord," he said, "Lords Muklah and Brakko have retired to their respective chambers, I do not expect to hear from them again tonight."

"Thank you Crall, wait for me in the kitchen."

Sisk made sure he spoke to both sets of guards before joining Troi and Crall in the kitchen, he made sure he had been seen to ask after the wellbeing of the pair of shits. He spent some time talking with Troi in the kitchen while Crall served them both a meal, he told Troi his Father was pleased for his progress and had received his letter, vetted of course, and his note for the pan-cover, he finished up his supper, stood up and said, "I'll bid you both goodnight, it's report-time for me," and he left.

Chapter 45

The Castle-siders, plus Tak, made way to the settlement across the Lake in the Queen Shaleena's pinnace, tied up at the smaller pier, unused on the Lake normally. The welcoming committee consisted of Nana, Gogon, Luron, the two Green-Islers Dauti and Doulen, and Nana's advisor Roqi, everyone was busy getting on with it, whatever it may be.

Shala leapt off the boat as soon as it came to a halt, and bolted to Nana, grabbing her around the waist and hugging into her bosom. "We've missed you, Nana."

"It's only been a couple of days, my precious girl!"

"Even so, Nana, what Shala says is true." And Anga threw her arms around them both. Toli and the lads tried their best to be aloof, manly, and were failing badly.

Nana saved the day when she said, "Right you lot, follow me," and she lead them to the new building, being used for community reasons, meals, meetings, stuff like that, it was the finished article stout beans and stout furniture with Nana's kitchen and pantry at the back.

"Their food is as good as, maybe better than ours, the blood sausage is wonderful!"

Nobody said, "We know Nana, we've eaten here already," but a couple of them thought it.

The fare was cooked Nana style at least, the company of sixteen chatted happily and casually as they ate, and in this manner, they brought each other up to date with all the new although most was known already, nothing hidden in the Valley.

It was late in the afternoon by the time they were boarding the pinnace again, in fine form, one and all, happy to see each other and happy to be so close together. The only new information from the Castle was that the Black-slugs flagship had now ten working cannon and the foot soldiers would be here sometime during the day, wagons were coming and going to bring them to their designated camps.

Entering the great house, it seemed so empty. Quor was alone in the cavernous hall, everyone else had duties, mainly military, so he was doing some paperwork, it was imperative to Quor that Valley lore be recorded and kept in safety, he would never allow their history to be lost again, not if he had a say in it.

He raised his eyes as the company walked in. "Ah, how was your visit, Sire?" He stood up.

"Please sit, Quor," Toli bid him, "there will be time for ceremony aplenty coming soon enough."

"Thank you Sire," and Quor related the cannon news to the company adding, "And the slug and his idiot Commander are back to drunken backslapping again."

"They've never really been involved, in any case," Tadesh growled, "and they're dead men regardless, they do not figure in anyone's plans." A hum of agreement went around.

"By the way, Sire, Xing wishes to invite you up to the training ground to examine his methods."

Shala grabbed Tak's arm and pulled him towards the doors. "Apologies, but Tak and I must find a place to fly a kite." And she dragged Tak out the building, almost bowling Bri, on his way in, over on his head.

"What do you think, Anga?"

"I think your men must go and be warriors, I'd like to be a daughter and spend some time with my Father, if he'd like that."

"I can think of nothing better." And Bri sat down next to Anga.

"Right," said Quor, "I'll show you the way." And they left Bri and Anga on their own.

"You were going to explain why I couldn't have been left with a family here, sorry Father, I must know."

"Anga, here on this Island, families are limited to two children, with the exception of royalty, who are not, if someone takes another's child, they risk not having their own second, the child becomes their own, you see Anga, the mountain guarantees a manageable population for the space we have, you should have known that had you been here on you 18th birthday, it's part of our passing here in the Valley, however you're still 18, and I am proud to tell you now, there are no more outside either, right?"

"Yes, right."

"So if a childless couple who maybe were only going to have one child, take on another's child, and they never get to have one of their own, and if a couple has a child already, the chance to have their own second, as I already explained, any other childless couple would have reared their own and in the quiet of their lives, had I not taken the way I did, I am certain neither of us would be here now."

"Toli's Father is not here to tell him, oh Father, poor Toli." Anga was in turmoil.

Bri laughed. "Toli had three older friends, I'm sure he's heard of it at least three times." He took Anga's cheek in the palm of his hand. "I'm so sorry, Anga; I left you all alone."

"Not alone, Father," Anga perked up, "just not with anyone my own age, I'm glad I heard it from you, now let's break out a flask of your gin and discuss the family recipe!"

Quor and the others looked across a field of one hundred warriors, Xing, on his own, out in front, each warrior was in mail, with Tarmin sword in hand, they began to sway, in absolute unison, swords above heads, waving like a field of silver rushes in a breeze, exactly in time, Xing made a swooping motion in slow motion, while slashing down to his right in an impossibly slow movement, and spun, on the ball of one heel through a whole turn, he smoothly changed hands and did it again in the opposite direction, each and every warrior a perfect part of the dance of war, more and more moves came into the rhythmic action of the field of swords, faster and faster, bodies spinning, swords whirling, then leaping, kicking and suddenly, all stop, dead in mid-movement, and one hundred warriors stood stalk still, heads bowed, swords held out in front, blade up.

The Castle-siders were stuck for words, so Quor spoke first, "Well, what do you think of our Master of arms' methods?"

"A thing of beauty, if you had fallen in there, you'd be shredded for sure, but so beautiful." It was Toli who recovered quickest.

"Yes Sire, beautiful and deadly, that is just a small part of Xing's fighting style, I can assure you Sire, he had many ways to kill, effortless ways."

The group moved off then, as light had begun to fade, but Xing had not finished with his students yet, as Tadesh had a last glance at the field, over his shoulder, Xing and his followers were slipping into one-piece, black, hooded suits, chainmail and all, they were heading who knows where, Xing's night training was not meant to be overt.

The men walked passed the great house towards Beeth, no one had seen a gathering like this anywhere on the Island, foot soldiers, mounted cavalry, archers and the many camp helpers, all doing what their personal preparations required of them.

"Even your coming, Sire, did not have this amount of folk in one place, and all the watch positions are still fully manned Sire."

"Yes, good, what are our comparative numbers."

"From his thirty ships, Sire, he has around two thousand five hundred warriors, about half of these are the murderous 'Kraken Brigade' led by a fanatical warrior, Bizzo, we expect a fight from these, the rest, in the main, seem to be disgruntled, so other than the personal guard, hand-picked from the Kraken Brigade, who will already have been dealt with, we'll have about half his force willing to fight, they won't get a chance, my King!"

"Yes, we'll return his surprise visit with a surprise of our own, what are our numbers, Quor?"

"Forgive me Sire, but the war council were unwilling to discuss tactics without all members being present."

Toli looked him in the eye and smiled. "Specifically Princess Shala, eh Quor?"

"Yes Sire."

"Well, as soon as my sister has completed her mission to find a place to fly from, we can sit down as one; in the meantime, let's go in for a bite of food, we can at least discuss opinions."

Shala and Tak managed to get themselves up to the lower tier watch station, by now everybody knew who Shala was, and nobody was willing to question her actions.

"It must be important, don't interrupt her," the duty Captain ordered his men.

This particular station had a big flat area of rock out in front facing east. "This is it, Tak we'll go from here, we'll have them place it tomorrow."

The flight deck, as Tak named it, was dead centre of the forest, beyond which, the two miles of meadow chosen by Shala as the main battlefield.

"Too dark soon, for tonight, so yes, place it tomorrow, we'll need to practice flying double, the harness is ready." Shala had given instructions after her day on the lake with Tak to somehow make a harness that can fly two.

"Already have 'em, Princess, I'll just take a few measurements and I'll do a made to measure for you." Which he did.

By the time the two did all they had to do and returned to the great house, the people inside were roaring and laughing, basically the head council members including Bri and Storq.

"What's so funny?" Shala asked Anga as she and Tak sat in their places.

"Storq was just telling me the story about the eagles and the fish," she said, tears in her eyes.

"But that's an old sto—" then she spotted the distinctive keg, the same as on the ship. "Ah, Bri's gin, that explains a lot."

"We were awaiting your presence in order to make decish, decish, decisions, Sister," Toli slurred.

"All decisions are made except timing, but I think that's best left for another day, it is not immediately urgent, for me I'm having my supper and an early night, we may have many long days ahead of us."

"Wise beyond your years, Shala," even Anga was slurring her speech. "We must all follow your lead. Toli!"

"Yesh my love?"

"Food and sleep for all, yes?"

"Yesh my love." There were no complaints.

Chapter 46

Sisk had left the Castle early in the morning to go and have a word with Troi and the wagoners before heading up the hill to check on the rail clearance, he was talking to Troi when Crall ran up soaked in blood. "My Lord! My Lord!"

Sisk left the dock to try and get out of earshot. "Calm Crall, Calm." And Crall immediately calmed himself. *Power is still there when needed.* Sisk had thought his powers depleted, they had been so seldom used.

"Now tell me about what happened."

"After you left, Lord, Lord Muklah woke up and called for a fresh barrel of ale, I was bringing in a tray of food I prepared for his awakening, he was screaming for ale, Lord, so I ran to get the cellarman, the only folk in the cellar at that time were Master Brewer Barri and his apprentice, so they helped me roll a big barrel to Lord Muklah's chamber; we got it up on its trestle with the help of his guards, and as the boy tapped the keg, a jet of ale spewed out and hit Lord Muklah in the crotch, while the apprentice struggled to stem the flow of ale, Lord." Now Crall was shaking again.

"Calm Crall, easy, friend." And again he was calm.

"Lord Muklah took a battle-axe off the wall and cleaved his head, Lord, right down to his shoulders." His knees weakened then and Sisk caught him.

"Easy now, Crall, my friend, I'll deal with this."

"That's not all, Lord, when Tukon, the boy, was cleaved, his master screamed at the sight, so he got cleaved too, this is his…" and he opened his arms to show the blood all over his tunic.

"I bolted straight here, Lord, in fear of my life."

"Who knows of this, Crall?"

"Me and the guards, both sets, I'd say Lord Brakko knows by now, Lord."

"And no-one else?"

"No Lord, some may have heard him scream for ale, but the act happened behind closed doors, Barri's scream could be attributed to Lord Muklah's frustration, he was screaming a lot, and the doors are closed now, Lord, Lord Muklah was still raving when I left."

"Get yourself up to the stables, take the long way around, find a quiet corner and wait for my command, and do not tell Horse anything." *Like that'll happen*, Sisk told himself.

Horse was the nickname of the stablemaster Strall, a cousin of Crall's. *This will spread like lava*, he thought.

He ordered the wagon up the hill saying he'd follow later, he had to report to the Castle. Khoul and Manni threw a glance at each other, and mounted the wagon, they left straight away, hoping there had been progress at the rail tracks, and wondering what was going on inside.

Sisk cast a calming aura as he came to the Castle, enjoying the use of it again, the guards were where they should have been, he nodded to them and stepped into the bloodbath, closing the doors behind him. Muklah sat at his table, horn of ale in hand calmly chewing on a chicken leg.

"What happened here, Brother?" Sisk asked him.

He pointed with his food. "That bugger there shot me in my balls with a jet of ale, it hurt and I got mad, so I cleaved him, and the other bugger wouldn't stop screaming so I silenced him." No problem, matter-of-factly stated.

"Who'll make your ale now, Muklah?"

"We have plenty in store until our lot learn the method."

"I suppose so." Sisk tried to make light of it. "Guards!" They ran in. "Wrap these two up and get rid of them, and do not let any Tolians see you!"

"Yes Lord." They wrapped them in blankets and threw them in a wagon at the back gate, after that two guards brought the mutilated corpses up into the dense forest and left them there for the wild things to feast on.

Crall felt terrible, as low as a man could get and lower again, he had been giving the Lords a beer which was part honey-draught which allowed drunkenness, but followed by the deepest of sleeps, the barrel that ran dry this day was a much different brew, and could provoke fights among the meekest of men, he couldn't think how it passed his attention, he was distraught.

Sisk said, "Right then, all's well, I'm off to check on progress up the hill."

Brakko staggered in then. "Everything okay then?"

"Yes, my friend, sit and have an ale with breakfast."

"I most certainly will, my friend," and he got himself a horn and filled it, emptied it and filled it again, he plonked himself on a chair and said, "Where's all the blood from?"

As Muklah made to begin his explanation, Sisk interrupted, "Well, if no-one minds I'll go to my chores."

And the two Lords cordially said, "Yep, have a good day, Sisk" and "Okay, see you when you get back," respectively.

The guards were standing outside again and he told them, "Two of you get in and clean the blood away; again, no Tolians may know."

"Yes Lord."

He went to the stables then and picked his horse, ready for him. "Crall, you stay here with Strall till I come back down, we'll go back in together."

"Yes Lord Sisk, thank you." Sisk left to go up the hill thinking, *Nothing escaped your attention, Crall, the barrel looked exactly as it should when you saw it.* He had hoped to provoke a reaction to make Muklah look irrational. He had provoked a reaction all right.

Chapter 47

It was early afternoon when Redwind flew in the open doors of the great house and grasped his perch. Worq crossed to him and listened. "Thank you, Redwind," he said and Redwind screeched and flew off again. Toli could tell by the look on Worq's face that things had turned for the worse.

"What is it, Worq?" Toli was concerned.

Worq related to the council members present, what had passed in the Castle a short time ago; as soon as he finished, Toli asked Quor, "Quor, can you get my sister here as soon as possible please, assemble the war council please Briq, it seems we do not have the luxury of time after all."

It took several hours for the whole council to assemble, Broq and Soq were all the way up at Beeth and were last to arrive, after the Brothers had been informed of the murders, they sat down to take part in the disorganised rabble. "We must go tonight!" Tadesh was yelling. "He's killing Tolians at his own hand, for what? Spilling ale? It has to be tonight! We can allow this maniac no more chances to take our people's lives, and that is it!" There was much thumping of tables and growls of angry agreement.

Toli stood up, there was silence. "My sister wishes to speak," and sat down again.

Shala was on her chair again. "General Tadesh, if I know, you are keen to avenge your wife, we all have someone to avenge, I am afraid it gets much worse, the apprentice who was killed was Tukon, your guard's son, Gogon's son, I ask you to wait another day, we are not ready tonight, but tomorrow is another tale, tomorrow we will be ready, maybe we Castle-siders should go to Gogon tonight, or maybe just you, Tadesh, you have been comrades for a long time, have you not?"

"Forgive me, Princess, you are right, of course I should go alone, with your permission Sire!"

"Of course Tadesh, Storq, please make sure General Tadesh is attended to." And Tadesh left the great house together with Storq.

Tak wanted to help, somehow take part, so he said, "Please excuse me, Shala, I'd like to help with the boat." And hurried out behind them, he would be useless at council, he thought.

Storq and Tak rowed the pinnace across to the far bank, and stayed in the boat as Tadesh had requested they do, a few minutes later, they heard the anguished cry of a man destroyed, his wife had been killed on the first night of the invasion, he did not know this either until a rescued shepherd picked up the courage to tell him, a few seconds later they heard Nana shrieking "No, no, no!" Nana had been close to the young apprentice, then Luron heard the desperate news, and his heart snapped in two. "Please, no more," he cried.

Across the lake in the great house the council heard the terrible noise of their sorrow. "Make sure Gogon and Luron are with me in the battle tomorrow," Toli choked out the words, while fighting emotions, so strong he was shaking.

"Broq, Soq, make sure you and your men keep that bastard alive, we all, from the Castle-side, would like a word with the spawn of evil."

"Yes Sire," the brothers said together.

When Tadesh and his two crew came back to the great house, Tadesh walked straight up to Toli and Anga, his eyes raw. "Please forgive me, my King, my Queen." And he bowed from the waist. "The days have taken their toll, with your permission, I'd like to retire now, so as to be fresh of thought tomorrow Sire."

"No need to ask, Tadesh, please do as you wish, my General, the murderous slug will have to face us all tomorrow."

"Thank you Toli," he said audible only to Toli and Anga, and left for his chambers, his friends, Shouk and Matak, stood, bowed and went out the door too, the three lads were staring at Toli now, Toli nodded and the lads quickly followed their fathers out the door.

Anga stood then. "I feel it would benefit us all to be fresh of thought tomorrow, perhaps we should all retire and clear our minds for we all need clarity in our thinking and planning on the morrow."

"Yes." Toli was on his feet again. "Please go to your troops and have them ready for orders tomorrow, everyone be here at first light."

Chapter 48

Sisk rode into the forge-yard to find the wagon already being loaded, and Troi had uncovered the ropes for the downhill drum and was shackling the strong wire-rope to the front of the bogey, the uphill drum had already been fitted and the bogey was full of stone chips to give more momentum going downhill. Khoul and Manni had told Troi about the fracas down the hill, but had no more to tell, only that something had gone on inside the Castle, but young Troi was safe, he was already at work on his guns, this all occurred after Troi left the Castle.

The wagon driver, Khoul, lit his lanterns again and asked to leave, permission granted, he walked his horses out the gate to begin his downhill trek, calling back, "For the sake of my horses, Troi, get this thing movin'." He pointed at the bogey on the way past.

The new barracks were only a few hours from completion now, and Sisk told Troi to split the soldiers into two crews, two men with himself, and the rest to begin marking out the new forge site for foundations, he spent a few hours in discussion with Troi and never once mentioned the episode at the Castle, nor did Troi ask. *Best to act ignorant, my boy is safe, that's all I care about right now,* he thought.

Sisk eventually left and Troi went into the forge, running smoothly now, worryingly. "What will be done with these lads when our Generals emerge again?" He had come to realise these men were good men, valuable men, and had stated no love for their leaders.

"Kile, the evening cannon poured yet?"

"Yes Troi, they are."

"Okay, lads, you head off and get cleaned up and have yourselves a treat, an early night and a few ales, eh? Kile and I will shut down for the night." They all said thank you and left for their early treat, Troi sat down by the forge and said to Kile, "We'll shut down early too, Kile, and you can go and join your friends, you deserve it!"

Kile had heard the conversation between Troi and the wagoners earlier and said, "Don't fret Troi, your son is safe, and it's entirely possible the blood came from one or the other of our revered Lords, they have drawn blood before on binges, Lord Muklah keel hauled three of his own men on the way here, keelhauled them for drinking water on duty, so it's possible they were hacking at each other, it's not unusual, Troi."

When Sisk arrived back at the castle, the two reprobates were sound asleep as planned, so Sisk went to the kitchen to find Troi and tell him of things up the hill; no need, he'd already been out to the stables to talk to Khoul and Manni, and Crall back with Sisk, more information forthcoming.

Chapter 49

The war council reported at break of day as ordered, Broq and Soq had to send a bird there was no headway to be made last night on the Beeth road, but after orders are given today, they'll make it to their warriors regardless of obstacles, the council had to be called to order, they were all loudly exchanging their opinions from all over the chamber at the same time. Quor, after several attempts at normal volume, screamed, "Silence! Silence for the King!"

Toli, already standing, announced, "My sister would like to speak," and sat again. The entire council were enraptured before she even spoke.

"We can influence the weather, yes Quor?"

"Yes Princess, as long as we are here with Tarmea; we know naught elsewhere."

"Good, here is my plan, if there is anyone here who feels a change is needed, in any way, please speak up, there must be no reservations, clear?"

"Clear Princess," the chorus returned.

"Thank you."

Shala's a queen, not a princess, Anga thought. *It's like she's been doing this for years.*

"You all know my original proposal, Broq and Soq take your forty men as soon as the sun drops beyond the horizon, the Castle will be in darkness on the east side, you Soq, go straight through till you meet Brakko's men, his men will fight, Broq you take your men immediately right till you meet Muklah's men, they will fight too, you may have to kill them all, once you have both Lords in chains, at the end of Muklah's corridor, the off duty guards should be asleep, through that door, but go through prepared to fight.

"When the Castle is yours, simply stay put, you'll find the traitor Sisk in his chamber next to the kitchen, this is your plan of the Castle, study it and send one man each to Sisk's chamber as you enter." And she passed a map around the council for Soq and Broq. "Any questions, Broq? Soq?"

"No, Princess."

"Then go to your men now you have a way to go, your signal will be one of Xing's fireworks from the deck of the Queen Shaleena."

"Yes Princess." And the Brothers left, glad of the time allowed them.

"Joi, you will send ten Bevalla up to the short side harbour wall, they must go out with Broq and Soq and take the long way around the Castle and up from the fitting docks, there is only one Kraken Brigade maniac on the wall and he's on the long side so just chain the Black-Islers up and gag them, and again wait, you're warriors are in for a royal box view of the battle, they must not leave their captors! Yes?"

"Yes Princess." Joi was bursting with pride.

"At the same signal from the Lake, you will take your warriors through, and do exactly the same, my guess is you'll have to kill the slug-soldier, but chain the rest, gag them and wait, most importantly keep my Queen safe, my pleas to remain in the valley have fallen on deaf ears."

"Yes Princess, we will."

"Good, go and pick your people to go out with Broq and Soq and send them up there now, here is a map for them." And a map was passed along to Joi. "Please return for Queen Anga when you are done."

"Yes Princess." And Joi left.

"Briq!"

"Yes Princess."

"Choose thirty men for each of the mines, at the same signal as the Bevalla and the Castle crew, go out above the mines and secure them all, we expect no resistance, there are none of the slug brigade anywhere up the hill, leave five men with the chained captives and carry on down to the forges, to do the same, captives from the mines and other forges must be brought to the cannon forge and, again wait, a fire-rocket will let you know to come down. Yes Briq?"

"Yes my Princess."

"The watchtowers on the strand and along the sea front are unmanned, we need not concern ourselves with them." Briq turned to go. Shala said, "Wait! Briq, come back here when you're done, you are going out with the King in the Vanguard, straight for the harbour."

"The King. The Vanguard!"

"Yes Briq, the King, the Vanguard, it is your King's decision, believe me."

"But Sire," Briq was aghast, "you must be protected."

"I have my Generals for that, Briq, and you, don't forget you, Briq."

"Never, Sire."

"Good, my friend, now, take your leaders and go and choose your order of mobilisation, mounted first, in the Vanguard."

"Yes Sire," then he left with Qwill, Luq, Shqin and Xing.

"Worq."

"Yes Princess?"

"Is it possible to ask Tarmea for a fog or a cloud for cover?"

"Yes, any one of us can control a breeze, but together, we'll lay a blanket of invisibility down."

"And it can be lifted easily?"

"Yes Princess."

"Good, we would not like to behave like the slug, we'll lift it at one thousand yards, they will at least hear us coming, but we will be seen eventually even in the dark, kill anyone who puts up a fight and chain the rest until Tarmea decides if they are fit to live upon her, we, that is the head council, minus me, will then go up and visit with the slug and his dung-beetle of a Commander, where you will do nothing but wait for my appearance, I need to see his last light go out."

Anga and Toli were taken aback by the venom in Shala's voice. *You are so changed, my little one*, Anga thought, for the first time with regret.

The light was fading now and Briq came in with Joi. "Right," said Toli, "get to your positions! We go to free our folk!"

They mounted behind the great house and rode out north, Gogon had joined the Vanguard with Luron at the Kings request, and they rode up the massed ranks, thirteen wide, Toli, Bri, the lads, the Generals, Quor, Worq, Briq, Gogon and Luron, with Shala and Tak behind on their ponies.

Toli rode to his position waving at the ranks the whole way, they responded by thumping their shields with spear or sword cheering wildly, the horses stamped and snickered, all in, one thousand Tolians, as he took his place he saw Shala and Tak gallop for the lookout position, their flight deck.

No point in complaining, I'd never have won! he thought, he'd known about the Kite the whole time.

Now they settled to wait for sunset and the signal, silence fell upon the Valley, from the west side a wolf howled, then a cacophony of animal howls and cries, roars and screams, from all over the Valley.

"What's going on, Quor?" Toli asked.

"The wild things cannot leave the Valley, they are expressing their support, and their regret that they cannot help in this."

"Well I never!" The sun dropped behind the peak then and the rockets went up and Joi and Anga led the Bevalla into the Mountain, as did Broq and Soq with their company. Five minutes later, Briq said to Toli, "You must say the words, my King."

"I don't know, I don't think I can!" Toli was confused.

"Say the words, Sire!"

"TARMEA WISTWA DALAKA," Toli shouted. The woods, sparse here, opened up to the Mountain, as the Mountain opened up in corridors to allow the passage of the army. Toli spurred his horse and the army was on the move.

Chapter 50

Sisk had left the Castle late, his Lords had awakened calling for food and ale and had kept him back with their stupid, dribbling questions; there was a feeling of unrest in the air, the absence of Barri and Tukon, coincidental with the Castle episode, had aroused suspicion to the point of certainty; he felt futile anger all around him, not from any Black-Islers though, just another one of Muklah's frequent fits, to them, a common occurrence.

He felt no animosity from Troi, it was there, he just couldn't feel it, again the slag and metals confused his senses. He spent several hours up the hill, he wanted to ensure the 'two morons' were out for the count when he got back. They were, so he made a show of checking on them, and said goodnight to the guards. He went to the kitchen for supper, he was enjoying his chats with young Troi in the evenings; it was late now, only the waning moon and the stars casting a faint glow. As he made his way to bed he imagined he heard the sound of far off explosions. *Too much cannon fire recently*, he thought.

Chapter 51

Broq and Soq watched the harbour from a point just above the back gate, they waited for the black silhouettes of the Bevalla to move into their positions silently, when they were, they made their move, they crept right up to the back door, they opened the door inwards, no one in plain sight, Soq and his men dashed straight on as quietly as they could, but they had been seen; one of Muklah's guards called out, "Hey, you lot!" And went to follow, now all the guards were alert, Broq came around the corner and drove his blade through the throat of the soldier who had called out, the surprise was lost, an off-duty guard looked into the corridor and shouted, "Intruders!" and rushed back in for his sword.

Soq had better luck, they were on Brakko's guards before they realised what the call was about, no mercy, slaughter, two men bolted into the chamber and chained Brakko, wrists and ankles together, not even awake yet, the two stayed with Brakko and the rest ran back to aid Broq and his men.

When Sisk heard the cry go up, he jumped to his feet and hauled the door open, he was immediately clamped in four strong hands by his arms; he was unceremoniously on his backside and shackled in short time, in the same fashion as Brakko, Tarmin manacles, no chance of escape, Sisk was mesmerised.

Who are these warriors? Where have they come from, and why are these manacles tingling?

One of his captors ran out the door to go and join his comrades in the fray, the other drew his word and held the tip of it a hairsbreadth from Sisk's eyeball.

"I'd rather be fighting than minding you, fool, give me a reason, please!"

By now Broq and his men had beat the guards back to the door, only enough room for three men fighting wide, they came forward, inexorably, Broq in the centre, stepping over dead guards, his blade whistling with speed, by now the stupefied Muklah had been shackled too. The last of the four guards left slammed the door, Broq kicked it in and stepped into the guards canteen closely followed by three of the others. The four guards had decided to make this their last stand, Broq and his three warriors fulfilled their last wishes without another thought. He went back into Muklah then, still only semi-conscious, screaming, "Take your hand off me, scum! Who are you?" Then he stopped; his head was breaking.

Broq grabbed him by his ankle chain and yanked him off the bed onto his back, Muklah yelped. Broq dragged him into the corridor and up to the kitchen door, he looked in and saw Sisk sitting on the floor. "Pick him up and follow me, pick him up like this," and he thrust his fist forward. Muklah's feet flipped up and he banged his head on the floor, and he went mercifully quiet.

They dragged their captives into the hall Muklah had burst into only days before, Brakko was already there, whimpering with the pain in his head, still no idea what was causing this ordeal.

"Who are you, and what do you want? There's an entire army here!"

"No, there are two armies here, traitor!" Broq said.

The Bevalla had overpowered the gun emplacement with ease, but for one exception, Joi and Anga had led a band of Bevalla up to the seventh position, at the end of the long side. When they got there, a guard had just finished urinating into the sea, he pulled his sword out and opened his mouth to yell, Anga stepped forward and took his head off with a single, calculated cut, the head rolled back and went over the edge into the sea, the torso stood till Anga put her boot to the corpse's chest, and he went over the low parapet wall, and followed his head into the sea. Anga wondered at her skill and composure for a moment, then helped chain up the compliant prisoners, the guard was Bizzo, son of Bizzo the beheader, who died in the castle. They watched the thick fog roll off the mountain from the harbour wall. "Here they come," Joi said to Anga.

The fog rolled slowly over the two miles of meadows, as it approached the harbour it stopped dead as a wall, a soldier somewhere shouted, "Oi, lads, come have a look at this." A few of the men wandered out, curious. When they saw it, they too began calling for mates to come have a look at the stationary wall of fog, a Kraken Brigade Captain said, "This ain't right."

As he watched, the fog began to clear, the first to show was Toli, the Captain jumped to the alarm bell just six feet from him, he rang the bronze ship's bell as fast and as loudly as he could, yelling at the top of his voice, "TO ARMS! TO ARMS! WE ARE UNDER ATTACK!"

Now there were Black-Isle soldiers pouring from their quarters, they were coming from the barracks and houses, confiscated from Tolians and given to more senior soldiers, the Kraken Brigade was forming fast, all hardened warriors, the night shifts had become almost non-existent, there was so much work getting done in the light of day, even the watch duties had become lax during the dark hours, as a result very few Black-Islers were wearing armour of any description.

But the Kraken Brigade were rushing to the alarm and forming ranks quickly. The Tolian army had come to a halt one hundred yards from the forming ranks of the invaders elite brigade, the other Black Isles soldiers, in the main, stood agape at the glittering wall of mail, most were not even armed yet, nor did they intend to be, most thinking, *Piss on Muklah and his poxy Empire*, or things similar.

When Toli decided that they, the Black-Islers, had had enough time to face his army, he raised his sword high above his head and shouted, "For the Valley! For the Harbour! And for TARMEA!"

Every warrior in the field screamed at the still forming ranks of hardcore fighters "TARMEA!", then Toli spurred his horse forward and joined by the rest of the Vanguard, rode full pelt at the front rank of the Invaders, the sound of the joining of battle, was like a storm wave, crashing off the harbour wall, the entire front lines of both armies were engaged in moments, the soldiers less inclined to be suicidal got on their knees and put their heads, forehead first, on the ground and wished for life and a chance to see their families again, should any of these decide to change their position, an eagle would drop a sixteen-pound cannon stone on their head, a little idea of Shala's, who could now communicate, in a rudimentary fashion, with the eagles; she was particularly friendly with Blacktail.

The Tolian and Black Isle swords flashed equally in the weak light of the waning, gibbous moon, unfortunately for the Black Isles maniacs, only the Tolian blades were making any impressions on the battle, the Invaders were worse, that useless, causing no injury at all and making the warriors more frustrated and more erratic, the Tolian spearmen were now involved in the battle, by now the Black Isles resistance was, like the moon, on the wane and the spearmen were only picking off already injured warriors. In the end only one maniac was left standing, without a word, Gogon who had fought like a demon alongside his brother, dismounted, head to toe drenched in blood, and without a word cleaved the soldier in his head, down to his shoulders, only Luron stopped him from chopping the man into small pieces, Luron had to throw his arms around his brother, pinning his arms to his side and saying in Gogon's ear, "Come back to me, Brother, come back."

Gogon's eyes cleared and focused through the blood. "Luron, my brother! Are we victorious?"

Luron released his grip and stepped back and said, "Yes beloved Brother, the day is won!"

A wounded soldier tried, groaning, to raise himself on his hands, a Tolian spearman ran forward and drove his spear through the back of the man's neck, as he pulled it out, he said to the corpse, "Didn't think I was getting one of you bastards today!"

Toli wheeled his horse around to face his army, he looked to the sky and saw Shala and Tak being reeled back to the mountain. *Good, safe*, he thought. As he lowered his eyes again, a bear-like shape caught his attention as it shambled into the closest of the trees.

Toli raised his sword and shouted to his army, "Victory!"

The battlefield erupted, not a single casualty, the horses had suffered cuts and gashes below the mail line, but nothing debilitating. The whole Vanguard were dripping blood and gore, screaming, "Victory!", when Anga came riding up bareback. *Another thing I've never done before*, she thought as she was mounting the borrowed horse.

When Toli saw her coming fast, the ranks making room for her speeding mount, he dismounted, where he stood with arms open. Anga dismounted at speed and flew into Toli's arms and they kissed passionately. The army went berserk, banging shields, clashing swords, leaping in the air, roaring and screaming and the horses rearing, the cowering prisoners were sure their ending was upon them.

They broke their embrace and Toli nodded towards the horse. "I did not know you could do that, my Queen."

"Nor did I, my King," and she kissed him again.

Eventually, Toli quieted the host. "My friends, today we made history…" A huge roar interrupted him, when he quietened them down, he continued, "But the day is not over yet, get these buggers chained together, and I mean all of them, together! Then have them throw this lot," and he indicated to the dead lunatics strewn all over the area, "into the harbour." Then he screamed at the prisoners, "And see you do a good job, lest you join them."

"Yes my King," they muttered into the dirt.

"Good, and now I must away to the Castle, I have an urgent council to attend, I mustn't be late for my sister, wouldn't do at all now, would it?"

Those who heard shouted, "No, my King," and laughed.

"Very well then, could the twelve men who rode with me in the Vanguard escort me to the Castle please." He hoisted Anga into his saddle and a soldier gave Toli a leg up. "Thank you, friend," Toli said as he settled in behind Anga.

Anga said, "Please soldier, what is your name?"

"Tisq, my Queen."

"Tisq, would you return my fine steed to its rightful owner, it's the first croft at the bottom of the causeway."

"I'll find them, my Queen, fear not."

"Thank you, Tisq." And Toli and Anga led the party of fourteen up to the castle.

They marched into the hall to find the three Lords, chained together now, "Toli!" Sisk gasped.

"Yes Tare, Toli, or should I call you Lord Sisk?" He ignored Sisk then and called Broq and Soq over to him, still standing in the entry end of the hall. When they came up to him, he hugged each of them and said, "Thank you, my friends, you are invaluable warriors, but I must ask one more thing of you."

"Yes my King."

"Broq, send messages to the leaders of the army who are council members, tell them to deploy or dismiss their troops as they see fit, tell them to send a message with a returning warrior, requesting all elders come to the Castle, on the morrow, to witness the trial of these three cretins, it concerns them too, have your messengers tell council members to make their way here when that's done, after your done come back and join your comrades-at-arms in council."

"Yes Sire." And Broq left for the harbour.

"Soq, you send a messenger up to the cannon forge and tell them to bring the prisoners down the hill in chains, and leave them in the battle field, if it's not already cleared, they can help feed the sharks, that done they can sit where they can, and await the judgement of Tarmea, and then, my friend, come back to us."

"Yes Sire." And he left too.

Toli turned to Anga and offered his arm. "My Queen." Anga took his arm and Toli showed her to Queen Shaleena's seat at the banquet table then he sat in his father's chair. *still mothers and fathers until I am crowned king.* He was adamant.

"Drag these three front and centre." He indicated to the stone floor in front of the huge table. "Then join us, please leave three places for the Princess, Tak and Storq. Crall!"

Crall ran in the door at the unexpected summons, panting with effort. "Yes Sire." He had stopped in front of Toli with his back to the stricken captives.

"Crall, we know who you are, I know you were friends with Saso, who the slug killed, is that right?"

"It is, Sire."

"We thank you for your service, Crall, we know as well how you kept these two quiet, at your own peril, and we know you did it all for your own folk, to keep them safe, now Crall, will you work for me?"

"Yes Sire, of course, Sire." He was overwhelmed.

"Then please set up the two long banquet tables down each side like we used to, we're expecting guests, and oh yes! Wine and ale aplenty and any food you can muster!"

"Yes, my King!" And he shot off like a coursing lurcher, as he reached the door, Toli shouted, "And Crall."

"Yes Sire?"

"Please make sure there are plenty of cots set up in good quarters for those who choose to stay overnight."

"Yes Sire," then he went out the door. Shala and Tak came in the same door with Storq, who had been on his ship to see his crew held up their end flawlessly, then Soq came in, again through the rear door, and took a place, Joi came in the front door then closely followed by Broq and Xing.

When they were all seated, Shala said, "So we have the three Lord slugs who decided to invade our land and kill our parents, eh?"

"Yes we do, Princess, yes we do," said Toli.

"And what shall we do with them, my King?"

"I know not, sweet Sister."

"I do; first drag these three of to a cell somewhere, and I'll share my thoughts with you, is anybody hungry? Don't look so hopeful, Tare," she said to Sisk as the three were being dragged out, "your days are done."

"But Princess! Shala! I was always good to you! Shala! Please!" He was ignored.

While this was going on, Crall and his people were flying through their chores, and places were set for everyone including those still expected, everybody went to a wash stand and washed hands and faces, their mail and everything under it remained immaculate. Shqin and Shivi walked in the front doors and when they saw the wash stands they made straight for them, before taking a place. They were all eating now and Shala said to Gogon, raising her voice to be heard by him, "Gogon."

"Yes, my Princess."

"The bugger who cleaved your son lies within these walls, he's the same bugger as killed my parents, would you like to hear my thoughts on the matter?"

"Most definitely, Princess."

Shala got up on her seat again, immediately Toli stood up. *Getting used to this now*, he thought.

"My sister wishes to speak." He sat down again.

"Friends," she began, "after the greatest battle ever seen and won…"—a round of cheering—"…we find ourselves with a dilemma, we have the fate of the invader and his spy in our hands, the other can share their fates for he is a murderous sea rat and we know of his plans of despotism, but Tare betrayed us all including King Jai and the Green Isle, he is responsible for getting these people here for his own ends. Muklah is directly responsible for the order to hang beloved children, wives, husbands and many others beside, he was also responsible, personally, for killing Gogon's son Tukon and Barri.

"In my opinion, we should build them each a stake with a pile of wood around them and a slug atop each of them, everyone who lost someone should take a torch for each slug-pile and light them afire all of us stoking all the fires, we should not light Muklah's fire until he witnesses the suffering of the others, their pyres should be built on the battlefield amid the ghosts of his failed army, those are my opinions, so please forgive me, I wish to retire to my very own room now, I have a sea battle to plan." She hopped off her chair and filled a plate with cheese, fruit and bread, kissed Anga and Toli, said goodnight to Tak, then the council and simply went to bed.

Toli looked at Anga, no longer shocked by his baby sister's meticulous logic.

"Despotism? Where did she learn a word like that at age 9?"

"She has been using that word since age 6, my King. I think the book was 'The Battle of the Red Isthmus'."

"The Battle of the Red Isthmus? Meer didn't give us that book until we were 16!"

"Shala couldn't wait for 16, so I got it for her, you really don't know your sister, do you, Toli?"

"Does not look like it, Anga." Then Toli had a thought. "Quor, may I have a word?"

Quor came over. "How may I help Sire?"

"Send birds to our allies on the Green Isle and Friendly Isle, tonight Quor, and tell them everything up to now, unfortunately we won't be able to stop them setting sail immediately, and we can't delay the inevitable, we must do what must be done on the morrow."

"There is total accord among all of us here with the Princess's solution, when the elders hear it, they will agree too, Sire."

"Yes, I know, Quor." Toli was getting weary now.

"I'll send the birds, Sire, then may I retire? I am drained."

"Yes, of course, Quor, goodnight."

"Goodnight Sire."

"Well Anga, I'll see you to your room."

"Yes, my King, soon it will be our room." They got up and said goodnight to the remainder, the lads and the Generals had gone to their homes to mourn their loss, father and son, together, Tak had found a cot as the remaining council members would. Anga kissed Bri on the way out and whispered, "I love you, Father."

"I love you too, Daughter."

"Goodnight."

"Goodnight."

When Crall had come back to the kitchen, Troi asked, "What's going on, Crall?"

"The King's out there with all his Generals, that's what, and the Princess, and apparently Anga is now our Queen!"

"Who's Anga?"

A brief explanation later and he said, "And they're all outside with a bunch of strange warriors, now you eat that and get a horse from Horse and move yourself up that hill, your Pa won't leave your Mother up there alone this night, now shift, you won't be missed in here but be back here early tomorrow, okay?"

"Okay Crall, thanks."

He pushed his horse as hard as he dared until a stream of chained captives came down the hill accompanied by tall, mail clad warriors, as he passed at a walk, at the end of the column he saw guards from the forges, they did not look too unhappy, Troi senior had told all the forge workers, come guards, he would vouch for them all personally.

Sitting in Mother's kitchen, Troi junior was glad to hear of his father's promise. "That means you and Mother can come with me in the morning, I can get you into the Castle, you can use the guards' horses left behind."

"Aye Son, we've been planning a trip down the hill for a while now, haven't we, Mother?"

"We have that, Father."

Chapter 52

As the sun began to show light through the tiny window of the damp cell, the cell had not been used since the smugglers' days, Muklah, now clear of thought, as was Brakko, said, "It'll be the gibbet, I hung them, nice and quick, crack and you're done." He was not speaking enthusiastically, but through the angry chagrin of his failure.

"Aye, and they may cleave our heads, that's quick too!" Brakko was in his own malaise of misery, unable to comprehend how it came to this.

"Both too quick, no, it's bad, I feel it."

The elders arrived early in the morning and after being briefed, the decision was unanimous in favour of Shala's 'suggestion'.

"Very well." Toli stood when he was given the foregone conclusion result. "Quor, prepare torches and the stakes."

"Already done, Sire, last night, by the friends of Barri."

"Right then." Toli sighed, dreading having to pass his first execution order. "Walk them out."

Two soldiers left to get the condemned trio. "Are you okay, my love?" Anga felt his emotions.

"Yes, my love, thank you." He stiffened himself, both physically and mentally.

The soldiers unlocked the ankle chains of the three, and pulled them to their feet, they left the ankle chains on, to be dragged along by their wrists, Brakko groaned the whole way to the hall, the captives were stood in front of Toli, Toli eyed them for a few seconds, you could hear a pin drop, had that happened, when he stood up he looked all three in the eye in turn, and declared, "All three of you have committed heinous crimes against the peoples of this land, too many to waste our time listing them here, so, by a unanimous decision, you will be taken from here to the scene of your defeat and burned at the stake."

Brakko's legs buckled and he had to be hauled to his feet again.

"It should be known that every torch thrown will be thrown by someone who lost family or friend at your hands, and YOU!" He stabbed his finger at a shaking Muklah. "You will watch and listen while these two burn and scream before you face your end."

Muklah began to scream, "You little shit! You can't do this to me!" And various other curses.

"Take them out to their fate," and the warriors marched them forcibly out into the sunlight.

They left the hall in procession behind the condemned men, now squealing for mercy. The Trois were on the roadside, along to the battlefield, chained soldiers lined the road sitting, heads on knees, not willing to look at the tormentor Muklah, as Sisk passed them pitifully.

"Help me, Troi, you know I'm not evil!" And he was gone squealing with the other two, they were chained to their stakes, by a hoop above their heads and another between their feet, Brakko vented his bowels and bladder as he saw the Tolians lighting their torches and surrounding his pyre.

He began to scream, "No, no, no, please, not fire. No! No! No!" But the Tolians remained unmoved and threw their torches on the mountain of wood, Brakko was hysterical now. The company moved to the next brazier, Sisk's brazier, they formed a queue to light their torches and walked around the pyre.

"No! You can't, I'm one of you, please Toli!"

They threw their torches just as Brakko's nightrobe went up in flames, in turn igniting his hair, his screams were heard everywhere, as if amplified, it went on for a while till he succumbed to the smoke, heat, and pain and he became unconscious, now Sisk's heavier robe caught and flared up his body, he had no hair, but his hood had been placed over his head, and the material had caught and was crackling atop Sisk's head, his teeth bared and eyeballs bulging, he too screamed until he blacked out, when they both fell silent for good, the torches were again lit, as they circled Muklah, he slid down his stake till he hung by his arms, blubbering incoherently.

"You first, Gogon," said Toli.

Without hesitation, Gogon threw his torch at Muklah's head; it bounced off the top of his head and fell to the ground but it caught a fire at the bottom and the flames grew stronger, the rest of the torches went on then, Muklah screamed till he snapped his vocal chords and then choked until he passed out.

The assembled crowd waited for the flames to die to nothing, as the last flame spluttered out, at the precise moment the Mountain turned a fiery, yellow and orange, the whole Mountain radiant, it stayed that way for a half dozen seconds and faded again, the only sound was the crackle of dying embers. Toli and Anga with Shala in hand, began the walk back to the Castle, the torch throwers in tow, with the rest of the council falling in behind.

It had been agreed at the morning council that any of the Valley-folk who wished to go to their families may do so, providing there were enough warriors to guard the prisoners, all the council members elected to go back till tomorrow, with the ulterior motive of giving the Castle-siders time to mourn among their own, actually Broq and Soq bunked in the stables with their men. Joi and Shivi joined the Bevalla encampment for the night, and Xing, Luq, Qwill and Shqin all joined their own men, which was where they would have been anyway, happy among their own.

The six Generals, as the lads and their fathers were now, and forever would be, had again gone to their own houses, which left Toli, Anga, Shala and Bri. The start of all the conversations that evening were how the Mountain had showed her delight at the final confirmation of the end of the pollution.

Toli called for Crall, "Bring us some supper please, Crall, I for one, wish to put this foul day behind me, bring honey-draught too, Crall, I may have trouble sleeping tonight."

Crall hesitated in front of Toli and Toli asked him, "What is it, Crall, what's wrong?"

"Sire, I beg your indulgence."

"You have it, my friend, please speak."

"Both Trois, the cannon forgers, Sire, are in the kitchen Sire, with Trois Wife, they wish to petition you, my King, for the lives of the Black-Islers who resided and worked side by side with Troi without complaint nor problem and—"

"Is it you who petitions me, Crall?"

"Well no, Sire, but—"

"Then please go and get supper sorted and while you're at it, ask Troi and his family if they would like to join us for supper!"

"At once, my King!"

Toli leaned back and sighed. "Are you okay, Toli?" Anga was becoming concerned.

"Yes, yes, Anga, not even properly dark yet and I'm exhausted."

"Toli, we all are, we have done nothing but pump our hearts at double, no, treble time, my own body and brain ache for a day without duty, to our subjects, we'll never have a day to ourselves again."

"Yes, we bloody will! You and I are going up in that flying contraption tomorrow, end of discussion!"

Crall's staff were filling the table, fit to creak, when Crall came in, leading young Troi and his mother and father. Crall was about to introduce the family, when Toli said, "Welcome, Troi, to you and your family, I am aware of your quandary, and I am aware of the men you wish to speak of, not the time to explain how, suffice to say I am aware of everything you wish to ask, you may retrieve your workers in the morning and bring them back up the hill, you will be allowed to take only the men that were there before, no exceptions, make it clear they have nowhere to go, and nothing to say, that we won't know about, now, join us Troi, Crall will find you and your wife comfortable quarters in the Castle tonight."

Shala filled a plate again and said, "Please excuse me, I hope I'm not being rude, my King!"

"Yes Shala?"

"Don't dare hurt my Xing wing tomorrow, okay?"

"I promise, Princess," and he leant down to kiss her on the cheek.

Shala bid them goodnight and after kissing Anga and Bri, left, apparently unaffected by anything. They chatted for a while, about cannon at sea and on land, until Toli called a halt, "I have no wish to offend anyone, but the honey-draught has worked its magic and I must sleep, Crall!"

"Sire!" He was there in a flash. "Please show our guests to their quarters."

"Sire." Crall escorted them to the kitchen, for a chat and a nightcap. Toli, Anga and Bri shuffled to bed themselves, giving weak goodnights and pecks on the cheek.

Chapter 53

Troi, Troi and Mother had a very pleasant, breakfast with Crall in his kitchen, senior was excited to be able to free his friends, sixteen in all, he was also excited to be able to carry on forging cannon, Toli had made it very clear during supper last night, that young Troi would be here, supervising fitting and training gunners at sea, he seemed to have a knack for the destructive maximisation of the guns, by hitting his target, first time usually, from a rolling and heaving deck, he was a natural on deck.

The family of three thanked Crall for his hospitality, and senior and Mother said their farewells, hoping they'd get a chance to visit with him again. They left the stables and rode straight to the ex-soldiers to give them the news and get them back up the hill, and back to work, as the guards unshackled them, senior was relating Toli's words to the group and a buzz of anticipation ran all the way up to the battlefield through the captive Black-Islers. The reunion was a happy one, with handshakes and hugs, and it gave others hope. Before they said their farewells, at the foot of the hill, senior dismounted and said, "Follow me, Son."

Young Troi dismounted and followed his father into an area overgrown with gorse.

"In there," Senior began, "is the downhill pull drum, you have no cannon today, yet, so could you grab a few men and uncover the thing, if it's in working order, fettle it for me, when I get 'my boys' up the hill, there will be at least two cannon coming down, that'll let you finish the 'Flying Princess', oh yes, keep it to yourself, but when the ship is ready, there will be a renaming ceremony, now I don't care how it's done, get these men onto the wagon somehow, and let's get back to work, me and Mother are going on ahead." They had planned a nice ride up the hill together, and it was very pleasant.

Khoul borrowed another two Garrons from Horse and hitched the team of four onto the wagon, the keen forge men crammed themselves in any, or no, fashion, they were about to embark on the most uncomfortable journey of their lives, and to date, the best.

Troi recruited his helpers from the ship, and soon they were hacking at the gorse, in no time at all, the drum and wheels were cleared, all in good order, Troi fettled the moving parts with axle grease, borrowed from Horse, all that was left to do was keep clearing the tracks going up till the cannon came back on the wagon.

Toli had sent messages to the Valley to say to them that there was no need to attend the Castle today and to spend time with their own folk and wait for a period of time, undecided, until they were contacted, and would Tak meet Shala at the flight deck after breakfast?

The royal and kings guards, who had never been more than twenty feet from the King since leaving the Valley, refused to go, as did the warriors who fought alongside them. "Someone has to mind the captives" was the logic given by Xing and Shqin, Luq and Qwill as their reason to stay, it was a valid reason, for now, the captive numbers were dwindling as more Tolians claimed their workers back, there would always be some soldiers around, not having had jobs, they were in a very nervous state, but they "needed minding!"

Tak was surprised when Toli and Anga showed up with Shala, he had been at the flight deck since first light, learning the operations of the Xing Wings equipment, part of Shala's plan to fly independent of help. The flight crew, again Shala's name for the operators, adjusted the double harness to fit Toli and Anga. Eventually, they were ready to go,

"You look ashen, Brother, are you unwell?" Shala mocked Toli.

"Don't be so cocky, Sister, you're not too big to be grounded," Toli said, provoking laughter from Anga and Shala.

"You keep believing that, Brother," and then she turned her face to the Mountain and spoke, "TARMEA WISTWA ZEPHRA," which meant 'Mountain Mother Breathe', and a breeze came up the face of the Mountain and took the weight of the kite. Toli and Anga began to feel weightless, then the breeze stiffened and picked them up off the flight deck, Shala said, "Just glide today, Tarmea will keep you safe, don't worry." Then she signalled to Tak to feed them out, as they soared above the forest the sea breeze was holding them up now, still controlled by the Mountain.

Tak fed them out further, which also meant higher, to the point where Shala said, "Leave them there for a while, let them get a feel for the changes in the air."

As they were being reeled out, Toli said to Anga, "Did you hear, Shala, enchanting spells and all!"

"Yes dear, and she has a rudimentary understanding of eagle as well."

"She what!"

"She can communicate with the eagles, early days but she's getting there."

"Well I never."

"Once again, you really don't know your sister at all."

"No I don't, but that's changing fast, my love, very fast!"

They stayed above the forest until Shala decided it would do their circulation no good to leave it any longer, they had hung there in solitude for hours saying very little, commenting how the battlefield had been cleared so quickly and completely by the captives, and things of that ilk, but mainly just hung there soaking in the peace, one thing had been decided though, they would be married in two days' time.

Shala had two operators from the flight crew reel in the couple, and when they were free of their harness, Anga hugged Shala saying, "Oh Shala, that was invigorating, thank you, thank you!"

"Okay," said Shala, "you must have really enjoyed it!" Had she known about the upcoming wedding, she would have understood.

"Yes, thank you, Shala, it's a great way to relax." Toli seemed distracted.

"If I have my way, we'll be able to do more than relax in them, Toli."

"What do you mean, Shala?"

"Flight without strings is what I mean, Brother, no strings attached!"

"You're mad!"

"We will see!" The four decided to visit Quor and the settlement before exiting the Valley now open to the harbour. Quor was in the great house already, bringing his documenting of recent history up to the present day.

"Quor, friend," Toli called as he entered.

"Sire, an unexpected but most welcome surprise." He had known about the flight but the visit was unplanned.

"We are on our way to see our folk in the settlement, could we borrow the pinnace and a couple of rowers?"

"Certainly Sire," and he brought them to the boat and told a couple of stevedores to take the party across to the settlement on the far bank.

Arriving at the settlement unannounced, the four made their way to the meeting house where Nana would be fussing over something no doubt. Dauti and Doulen spotted them first and rushed to meet them. Before they could speak, Toli stopped them and said, "The people of this Island thank you for your contribution in the conflict passed, and for your contribution in the difficult executions." They had been the only non-Tolians to throw torches the day before.

"Had we gotten our way, Sire, we would have been skinning them alive for days, but thank you for the honour of some revenge for King Jai," Dauti said.

"King Jai was my father's friend, I called him uncle as I called Queen Prina aunt, I was betrothed to Princess Prina, I called Admiral Tors and his wife, uncle and aunt, and I saw them all hanging from gibbets alongside my Parents and Brothers, skinning would have been my choice too, had there been a vote, the executions would have lasted weeks."

They said hello to all in the settlement before going into the meeting house. The assembly listened intently to Toli.

"In two days' time, time enough for a rest, eh?" The small crowd sniggered, "We have a ceremony, to rename the Invader's ship, his flagship the Black Kraken, The Flying Princess, there will be a short ceremony in the throne room before and would like your council to attend."

"Yes Sire," an enthusiastic chorus went up.

Shala hadn't heard. "Is there, Toli, really?"

"Yes my Princess really." He did not mention the nature of the 'short ceremony'. "We would like to see you all at twelve noon, would that suit?"

"Yes Sire!" a shout this time.

"I look forward to it, see you there," and he left and tracked back to the boat. Back with Quor, they gave exactly the same tale but more, "It'll be a formal affair, and pass the news on to the appropriate elders and leaders, a day tomorrow to prepare, and the throne room, day after, yes?"

"Yes, my King, got it all, would you take some ale with me? Maybe some wine?"

"Very kind, Quor," Anga said. "But we must attend to our own preparation, and our carriage awaits."

"Of course my Queen, I completely understand."

"Right then, Shala, you and Tak coming?"

"Might as well. Preparations eh?" And she winked at Quor. The decision about the ship had been made in the Castle, so Shala had been genuinely surprised, but they had spent the entire morning surrounded with birds, no secrets in the Valley.

They got back and had Crall bring back some food to the royal dining room, it was late afternoon. Crall brought the food in and told Toli, "Sire, the two cannon are being fitted aboard as we speak, the wagoners came straight back, the four horse team made everything quicker, the ship will definitely be ready for the ceremony."

"How did you know about the ceremony?"

"Everybody knows Sire, a ship-naming is a rare occasion these days, Troi has men painting the ship now, but apparently there is a problem he would like a word, Sire."

"Please tell Troi I wish him to join us for supper later, we have family matters to discuss now, thank you, Crall," and he swiftly ran up to Troi at the ship, they had become great friends.

Anga decided to take the lead, "Shala, we have something to tell you."

"Toli is being crowned king the day after tomorrow, immediately after that you will be married to my brother, immediately after that you will be crowned queen, then, and only then, we will get to my ship, really, you two should know better, after all you'll be king and queen, don't worry, your secret's safe outside the Valley, so far."

Toli at first was shocked by Shala's knowledge and after a very few seconds, Anga's brain clicked in. "Ahhh, Toli, we must mind what we say among the birds."

Toli sat, slouched, in his chair, with a sign of resignation in his face, lids half over his eyes and fingers meshed on his stomach, and said, "I give in!"

They talked excitedly, now about the wedding more than anything, Bri came in, he had been crying, he tried his best to hide his emotions until Anga could tease him no longer. "Father, we know you know!"

Bri picked Anga up and grabbed her around the waist, then spun her around, crying again, "I tried to wait, I did, but I had to see your face."

They calmed down and eventually sat down, Toli, still slouched half lidded, and finger meshed said, "I give in!" and sighed.

The afternoon had since passed unnoticed by the new family, Tak was included in everything and felt part of it. The conversation had come around to supper, when Troi walked in with Crall.

"Sire, Master Troi is here as requested, shall I serve supper?."

"Immaculate timing, Crall. Yes do!" His mood had lifted and it was evident. "Please Troi, sit, tell is of our problem, oh, and Crall?"

"Yes Sire?"

"Please bring in a round of Bri's gin, large if you please, and a keg of harbour ale, Tak and Shala will have small wines."

"At once Sire." And he was off.

Troi sat down. "So what's the problem, Troi?" Toli asked.

"My King, the ship is now fitted with its full complement of cannon, the ship is sound to the eye, but as we went down the ship, below the water line, lower into the dock, now drained Sire, for caulk and tar,"—new vocabulary for Troi—"and your shipwright found shipworm, Sire."—again new learning—"He says the ship will fall apart soon, he thinks it hasn't been careened since it was built."

"Sail it upriver."

"What, Shala?" Toli got a shock, he jumped with the suddenness of the declaration.

"Float the ship, sail to the river mouth, and ask Tarmea to open, sail the ship up to the falls, turn around and come back again, the river mist will scour the upper ship, and the river will take care of the rest, remember Beeth, Toli? About the water and timber?"

"It'll work," Bri enthused. "I'm certain."

Then Toli said, "Yes Shala, I do remember."

Troi was baffled, "Forgive me Sire, river, water, mist?"

There and the Toli decided to explain the strange warriors, and how they came to be here, and how they always had been here, at least on this Island, it was getting late now, and Troi asked, "Please Sire, might I retire now, there is a lot to do on the 'Flying Princess' for the renaming ceremony."

"Please do, Troi, be back here for breakfast, and we'll follow my sister's advice and go for a little cruise, eh Troi?"

"Thank you Sire," and he left thinking, *Supper with the King, breakfast with the King, cruising with the King, it just can't get any better!*

After Troi had gone, Anga said, "Well done Toli!"

"Thank you Anga." Toli looked pleased with himself. He knew Troi would tell Crall, and Crall would see to it the entire population would know by this time tomorrow. He had just taken one, long drawn speech off the list of speeches.

Chapter 54

At Toli's request, the party walking up to the Flying Princess consisted of the six Generals—Troi, Bri, Storq, Shala, Tak, Anga and himself. The crew and the shipwright, Shai, were on the dock, ready to float the ship, Troi insisted the King actually saw the extent of the natural damage, Troi was becoming a proper seasider now.

"It looks like a beekeeper's honeycomb, Sire, it'll never survive another voyage, let's hope the Princess's plan works."

"It'll work," Bri stated.

"Get some of the crew up here that brought the ship here, I think we should use the thing here to get us up the river." He was pointing at the propeller, it fascinated him.

"Already aboard, Sire, already below," and Troi waved a signal to open the dock to the sea again and float the ship. When the ship was floating again the party boarded and when the ships propeller had cleared the big stands, he signalled to the helmsman, a Black-Isler who knew the ship and how to manage her, he called into his talking device, trumpet like, direct to the prop crew.

"Slow ahead!" he called, slowly the propeller strained into movement, the ship began to move, as it moved the strain on the crew below loosened, and headway became easier.

"Incredible," Storq gasped.

They left the harbour and headed south for the river mouth, Troi was hanging over the transom watching the action of the prop.

"What is it Troi?" Toli asked him.

"We can improve this, Sire."

"How Troi?"

"Not sure, Sire, not yet."

They came to the river mouth and turned into it. "TARMEA WISTWA DALAKA," Bri shouted over the rush of the rapid, the rapids quickly settled to a quiet docile flow, the Black-Islers aboard were aghast, they knew about magic, but this! As they made their way up river they could clearly see, the ridge-path the explorers had been rescued from, Sisk hadn't seen it, Tarmea did not allow it.

Abruptly, they came into kind of a lagoon, with the falls from the lake throwing a thick mist into the air at the far end, allowing them to come about in a big circle, taking the ship beneath the mist on the way. As they passed into the mist the ship began to creak, crack and moan, coming out into the sea water again the ship seemed to be slicing the water more easily than the outbound sail. This cruise became a ritual for all ships still to be named.

Troi went to work, he got the ship into dock as quickly as was possible, and ordered it drained, he hadn't even asked the Kings permission, no-one noticed, as soon as the ship was rested in its cradles and made safe Troi slid down a ladder into the dry dock still knee deep on him.

He wandered up and down both sides of the ship, joined now by the shipwright, they spent an hour going around they ship muttering, inaudible from above, When they stepped onto the dock again, Toli asked, "Well?" and spread his arms.

"It's beyond belief, Sire," Troi said in a puzzled way. "The shipwright says it looks like it's never seen a worm, nor barnacle, and he says the joints may never leak again!"

"Tarmea!" Toli said.

"Yes Sire, Tarmea!" Troi said through his grin. Troi immediately called to flood the dock again, no work to do below the waterline, probably never again. As the ship re-floated, Troi noticed that nothing above the waterline needed doing either, even the cannon were gleaming.

Strange thing, he thought. *The guns never need cooling either*.

"Right," he said to Shai, "let's get the figurehead out of hiding and onto the 'Princess'." They ran up to the big storage shed and threw open the big double doors the figurehead was right there on a specifically made bogey, resplendent in the sun, silver mail, golden Princess's crown atop her head, red wings swept back to exactly the sweep of the bow, and a hole in her chest to take the new Tarmin Cannon.

"Beautiful," Shai declared breathlessly.

It had been made in a day in Beeth and stored in the dead of night, last night.

"These folk are a bit special," Troi said to Shai.

"Just a bit," Shai replied.

Toli called for Crall to bring food and drink into the dining chamber. When they were all seated and eating, Toli said to his Generals, "Friends, we have, Anga and I that is, have something to say to you all."

Dovitt laughed, "We know Toli, crown, ring, boat right?"

Toli dumped himself into the slouched, resigned position again. "I can't win! Crall!"

Crall trotted into the room pushing a tray with twelve tall glasses on it and a small keg of Bri's gin, he stopped in front of Toli and said, "Yes Sire? Gin Sire?"

"How did you—? Yes Crall, gin, thank you." Crall gave everyone a measure, double measure actually, and small wines for Shala and Tak.

"Oh and Crall?"

"Yes Sire?"

"Please send for Worq, and bring out a glass for him too."

"Beg your indulgence Sire, but Worq will only drink ale, I'll go to get it now, and Worq is on his way Sire."

Toli looked at Anga in the eye, "Worq knows too, doesn't he?"

"That would be my guess," she replied.

Worq came in with Crall who was carrying a small keg of ale. Worq stood in front of Toli. "My King, may I say how proud I am to be chosen to conduct the ceremonial duties tomorrow."

"I haven't asked—never mind, carry on!"

"Thank you Sire, I never had the honour of meeting your sage, Meer, but he was known to be sage indeed, I mourn his loss Sire, I hope I can do him justice, I'd like to dedicate my work tomorrow to him."

"Thank you Worq, he was sage indeed, and kind, patient and strong too, he always spoke the truth, and he would have been honoured to meet you, I know it." And he bid Worq sit.

"There is one more thing, my King, you ceremonial clothing is waiting in the ante-chamber of the throne room, perhaps you would all like to see, we think you will like them."

"Come on, Anga." Shala grabbed her by the hand; she thought she may have to drag Anga, but Anga was keener then her, she thought she had a day of secret rehearsal and dressing, but all seemed to be in hand, she knew she would love her dress, no question, she knew.

They burst into the room to see a row of mannequins, King and Queen out in front, they stood speechless when the men arrived. Anga's and Shala's dressing mannequins bore identical dresses, made from spun Tarmin, so beautiful they could not speak, the three royal mannequins had Tarmin crowns atop their heads. Toli wore a suit of the same material, matching the other men's exactly, shirts and leggings of Tarmin, knee high leather boots, ox blood and shining, the only difference was in the tabards. Toli's bore a crown of Tarmin stitches on its chest, glowing from the deep purple tabard, the other tabards were a lighter shade of purple and bore smaller crowns, but the other guests would be wearing their own tabards, blue for guards, white for navy, and grey for army and cavalry, and so on. Anga and Shala saw Tarmin slippers twinkling out from the hem of their dresses, that was it.

"Where do we put them on, Worq?" Anga couldn't wait.

"You and the Princess may dress in here." And he showed them into a room with three mirrored walls, some staff quickly moved the dresses into the room and the dressers went to work.

Before he left, he said to Anga, "My Queen, please don't leave this room wearing your gown, it would be bad luck."

"I know, Worq, don't worry, now get out!"

The men had already gone to their respective rooms leaving Bri and Toli alone. "Bri," Toli said.

"Yes Toli."

"When you give Anga to me tomorrow, would you give me the honour of standing by me at the altar?"

"I would, Toli, my honour."

"Good," said Worq, "I took the liberty of putting Bri's clothing in the same room as yours Sire, I hope that suits."

"Thank you, Worq," and Toli hugged him, which made Worq very uncomfortable. By the end of the night, each and every one of them knew exactly where and when they were going and what they were doing.

Chapter 55

At noon the next day, the people started flooding into the throne room, the head council stood a half pace behind the throne and Worq stood before the throne, resplendent in Tarmin robes.

Dauti and Doulen were in the front row sitting by the Trois and Mother, Nana and the rest of the Castle-siders, Luron and Gogon next to Nana, were also in the front, behind came the elders and leaders and the throne room filled to bursting with merchants, carpenters, all walks of life on the Island, when the guards had to close the doors, leaving many outside.

Troi and the lads came from a room, left of the centre, Toli in front, they walked to the centre aisle and turned right to approach the throne. "They look splendid, splendid!" an excited onlooker exclaimed. And they really did.

"Who approaches the throne!" Worq challenged.

"I, Toli, rightful King of this land, come to take my crown!"

"Pass Toli King, take your throne." Worq moved aside to allow Toli to sit atop the throne, he glanced at Anga and Shala sat to the right of his throne, only slightly behind, Shala the only one wearing a crown at this time, a fact she just reminded Anga of, for the third time.

Toli sat and the lads joined their fathers behind the throne.

"Toli King, do you swear by your life to defend this land and its folk?"

"I so swear."

"And do you swear to listen to grievance and attend to need?"

"I so swear."

An acolyte came from somewhere unseen and walked over to Worq with Toli's Tarmin crown atop a velvet cushion, shining deep purple. Worq took up his crown between forefingers and thumbs and stood before Toli holding the crown above Toli's head.

"Toli, you are King and this is your Crown." Worq placed the crown, firmly, on Toli's head and, as expected, the throne room exploded in a riot of sound.

Bri moved forward and offered Anga his hand, she took it and stood with Shala on her other side. Bri walked her over to Toli and Worq, he kissed his daughter on the cheek and walked to the other side and stood by the lads. Toli nodded thank you to Bri.

"Anga, you have been given to me by your father so that you may marry this man, King Toli, are you in accord with these sentiments?" He hadn't used the word Queen yet, rightly so.

"I am."

"And do you swear to uphold your husband's oath as he has sworn to?"

"I do."

"Take a knee please."

They both got down on one knee, another acolyte appeared with Anga's crown, and Worq picked it up and placed it on Anga's head and declared, "Arise, Toli King and Anga Queen, man and wife!"

The noise was unbearable, but it didn't stop, they heard it up at the forges, manned today solely by Black-Islers, aware of the punishment for treachery.

Anga and Toli stood waving for a while, Toli, a true King, and looking every inch of it, and Anga his Queen, her gown, and Shala's, glittering like stars in a silver sky. Worq threw his hands up for silence, eventually, the din receded all the way back to the battlefield, now occupied by a Black Isle encampment.

"We will progress to the fitting dock now to name the new flagship." A path was immediately cleared from the throne all the way to the harbour and then the fitting dock. The noise outside was incredible, the people jostling to see the new King and Queen. The happy royal procession walked along waving all the way, there had been a podium built at the bow end of the dock for the Princess and Worq with the King and Queen, they stepped up on the podium, Toli whispered, or rather, shouted in Worq's ear, "Well done, Worq, all the pomp and ceremony, without the pomp and ceremony, well, kept to a minimum anyway."

"Yes Sire, and all in daylight still."

The Flying Princess looked glorious in her new livery, the likeness of Shala on the figurehead was incredible, her wings perfectly matching her curves, shining so white it blinded the folk who caught the glare of the sun off her hull, stunning! Shala stepped forward with a bottle of Bris gin in her hand, she insisted. Worq held up his hands for quiet again.

Shala shouted, "I name this ship the 'Flying Princess'; may the elements be kind to her and her crew!" Then she smashed the bottle by the neck of her own likeness, the crowd went berserk.

Senior shouted in Mother's ear, "They don't half do things quick around here, eh Mother?"

She laughed and kissed him on the lips. "You ain't such a slouch yourself, Husband," she said lovingly. The main party were cheered all the way back to the banquet hall, and when they got back the tables were laden with food, and the walls were lined with various barrels containing various beverages, Toli and Anga tried not to be too engrossed in one another, and tried to show a modicum of interest in conversation with other people.

Outside, Toli had barrels of ale set all over the area, and many a toast went up for Barri and Tukon before the night was done, cooking food was everywhere, braziers lighting the faces of the diners tearing pieces of meat from spits in the growing darkness.

Shala and Tak had gone to their separate quarters hours ago, when suddenly there were loud explosions outside, Xing had arranged a treat, a fireworks display, there were rockets, spinning cartwheels and bangers and sparklers for children, the display above the harbour was stupendous, every pair of eyes was on the spectacle.

Toli and Anga slipped out to the royal bedchamber during the display, thanking Worq again. The night continued without anyone asking for the King or Queen.

Anga and Toli stood naked before each other, each one having as much experience as the other—none. Anga stepped up to Toli and turned her face to his, he kissed her hotly, then Anga stopped and led Toli to the enormous bed, she climbed up on the bed and pulled Toli up after her. Anga laid Toli on his back and sat astride him awkwardly; she took Toli's hand and placed it on her breast, leant forward and kissed Toli, tenderly, repetitively, then as natural as if they'd been lovers for years, they co-joined, and it was perfect, they made tender love for the rest of the night, until exhaustion overtook them.

Chapter 56

It had been three days since the day of ceremonies, as the wedding day had been called around a brazier that night. "Well, that was a day for ceremonies, wasn't it?" a drunk minstrel said, waving a horn of ale around, and it was taken up, and by the morning it had become a common phrase, and Quor wrote it so into history. The King and Queen had surprisingly little to do, the rail was open and six cannon a day were coming in their bogey with a second bogey not full of shot, and up at the forge another cannon forge was being planned, the ships were being armed quicker now, this second ship was almost ready for its naming cruise.

All the captives were happily keeping themselves busy making themselves available to help anyone who needs it, in the meantime, they'll maintain the struts and keep things clean, some of them had formed a crew to paint the ships before fitting, only leaving finishing touches after the guns were fitted, and Troi was conferring with Slaq about his idea for a new propeller shape, could he form this from Tarmin or would it be best to have it beaten out of steel, they were poring over Trois drawing of a rounded propeller with twisted blades, giving a screw effect, and forcing the ship along more efficiently and speedily, Slaq put the drawing in his leather satchel and made his way back to the Valley.

There would be twelve guns fitted by the end of the day and eighteen tomorrow.

"I'll take her around to the river with eighteen and fit the two absentees when I dock again, at that rate, I should arm one ship every three days," Troi said out loud.

Toli and Anga walked along the strand in an idyllic daze, the guards had been told to stand down and go home to their folks for a while, Toli knew they were lurking around somewhere, at least they were keeping their distance and people were just going about their business, leaving the newly-weds alone, Toli spotted

Crall galloping from the Castle, two horses behind him, he pulled up at Toli and Anga.

"Sire, you are needed at the Castle, there has been a bird."

The three of them galloped the short distance back to the Castle, Quor was already inside with Bri, Briq, the six Generals and Tak, Shala, Storq and Troi were there already discussing Shala's plan for flying at sea.

"What's so urgent, Quor?" Toli asked him.

"The second fleet left the Black Isles a month ago, we reckon no less than eight weeks before they get here, they have a mage on every ship Sire, these buggers are extremely serious people!"

"So were the last lot, Quor, this lot won't even get to set one slimy tentacle upon our homeland. Troi, what will we have in numbers?"

"If we say eight weeks is our deadline, that's fifty-six days, which means by the end of the fifty-sixth day, you'll have eighteen men o' war." Another name that was to stick around.

"Plus the two ready right now, twenty ships Sire, each one capable of sinking twenty enemy ships on its own." He was counting the ship in dry-dock being fitted still, eighteen cannon by the end of the next day, full complement by the next, he would make twenty, he said so, so he would.

"How many ships are coming, Quor?" Shala asked.

"Twenty, Princess, we expected thirty, but he has left ten behind, we don't know why, we think to defend the capital in his absence, this Vakkra fellow seems to have a brain in his head, to carry a mage on every ship, I think, shows his intent to be rid of his competition on his arrival, and they will be almost impossible to defeat at sea, by conventional methods, at least, but we are not conventional, Princess Shala, are we?"

"We most certainly are not, Quor. Troi!"

"Yes Princess."

"I hear your Black-Isles helmsmen has been vocal in his hatred of Muklah and his regime, even cursing mages occasionally."

"That's right, Princess, his hatred is real, even venomous."

"Please bring him here, Troi, I wish to speak with him."

"At once, Princess." And Troi went to fetch the helmsman, Koto.

Shala spoke to them all, "This man has first-hand experience of their battle tactics and his hatred is real or Tarmea would have weeded him out by now."

A hum of agreement went around.

Toli and Anga had not yet taken part in this discussion, they could not believe their idyllic honeymoon was over so soon. When Troi returned with Koto, the helmsmen being used by Troi, and who was aboard the Black Kraken getting here, Toli and Anga came around. Shala decided to involve them.

"Koto, could you give our King and Queen any information on the likely approach of the Black-Isles fleet?" Toli and Anga were alert now.

Koto addressed the couple, "My King, my Queen," he began, "I can tell you exactly how the fleet will approach, it never varies."

"Then tell us, and the outcome may determine whether we are your King and Queen or not."

"I understand, Sire, they will move into sight at four knots, under sail or man power, they will be sailing ten in line, two abreast, one hundred feet between them, you could slip up the middle and blow them all to the depths, these ships, I'm sure Sire, will be full to the gunwales with assault warriors, maniacs who call themselves the Vakkra Wind, much worse than the Kraken Brigade, Vakkra himself will not tolerate civilians pressed into service, aboard his ships; one word of advice, Sire."

"Tell us, Koto." Anga liked the idea of blowing the Black-fleet out of the water, then she and Toli could get back to their very happy marriage.

"If they see gleaming white ships coming at them, they will instantly stand to arms and the mages will cloak them in cloud, where they will disperse and come from many different directions."

"Right," Toli said. "Get the Flying Princess into the harbour, stand her at anchor under the north wall, if she's spotted from above they'll assume she's a captured vessel, the rest, restore to their original colour, he'll see the Black Kraken is not there to welcome him but he'll soon find there is no welcome for him here in any form."

"If we are on deck dressed as Black-Islanders, Vakkra will assume Muklah has sent a delegation rather than bother to come himself, their hatred of each other is legendary, and this would probably have happened anyway." Koto was excited, no chance of killing a friend in this engagement, and another tyrant gone, "Maybe I'll see my son again someday, hope is not lost!"

Quor said, "There is no deceit in his words, Sire."

"I know, Quor." Toli said to Koto, "Be sure, Koto, every member of this council knows you are being honest, it seems we are your King and Queen, Shala, Princess, have you anything to say."

"I have, Koto, you will go a pick your best prop crews, enough for twenty ships, get another nineteen Black Isles helmsmen."

"Princess!" Admiral Shouk protested.

"Admiral, these are Black Isles ships and must be sailed in a Black Isles way, there is no question even if we had time to train gunners and crews for twenty ships."

"Yes, sorry, Princess." Shouk was cowed.

"Troi, you will train gunners as guns become available, the crews, including Black-Islers, will go to their allocated ships and prepare themselves and their ships for battle at sea while they await fitting, take them upriver for the remaining cruise as soon as they are fully equipped, the timbers will not cede to our saws after the cruise, however if a ship is fully prepared, waiting for guns, get her upriver too. Tarmea is sending an endless supply of shot, and powder stores are at full, our mail and ships and folk belong to Tarmea and that will negate any interference from their mages, and I believe Koto's plan is the one we should train for. WHAT SAY ALL HERE?"

"ALL HERE SAY AYE!" And it was settled.

Later that day, a solitary ship was spotted coming from the south and east, the sail soon became clear, green sail, with a blue trident, Admiral Tors.

"Crall!" Toli yelled.

"Yes Sire." He was there in an instant.

"Send for Dauti and Doulen, get them here in an hour, tell them they have a visitor, to dress like Green-Islers, and to wait with you until I summon them."

"At once, my King," and out he went, he hadn't far to look, Dauti and Doulen were already in the kitchen picking clothes out of a pile of Green Isle dignitaries, unfortunately now all dead. They had been in the square cleaning their statues of bloody vandalism, unintelligible words daubed in blood across them all, when Crall found them, they were ecstatic at the news.

A few hours later, Toli was welcoming Admiral Gous and General Hiro with the delegation from the Green Isle, they all knelt as one, and said as one, "Hail to the King!" Then they rose and Gous stepped up and hugged Toli fondly.

"Toli, we are so grateful for your swift action, we are sorry, personally, that we, Hiro and I, could not be here to help."

"Had you been here, Uncles, you would have, for sure, gone the same way as your brothers. I, for one, am very happy you're still here!"

"Thank you, my King." He side-stepped to Anga and took her hands in his, while Hiro embraced Toli.

"I can see you are a Queen indeed," and he threw his hands in the air, then hugged Anga, laughing. Anga was immediately taken by the Admiral and the General, who also hugged her, the two even had Shala giggling and wriggling as they poked at her and tickled and teased her.

"Right!" Gous said, straightening. "If you would indulge me Sire, I'd like to meet the two men who represented us throughout all this, the legendary, Dauti and Doulen!"

"They await your call, my friend." Toli led the way back to the banquet hall big enough to take everybody, the entire war council including elders and now Troi and Tak, the Black-Islers would be introduced at a later date, a safer date.

Crall already had Dauti and Doulen in the hall awaiting their fellow Green-Islanders, the same age as themselves, having grown up together, the reunion was emotional. When they settled around the tables, Crall brought them food and drink, and the Green-Islers were informed of everything but the Black Isles crew members, when Gous said, "I assume the Green Isle will be allocated places on these ships," it was time to explain, at the end of the explanation, an unexpected reaction returned.

"Good, makes perfect sense, Toli, great tactics, you're a great General!"

"Not my plan, we all have Shala to thank for that."

"Then thank you Shala, very clever, you get that from your Mother, you know." Her mother, Queen Shaleena, had been a Green-Isler known for exceptional organisational skills.

"Thank you Uncle, I appreciate your words."

They spent the rest of the day and evening in catching up, the plan was set, nothing to discuss there. Shala made it clear it was Koto's plan.

Chapter 57

The next two months passed in a flurry of activity all over the Island; come the fifty-sixth day, Troi had twenty battle-ready ships, each one filled with the new Tarmin propeller which was a huge improvement in performance and ease on the prop crews, each one armed and ready for battle. The bird came late in the evening, the Black-Isles fleet would be in view at dawn, the day after tomorrow, they were doing four knots under sail trimmed perfectly to maintain that speed, and were two lines, ten a line travelling one hundred feet apart.

In their bedchamber, Toli and Anga laying in each other's arms after their love making had once again exhausted them.

"I can't accept war will be so frequent in our lives forever!" Anga was concerned about something, hiding it.

"It's not forever, Anga."

"I know, sorry." And she pretended to fall asleep.

In the morning, after breakfast, it was time to organise the order of the single line of attack, the only thing left to do. Shala took over.

"My brother will not be moved, he's going in the Hurricane, the first ship, he knows his crew, as you all do at this point, he'll be followed by Admiral Shouk, then Admiral Gous, then Storq, the Generals in line next the rest of the commanders know their places, the King will be with Captain Troi and the helmsman Koto, Koto will be taking the lead in the battle, he will be timing the first shot, please Koto, take over." Koto was now trusted as a Tolian would be, he has proved himself as a loyal man. Troi hadn't missed the promotion either.

Koto took the floor. "Tomorrow you must follow my actions, we will sail out and approach the Black fleet at four knots in line. This is expected, we will sail fifty feet apart as they will, they will recognise the Hurricane. And that'll keep them thinking, but they will notice the lack of sail and mast, and then the cannon, at this point the mages will begin to form a hiding place for the fleet, it'll be a thick cloud, and you won't see the end of your nose, but I'm told you may have a solution for that, in any case, I'll be counting, when I yell fire! The first ten ships let go their cannon, port and starboard as close together as possible, when the first gun goes off, the lead ship of the second wave of ten, count to one hundred and let loose again, they will not be able to scatter as they'd like and this wave will finish them off.

"I suggest we spend today lining up properly, come ashore for a final meal before spending the night aboard the ship, this is what Black-Islanders would do, in case they have eyes, they control evil birds, and they talk to them, they will be collecting information at first light, best if we keep it traditional Black Isles."

So they did all this dressed as Black-Islanders, but with Tarmin mail below, every single person going to sea had been given one, the crews came ashore after lining up at anchor, when the council came in for food, outside the Black Islanders lit braziers and ate roast boar late into the night, traditional.

When it was time to board for the night, Anga wept in the bedchamber. "You come back to me, right?"

"Right!" Toli kissed Anga and left to join the men, there would be no public farewells—tradition.

The rain hammered down, Toli, Troi and Koto listened to it all night, they sat together in the cabin reserved for the Captain of the ship. "When it stops, it'll be time to up anchor sire, the harbinger of dawn, normal when magi are around." Koto was the calmest man there.

Troi said, "My gunners can shoot blind anyway, Sire, we create our own clouds."

"What do you mean, Troi?" Toli asked.

"As soon as we, the first ship, fires our first cannon, the rest will follow ten at a time, ships that is, the second ten would be blind anyway, as will any ship behind ourselves."

The rain stopped with such suddenness it woke the sleeping, the crew started manning their guns, they had been loaded in the sun the day before the caps Troi had made to protect the primer powder worked perfectly, all guns ready to go!

They upped anchor and began to make headway north.

"How do you know when it's four knots, Koto?" Toli asked him.

"We learn all our seafaring at this speed, it's inbred, even me, I'm a fisherman and we use it when learning."

As they reached the four knots traditional speed, the first sails hove into view, as Koto commented, "In their arrogance, they have no birds out, maybe never brought any, so sure are they of your demise, Sire."

"How do you know?" Troi asked.

"They would be under manpower, Sire, no sail showing, no idea, they think were showing off our new guns, the problem now is when they notice the masts aren't even aboard, this is not traditional, Sire."

They were close enough now to pick out individuals and Vakkra, stood in the bow, with a mage studying the approaching ships through a telescope, he snapped the leather tube closed.

"That's Koto at the helm, I know Koto, good man, don't see Muklah, didn't think I would anyway."

As the 'Hurricane' entered the gap between the two small flotillas, Vakkra actually waved to Koto, who waved back; he could not believe his luck.

As the ninth ship passed between them, only thirty or so feet, hull to hull, Vakkra saw a gunner flip a lid on his gun and lift a taper to his lips to blow it alight.

"What are they doing!? Man the bows." Too late, further up the line a voice yelled Fire!

There was an almighty crash as the cannon went off, almost, simultaneously, the smoke was thick and black and coated everything it touched, one hundred seconds later the second ten ships let loose, again the cloud, Koto let the flotilla in a big turn to bring the ships about in line, but this time abreast, should there be something left to chase.

As the whisper of the breeze cleared the smoke, leaving small wisping threads of smoke, it became clear, there was nothing left to chase, what flotsam there was, were only splinters, there was no sign of bodies, no crying out for help, no screaming, nothing.

The crews were cheering wildly. Koto ordered, "Slow ahead," and the Hurricane made way slowly, silently and the rest followed in line, in order, behind the Hurricane, again on a heading for home.

Koto ordered, "Four knots," and the prop crew knew exactly what to do.

Both Tolian and Black-Islanders fell into silence on the way back, both had realised the battle they had just taken part in, had contained a weapon of total destruction, the Black-Islers hoped taking part may get a voyage home to their families, at least some did, while they were deep in thought about their families, the majority of the single warriors, some of whom knew their families were already dead, and perhaps had an eye for a young Tolian maiden, were wondering how they would go about not going home, how perhaps they may be allowed to stay.

The Tolians plus one Black-Isler, Koto, were thinking, *This fleet is invincible, indestructible*; however, Toli and his leaders were all thinking, *Every bugger with a notion of conquest is coming after those guns.*

In any case, the harbour was packed with celebrating people and the thoughtful and hopeful crews began waving and dancing little jigs on deck.

Anga and Shala were there on the dock with Tak, Anga was smiling but weeping silent tears, tears of relief that her love had come back, safely. Tak and Shala on the other hand were dancing a lake-jig that Tak had taught Shala on the Queen Shaleena.

On coming ashore, Toli and Anga almost crushed each other in embrace, they kissed and parted, and Toli shouted, "Bring out the ale, light the braziers, time for celebration!" And the crowd rushed to do their King's bidding with gusto; Crall had everything all around ready just to uncover.

Troi senior, and Mother, and the Black-Islanders up at the forge, had watched the disintegration of the Black-fleet from the best position on the Island, after the shock of what they had witnessed had worn off, Troi and Mother walked back to their cottage, Troi, in the realisation of the power he was creating, said to Mother, "Well I never."

And Mother said, "As long as you don't end up wishing you never had, my love," and she took his arm and went inside and didn't come out again that day. He and Mother will go down to Troi in the morning, there can be no doubt that he was unharmed.

As their day passed into darkness, noticed that Toli and the Generals were not taking part wholeheartedly, even Shala was throwing furtive glances at times, they all knew this was not finished, but that could wait for another day. Toli was concerned about the lack of a ship from the Friendly Isles.

One day Anga said, "Come walk." They took the path they so enjoyed on those idyllic days of total peace.

They sat on the harbour wall and Anga said, "You're miles away, Toli, this isn't over, my love, I know it too, but for now, it's over for you!"

"What do you mean, Anga?"

"You're going nowhere nor doing any warlike activities for the next seven months or so."

"Oh really, and why would that be?" Still really a clueless teenager.

"Because, my love, I want you here for the birth of our first child."